Ruins of the Earth

Book 1 in the Ruins of the Earth Series

Written by
Christopher Hopper
and
J.N. Chaney

Copyright © 2020
Variant Publications, LLC / Hopper Creative Group, LLC

RUINS
OF THE
EARTH

CHRISTOPHER HOPPER
J.N. CHANEY

VARIANT
PUBLICATIONS

LAS VEGAS, NV • NEW YORK, NY

Your spirit inspires us—those near and in galaxies yet unknown.

—Christopher

JOIN THE RUINS TRIBE

Visit **ruinsofthegalaxy.com** today and join the tribe.
Once there, you can sign up for our reader group, join our
Facebook community, and find us on Twitter and Instagram.

If you'd like to email us with comments or questions, we respond to
all emails sent to ruinsofthegalaxy@gmail.com, and love to hear
from our readers.

See you in the Ruins!

STAY CONNECTED

Join **JN Chaney's Renegade Readers Facebook group** where readers come together and share their lives and interests, discuss the series, and speak directly to the authors. Please check it out and join whenever you get the chance!

For updates about new releases, as well as exclusive promotions, sign up for the newsletter at ***https://www.jnchaney.com/ruins-of-the-earth-subscribe***

Enjoying the series? Help others discover the Ruins of the Earth series by leaving a review on **Amazon.**

CONTENTS

Prologue   1

PART ONE

Chapter 1   15
Chapter 2   27
Chapter 3   39
Chapter 4   49
Chapter 5   63
Chapter 6   75
Chapter 7   95

PART TWO

Chapter 8   109
Chapter 9   123
Chapter 10   139
Chapter 11   151
Chapter 12   177
Chapter 13   199
Chapter 14   211
Chapter 15   229
Chapter 16   241
Chapter 17   253
Chapter 18   265
Chapter 19   277
Chapter 20   301
Chapter 21   321
Chapter 22   333
Chapter 23   347
Chapter 24   369
Chapter 25   387
Chapter 26   409

PART THREE

Chapter 27	423
Chapter 28	433
Chapter 29	445
Chapter 30	457
Chapter 31	463
Chapter 32	479
Chapter 33	495
Chapter 34	507
Chapter 35	517
Chapter 36	533
Chapter 37	551
Chapter 38	567
Chapter 39	579
Chapter 40	587
The Story Continues	625
Super Good Time Feelings Merchandise Store	627
Stay Connected	631
Acknowledgments	633
About the Authors	635

PROLOGUE

1048, Tuesday, March 9, 2004
Al Qa'im, Iraq
South of Route Jade

INCOMING bullets snap against the house's corner like a spatula slapping a kitchen table. I grab Jack and pull him off the sidewalk as bits of cement sting the side of my neck. This isn't the first time I've been shot at, but it's definitely the closest I've come to getting hit. I'm pissed and scared all at the same time.

"You see 'em?" Jack asks.

"One block south, other side of the street, I think." I'm doing my best to slow my heart rate, but I can't remember how many breaths per second I'm supposed to be at. "Up on the, uh, second story window."

"Roger."

Jack takes a knee, waits for a break, and then sticks his M4 around the corner. "I see 'em." But before he can get a shot off, more rounds take chunks from the building's edge. Jack pulls back. "Three more. Street level, red Toyota."

"It's like they knew we were coming." I adjust my grip on my M4. "Ten bucks says it's Yasin."

Jack looks up at me. "Mr. Giggles?"

I nod. "Think I saw him a block west on his cell."

"You sure?"

"Pretty sure, yut. Where's Clark?" I'd lost track of the private running point.

"Donkey cart, fifteen yards ahead. He's down, but still moving."

"Shit."

I glance back the way we came. The rest of Echo Four One has taken cover along the street, but they're pinned down too and returning one round for every five that come in. Fortunately, Corporal Shaft—yut, real name—staggered the squad and spread us down both sides of the street.

While Jack and I have spotted a total of four tangos, there's gotta be plenty more based on the amount of incoming AK fire. This is an ambush. And right now, the enemy has us clinging to indents in the low, one-story mud and cement homes like cats avoiding water. My heart's pounding in my chest, and I'm forcing my hands to stop shaking.

Just then, one of the squad's Humvees with the M240B, a belt-fed, gas-operated medium machine gun, opens up from the rear of our patrol. Aside from killing tangos with extreme prejudice, it's meant to intimidate the hell out of the enemy in situations just like this so Marines on the pavement can get done what we need to.

"'Bout time," Jack says. "Go for Clark?"

It takes me a second to realize that Jack wants to run out and attempt to pull the private back. "Yut. Of course. Musketeers, right?"

"Thicker than blood," he replies.

But I'm still hesitating.

Just then, our squad's 249 gunner, Private First Class Garcia, starts massing fire with the Humvee. It's enough to give me the boost I need. "All right. Let's do it."

Jack hunches over and leads, while I hang back a little with my M4 pointed downrange. I send a few shots toward the enemy, but I'm too jacked up on adrenaline to know if they hit anyone. As soon as Jack's behind the donkey cart, we trade roles, and I dash the rest of the way to cover while he lays down suppressive fire. Enemy rounds skip across the hardpack as we flip the wood and metal wagon on its side in the middle of the street.

"How you doing, Clark?" I ask as AK rounds pepper the rail above me. But the question's barely out of my mouth when I notice the blood pooling under his legs and the open flesh around his knees. I don't know how to handle this. It's not like the movies. Or my games. It's—

"Did he get my dick?" Clark grabs my vest. "Are my nads gone?"

Honestly, I can't tell if Clark's dick is gone or not. It's a goddamn mess down there. I'm more worried about his femoral artery than his manhood, but he has every right to be scared. "You're gonna be okay, Clark. You hear me?"

"It's bad, isn't it."

I lie and shake my head just as two bullets pop in the dead donkey's corpse beside me. Air smells like ass and burning rubber. "You just keep breathing nice and slow. Roger?"

He nods.

I reach behind Clark and grab the medkit on his utility belt that we all stow between our buttpack and canteen. With Jack combining fire with the machine guns, I remove the tourniquet. Thing's dancing in my hands as I try to assess which of Clark's legs is worse. The right one, I think. "This is gonna hurt, bro."

"Do it," he replies.

I nod and then get to work. Jack helps hold Clark still as the private swears and struggles against the pain. When it's done, I pull my hands away and feel shocked at how much blood is on them. Not sure what I was expecting, but suddenly the extra grip tape Sergeant Michaels told us to put on our M4 handles makes a lot more sense.

Now it's time to get Clark outta here.

While the squads 240, 249, and M4s are keeping most of the hajjis suppressed, one insurgent in particular seems to have a bead on us that's out of the squad's field of fire. Dragging Clark from the danger area won't be too effective if Jack and I get gunned down in the process.

With a quick peek around the cart's left corner, I spot a man in a red-and-white-checkered scarf and a black tracksuit just inside a first-story window. "Contact left," I say to Jack.

He nods, and while lacking a good sightline, Jack opens up on the house, which forces the target to step away.

Then I lean out and look down my scope. "Come on, you son of a bitch. Where'd you go?" Two beats later, the enemy steps back into the window and right behind my chevrons. My heart stops. I squeeze twice, and my M4 barks and flings brass. The hajji disappears.

"You got him," Jack yells as I pull back behind the cart.

I take his word for it. "Tango down."

"We're gonna get you outta here, Clark," Jack yells. "Can you still shoot?"

The private looks down at his M4, then nods at Jack and me. His face and lips are white as a sheet.

"Good," Jack says and then looks at me. "You ready?"

"Wait." I pull an M67 fragmentation grenade from a pouch attached to my load-bearing vest. "Now I'm ready."

Jack smiles and takes hold of the canvas handle on the back of Clark's flak vest. "Party time."

I pull the pin. "Frag out." The spoon spins away as I toss the grenade down the street. Then both of us are hauling ass as AK rounds zip into the hardpack. Clark's flipped his giggle switch and is firing full-auto as we run, and I can't say I blame him. I'd drain my magazine too.

We're almost back to cover between buildings when the subconscious alarm clock in my head goes off. A split second later, my frag detonates. The ground shakes, and my ears ring. But the enemy fire abates just long enough for Corporal Shaft and Lance Corporal Anderson to grab our arms and pull us into the alley.

"Shoulda waited for more fire support, Finnegan," Shaft says.

I slump down against the block wall, but I'm too nervous to respond with anything more than a, "Yes, Corporal." I wanna tell him that I saw Yasin—wanna tell everyone that I think he's giving away our positions and letting the insurgents know exactly where to find us. But the blood on my hands and the fact that I just ran through a hailstorm of bullets and survived is freakin' me out.

"Corpsman up," Anderson yells down the street. Then he hits my shoulder. "Hey. You good?"

I nod, but I don't feel good.

"You did right by him." Anderson nods at Clark.

"Thanks."

Jack's at the private's other side, keeping the kid talking. "Breathe with me. Come on."

"Did I get any?" Clark asks.

"Yeah. Hit the donkey twice too."

Clark smiles.

"Where's my goddamn corpsman?" Anderson yells again.

Plastic shopping bags tumble past the alley's mouth as I think back to Yasin on his cell. "I saw him," I say to Shaft. "One block west."

"Saw who?"

"Yasin." The man is a member of the Iraqi Civil Defense Corps and routinely serves as one of our unit's translators when working with Al Qa'im's latest police chief. I've had a gut feeling since day one that both men were working with Al-Qaeda but had no proof. And who's gonna listen to a private first class from Brooklyn when he says he doesn't like some hajji with a crooked smile?

"You saw shit, Marine," Shaft says. "The Major's counting on our partnership here to work, and you're not gonna screw that up. Roger?"

"Roger."

Sure, I wanna punch this guy in the mouth so bad. Every movie I've ever seen where some boot hits an idiotic NCO plays in my head. But unlike the actors, I have to live with the real-life consequences of nonjudicial punishment. It's not worth the fight.

Just then, the corpsman slides into the alley. Likewise, the Humvee with the 240 pulls up, and Shaft orders Clark into the back. I'm about ready to lend a hand when someone shouts, "RPG."

I fall back against the building while Jack leans over to cover the private from the blast. In the split second where the rocket-propelled grenade skips by the vehicle's side and detonates against the building behind us, I realize that what I've always felt about Jack is true: my childhood friend's a goddamn hero. Never tell a devil dog that. But of all the guys I've ever met who were fit to kill the enemy and save a brother at the same time, it's him—Captain America, in the flesh.

Cement and shrapnel rain down on us, and my ears ring louder. I blink several times and see Jack yelling in Clark's face, both men covered in moon dust. I can't hear what he's saying, but I see Jack pulling on Clark's vest.

"Get him loaded," Shaft yells.

I snap upright and help shield Jack and the corpsman as they haul Clark out of the alley's safety. But AK rounds slap the Humvee's windshield and force us back.

"I got you," the driver says as he opens his door to help cover us and then returns fire. Spider veins splinter across the bulletproof glass, and more bullets skip off the steel plating. But it's enough to get Clark where he needs to go. Two more Marines, Private Clapper and Private First Class Wood, are helped up behind Clark. Clapper looks like he's taken a round to the shin, and Wood's left sleeve is soaked in blood.

With our thirteen-man squad down to ten, and the remaining three Marines taking cover behind the Humvee, Shaft gives the order to fall back. The unit moves with the vehicle as it returns the way it came. It's humiliating, and I hate it, but I'm also glad to be getting out of this hellhole. The enemy has amassed too much fire and has superior positions.

We pass a side street on the right, and I spot a man at the opposite end in the solid brown uniform and a red baseball cap of the ICDC. It's Yasin. And he's still on his damn cell phone.

"Son of a bitch." I get my NCO's attention and point down the alley. "Corporal Shaft. It's Yasin."

Shaft sends a few more rounds downrange and then looks to where I've gestured. "God damn."

"I can take 'em."

"Negative. He's unarmed."

"But he's calling—"

"Negative, Finnegan! Return fire."

"Roger." It's the wrong call. This hajji asshole's gotta be orchestrating the insurgent ambush on us, right? And based on chatter I'm hearing over comms plus a red star-cluster firework and some purple smoke four blocks west of our position, I'm guessing Yasin has called in hits against Second and Third Squads too.

I grit my teeth and let the alley disappear with Yasin in it. My hands aren't shaking as much, but I'm still pissed. So I take out my aggression on a punk in shorts and flip flops running up behind the donkey cart carrying an RPG—the great equalizer of the Third World enemy combatants everywhere. My round hits him in the shoulder, and he spins out of view. Two seconds later, his buddy hoists the shoulder-fired weapon and aims at our Humvee. My next shot hits the hajji in the head. But not before his finger squeezes the trigger.

When the ordnance hits the Humvee's windshield, molten glass shoots out the vehicle's rear. Two men go down, and a third gets pinned against a house when the Humvee bucks. I'm on my back but climbing to my feet as Jack has the presence of mind to pull Clark out of the vehicle. The private's legs are partially on fire, but he looks in too much shock to be feeling it. Still, Jack beats out the flames and starts dragging Clark down the street.

I grab the private by the arm and look north to see that we're less than twenty yards from Route Jade, the main road that runs due west to Camp Husaybah. With any luck, Major Corrigan's convoy at the police station is closing in for support. Unless, of course, he's under attack too, in which case we need a QRF.

Look at me, I'm a goddamn private playing chess while bullets are flying over my head—Mother Mary and Jesus.

I glance over my shoulder to see the hajjis start falling in behind us. They must smell blood in the water.

"Frag out," gets yelled two, maybe three times, followed by several explosions. The street's filled with dust and smoke, but the AK rounds are still coming. Just then, my left knee goes limp as what feels like a red-hot iron pokes through my upper calf. But somehow, I manage to stay upright and keep pulling on Clark's arm. I see blood on my pants leg. Yut, I've been shot. Oh, God! I've been shot in the goddamn leg.

We're ten yards from the main road when a high-backed Humvee noses around the corner bearing an improvised weapon's mount for a Mk 19 belt-fed automatic grenade launcher. Apparently, Mary and Jesus were listening. The Humvee's canvas has been rolled back to make room for improvised armor. Thing looks like something out of Mad Max.

The Marine atop doesn't waste a second. He summons the Mk 19 to life, and I hear the trademark *thug-thug-thug* rip down the street as 40mm rounds explode on the enemy's position. Despite my injury, the grenade launcher's rhythmic cadence gives me something to march to, and Jack and I swing Clark free of the danger area and behind cover along Route Jade.

I'm back around the corner, M4 pointed south, as the rest of my squad charges toward me. I'm searching for tangos in the background, but the Mk 19 has made a meal of them, and the AK-47s have gone silent. Instinctively, I start counting our fire teams and then add one more Marine for Corporal Shaft, who's emerged completely unscathed. Imagine that.

I look down at Clark. The corpsman has just finished injecting him with morphine and writing the time and dosage on his arm. But then I catch Jack's eye and a slight shake of his head and realize that the drug is meant to help ease Clark's passing, not his recovery.

I DON'T TELL this story. At least not all the details. But I do talk about how bad it was having to abide by the general's "first do no harm" mandates in order to promote the "pro-coalition mentality." Granted, I was just an Irish Catholic redhead from Brooklyn; what did I know?

"We learned from Vietnam," they said.

"Embed with the locals, patrol with the police, win hearts and minds," they ordered.

And I get it. Our commanders said they believed those policies were the fastest way to end the fight. And I think that most of them wanted to get home just as badly as we did.

But it wasn't the best way.

And it cost lives.

Private Samuel K. Clark, a grocery store clerk who loved to hunt elk outside his hometown of Flagstaff, Arizona, died before we reached Camp Husaybah. No medal. No explanation to his family. And seeing him die tore me up inside. Still does.

Jack deserved a medal too. But no commendations came despite the after-action reports I sat through and the letters we helped write to the brass. But you can bet that dumbass lieutenant who got us into this mess received something.

The Major, God bless him, needed a win, not multiple ambushes. Politicians in leatherback chairs and leather-bound note-books needed leathernecks to help ensure their reelections. Needed to hear that their plans had worked.

And what did we need?

I think about that a lot. The way I see it, we needed permission to fight the war the way we'd trained to fight it. To win. But the country wasn't ready for that. They'd lost their stomach for the kind of violence we knew how to unleash. It's ugly. And I don't blame them one bit. But that's the difference between trained warriors and civilians. We have the constitution to head outside the wire and do what no one else can, or wants to. It's called war. And we needed to win it. Instead, all we got was a slowly festering wound that still hasn't found a way to heal.

What happened in the checkpoint border town with Syria was swept under the rug. Sure, news came out here and there, eventu-ally. But it wasn't a true reflection of the way Echo Company saw it.

Ironically, by late April of 2004, all personnel, facilities, and equipment of the Civil Defense Corps were transferred to the Iraqi Ministry of Defence under the Iraqi Armed Forces. But it wouldn't be the last time Marines came under attack in Al Qa'im. Three weeks later, those who survived and those who fell would get the recognition they rightly deserved. Oorah.

As for Jack and me, we returned to our unit after some Jell-O and Band-Aids. I never saw Corporal Shaft again, which was for the best. And every time we went out on patrol, Jack always asked to take point.

"It's for Clark," he'd say.

And he was a son of a bitch for saying it like that, 'cause he knew I couldn't say no.

And I should have.

Damn, I should have.

PART ONE

TWENTY-THREE YEARS LATER

1

1415, Monday, April 25, 2027
West Antarctica
Ellsworth Subglacial Highlands Research Facility

I've given up fighting. But sometimes us old devil dogs aren't given much of a choice, are we.

So I jab once at Vlad's mouth.

The six foot, three inch Muscovite's monobrow raises in a look of surprise. Then he smiles, displaying two rows of red-smeared teeth—one freshly out of place.

"Might wanna have that looked at," I say.

He growls and spits the tooth away.

"Or get rid of it," I add. "Cheaper that way."

I lean away from his counterpunch and throw a right cross at his cheek. Again, the brute seems calm. But the crowd isn't—they whoop and holler around the mess hall, a third of them in Russian, chanting something about "the old man and the monster." Sounds like a bad Hemingway novel. Or an even worse 80s action flick.

My opponent's next two punches land against my forearms. Guy's a damn tank. I avoid his third strike and deliver a rib shot to his left side. Something cracks under my fist. He grunts—I'm guessing he feels it too. So I go for a second punch to the new sweet spot, but he captures my fist under his arm and twists.

The sudden force yanks me off my feet, and I crash into some of the mess hall's folding metal furniture. The Russians roar and start pounding tables.

When I turn to face my opponent, there's a fist coming at my head. I duck and feel the wind brush over my ear. Then he grunts again as I land a second blow on his ribs. That sends him to the ground and the audience to their feet—half out of surprise, half out of excitement.

From the moment the international "joint military contingents" on "non-weaponized field training maneuvers" got here a month ago, Vlad had labeled me the "red-bearded American dog alpha top." I don't mind the moniker, but it's not the easiest to tattoo. From bumping into me at the gym to long looks across the mess hall, I couldn't tell if Vlad was trying to size me up or ask me out.

"Stay down," I tell him, knowing that if he gets up, he'll end up uglier than when he started, and that was saying something. I hadn't been in the mood to fight when this started, and I'd make sure there wouldn't be a second confrontation when it was over. My opponent, however, seems that he won't stop fighting until he's unconscious. Based on the ink across his hands, that's not surprising.

Vlad spits blood on the linoleum floor, then he barrels into my stomach and wraps both arms around my waist. I backpedal hard, trying to keep up with him, but I'm not fast enough. The crowd parts, and we crash into a line of metal folding chairs. I use the chaos to my advantage and manage to roll away from his grasp.

A beat later, I'm on my feet, steady and still, while he struggles to get off the floor. Sure, I could jump him now, and probably win too. But I don't believe in kicking a man while he's down. That, and I don't need to. The mere fact that I'm up first is doing the work for me.

Vlad here is ten years my junior and has both height and size on his side. Whereas I'm the old man at the station—two inches shorter and fifty pounds lighter. While we both might be fighters and patriots, I'm one thing Vlad isn't.

A student of chess.

Most people think a brawl is all about brute force and knowing how to take a punch. Yeah, that plays into it, of course. But winning a fistfight, or any fight, has a lot more to do with strategy than most people assume. It's a mind game, a true battle of wits, to quote the Princess Bride, where we find out "who is right, and who is dead." God, I'm a sucker for that movie.

In the course of studying my opponent over the last month, I noticed Vlad suffers from a short temper, which means his amygdala is currently trying to overtake his prefrontal cortex for dominance.

To prove my point, Vlad throws a chair at me. I deflect it and wait for him to get up. He tosses his head like a bull, and then, with predictable rage, Vlad drops his shoulders and charges. I sidestep him like I'm a matador and watch several of his men catch and spin him around. He's bleeding from his mouth and reflexively protecting his left side.

He charges again, so I pull out a little more from the Marine Corps Martial Arts Program toolbox. I lean left to avoid a right cross, and then leverage my shift in balance to deliver a quick kick to his left side. My lower shin strikes his ribs. He buckles into the blow but recovers quickly. Then he jabs with his left hand, but too slow to be effective. So I lock his wrist and curl his hand down and away. His nerve pain is explosive though non-destructive, and Vlad instinctively tries to ease the pressure by arching his back.

Knowing that Russians are taught to be ruthless—as the thrown chair mildly demonstrated—I decide to encourage Vlad to give up this fight while he has a chance. With his hand still locked, I deliver a quick strike to his left knee. Not enough to break the joint, but he'll be limping for a week or two.

Vlad pulls away and emits a low growl.

"Listen, big man," I say, lowering my hands in a symbolic gesture. It's a move that gives tired opponents an out and aggressive opponents an excuse to keep fighting. "We can drop this now and we both—"

He's aggressive.

Vlad's comrades thrust him back into the makeshift ring, and he throws a left hook at my head. I duck to the left. He uppercuts with his right. I dodge right. After his next failed left hook, I strike him in the ribcage for the fourth time. He curls over and backs away.

What my oversized contender doesn't know is that I'm in pain too. This forty-four-year-old body isn't what it used to be. My knuckles are screaming, hands and arms aching, and something in my back is messed up from hitting the table and chairs. But that's the other thing that comes with age—the ability to hide your crap. And as simple as it sounds, if the enemy doesn't think they're affecting you, there's less fire in their fight.

Which is fine with me. I want less action right now, not more. This was supposed to be easy, remember?

Two more weeks and I'm out. Sipping lemonade and watching rural Pennsylvania sunsets where no one can find me.

People say I'm gonna miss games like this. Maybe I will. What I won't miss, however, is not bringing everybody home at the end of an op. That part can stay the hell away from me. And so can all the claims that we're fighting for something bigger than ourselves. We were once. But now? I don't know. Maybe we're just boxing younger versions of ourselves, and at the end of the day, none of it matters. No one cares. And the world is gonna do what the world wants to do with or without us.

Vlad cracks the vertebrae in his neck. Posturing.

I grab my sandwich from the mess hall table and take a bite. "You sure you don't want to stop?" Then I swallow the flavorless ham and cheese on rye.

Vlad motions me toward him with curled fingers.

"Suit yourself."

Hands raised, we circle one another once, heads moving left and right like snakes playing hide-and-seek between stone columns. Vlad throws a left-right combo that actually forces me back. A third punch clips my chin—not enough to do any real damage. It hurts, but not nearly as bad as my left jab to his face and right hook into his ribs. He swears in Russian, steps away, and gives his head a shake.

I'm one move away from checkmate. My research says so. Every time Vlad attempts his last bench press in the gym, he does some sort of Lamaze breathing technique, like he's gonna give birth to a deranged Mini-Me. It's the same thing he's doing now, only there's blood flinging off his lips.

"Last chance, Vlad," I say. "We shake hands and—"

"Mother Russia never walks away from fight, Brooklyn New

CHRISTOPHER HOPPER & J.N. CHANEY

York," he says and then spits a wad of blood and phlegm. That was something else he called me after he learned where I grew up. If my stint on Antarctica lasts longer, who knows how many more nicknames I'll walk away with.

"God, it must be painful being so stubborn," I say.

Vlad uses the back of a forearm to wipe blood across his face. "Not as painful as watching American flag fly over compound like underwear of old hooker."

A round of boos and "Awe, no he didn't" comes from the Marines behind me. Even some of the Brits seem to champion the American cause.

Time to end this.

I move toward Vlad, dodge two hasty punches, and then step inside his reach. Unable to account for my sudden proximity, Vlad leans back, but not far enough. My right uppercut smashes his jaw closed, throws his head back, and sends him crashing to the floor like a felled tree.

The Russian contingent gasps, and there's a moment of silence where everyone waits to see if Vlad is going to move.

He doesn't.

My squad of thirteen Marines and at least half the Brits start collecting their earnings, and I head to my rucksack to get a bottle of Motrin. Damn cold-weather training.

THERE'S a knock on my barrack's door.

"You'd better have some Redbreast," I say, noting my preferred whiskey when someone else is buying.

Simmons laughs and then opens the door, holding a bottle of

something clear and two glasses. "One of the Russians couldn't pay up, so he offered a bottle of——" Simmons tries to pronounce the Cyrillic text but knows as much of it as I do. Giving up, he says, "Well, it's wet, and I think it's vodka."

"Pour it."

I offer Simmons a seat, and he tips the bottle. He's my squad's Sergeant for this "exercise" and a good Marine. Honest, treats the men with respect, and knows when to lighten up—like this. I appreciate that. And the vodka. Nothing worse than a Marine who takes things too seriously when they don't need to.

Officially, we're at a remote civilian research facility in western Antarctica to conduct cold-weather training. Apparently, the Pentagon wanted to spend a lot of money to give some NCOs and a bunch of boots—what we call anyone who hasn't seen action yet—their merit badges in cold weather camping.

Off the record, this is something different—but no less expensive or boring. According to the Antarctic Treaty, signed in 1959 and enforced in 1961, no country's allowed to pick a fight on the world's coldest continent. Which, as far as I'm concerned, is stupid because there's little else to do. That, and everyone's pissed off 'cause they're so damn cold, so I'm pretty sure mess hall brawls are excluded.

All that said, if a government wants a military presence on the world's coldest continent, they've got to be sneaky about it. Like tasking a nearly retired Marine Raider to conduct a cold-weather training evolution hosted by a pop-up civilian research facility. Though tasking is too kind a word—*conning* is more like it.

"Your hands okay?" Simmons asks.

I flex my right hand. "Figure it's the last time I'll be able to drop a guy without a lawsuit."

Simmons laughs. "Goddamn military's good for something."

We clink glasses and down the shots.

Simmons sucks in air after the eighty-proof libation and then looks at his glass. "No wonder they're pissed off all the time."

"Not a vodka fan?"

"More of a whiskey guy."

I salute him with my glass. "Good man."

"Which is more than I can say about your sparring partner back there." Simmons pours us another round.

"Eh, he's not so bad. Just some cabin fever."

"He was asking for it."

"Maybe." I look at my drink and then flex my hand. "But if that's all the action we see down here, then I'm fine with that."

Simmons knows I'm just weeks away from retirement. Did this op as a favor to an old friend. And that's the only reason.

After a beat, Simmons says, "I can take the next patrol if you want."

I glance up. "You offering 'cause I'm old?"

"Nah, I was just—"

"It's a sin to insult your elders, Simmons." I point a finger at him like I'm aiming down my Glock 19. "And I don't see any priests on this ice block."

"Then you can say an extra Hail Mary for me."

I give Simmons a grin. "It'll cost you."

"I expect nothing less, Wic."

The nickname WIC—White Irish Catholic—had been a holdover from my first deployment to Iraq. Ironically, I hadn't attended mass since I was a kid, nor had I ever stepped foot on my grandmother's homeland. But I was white, freckled, and redhaired, so the semi-derogatory label of a Brooklyn boy of Irish heritage stuck. Sure as hell beat some of the other names guys got stuck with. Plus, I liked the head-nod to my favorite fictional anti-hero, John Wick. If I owned a dog and somebody killed it, I'd be pissed too. Other than that, leave me the hell alone, 'cause I'm out.

Simmons and I had been taking turns running patrols outside the dig site and reporting back to the spook we'd been assigned. I don't like the CIA, they don't like me, and that's just fine. A daily call to report "no new intel" about our British and Russian counterpart's activities is as much contact with the Agency as I want. Sure, plenty of my former COs had slid over to serve at Langley—even asked me to tag along.

"We can always use someone like you," they'd said. "Research, plan, execute. Right up your alley." They spoke like spy work was going to make more of a difference than what I'd already done.

Nice try.

I nod at Simmons. "If you're serious about covering for me"—cause Lord knows I can use a shower and more Motrin—"just keep an eye on our pals. They might be looking for a little friendly payback. Rope the Brits in if you need to; some old SAS in there."

"Copy. Nothing we can't handle."

"Nothing *you* can't handle," I say in a corrective tone. "Some of the boots, not so much."

Simmons nods. "Think the ruskies are former mafia?"

"Former?" I give him a blue-eyed wink. "Who says they left?"

"You mean the tats on the hands?"

I tip my glass toward him. "Once in the family—"

"Always in the family," Simmons says.

The adage was that the only thing that separated Russian soldiers from Russian mobsters was in which order you got your ink for each org. And, like us, these lads were here to make sure no one got too close to what they believed was rightfully theirs. Welcome back, Cold War. We missed you.

Ah, hell. All the talk of the Russian mafia brings up bad memories of seeing the Bratva work in my native Brooklyn. I can't let Simmons take my patrol because of that scuffle. But I also don't want to go outside right now. Just too damn tired. And I know I don't have enough credit to buy myself out of this particular purgatory.

A channel on my MURS handset cracks open. "Mr. Finnegan?" says the hesitant voice of a grad student named Lewis. "Are you copying me, sir?"

I give Simmons a raised eyebrow and pick up the radio. "Send it."

"Hi, sir. Uh, Dr. Campbell says he wants you down here."

"Say again." I'm both simultaneously annoyed and understanding that the kid has no common sense about how to speak over comms.

"In the pit, I mean."

I cast Simmons a curious glance. This is a first. "Acknowledged. I'll be on the way after lunch."

"Uh, he says as soon as you can, sir."

"Is there a problem?"

There's a noticeable delay in Lewis's reply. "Uh, no, sir. It's just... well, he thinks he is close to doing something of importance and would like you here. You know, just in case there are *complications with distributing the Easter baskets.*"

Using the code phrase for hostile intent is the one thing Lewis is getting right. And that right there is the whole mission—keep whatever Dr. Aaron Campbell finds from falling into the wrong hands.

Like the Russian's. That is, of course, assuming the doc finds what he is looking for in this godforsaken wasteland.

Lewis's use of the code phrase also puts me on heightened alert. It means I'm not going alone. But I don't want to risk saying anything more over the radio.

"And, Mr. Finnegan? Dr. Campbell asked specifically for you."

I raise an eyebrow at Simmons and say off-comm, "See? Not everyone thinks I'm senile."

"They need glasses."

I give Simmons the one-finger salute and then open the channel. "I'll be down in twenty, kid."

"Thank you, sir. I'll let him know."

"Finnegan out."

"Okay, I'm out too, sir. I mean, over and out."

Says no one ever.

I set the radio on the desk and stand, stretching my back. "Tell the boys to get their mittens on. Storm might be rolling in."

"You want all three teams?" Simmons asks. "Isn't that a bit much?"

"Just being prepared."

"But it sounded like he just—"

"I heard him, Simmons. And it doesn't change my decision. Ready the teams."

"Roger that."

God, I can't wait to get off this damn rock.

2

1447, Monday, April 25, 2027
West Antarctica
En Route to the Ellsworth Subglacial Highlands Excavation Site

WITH EVERYONE PACKED into the white Bv 206 SUSV and matching trailer—known as a susvee, short for small unit support vehicle—Simmons puts the beast in drive and eases the Mercedes six-cylinder diesel engine to take us into the near-whiteout conditions. The Hägglunds developed, BAE Systems built, Bandvagn 206 is the only way anyone can travel safely as the beginning of winter sets in. Snowmobiles are also permitted, but only when visibility is better than it is right now. Plus, at a balmy five degrees below zero Fahrenheit, everyone's happy for the susvee's heaters.

Simmons takes us around the east side of the research facility—a cluster of eight insulated shipping containers and smaller outbuildings—and points due north toward the Ellsworth Subglacial Highlands excavation site. It's a ten-minute drive in good conditions, fifteen if there's some weather.

While our team has only been here a few weeks, Aaron and various staff members have been here for almost seven months—and that's just this trip. His previous expeditions have lasted even longer and included researchers from Cornell University, the Environment Department at York, University of Bristol, and Lomonosov Moscow State University, to name a few. But, according to the rumors, none of them were as committed and determined as Rutgers University's very own Dr. Aaron Campbell, which sounded about right. Aaron always was a stubborn pain in the ass, which is probably why we got along so well.

"I think we have it this time," Aaron had said to me over the phone back in January. It was the height of the Antarctic summer, and he and his team had apparently made a lot of progress on whatever it was they were looking for.

"You're not going to give me any details, are you." I didn't need to be on a video call to know he was smiling.

"Sorry, Patrick. You know the drill." That was code for his phone line was probably being recorded, and whatever he was researching was classified.

"I do. And to all those sorry sons a' bitches out there who have nothing better to do than hack this call, sorry your job sucks."

Aaron forged ahead. "The suits are interested, and they've asked me if I want anyone specific."

It actually took me a second to realize what he was saying. "Man, I'm honored. But I'm gettin' out the first week of May. So I'll be tied up with—"

"Your CO said you could do it."

I pulled the cell phone away and looked at it. "Who'd you call? Colonel Rodriguez?"

"Seems like a nice guy."

"Pain in the ass," I said. "You. Not him."

"Funny."

I let out a sigh and tried to explain how tired I was without sounding like a deadbeat, but it wasn't going well. That, and Aaron had other plans. "Listen, Aaron. You need help, you know I'm there for you. But I'm—"

"I knew I could count on you, Patrick. Said there's no one else I'd rather have watching my back."

"Sure, but—"

"Banks agreed. Said he'd get your commander to set you up with a small team, and then your Agency handler will take care of logistics. You'll report directly to him so it stays off the military's official airwaves."

Son of a bitch.

I sighed and rubbed my temples. After all I'd been through, the last thing I wanted was another deployment, especially if it was one to the middle of nowhere overseen by spooks. Then again, maybe that's just what I needed to get my mind off things. Plus, the middle of nowhere meant no one would be shooting at my team. I could live with that. And so could they. It also meant no nightly news, no political BS on post, and fake smiles and false handshakes. Not that I'd ever doled those out—I just hated other people giving them to me.

Still, if I didn't have to go, I'd rather not. "Did the Colonel say I had a choice in the matter?"

Aaron hesitated. I could practically hear him wringing his

hands. "He did, yes. Of course. You don't have to if you don't want to."

That's when Aaron played the lowest card of all.

"I just figured you might do it for the Musketeers."

"You're an asshole, Aaron."

"I've been called worse." He sighed. "But we made a promise."

"It was a long time ago."

He laughed. "And isn't that the curious thing about promises? They endure."

"Eh, not all are supposed to."

"Jack would want——"

"No." I didn't like where the phone call was going. "Don't make this about Jack."

But it was. Hell, how could anything having to do with Aaron and me *not* be about Jack?

"I'm sorry," Aaron said. "I just... man, I need you. Need someone I can trust."

I don't believe in ghosts—in people talking from beyond the grave. That's because they all still live in my head. And I can practically hear Jack now. "We're always gonna stick together, right? Hands in the middle."

We would. And we'd chant. "Thicker than blood, through fire and mud, let everyone fear, us Musketeers." We were kids, but damn if that rhyme hadn't haunted me halfway across the world.

"Thicker than blood," I said to Aaron over the phone. "I'll give you a month—six weeks max," I said. "Then I got this sweet little cabin in the—somewhere, that I'm disappearing to. You come visit when you want. And after this, I'm not leaving it, even for you."

"Deal."

Campbell grew quiet. Something about this… it was serious for him.

"Everything good?"

When he spoke again, it was soft, like he'd seen his own ghost of Jack. "They're not gonna laugh at me anymore after this. No one will. Not once they see it."

Again, I had no idea what the "it" was. That was classified. Given my childhood friend's notoriety as one of North America's leading dirt sniffers and fossil diggers, I guessed it had something to do with a rare mineral deposit or the remains of a badass Neanderthal riding a T-Rex.

"I'm sure they won't," I said. "I'll see you in March."

Oddly enough, that was the last time I'd talked to Aaron, even since arriving at the research facility. He'd done all his communicating through his grad assistant, Lewis. Even our spook handler said Aaron was living at the excavation site twenty-four seven. The closest our patrols got was to the entrance of the snow cave in the side of a low mountain. Whatever was inside was being closely guarded—so close that not even my childhood best friend would fill me in.

Simmons parks the susvee but keeps the engine running and then calls for everyone to load out. Unlike all our other patrols in which we packed concealed Glock 19s in accordance with the spirit of the Antarctic Treaty, now we carry suppressed Raider-issue FN SCAR 17s in a white "rattle can" finish. To everyone else, that's spray paint. Even our magazines and Trijicon Advanced Combat Optical Gunsights are coated to blend in with the winter landscape. Likewise, the squad wears their Kevlar helmets and metal plate carriers atop white camo winter fatigues. It feels like overkill for an Indiana Jones meets Frosty the Snowman-style op. But with Russian muscle hidden in plain sight at the station, having a .308 round in the chamber against my chest makes me feel a little warmer on the inside.

With so much secrecy, the only thing I figure Campbell has found is Ernest Shackleton's buried treasure. That or we're back to something like a dinosaur with lasers on its head. Either way, today we're being allowed into the inner sanctum.

I nod to Simmons, and he gives orders for Third Fire Team to guard the entrance while One and Two follow us inside. "If you get cold, take turns cycling through the susvee," he says.

They acknowledge and take up positions around the opening. My fingers and toes are already fighting off the subzero temp, so I know it won't be long before these guys are back inside the support vehicle.

The cave's interior is lined with cold-weather work lights along its rippling blue walls. Place looks like it's carved straight out of a damn glacier. After twenty yards, the path begins to descend and curves to the right. I glance back to make sure everyone's following. Teams One and Two taking in the sights—weapon hands relaxed.

The tunnel turns left and ends at a large metallic door. It feels entirely out of place—more like the entrance to an underground missile defense system than an academic dig site.

I see a keypad. Without a code, working the panel is pointless. So I pull out my radio and hail Lewis.

"I'll be right there, Mr. Finnegan. Please stand by."

A minute elapses before a motor strains behind the overhead door. The barrier creeps up, revealing yellow-painted tines and recessed holes in a steel threshold. It's not even halfway up when Lewis bends down in his orange oversized North Face winter coat and waves us in.

"Hi, Mr. Finnegan. Please, come. Dr. Campbell's waiting for you."

I give the tines a look and then pass beneath them. On the other side, I'm greeted by a sunken dig site at least four football fields wide and just as deep. The ceiling is a domed ice sheet some one hundred yards above, supported by a network of aluminum trusses. Throughout the cavern floor are cranes, work lights, ATVs, scaffolding, and translucent plastic walls blocking off large sections of the site. And in the air, there's the constant background sound of Salamander heaters and the odor of diesel fumes. There must be two dozen people walking around the site, each in coveralls or orange coats.

"Hey." Simmons nudges me. "I think I see Tom Cruise down there."

"That's Dwayne Johnson. But you're right; they're practically the same when they smile."

Simmons isn't far off in his larger assessment: this feels more like a Hollywood movie set than an archeological dig site. And by the looks on my squad's faces, everyone else is just as surprised.

My Spidey Sense is also piqued. And, apparently, so is Simmons's.

"Feels like Jeff Goldblum's about to come running out of there chased by a tyrannosaurus rex." His tone suggests he's not entirely joking either.

"Relax," I say. "Hundred bucks and your bottle of Russian booze says this is about gold or oil. If it's a fancy-ass dino, living or dead, you win."

"You're on."

Simmons and I fist bump to seal the deal.

"This way, please," Lewis says as he descends a metal switch-back staircase to the dig site floor.

By the time we step onto the hardpack below, I feel the uptick in the temp. It's not shorts weather, but it sure as hell ain't negative five.

Lewis leads us along the main thoroughfare bordered on each side by large, cube-like structures covered in plastic. The scene reminds me of a small town covered in cloudy Saran wrap, which sets me to wondering what's behind the sheets.

I reach toward a flap when Lewis catches me.

"Please don't, Mr. Finnegan. There will be plenty to see in just a moment."

I don't reply verbally, because I don't much like being told what to do by a brain in a coat, but I nod and leave the plastic flap alone.

"Busted," Simmons says.

I don't give him the pleasure of a response and stay after North Face. "Seems like you guys have been busy," I say to Lewis.

"We have, yes."

"And well funded," I add.

"Also, yes. The small group of people who have been following Dr. Campbell's work have invested heavily in his success."

"And he's clearly done a lot with their money," I say, looking up at a crane arm that towers over the site. "Always was a hard worker."

We pass several more plastic-covered structures before arriving at the largest translucent sheet, which spans about a football field left to right—easily the largest object in the pit. Several ATVs, equipment containers, and computer workstations are scattered in front of it.

Lewis stops just in front of a yellow-outlined doorway in the plastic. "You're the only one allowed inside, Mr. Finnegan."

"Don't miss me too much," Simmons says.

I give him a cheer-up nod with my chin. "If I see any velociraptors, I'll be sure to tell them you're dying to meet them."

"Screw you."

Lewis gestures toward the plastic and then pulls it aside. I step into a small intermediary room and then out through a second plastic drape. On the other side, I'm met by one hell of a giant-ass ring. It's gotta be eighty, maybe ninety yards across. Looks like something outta Stargate, only bigger. Two halves of a second ring rise to the right and left sides of the main one. Whereas the central ring is comprised of geometric shapes, the outer halves are layered like bands of plywood—only the material looks metallic.

"Welcome to the Orion Theta Project, Patrick," says a familiar voice from behind a formidable four-sided work area composed of curved computer monitors. The quad is about twenty yards ahead and not far from the ring's base. "And, damn, if it isn't good to see you." It's Aaron, dressed in a similar orange North Face coat to Lewis, bearing the Rutgers University logo on the breast. He adjusts his glasses and walks out to greet me with his arms spread wide.

Always was a hugger.

"Good to see you too." I brace myself against Aaron's double-armed greeting, then nod toward the massive ring and another twenty or so people working throughout the space. "Seems you found something after all."

He spins around. "Isn't it magnificent?"

"Sure. And I bet you have Richard Dean Anderson on retainer somewhere?" I'm trying to ease the strangeness of the situation, but now I'm suddenly wondering if I might owe Simmons a Benjamin and some booze. Still, logic says there's a perfectly reasonable *human* reason for whatever this is.

"Richard Dean Anderson," Aaron says with a bemused smile. "You're not actually that far from the truth, Patrick. Come on."

I attempt an inquiry, but Aaron's on the move. I follow him toward the ring and then head up a stone staircase that looks like it belongs in Rome. The ring's apex looms overhead, and I get my first sense of just how thick the structure is—twelve, thirteen feet, easy. And all over it is some sort of design, like an ancient language, carved into the irregular surface.

"What do you think?" Aaron says as he spreads his arms and spins around to gauge my reaction.

"It… looks like you managed to build an old Ferris wheel without cars. Congratulations."

I've never been the best with expressing my emotions, and right now is no exception. Obviously, I'm curious about the object. And if I'm being honest, somewhat apprehensive too. I'm really hoping that Aaron is going to tell me this is all his making, but I can't think of a single good reason why one would build whatever the hell this is all the way in Antarctica. Instead, I'm imagining weird invasion scenarios, none based in reality. And the fact that my brain keeps going there is proof that my old man was right—too many sci-fi movies too late at night *does* mess with your head. Never mind the fact that it was my only escape from everything else that was messing with my head back then.

"It is really old," Aaron replies, repeating my very technical description. "But it's definitely not a Ferris wheel."

"So what'd you build then?"

"Ha! *We* didn't build anything. But *they* did."

"They?"

"Come on."

Before I can get anything else out of him, Aaron quicksteps down the stairs, dashes into the quad of computer stations, and shoos away a few staffers.

I follow as he pulls up some sort of data chart on several screens showing what looks to be microscopic cross-sections of various materials.

"What are we looking at?" I ask.

He dismisses the question with a wave of his hand. "Eh, it's spectral imaging combined with microscopy and carbon dating, plus some other stuff."

"And it tells you…?"

Aaron expands one of the x-ray-like images and steps away from the screen. It's his silent cue that I'm supposed to examine it.

"That's, uh… real interesting."

"Pleistocene epoch," he says, tapping the screen. "Pleistocene, Patrick!"

I must look like a deer in headlights because he gets exasperated and throws his hands up. "Twenty-thousand years ago."

"So, you didn't build this," I say, more to assure myself of the facts than to reiterate his— well, let's just call them "speculations."

"Certainly not." He brings up another image and more data, and then he taps the screen, as if I'm supposed to read it all in one sitting and come to whatever conclusion he's arrived at. "We've got Homo sapiens, and nearly extinct Neanderthals and Denisovans— they're all running around in the late Pleistocene epoch. Quaternary period, Cenozoic era. Follow?"

I laugh. "We're knuckle-draggers, and it's a long time ago. I think I've got it."

"Hardly. But…" He tries to find his words. "Back then, we're improving tools, language, shelters… but nothing like this."

"It's a stone circle," I say. "Maybe it's a… a giant fire-pit ring that got tipped up on its end after melting a spot in the glacier."

Shows you how much I know about geology.

Now it's Aaron's turn to laugh. "The region wasn't frozen back then. The Ellsworth *Subglacial* Highlands are *sub*-glacial. This was once as pretty as Camp Cayuga."

"Hey. Nothing's as pretty as camp," I reply, careful not to let my friend tread upon our youth's sacred summer grounds.

He gives me an acquiescing nod. "While that may be, someone placed this ring exactly where it stands a very long time ago."

"And you're here to figure out who," I say.

"No." He stares at me for a beat. "I'm here because I'm going to open it."

3

1505, Monday, April 25, 2027
West Antarctica
Ellsworth Subglacial Highlands Excavation Site
The Ring

"YOU'RE WHAT?"

"Opening it," Aaron replies.

"As in…"

"It's a portal."

The cold weather's gotten to his head. Or maybe to mine. Either way, one of us is delusional. And since I know Aaron isn't an idiot, and I feel just fine, I realize that he's playing me like a fiddle. "Hold on. I'll go grab my Egyptian headdress," I say with a chuckle. "Don't go through without me."

Aaron tilts his head at me. He isn't laughing. "I'm not kidding, Patrick."

I take it back. Maybe he is delusional.

I point up at the ring. "This is a…"

"A portal."

"Built by…"

He shrugs. "No one from around here."

"As in, E.T.?"

He nods.

"Holy Mary and all the saints." I stare at him for a three count to make sure he's not busting my chops. "You're really serious right now."

"Completely."

I turn away and growl. I can't believe I got roped into this. "You got me, Aaron. Got me good. And Lord knows how you fooled all those investors into giving you this stuff. But I'm not buying it."

"Patrick, listen."

I spin on him. "And you know what chaps my ass the most? You used Jack. *Jack*, goddammit."

"I can explain."

"What's to explain?" I raise a hand at the ring. Everyone else in the workspace has stopped their side conversations. "You found some ancient circle, and instead of using your head like you used to, you've gone and invented some ass-crazy story because you…"

"Because I what?"

"Nah. Never mind."

"No. I want to hear it, Pat. You got something to say, then say it."

"You wanted fame."

"Uh-huh. That all?"

"And you wanted to stop being the punchline of everyone's jokes."

Aaron's face reddens.

"Hey, you said it yourself, Aaron. Said they wouldn't laugh about what you found. But this? I…"

"And if I had explained that over the phone"—he thrusts a finger to the ring—"would you have come, Pat? Would you have taken me at my word? Because it seems to me that the way I even got you here wasn't by saying I needed you, it was by saying all this was for Jack."

I grit my teeth at him. If we didn't have so much history together, I'd punch him right now. Or maybe a long past is precisely why I *should* hit him. "You know I've got your back. But this?" I nod at the ring. "You don't need me for whatever the hell this is."

"I can explain it," he says.

I turn and walk away. The government was wrong to get involved. "I'm not the one lending you money, Aaron. Save it for the people who care."

"Dammit, Pat. I said I can explain it."

"Congratulations."

I'm far enough away that he shouts his next words. "It's made from an element we've never seen before."

"Well, congrats on that too." I'm still walking straight out of here and telling my spook handler where he can shove this op. I should have known—damn freaks.

"In case you're wondering, that new element is why all the governments are interested. That's why the universities have sent teams of their best researchers."

I slow, but I'm not turning around.

Aaron keeps talking. "Think about it. A 200,000-year-old structure made from a synthetic element we've never encountered anywhere else? What would you conclude?"

"I dunno, Aaron. But I'm guessing I'd exhaust all other possibilities before I jumped to yours."

"And you think I haven't?"

I'd insulted him once. I knew I couldn't do it again without walking out on our friendship completely.

I stop and turn to face him, still about fifteen yards away, and then point toward the ring. "You're saying you're not the only kook who thinks that's the real-life version of SG-1?"

He raises an eyebrow and shakes his head as if taking pity on me.

"And Richard Dean Anderson isn't about to yell 'Cut' and say, 'Great take, everybody. But let's do it one more time'?"

Again, Aaron shakes his head.

"Crap." I gesture toward the computer quad. "Then you better show me what you've got."

THERE SEEMS to be a mutual sense of relief shared between Aaron and me as he presents his findings: I'm glad he's not completely lost his mind, and he seems happy that I'm at least listening to his evidence with interest. And the truth is, I am interested, even if it's to reinforce my case against him. But as Lewis hands me a hot cup of coffee and a protein bar, I have the sense that I'm not the first person Dr. Aaron Campbell and his team have had to court.

"Thanks," I say to Lewis.

"Need anything else, just let me know."

"That will be all, Lewis," Aaron adds without looking from his screen. "Now. See here?"

I sip from the metal mug and adjust the stool under my ass. "Yut. Looks like a fractal or something."

"Yes," Aaron exclaims. "That's exactly right. Just like the base element, we have no record of it. That, and it has some very peculiar properties."

"Like what?"

"Well, first we used portable X-ray fluorescence spectrometry, then inductively coupled plasma mass spectrometry, and then ICP-atomic emission spectrometry…" He pauses, hopefully sensing that he's lost me, and turns around to look at the ring for a moment. "Why don't I just show you. Come."

I take a bite from the protein bar and follow him back up the stairs, careful not to spill my coffee. Aaron motions me to the ring and then points to one of the many block-like protrusions along the circumference.

"You ready?" he asks.

"Uh. Sure."

Aaron slides the block three inches to the left. The moment he does, a square yard of the ring's surface lights up in blue.

I step away and nearly spill my drink. "Sweet Mother of Mary. What the hell'd you do?"

"Turned it on," Aaron said with a grin.

"Thing's got batteries?"

"Not as far as we can tell. Those fractals I showed you? They're able to grab energy and channel it here."

I open my mouth to say something but can't think of anything intelligent.

"Don't worry," he says with a hand on my arm. "We're not sure how it works either. But we do know this. Look." Aaron motions me closer. There are hundreds of tiny symbols and hash marks illuminated in yellow against the glowing blue surface.

"What is it?" I ask

"We didn't know at first. A language, a codex?"

"And now?"

He chuckles. "The easiest thing of all. A puzzle."

"That's easy?"

"Of course. Didn't you play with blocks as a kid?"

"I guess."

"And didn't you find the interaction stimulating as you tried to work out how to balance one atop the other?"

"I wouldn't go so far as to call it stimulating, but—"

"This is like playing with blocks." Aaron touches a second block near the edge of the blue region that activates a second patch along the ring's metallic surface.

"But what do all the tiny symbols mean?"

"That's the beauty of a puzzle. Symbols don't have to mean anything. In fact, if you're trying to communicate with a foriegn group, the less meaning, the better. Instead, you're trying to establish patterns."

"And why's that?"

"Well, because meaning can be tough to interpret. Words are filled with polysemy."

"Poly who?"

He shakes his head. "Multiple meanings, double entendre. And for each use, you need subtext to understand it. Consider, for example, the simple phrasal verb to take off. I can take off a hat, watch the plane as it takes off, a new song can take off in popularity, take off some time from work, or tell an annoying child to take off."

"I can see how that could be problematic, yeah."

"If you add another phrase to the first, now you're talking about several permutations of possible meanings. Worse still is the issue of tone. Ever seen that classic one on the Internet?"

I have no idea what Aaron's talking about, so I'm grateful when he continues without me having to ask.

"I never said she stole my money," he says.

I give him a look. "Come again?"

"No, the phrase: I never said she stole my money. Depending on which word you stress, those seven words can create a sentence that means seven different things. '*I* never said she stole my money,' implies the speaker's innocence while simultaneously implicating someone's guilt, whereas 'I never said she *stole* my money,' asserts that the woman in question might not be a klepto-maniac but could have done something else scandalous with the money."

"Ah. Gotcha," I say.

"So, as you can see, from an anthropological standpoint, language is inherently troublesome, whereas puzzles are far more effective in establishing a connection."

"And you've found them? Puzzles, I mean?"

"Oh, have we ever." Aaron gives me a smile so big that his eyes disappear, then he shouts down to his staff and moves his hand in a circle. "Let's fire it up."

I'M STANDING beside Aaron in the computer quad as a small army of researchers starts rolling towers of scaffolding into place around the ring. A few platforms are lowered down from trusses along the ceiling too. The affair takes about fifteen minutes before Aaron gives them the go-ahead to "initiate level upsilon."

At his word, people take turns sliding, pushing, and twisting the various geometric shapes scattered across the ring's surface. Each person keeps referencing an iPad and talking into an in-ear comm. The four staffers behind the main computer stations, each under Aaron's watchful eye, talk back to the teams on the scaffolding while monitoring a dozen screens.

With each action on the ring, a new section lights up. The blue patches and yellow text cover about 20 percent of the surface.

"Level upsilon complete," Lewis says to Aaron. "All readings are nominal. We're clear for level phi."

"Initiate," Aaron replies as he gives a knife-edge hand chop through the air.

Again, the researchers move shapes across the ring's surface, and more of the structure lights up. There's also a new tremor in the ground.

Just then, my radio chirps, followed by a voice. "Wic, this is Simmons."

"Send it."

"We're getting some sort of low energy vibration out here."

"It's all right," I reply as I work to keep my voice calm. "Dr. Campbell's just showing me something."

"Copy. And the light coming from behind the plastic?"

"That's Dr. Campbell's doing too. Everything's green."

"Understood. Simmons out."

Aaron watches me let go of the radio attached to my chest and then looks back at Lewis.

"Psi complete, Doctor," Lewis says. "Clear for chi."

Aaron nods. "Initiate chi."

Again, his staff moves through the scaffolding like worker ants on a mission for their queen, moving the ring's protrusions and causing more of the object to light up. The hum in the ground is getting louder too.

Aaron must sense my apprehension and says, "It's okay. All part of the puzzle."

His words of encouragement don't alleviate my concerns, however, and I find myself squeezing my SCAR17's pistol grips tighter.

By the time Aaron orders level psi, I swear there's some sort of energy flickering across the ring's imaginary plane. It's like a thin veil of haze with an electrical storm behind. The hum is growing louder too, to the point that I have to raise my voice at Aaron.

"The last five letters of the Greek alphabet," I say in his ear.

He nods.

"What happens when you get to omega?"

He holds his hood to keep it from whipping his face as a gust of wind kicks up from the ring. "We don't know. Never got that far."

"Why not?"

"Was waiting for you, Musketeer."

This all feels impulsive. I need to think it through and talk Aaron down, but there's no time. Two of the main towers are swaying, and I'm concerned these researchers are too much scientist and not enough engineer.

"All systems look good," Lewis yells back to Aaron.

"Let's do it," he replies.

I grab Aaron's shoulder. "I want Simmons and the rest of the teams in here."

"No, no, no." He casts me a forlorn look. "You're always preparing for and assuming the worst. But this isn't the worst, Pat.

We're about to do something amazing here. Don't ruin this moment for me."

My gut doesn't like this. But he's got a point: I do always anticipate the worst. But only because the worst is what tends to happen in real life. Meanwhile, the best remains just out of reach. It's called being realistic. "You sure about this?"

"Through fire and mud." He puts out his hand. We hadn't done this since before I dropped out of college. Jeez.

What are you doing here, Wic? This is crazy.

I place my hand on top of his, then say, "Through fire and mud."

Aaron gives me an electric smile then yells at Lewis. "Initiate level omega."

4

1548, Monday, April 25, 2027
West Antarctica
Ellsworth Subglacial Highlands Excavation Site
The Ring

A FLASH of light leaps across the ring's plane as Lewis gives orders over comms. To my surprise, the researchers on the scaffolding start descending. That's a relief. The last report I want to send is that someone fell to their deaths because no one knew how to set up a simple safety harness. But the retreat doesn't explain what "initiating level omega" entails.

"That's our cue." Aaron touches my shoulder. "Come on."

"Our cue for what?" I shout. But Aaron steps out of the quad and heads toward the steps. I lunge and grab his arm. "What are you doing?"

"The last piece of the puzzle."

Another arc of electricity snaps across the ring. The distinct scent of ozone is making the hairs in my nose curl. The wind is picking up too. "Do you even know what this is, Aaron?"

He gives me a sideways look but says nothing.

"I'll take that as a no."

"It's an opportunity," he says finally. "Someone put this here and left us clues. As far as I can tell, we're the first ones with the tools and intelligence to put the pieces together. And we've exhausted what there is to learn. This"—he thrusts a finger at the glowing ring —"this is our next step. And we've got to take it, Pat."

You know that part in a movie where the main character is about to walk through a door, but you know there's something bad waiting on the other side? You're yelling at the screen, "Don't do it!" but they can't hear you? This is that moment, only it's not pre-recorded. It's happening in real-time. And unlike actors and their stunt doubles who get up off the floor when the director yells "Cut," people die in situations like this—*have* died. And I've been there to see it—more times than I care to talk about.

It's the improvised explosive under a pile of garbage that takes out your point. It's the kid you let go yesterday who decides to pick up a Dragunov SVD semi-automatic sniper rifle and blow the brains out of your corporal today. And it's the eighty-two-millimeter Soviet mortar round that crashes through the southeast corner of your FOB in the middle of the night and takes out the latrine. Sure, it's just a restroom, people think. Until they realize Murphy and Higgins weren't in their bunks. Those kids didn't die killing bad guys. They died taking a goddamn shit. And for what?

"Patrick. Please let go," Aaron says, looking down at my hand.

I pull away and grab my SCAR17's forward grip.

You know what? If Aaron wants to do whatever he's determined to do, then I won't stop him. Not like I could anyway—people are gonna do what people wanna do.

Sure, I want to tell him I feel like this is a bad idea. That someone needs to do more research about whatever the hell this thing is. That there needs to be a larger team, more equipment— maybe an entire battalion at the ready. I don't know. Just, not this.

But it's not my call. And even if it was, I doubt it would do anything. At the end of the day, people die whether you want them to or not. And when you get home, you're left with bad memories and that sense of—what is it again? Yut, there it is. *Helplessness*.

"Be careful," I say to Aaron.

He nods and then starts up the ancient-looking set of stairs. My pulse has picked up, and I'm willing my breathing to slow down to a target rate of eight breaths per minute. Any faster, and I won't be in the right headspace.

I raise my SCAR17 and watch Aaron reach the summit through my ACOG. I have no idea what I'm targeting should something happen, but this is what I do—cover my team and wait. Sure, images of little green men and Pharaohs with plasma spears tempt my imagination. But that crap's not real. This is.

Aaron reaches for a shape at the center of the ring's lower arc. It's the only section not illuminated. This must be it: the final button push. Level omega.

I lift my right cheek off my weapon and blink twice to clear my vision. Then I'm back on the scope. The ring is more active, as if sensing that someone is about to awaken it like a dragon from a long sleep.

Aaron's working the block, pushing it to the left, when a bolt of electricity jumps out of the ring's center and licks at one of the scaffolding towers. Sparks shoot in all directions, and some plastic catches on fire.

Eh, screw this. I grab the radio and open the channel. "Simmons. I need two teams now," I yell. "Set up on me."

"Say again?"

"Teams One and Two, double time!"

"Roger that."

Aaron's still working the button when two more lightning bolts snap through the air. One strikes a truss along the ceiling, and another crashes into a cluster of equipment containers. Both hits result in more strikes and small fires. And yet Aaron seems completely calm. Fearless even. Maybe he missed his calling as a Marine.

Aaron's body jerks as the block slides to a halt, and then he stands back. All at once, the wind dies, the electrical energy dissipates, and a shimmering blue energy field pops across the ring's inner plane. It's semi-translucent, like looking through shallow waters from the open side of a Blackhawk. Beyond the thin film is a second smaller ring, and past the film across its surface is a third even smaller ring. The circles seem to repeat and fade away into infinity.

All is quiet save for the low, slowly pulsing hum in the ground and the occasional soft snap of a small lightning bolt spider-walking its way along the ring's edge.

Aaron throws his arms out to the sides and lets out a cowboy-like *wah-hoooo!* He spins to face me and then his team. "We did it!"

I glance to my left and see Simmons. His eyes are wide and locked on the ring, and my other Marines are just as bewildered.

"Lewis," Aaron shouts as he bounds back down the steps. "Sensors! What do they say?"

While Lewis gives Aaron an update, Simmons leans over. "What the hell, Wic? I mean, what the actual hell?"

"I dunno. Just keep weapons trained on that." I nod toward the ring.

"This for real?"

I nod. "Seems like I lost the bet."

"Ya think? I have the sudden impression that Sigourney Weaver is the only one getting out of here alive."

"Easy, Simmons." I pump the flat of my hand to calm him. "Let's stay cool. I'll go talk to the professor. You have the teams."

"Roger."

With my SCAR trained on the ring, I move toward the quad. It's filled with even more researchers than before. They're scurrying around like kids on Christmas morning, shaking boxes and making guesses. Only, in this case, they're tapping screens and comparing notes.

"Whadda we got, Aaron?" I ask, far from sharing his team's visible sense of wonder and delight.

Aaron adjusts his glasses and waves me toward one of the larger computer monitors. "Look here. You see these lines?"

It looks like a cross-section of the stock market index, climbing steadily from left to right. Several different colored lines are crisscrossing one another, but all seem to be on an upward trend.

"This is tracking several different kinds of radiation. As you can see, it's climbing steadily as we activate each level." He notes the stages labeled upsilon, phi, chi, and psi.

"And what's that?" I point to a sharp spike in a few colors that

53

shoots clear off the chart, while the other colors take an equally sharp nosedive. "Looks dramatic."

"Oh, it is. That's when we initiated level omega."

"And it means what?"

"Well, first of all, the ring is putting out a lot of different kinds of radiation, most of which we can track. Fits within the range of the ionizing and non-ionizing radiation spectrum."

"Layman's terms?"

"Uh"—Aaron thinks for a second—"Non-ionizing radiation won't kill you, whereas ionizing will."

"So, like my TV remote versus a nuke."

"Something like that, yes. We see both types slowly climbing with each level we activate. Nothing that will kill you, of course. But enough that you wouldn't want to play with those buttons all day without a suit on. And this is exactly what we've seen with all our previous tests."

"And then here?" I point to the spike and drop off region just after level omega was initiated .

"That's what all the fuss is about. All the ionizing—the dangerous type—all those waves drop to nil. While the non-ionizing spike off the charts."

"And what's it mean?"

Aaron looks at Lewis and then a few of the other researchers who've been listening in on our conversation. They cast each other all sorts of smiles and raised eyebrows like they've all heard the punchline of an unspoken joke.

"It means that whatever's on the other side of that plane is putting out an amazing amount of power, energy that is not harmful to living organisms."

"So it's an energy source?" I ask, hoping that's all it is.

"No, not really. At least not in ways that would help us as a civilization. Remember, it's uranium that fuels nuclear power plants, not your TV remote."

"So if it's not an energy source"—I turn to look up at the ring —"what is it?"

Aaron adjusts his glasses and looks at his colleagues. God, they're all acting so damn giddy that it's getting on my nerves.

"We believe it's a portal to another dimension," Aaron says.

I can't help but laugh. Loud, man. Like they're all pulling my leg. My outburst has an interesting effect on them, though—their faces grow stone cold. I mean, like they want to murder me with their eyes but lack the superpower to do it kinda cold.

"God. You're all actually serious about this."

"Quite." Aaron pushes out his chin and smooths his coat. "And we expect everyone else in here to act professionally with what is, need I remind you, a matter of national security."

Is the college professor really grandstanding me on national security? Jesus, James, and Joseph—I've gotta get out of this job.

I run a gloved hand over my beard. "So, it's a portal then. To where?"

"Your guess is as good as ours," Aaron replies. He's still eyeing me cautiously but seems satisfied enough to keep expounding. "But the destination isn't our greatest concern."

Two men behind Aaron clear their throats.

"At least not to me," Aaron says as if to clarify his previous statement. "The astrophysicists, on the other hand—"

"*We* very much do care," one of the stargazers said. No, that's astronomy. Same stuff, whatever.

"And yet the primary objective of this particular research project is not where the portal leads," Aaron says, clearly directing most of his speech to the astrophysicists by way of a pointed reminder. "It's who put it here and whether or not they are still willing to converse with us."

"Anthropology over stargazing. Got it."

The two astrophysicists bristle at my conclusion, but Aaron seems downright proud.

"So whadda we do now? Go through?"

"Lord, no," Aaron says. "What do you think this is, the movies?"

"Uh, yut." I raise a hand to the ring. "Material evidence A."

"Patrick, there's no telling what might happen to our physiology if we attempt to cross that plane."

"I thought you said it was projecting non-ionizing radiation."

"It is. But that doesn't mean we just send anybody into it. That's a death wish, and far outside the scope of our ethical standards. North Korea? Fine. But we're not them."

"So, what do we do then? Just sit around and wait?"

"Actually, that's precisely what we are going to do." Again, Aaron seems proud of my conclusion and is returning to his more relaxed self. "Logic insists that whatever sentient species created this ring and placed it here is also more than capable of returning through it on their own accord."

"So why haven't they already? I mean, not as in right now, but as in, ever."

Aaron pushes his glasses up the bridge of his nose. "Who's to say they haven't?"

I freeze, unsure how to respond.

"But let's say for the sake of argument that they haven't. By the way, our research suggests that this site has sat undisturbed for millennia. Do you even know how long it took us to open this subglacial cavity? Just be glad you got to skip to the end, Patrick.

"Anyway, I digress. There are several explanations as to why the species responsible for this ring have remained aloof. For one—"

"Uh, for one, perhaps you'd better leave this to SETI," says a long-bearded man in orange bib suspenders over a wool sweater. He reaches out to shake my hand. "Hi, Sergeant Finnegan."

"That's Master Gunnery Sergeant," Aaron says.

I give my friend an approving look. Somebody's been paying attention.

"Sorry, Sergeant." The scientist clears his throat. "Dr. John Walker, SETI Institute, Mountain View, California."

"Nice to meet you." I shake his hand. "Big fan of your whiskey."

"What? Oh, right. Me too."

I still can't believe how relaxed everyone seems in light of the present situation. Then again, live with anything long enough and it becomes normative. "You were saying, Dr. Walker?"

"Right, yes. Most plausible explanations are based upon the Fermi Paradox, though several have been ruled out. The derivatives, however, are far more interesting."

"You'll have to excuse me, but Furby Paradox?"

"Fermi," he stresses. "Encino Fermi, Italian physicist who created the first nuclear reactor? No?"

I stare at him as if that's supposed to mean anything to me.

"Never mind," Dr. Walker says. "Suffice to say, Fermi was the first to hypothesize why, in a universe so vast, we had yet to encounter extraterrestrial intelligent life."

"Hold up. Are you saying aliens, doc?"

"We prefer extraterrestrial life."

"But still, aliens?"

Walker sighs—irritated. "Yes, *aliens* if you must."

I run a hand down my beard again. I need a drink. Bad. This is —well, it's insane, really. The fact that there are whole groups of people who've been waiting for a moment just like this makes everything even more unsettling.

"Go on."

"One of the resulting hypotheses that might apply here is one which postulates that a species may in fact meet its end before it is able to make, or in this case, re-make contact with Earth. They are just as prone as we are to cataclysmic natural disasters as well as self-eradication."

I look at the ring and then back to Dr. Walker. "So you're saying that they could have placed this here thousands of years ago only to go extinct later on because of a nuclear war over a territory dispute?"

"Among other scenarios, yes."

Aaron jumps in. "It would go a long way in explaining why the ring was never activated from their side again."

"Again? As in, you have evidence that it was active once before?"

"My apologies. That was a bit of a slip up on my part. The causality arguments are plentiful, and I didn't mean to suggest that this ring got here on its own. But it stands to reason that a mechanism of this magnitude would not go unused, especially upon its construction."

"Dandy. But what I need to know right now is what you think the chances are that something hostile is going to come through that gate?"

Aaron and Dr. Walker look at each other and grin.

"Hostile?" Aaron says and shares a chuckle with Dr. Walker. "Zero. If some ancient extraterrestrial civilization wanted to conqueror us, don't you think they would have done it when humanity was, as you say, knuckle draggers?"

Now most of the scientists in the quad are laughing.

"Fair enough," I reply. "But where your job is to infer that all yellow brick roads lead to Oz, my job is to assume everyone wants to kill Dorothy. So you'll have to forgive me if I don't really buy your arguments."

"Sergeant Finnegan," Dr. Walker says as he puts his hands together like a hippy. "Please understand that we have the very best and brightest minds at work here."

"And Greece had Aristotle. Know who built roads straight through their vineyards? The Romans."

"Sergeant Finnegan, I—"

"Listen, you guys keep doing your thing. That's not my call. But if anything comes through that, and it so much as looks at any one of us the wrong way, my orders are to protect every person in this facility with extreme prejudice. And that will include shutting down the ring ASAP—no questions asked. Copy?"

Aaron doesn't even look at his counterparts. "Of course, Patrick. We all understand."

"Good. Now what's your ETA on possible contact?"

"We… we have none." He shrugs and offers me a bemused smile. "There's no precedent for any of this."

"So it could be in three minutes or three days."

"Or three decades," he adds. "We really don't know."

"Oh no you don't," I say to Aaron. "You're not roping me into staying one day longer than the month I gave you."

"You said six weeks maximum."

Son of a bitch. "Yut. I sure did."

"So that gives us two more weeks together."

"I can do the math, Aaron."

"Great. Then my official request, according to your own mandate of national security, is that you set up whatever kind of watch you deem sufficient up until you are relieved."

"Don't forget to include our comrades in the roster," says one researcher with a heavy Russian accent.

"Nor our specialists," says another brain in a fluffy coat—this one speaking Queens English if I'm not mistaken.

I get the feeling that Aaron has denied requests for any other military presence to be admitted besides my team. Now that things have escalated, and the researchers are face to face with the guy who'll be calling the shots from here on out, they seem only too eager for their own country's military attachments to get a hand in the cookie jar. Can't say I blame them, either. Were the roles reversed, hell knows I'd be kicking down doors to let Uncle Sam in.

At the end of the day, however, I'm just a jarhead on his last op. What do I care about little green men and professors in lab coats? As far as I'm concerned, they can all stay down here and freeze their balls off, giggling over radiation stock tickers until their dicks glow.

"We'll make sure everyone gets a turn," I say. "But I'm the head of the chain of command. Anything happens down here while I'm away—and I mean anything—I'm the first to know. Not your Aunt Sarah or your best friend on Twitter. Me. And I'll detain whoever the hell I want if that's not followed to the letter. Copy?"

Heads nod, and nervous exchanges are shared. Apparently, that's not how people talk to each other in college.

"Anything you need," Aaron says. "Just say the word."

"You can start by giving my men something warm to drink and a few chairs."

"Of course."

"And if you have any extra tables, we could use a few for gear. Then Simmons"—I glance over my shoulder and wave him over —"Simmons here is going to provide you with a materials list to build a shield wall."

"A shield wall?" Dr. Walker says. He looks at Aaron. "Is this really necessary, Campbell?" Then he looks to me. "This is a secure research facility, not your personal playground for blowing up—"

"Listen, Dr. Whiskey," I say, stepping toward the man. "You have your expertise, I have mine. And you also have my word that if nothing hostile comes through that *thing*, then we won't get in your way. Promise. But if things go sideways, it's my job to be ready. And part of battle readiness includes having something to hide your skinny ass behind if the aliens turn out to be a lot more like Xenomorphs than Marvin the Martian."

"I can live with that," Dr. Walker said.

"Fine and dandy. Then we have ourselves an understanding." I look at Aaron. "I'll leave you all to your work then, and we'll see to ours."

"Sounds like a plan," Aaron replied. Then he extended his hand to me, and we shook. Not a hug, not a head nod. Just a handshake between professionals. "Thanks for coming, Patrick. I'm glad you're here."

"Sure." The natural thing to say is I am happy to be here too. But I'm not, and I don't feel like lying just to be courteous. Instead, all I can manage is, "Glad we're able to be of service." And even that sickens me a little.

I walk out of the quad with Simmons and head back toward teams One and Two.

"Hey," Simmons says. "Nice speech. I think they'll stay out of our way now."

"Let's hope."

"Just one problem with what you said."

"Oh?"

"Even Marvin the Martian had a badass ray gun."

Son of a bitch.

5

0601, Tuesday, April 26, 2027
West Antarctica
Ellsworth Subglacial Highlands Excavation Site
The Ring

"You're late," Simmons says as I step through the plastic for my morning shift. The ring looks the same as I left it yesterday—still on and still asking for trouble.

"What's the matter?" I ask. "Did room service forget to put chocolate on your pillow last night?"

"Cute." Simmons thumbs over his shoulder. "Keeping Vlad and his two fire teams in their corner is like trying to herd cats."

"They're just curious, I'm sure."

But Simmons shakes his head. "I had to threaten to take the guy's phone away just to keep him from Tweeting pics."

"Perfect." One more reason I hate cell phones.

"So, yeah. If housekeeping did forget the turndown service, that would be the least of my problems."

"Coffee?" I offer a thermos I topped off in the mess hall.

"Actually, no." Simmons nods to a cluster of steel tables in a back corner of the plastic-walled enclave. It appears to be brimming with all sorts of culinary equipment. "Seems that whoever's funding the good doctor didn't want to skimp on the researcher's gastrointestinal health. Got a damn espresso machine from Italy."

"Don't ever let them fool you, Simmons."

He casts me a questioning look. "How's that?"

"Money does buy love, and a whole lot more." I toss him the thermos and then head for the computer quad.

Aaron looks like he hasn't moved since I left him the night before. The bags under his eyes confirm my suspicions. "How goes it?"

Aaron looks up. "Patrick! You're just in time."

The guy's hopped up on coffee—that, or he's got a natural high from his discovery. Can't say that I blame him, only my version of happiness would revolve around blowing this ring to ash.

"In time for what?"

"Come, come." He waves me over. I give a quick nod to Walker, who also looks like he hasn't slept a wink.

"Check this out," Aaron says.

The monitor he's pointing at shows more stock market lines. I guess I should be honored that he has so much confidence in my powers of observation. Still, without an extended tutorial on this stuff, I'm pretty much worthless.

"So," I say, taking in the displays. "Looks like the DeLorean's still going eighty-eight miles per hour. Flux capacitor looks good as well. Holding steady at 1.21 gigawatts."

Aaron is nodding absently, then turns toward me with a wide grin. "Nice one."

"Just keeping you on your toes."

"Doc Brown aside," he says, leaning toward the monitor. "We're detecting some new radiation emissions. Here, and here." He indicates two new colored lines that I don't remember from the night before.

"And they mean?"

Aaron pushes up his glasses. "Well, up until now, we've had steady emissions of MW, RF, and ELF waves."

"Lost me."

"Microwaves, radio frequency, and extremely low frequencies. And plenty of emission in the visible light spectrum, but most of those seem to be originating from the ring's structure."

"As in, the physical object is producing all that?"

"More like gathering the energy from around it and redirecting it in a focused application. But these lines here are introducing something very different."

He pauses so long that I have to ask him to continue.

"Right. Sorry." He blinks several times. "What we're seeing now are variations in UV and IR spectrums. That's—"

"Ultraviolet and infrared. I know those."

"Very good."

"And they interest you because?"

"Well. For one, as I said, they're new. They've been introduced recently."

"Meaning, you think something started kicking them out on purpose."

"Potentially, yes. But their presence alone isn't what's so intriguing." Aaron taps on the screen, click-grabs one of the lines, and pulls it away from the graph. As he spins it into a three-dimensional shape, I see that its cross-section is shaped like a U. At the top of the shape's left stem, I see the negative sign symbol, whereas, at the top of the right side, I see the positive sign symbol. There's a zero under the middle of the U's trough.

"What's it mean?" I ask.

"It's oscillating," he replies.

"Not following. Don't all waves oscillate?"

"Of course. But…" Aaron pats his coat and then reaches into a pocket to pull out a small Mini Maglite. He switches it on and starts passing it back and forth across my face. "Like this."

I wince and lean away. "Okay?"

"Don't you get it?"

"No, Aaron."

He points the flashlight toward the ring. "It's scanning."

I look from Aaron to the ring to the computer monitor and back to the ring. "Right now."

"Yes. Right now."

I felt out in the open when the ring turned on last night, but this news takes me to a new level of vigilance. "Somehow, I liked it better when it was just a static wall."

"Extraterrestrial multi-spectrum portal node," Walker interjects.

I ignore him. "Can we send something of our own through? Maybe a drone?"

"Of course not," Aaron says—and a little too quickly for my taste. Not that I'm easily offended about much of anything, but let's at least talk it through, people.

"Care to elaborate?" I ask.

"Well, how would you feel if they sent a drone through?" Walker asks.

I cast him an irritated look, but it's an honest question. I imagine a bunch of scientists in an underground lab in Moscow or Beijing. "Probably pretty leery of it. Would want to know who's watching and why."

"Then it's safe to assume the same on their end," he concludes. "If we present even the slightest hint of hostility or suspicion, we could start things off on the wrong foot. And doing that with what is, by far, the greatest discovery in human history would be"—he lets out a forced breath—"well, let me tell you, it wouldn't be good."

"Except that they're the ones who put the ring on our planet, Doc. Where I come from, that means we have a right to investigate."

"Moral prerogatives aside," Aaron said in an apparent desire to keep things amicable. "Even if we did send a drone through, we have no guarantee that we could maintain a connection with it. Therefore, we'd be needlessly muddying the waters, as it were. Better to wait and see."

"Said no intelligence operative ever," I reply with no attempt to hide my disdain. My additional two-week commitment is beginning to feel like I signed up for couples therapy, and I'm pissed. "Listen, I get the idea of not wanting to project hostility. But we could quite literally be staring down the barrel of a gun. And we're just standing around here with our thumbs up our asses waiting to get taken out by God-knows-what? No. No way."

"Patrick, please."

Aaron reaches up to touch my shoulder, but I push his hand away.

"We already established that you have your role to play here and I have mine," I say. "But right now, I have zero intel on what this thing is meant for, who put it here, or why the hell they're currently scanning us. I get that it's your job to be scientifically curious and optimistic. Well, it's my job to believe that everyone who wants to kill you will take every chance they can to make their dreams come true—aliens or not."

"Extraterres—"

"Clamp it, Walker."

The SETI expert rocks back.

"If you want my opinion, we're sitting ducks out here even with the barricades we've set up. And where are all the kill switches? I'd much rather find out these bastards are frickin' Mary Poppins and have to apologize than be caught with a BB gun trying to take out the Predator. You feel me?"

"Give me your goddamn phone, Sergeant," Simmons yells.

I spin around to see Vlad fending off Simmons' attempt to keep the Russian from taking another pic of the ring.

"Sergeant Petrov," I yell at the Russian commander, and then I snap and point toward Vlad. "Get ahold of yourself before I relocate you to a medical unit."

"Is that a threat, Brooklyn America?" Vlad says as he pushes Simmons away.

"It's a promise, Vlad. Hand over the phone."

"Professor," Lewis says behind me. "We're getting some new activity."

I want to look at whatever Lewis is talking about, but Vlad has just punched Simmons in the face. I take off toward Vlad. But I'm not the only one—our guys and some of the Russians are running toward the confrontation. And here I thought we were supposed to be professionals. Shoulda' never accepted this mission.

I'm in the middle of Vlad and Simmons when one of the Brits yells, "Holy Queen Mother Almighty."

I catch one of Vlad's punches in my shoulder, knock his arms down, and turn around. There, hovering just in front of the ring mid-level, is a magenta-colored pancake the size of a garbage can lid. It's got what looks to be small black lenses on five sides and five blue-glowing square panels on the bottom.

The researchers throw themselves into chaos, grabbing recording devices and chattering like a bunch of concertgoers at a Taylor Swift show. Meanwhile, the security forces are staring at the thing slack-jawed.

"Cover down," I yell. "Safeties off. And keep your fingers off your triggers until I give the order."

I grab Simmons, who's nursing a swollen jaw. "You okay?"

"Stroganoff-eating bastard," Simmons replies and then spits out a mouthful of blood. "I'll be fine."

"Get to cover. Call the other teams down from the entrance. I want every barrel we have on that thing."

"On it."

My SCAR is in the high-ready position, and I'm moving back toward Aaron's position in the computer station quad. "Aaron?"

"Are you seeing this?" he exclaims.

"I am. And I need to insist that you and your team take cover with us."

He laughs. "Don't be ridiculous, Pat. Look!"

"This isn't an option. It's an order."

"It's investigating." Aaron spins to Walker. "We've made contact!"

The two scientists embrace and start celebrating like they just won the nerd Super Bowl. It takes me several seconds to get their attention while never taking my ACOG off the drone.

"Gentlemen, I need you to get to cover right—"

The drone's engine panels flare, and the thing creeps toward our position. Several people gasp and duck as the drone descends. Then a bright light sweeps around the drone's perimeter and, with it, the projection of a vertical laser-like wave of blue light. The beam seems harmless enough, but I hate feeling that I've just been scanned.

"Please put down your weapon," Aaron says, reaching toward my rifle.

"Not a chance in hell, buddy," I reply without taking my eyes off the drone. This here is a pawn, sent across the board to probe the enemy's front line. I can feel it.

The blue wave disappears, and a small red beam shoots across to the central hard drive locker. My gut says it's a laser sight for a weapon, and I'm a fraction of a second from taking down the drone when Aaron steps in front of my weapon.

"Dammit, Aaron," I yell and push him aside.

"It's just scanning," he replies. "Look!"

I cast a glance over my shoulder and see that the red laser is creating an intricate grid pattern on the locker's black wall about the size of a frisbee.

"Whoa," Lewis says, looking up at a computer monitor from his hiding spot on the floor. "CPU usage is—it's at 100 percent."

Aaron runs over. "It must be accessing our servers."

"Shut it down," I say, baffled that I'm the one who's watched more alien invasion movies than these brains. If I'm wrong, I'll send them "I'm so sorry" cards for life. But if I'm right? Damn, I don't wanna be right.

"I said, shut it down!" I'm walking toward what looks like a breaker box. With any luck, there's a master switch that will kill the computer quad.

"That's not your call." Aaron jumps in my way, but I push him aside. Hate getting physical with my friend, but we don't have time to argue.

"CPUs are reaching critical temps," Lewis announces.

I sidestep Aaron and bolt toward the electrical box. I throw the door open when the red laser grid on the lock disappears.

"Temps lowering," Lewis says.

The towers' cooling fans sound like the locker's about to take off. Meanwhile, the drone is hovering in place. No blue waves, no laser beams. It's just chilling, and all the researchers start to regain their confidence.

Lewis is back on his feet when Aaron orders him to start recording the drone again. The kid fumbles with a Sony video camera and eventually gets it up. He's so excited I don't think he realizes that he's getting dangerously close to the alien craft.

"Lewis," I say. "Back it on up, champ."

But he's too preoccupied—now narrating what he sees to the camera.

"Lewis." He's still not listening. God, these people are worse than Vlad. "Lewis, I need you to—"

Something pops beneath the drone and a projectile streaks toward Lewis. The kid screams as the video camera goes flying. Then his body jerks forward like something's hooked him. I noticed a filament connecting his chest to the drone's belly—and the thing's reeling him in like a fish.

"Open fire," I yell over comms, then aim at the drone. My SCAR barks as .308 rounds punch the target.

The drone rocks backward with every hit but rights itself almost immediately. And with each blow, Lewis is yanked a little further out of the quad. He crashes into a table and knocks over several monitors.

More rounds from the security forces crash against the drone's body and send out sparks. But the thing is surprisingly tough, and it's picking up speed toward the portal. That's when it dawns on me that the drone's taking Lewis with it.

The kid's screaming for Aaron—for anyone. But whatever's clamped to his chest isn't letting go. The Hollywood in me envisions breaking the line with a round, but the odds of that happening are slim to none and a waste of ammunition. Better just knock the thing out of the sky.

My ears are ringing from all the weapons fire, and the smell of spent cordite burns my nostrils. The researchers have their heads down, arms covering—crying for this to stop. But I'm not letting up, and neither are the teams.

Someone's round takes out one of the engine panels on the drone's belly. The explosion sends the drone wobbling sideways. Lewis slams into the ancient stairway and lets out a wail. But the drone rights itself and starts flying faster toward the portal. Whatever this thing is made of, it's strong, apparently opting for shielding over weaponry as it hasn't begun shooting munitions at us—at least not yet. No way anything we'd make could stand up to this much firepower unless welded to the side of an MBT.

"Changing," I yell out of habit, even though no one around me gives a damn. I drop the spent magazine and slam a new one home in under three seconds, all while moving forward after my target. As soon as I rack the first round, I send another volley at the drone, this time on full auto. I risk overheating the barrel and causing a malfunction, but I need to put as much lead on target as possible. The drone is closing on the portal, but as I drill it—taking out one of the lenses and a second engine panel—each .308 round sends the craft closer to the plane.

Lewis is getting dragged up the steps. He's stopped screaming, which means he's been knocked out, hit by a stray round, or incapacitated by something the drone's sent down the filament. Either way, his limp body is sliding across the summit toward the portal.

My whole life, I've tried to be useful, tried to solve problems before they become even bigger problems. But watching Lewis slide toward the gate is reminding me that my best years are probably behind me, and that I'm not thinking fast enough to solve this particular situation. Deep down, I hate myself for it.

"What are you doing?" Aaron screams at me—glasses gone, hair mussed. "Go get him!"

I curse and then make for the platform, hoping my Marines and the rest of the security forces have the presence of mind to stop firing. There's no time to wave them off.

My legs pump up the stairs, and I near Lewis. But the drone is pulling him too fast. So I dive toward the kid, my left hand extended. I manage to grab his boot just as my hip slams down on the stone.

The *ping-ping whap* of bullets smacking the drone slows as shouts of "Check fire" move down the line. With one hand still on Lewis's leg, I raise my SCAR and shoot at the flying bot. The action produces more sparks and loud *pings* but neither my added weight nor the weapon's fire seem to be dissuading the drone from its mission: it's still dragging Lewis and me toward the gate.

I aim at the spot where the tether protrudes from the drone's belly, hoping to break Lewis free, but it's no good. The drone intersects the portal's plane and vanishes a beat later.

We're sliding faster. Either I go in with him or let go right now.

I'm not sure if my hand gives out 'cause I'm old and can't hang on anymore, or if it's because I'm too afraid of what's on the other side. But I lose my grip and watch as Lewis's puffy orange North Face coat slips through the portal wall.

6

0630, Tuesday, April 26, 2027
West Antarctica
Ellsworth Subglacial Highlands Excavation Site
The Ring

"WHAT HAVE YOU DONE?" Aaron charges up the steps at me. "You let him go."

"Lost my grip." I push myself up and wince at the pain radiating from my hip.

"No, you"—Aaron pulls off his glasses—"you didn't try hard enough."

"Aaron, I was—"

"You just… you let him go. And, this isn't…" He turns away from me. "This isn't how it's supposed to go. How any of this is supposed to go."

"Listen, buddy. I'm sorry. But right now, we've—"

"We must continue the work." Aaron's eyes look glazed over as he stares at the portal. He's not thinking clearly.

I'm on my feet and trying to get in his face. "We've gotta ensure the safety of everyone else in here, Aaron. This gets shut down right now."

"Shut it down?" Aaron's eyes focus on mine. "It's been waiting to be opened for thousands of generations. We can't shut it down. Are you mad?"

When it comes to arguments, I don't mind when people have differences of opinion, so long as they're reasonable. And right now, my old friend is far from thinking clearly. "Aaron, listen. I think you need to take a breather and—"

"A breather?"

"Dr. Campbell, please," Walker says, coming up the steps behind Aaron. The SETI looks shaken too but appears to be less anxious than Aaron. That's good. "Why don't we just go sit down and—"

Aaron throws off Walker's hands. "No."

But the SETI expert isn't taking no for an answer. "Why don't we sit down and figure this out."

"There's nothing to figure out. We have the portal open. The work must continue, and we need to get Lewis back."

"Great. Let's talk it through." Walker is leading Aaron down the stairs. "If the extraterrestrial species determined that Lewis's biology could pass through the portal, perhaps it's possible to plan a rescue mission."

Aaron nods at this. "Yes. A rescue mission."

Walker's plan is horrible. But it's got Aaron engaged, and that's good. Walker gets Aaron seated and hands him a water bottle. "Just sit here while I speak with Sergeant Finnegan."

Walker pulls me aside as the researchers start to climb out of hiding and look around. One fluffy coat hands Aaron an iPad and turns his chair away from me.

"He's been under a lot of stress lately." Walker leads me outside the computer quad. "We all have. And first contact didn't go exactly as planned."

I manage a small laugh. "What were you expecting? A prom date?"

Walker blinks at me.

"Never mind."

"Right." Walker clears his throat. "Now, about what to do next."

"You're gonna shut it down."

Both his eyebrows go up. "But we just got it open."

"I don't care if it's Christmas Morning and Santa gave it to you personally. Do you have any idea what happens to people when they go through it?"

"Well, no. But—"

"Or what that drone intends to do with Lewis?"

"Of course not."

"Then we both agree that we're underprepared for this threat. Until we have a more robust plan of action and a hell of a lot more intel, we're shutting that thing down. I don't want anyone else getting pulled through, and that's the end of it."

"But Sergeant Finnegan, we—"

I thrust my left hand toward the ring. "Shut. It. Down."

Walker seems taken aback but compliant. "Yes. Yes, I suppose you're right." Maybe the E.T. freak is sensible after all.

"How do we do it?"

"There." He points to the lower right section that's half immersed in the platform. "The same component Dr. Campbell used to initiate level omega. Moving it back into place will—"

"I'm on it," I say before Walker has a chance to continue. Then I yell back to Simmons and the rest of the security elements. "Cover me. I'm headed up."

"Roger," Simmons replies and then relays my order.

As I mount the steps and clear the summit, I'm struck by how massive the energy field is. And I'm more than a little concerned that another drone might slide out and snag me. Knowing that something or someone could be just on the other side of this wall, staring at me, is unsettling. Granted, I'm trained for unsettling—my whole damn career's been unsettling. But this is a new level of crazy.

I edge toward the plane, one eye on my ACOG, and the other scanning for the spot where Aaron manipulated the ring's right side as it rose from the summit path. Thanks to Simmons and my own overactive imagination, I can't help but see Marvin the Martian pointing his ray gun at me from the wall's other side. Sure, and a Xenomorph XX121 ready to eat my face with its second sub-cranial mouth extension.

The button Aaron manipulated is two yards away. I release my left hand and cross it under my SCAR while still keeping my weapon aimed at the shimmering blue wall. The subsonic hum is even louder up here—damn thing's making my feet tingle.

I reach for the button when I hear Aaron shout from below.

"What are you doing?"

I ignore his question even as I hear him tear through the

computer quad and start running for the steps. Walker calls after Aaron—yut, he's sensible.

"Dr. Campbell, please come back! Until we know more, there's just—"

"No! We can't afford to close it."

But before he can protest more, my hand is moving the block back into place. Or at least I'm trying to move it. Thing won't budge. I'm gonna have to use two hands, but that means letting go of my SCAR. Dammit.

Aaron is bounding up the stairs with Walker on his heels. There's no time to argue this one through.

I release my weapon and apply both hands to the block, throwing all my weight into moving it. My head is mere inches from the energy wall. I can practically feel it wanting to zap me with a mini lightning bolt.

"Come on," I say through tight lips. But the thing is barely moving.

Aaron slams into my back and almost knocks me over. "You can't do this!"

"That's not your decision," I say, boxing him out with my left hip.

"Patrick, stop! Please."

I'm about to let go of the block and shove him back when Walker pulls Aaron away. "Dr. Campbell, please."

"Let me go!"

"We've got to shut it down until—"

"We've got to save Lewis."

I can't fault him for having his heart in the right place, but some things the heart can't fix.

I'm straining against the block when I sense a presence to my left. It's a body—stepping through the wall.

"My God," Walker exclaims.

I bring my SCAR up and try to make sense of the figure two yards away. It's a robot of some type—arms and legs like a muscular human, maybe eight feet tall. Thing's got a head like a fat pistachio shell tipped on its end with five lenses around the skull. It's body's clad in magenta plating, like the drone's, and the bot has a black skeletal structure underneath. Odd yellow and white markings adorn its chest, shoulders, and the side of its head.

My first instinct is to shoot it, but my training overrides the gut-level reaction. If that armor is anything like the drone's, I risk getting struck by a ricochet, as do Aaron and Walker. Instead, I start backpedaling to put some distance between me and the contraption —waving Arron and Walker back.

"Wait for my go," I say to Simmons over comms.

"Roger."

So far, the robot isn't moving, it's just standing there, which is all right by me. I hear one of the two men behind me falter.

"We don't know if it's hostile, Pat," Aaron says.

Is this the same guy who just chewed me out for *killing* Lewis? "Get behind the barricades, Aaron. Walker, take everyone else with you. Now."

"But, Pat, I think—"

"Now," I seethe.

"Come on, Dr. Campbell," Walker says. "Everyone, let's go!"

I'm moving backward, nice and smooth, when the bot's head turns and points its forward-most eyes at me. A chill goes down my spine. I'm in the open and need to get to cover, but I'm the only defense between the bot and the retreating researchers.

Among the footfalls and nervous whispers, I hear someone trip beside me. The bot tilts its head, almost as if it's curious.

"Awaiting your order," Simmons says.

The bot's head straightens and looks back at me.

I'm about to say open fire when the thing raises an arm and shoots something from its claw-like palm. A round of blue energy hits the researcher who tripped and renders her unconscious.

"Engage," I yell and lay into the bot with my SCAR.

The first rounds produce impact sparks but appear to do nothing more than rattle the bot's torso a little.

Between shots, I glance at the downed woman and try to call for someone to help her up. But everyone's running, covering their ears at the gunfire. I'm gonna have to do this myself.

When I look back at the bot, it takes its first stride. It's long and confident, like a rook moving out from behind a wall of pawns. It has nothing to lose—the action of a chess piece who knows it has an army behind it.

I've gotta get this woman outta here. My left hand reaches for her wrist, when a blast of blue light fills my vision. I blink it away, sure I've been hit, then I hear more screams behind me. Another researcher's been struck, and I see a scorch mark on the ground between us. The blast must've been meant for my hand and glanced off the stone. Either way, I grab the woman's wrist and drag her across the ground while firing on the bot.

Still, the thing appears unaffected and takes the steps three at a time. Rounds pelt its chest and head in tight, relentless groupings. The bot's throwing off sparks like a Roman candle on the fourth of July.

My SCAR's bolt locks open. "Changing." I can barely hear myself say the word. I drop the woman's arm, eject the spent mag, and replenish. As soon as I've sent the bolt home, I hoist the woman over my shoulder and continue engaging the bot.

"Coming to you," I yell to Simmons.

He waves me toward him as researchers dash behind the improvised barricades. Another flash of blue light explodes somewhere behind me just as Simmons pulls me and the woman behind cover.

"Check her," I yell to McGarret, First Platoon's Corpsman. Meanwhile, I lean out to put a few more rounds on Mr. Bucket-O-Bolts. To my surprise, it's missing part of its right arm, and it's walking with a limp. Some electrical sparks spit from a knee and shoulder joints, and I hear a few shouts go up from among the security forces.

When the bot's head finally spins free of its shoulders, the men cry out in cheers and unit mantras. A beat later, the machine pitches forward and slams to the ground.

"Oorah," Simmons yells to our Marine unit, and he gets unanimous replies.

"She's got a pulse," the corpsman says. "But it's weak."

"See if you can stabilize her," I reply. "Get her out."

"We still need to shut it down," says a voice behind me. It's Dr. Walker.

I raise an upturned hand toward the ring. "Be my guest, Doctor."

His eyes widen.

"I'm messing with you, Doc." I look to Simmons. "Cover me."

"Hell no, Wic." He grabs my arm and yanks me back. "That ain't chain." He means the chain of command, and he's right: Master Gunnery Sergeants don't run point. That's for Privates. But I don't have time to tell anyone which block I was moving and in which direction, nor do I want anyone else getting taken. Lewis was my fault, and I'm sure as hell not parting with a Marine. I want this damn op to be over and everyone to leave me the hell alone.

"Who do you think should go?" I ask.

As soon as Simmons looks at our teams, I turn out and beat toward the ring. I hear him yelling at me, followed by the sound of boots striking the ground as several Marines follow me. A glance over my shoulder shows it's First Fire Team.

I run past the downed robot and notice the thing is twitching. Smoke curls up from still-sparking holes throughout its body, most notably its severed neck. Seeing the corpse gives me at least a little courage—the thing wasn't invincible.

I'm almost to the stairs when I hear someone yell behind me.

"Contact."

Ahead, there's another bot stepping through the portal. And then another. And another. These look similar to the one before, but they have magenta-colored plates on their heads and large rifles in their hands.

I brake hard and whip around. "Everyone back."

We race toward the barricades as the bots start firing. I can't tell if they're shooting more of the paralyzing rounds or something more lethal, but I don't want any of us to find out the hard way.

A Marine just ahead of me takes a hit to the middle of the back and sprawls forward. Before he lands facedown, I notice a hole in his rear plate holder. I'm running too fast to see whether it just burned through the fabric sleeve or went straight through.

No. That's… that's crazy.

What—crazier than giant robots stepping through a portal from another world?

"Man down," I yell.

CHRISTOPHER HOPPER & J.N. CHANEY

A beat later, a second Marine hits the deck. I think he tripped. But then I see a hole in the back of his head.

Dammit.

I run as fast as I can, urging everyone to take cover. Fortunately, no one else falls in our final few yards to the barricades: the Russian and British contingents are laying down heavy suppressive fire for us.

"SITREP," I yell at Simmons as I throw my back against the wall and suck in air.

"Two Marines down. Greaves and McClintock. Three hostiles advancing on our position."

I swear, then peek around the corner. Sure enough, the new bots have split up and are moving toward us. Opening the all-squad channel, I give orders for the Brits to break left. I take extra care to make sure the overly zealous Russians on our right hold position. If two elements flank during an envelopment tactic, they risk firing on friendlies. Instead, one element sweeps while the other two adjust fire. "And focus on their heads," I yell before releasing the talk button.

My SCAR is up, firing on the middle bot, landing one round after another on target. But the head's clamshell-like shape is deflecting almost all of my shots. Its armor is damn near impregnable too.

"Corpsman," someone shouts.

"Man down," says another.

More enemy rounds berate our barricades, throwing up showers of sparks. Whatever ordnance this is, it's not what paralyzed the woman from before. These chess pieces are knights, and they're playing for keeps.

"Frag out," someone from Second Team calls. It's Josephs. He's "milked" the M67 fragmentation grenade, letting three of the fuse's five seconds tick by with the pin pulled and spoon free. It's risky and, in my opinion, downright stupid—belongs in Hollywood, not the battlefield. Josephs tosses the ball-like device and takes cover behind the wall. Two seconds later, the frag detonates and shakes the ground. Lucky Devil.

I turn out and start shooting, taking advantage of the robot's momentary confusion. I select my SCAR's three-round burst mode and spend the rest of my second magazine on the enemy. The bot singles me out and sends a round my way, but I'm concealed before it blows a chunk from the barricade's side.

"Changing," I yell and eject the spent mag.

As I slam home the fresh magazine, I notice my ears are ringing. Most of the units are devouring ammunition way faster than they should. Not that I'm arguing against sending streams of lead down-range. But there's a world of difference between effective fire and spraying the enemy haphazardly. In fact, all the security forces seem largely inexperienced. Dammit. What I wouldn't give for a single seasoned sniper with a Barrett .50-caliber rifle to put some rounds on target. That and someone who knows their way around an M-249 SAW.

The thought crosses my mind to get out my 3M CAEv2s—combat arms earplugs version 2—but given the choice of protecting my hearing or firing on the enemy, I know which I'm choosing, all day, every day. Especially when getting our asses handed to us.

With my SCAR ready, I lean around the barricade again. My ACOG's chevron is on target when a bright blue light fills the scope. The round's heat flashes against my face, and I pull back. Somehow, it's missed me. I'm okay, which is more than I can say for the plastic wall separating us from the rest of the dig site to the rear. It's riddled with hundreds of holes, and half of it's on fire. Flaming plastic drips down like napalm. The researchers are taking turns running beneath the veil, but only a few sneak through completely unscathed. Most suffer minor burns, while four twirl about in a desperate attempt to extinguish themselves. The flaming death dance brings back nightmares from Iraq and Afghanistan, and I force myself to look away. The enemy awaits.

"Tango down," someone shouts.

I look downrange again and see that our target has fallen. Several more M67s have detonated—but the bot's not out. Instead, it's lying on its chest, firing on our position. And the damn thing is deadly accurate.

I hear someone else say a Marine is hit, but between the gunfire and the screams, I can't be sure. The ringing in my ears is keeping me from thinking straight. We're taking casualties faster than I can count.

As yet another Marine slumps down beside me, I wonder if this is it. If this is how I'm going out. Stuck on some goddamn ice cube in the middle of nowhere gunned down by alien robots. I laugh, but only because of how much it feels like a movie. That, and no one's ever going to find us if these things win. I imagine a cave-in's gonna happen any second, and then it's all over. Fitting, I suppose, given that the country's already forgotten us. Forgotten me. Or maybe that's just me wanting to forget it.

I look over at Simmons. He's screaming something at me. Feels like he's speaking in slow motion.

I blink and shake my head.

"Another hostile," he says for maybe the third or fourth time—I can't be sure. "And another drone."

"What?" I chance a glance back toward the portal, and, sure

enough, there's another recon bot that looks like the first rook that came through, plus another one of the drones. It seems like a strange strategic choice—why not send more assault bots to finish us off first?

Unless the enemy thinks there's no way we can win.

"Son of a bitch," I say to no one in particular.

"What is it?" Simmons asks.

"It—*they* think this is all over. That's one of the recon bots along with another collection drone to drag some bodies away."

Simmons swears. "I've still got some fight in me if Marvin does."

I laugh. "Me too."

We bump fists and then lean out on either side of our barricade to send heat toward the new bot and the drones.

As I fire, I notice that the middle robot has been finished off while the other two are still being worked over by the international elements. But even from here, I can see that both squads have taken casualties.

I pull back behind the wall and ask for a SITREP over the all-squad channel.

"We have lost eight men," says the Russian commander. "No. Nine."

"We're down to four men," says the British commander.

"Say again," I reply. I think I've misunderstood him. "You're down by four men?"

"Negative. Four men remaining."

This was unbelievable. "Understood. Keep the pressure on."

"Roger."

I release the radio and look at Simmons. "We've got to get the gate shut before any more come through."

"Any bright ideas?"

I shake my head. "Not unless shooting the off-button is an option, and I highly doubt it is."

"Yeah. And I don't see heads or tails of Campbell or Walker."

I sigh. "Shift the elements left, I'll head right."

"But, Wic—"

"That's an order, Simmons."

"Roger. Shifting left." He grabs my arm. "Good luck."

"You too."

Simmons is on the move, ordering all remaining forces to get behind the defenses and toward the left side.

As I make for the right end, I pass several Russians, including Vlad. They've lost almost their entire unit and look like hell. My former boxing partner gives me a small nod and then carries on.

By the time I reach the far end of our cover, I notice all enemies have shifted their focus, leaving me a straight shot to the stairs. So far, so good.

As another grenade explosion shakes some ice from the ceiling, I steal my resolve and then take off for the ring. I'm halfway across when the drone takes notice and speeds my way. But I'm going too fast to stop now. I'm committed.

A heavy stream of machine gun fire pings and pops against the drone above me. The garbage can lid even fires its harpoon at me but misses thanks to the constant barrage. I want to charge up the stairs, but now one of the bots is shooting at me, so I drop and slide into a shadow to the platform's right.

As I come to a stop, I realize the drone has lost track of me. It crisscrosses overhead and then moves off to antagonize our main body. That's the good news. The bad news is that the damn robots are now directly between me and my unit, which means I'm in the line of fire. To prove my point, stray rounds pepper the stairs and zip over my head. The classic *pih-twang bwit-toon* sounds of glancing bullets spiraling off into the distance fill the air.

Trapped, I move back in the shadows and see that I'm about ten feet below the exact spot on the ring where the master button sits. I want there to be a ladder or chair around here, but all the equipment is back in the open.

"Hey," someone says as they slide in beside me.

I spin and almost shoot the person in the chest. "Walker? The hell? How'd you—?"

"Figured you'd want to make another go at this." He nods up at the ring. "So I worked my way around the outside of the site."

"Listen, you gotta—"

"Nice to see you too. So, are we doing this? Or do you just want to stare longingly into my eyes?"

The shake in his voice lets me know Walker's more afraid than he probably wants to be. Still, a one-liner in combat is worth two lines in a bar. Props. Seems I've underestimated Dr. Walker's spine, and I'd be lying if I said I wasn't at least a little impressed. Or the guy's a few French fries short of a Happy Meal. Aren't we all.

"You're one crazy son of a bitch," I say.

He smiles. "Yeah. I get that a lot."

"We need to get up there." I point straight up. Then I realize he, of all people, doesn't need to be told where we need to go. "But we also don't want to get shot. I'm gonna call off the dogs for a short window, which should buy us the time we need to run around. But it also means—"

"The robots could turn on us."

"Yut."

"I got it, Sergeant. Let's, you know, do this."

Damn, I really have underestimated this guy.

A loud explosion comes from the bots' vicinity. Sounds like another one of them's been taken out. I glance around the platform's corner and see that, yut, the second assault bot is down, leaving the third redhead plus the slightly less formidable recon bot.

As for Walker and me, we're still in the line of fire and outmatched armament-wise. Strategically, however, being behind enemy lines isn't always a bad thing. If you can sneak a rook along the enemy's back row and trap a king behind his own pawns, then you win, baby. And they don't even see it coming.

Then again, getting shot by your own people sucks too. I duck as a stray bullet smacks into the steps and sends up bits of stone.

I grab my radio and open the channel. "Simmons."

"Go."

"Need you to check fire on my command. I say again, check fire on my command."

"Roger."

Walker and I crouch, still tight against the platform's side. One last look shows the robot moving fast toward the barricades.

"You ready?" I ask Walker.

"Let's do it."

I nod and then call up Simmons. "Check fire. Check fire."

Walker makes to jump past me, but I grab him by the arm. "Not yet. Takes a second."

He looks sheepish as he nods and cowers down behind me again.

The call for a check-fire travels through the ranks. When the last round barks, I nod at Walker. "Now."

We run from cover, turn at the bottom of the stairs, and charge toward the summit. We're halfway to the ring when I hear Simmons's voice break over the radio.

"You're spotted."

I'm grateful for the heads up, but we can't do anything about it. And neither can the security forces—any shots from their position put us in harm's way.

Walker and I slide to a halt at the ring's upswept arm and start working the button. It's moving faster this time, but still not fast enough.

A blue energy bolt strikes the ring's edge less than ten inches from Walker's hip. He jumps away but goes back to work.

I spin to see the recon robot moving back toward the stairs, hand raised, when I notice someone running with a limp in the background. It's a person in Russian winter fatigues. He's making a beeline for the bot, weapon still on his shoulder.

I want to shout the man down, but that would give away his element of surprise. Whoever it is, he's positioning himself to fire without risk of hitting us. And he's coming in close. Meanwhile, the rest of the security forces have moved from cover and are taking on the last assault bot—moving themselves to keep Walker and me out of their line of fire. It's suicide. But if they don't keep the assault bot distracted, this gate won't get closed.

I'm a split second from firing when the recon bot fires another round from its palm. The shot smacks into my SCAR. A jolt of electricity shoots up my arms. Feels like the family toaster finally got revenge on me for all those errant knife jabs. I stumble backward. Stars fill my vision, and I blink to keep myself upright.

"Gotcha," Walker says, bracing me from behind.

This was a bad idea.

"And the gate's closed," he adds.

I'm still stunned but manage to verify his claim with a glance over my shoulder. Doc's done it.

"Can you walk?" he asks.

"Yeah." I aim at the bot through my ACOG, but the enemy fires again. The round misses me and snaps against something over my shoulder.

Walker's taken the blow to the head. Before I can grab him, he goes limp and sails off the summit's edge. I look to repay the bot's hostility, but the Russian soldier is too close and blasting away at the bot with his AK-74M.

Ricocheting lead cuts through the air around me. I shy away from the bullets and try to regain a sight picture. But the bot appears to be more irritated than I am. It spins around, takes three long strides toward the soldier, and bats his weapon away. As soon as the robot lifts the soldier, I recognize the man.

It's Vlad.

I can't shoot the enemy without risk of hitting the guy, so I sling my SCAR and start charging the bot. I reach the top step and leap toward the eight-foot-tall robot. The collision knocks the air out of me, and my hip and elbows are burning. But I'm on, arms wrapped around the bot's neck.

The robot's twisting its torso and flailing its free arm, trying to work me off its back. But I'm going to finish this. Just as I reach for my Glock 19, there's another explosion. The last assault bot's been taken out, and the remaining security forces are firing on the final drone.

Emboldened by the taste of victory, I ram my pistol's barrel behind my bot's backplate and wedge it against the base of the bot's neck. Then I squeeze the trigger twice. A duet of bright flashes accompanies the pistol's bark, and the ringing in my ears intensifies.

This bot isn't dropping, so I fire one more round into its trunk.

Something breaks inside the chest, and Vlad hits the ground and rolls away. Finally, after what feels like an eternity, the robot pitches forward. I ride it down until its chest slams against the deck. Pain shoots up my chin, and more stars erupt in my vision. But I'm alive. And the robot isn't.

Checkmate.

7

0651, Tuesday, April 26, 2027
West Antarctica
Ellsworth Subglacial Highlands Excavation Site
The Ring

"BROOKLYN NEW YORK," says a voice. "Are you being all right?"

I blink several times and feel blood pooling in my mouth. After spitting, I say, "Yeah, Vlad. I'm being all right."

He offers me one of his heavily tattooed hands and pulls me up —a little faster than I want. I'm lightheaded, but I manage.

"Nice work," he says. "You kill bitch like true red-bearded American dog alpha top."

"You're not so bad yourself."

He pouts. "I have done better work. But not worse work. I say, average."

"Right." I'm looking around the space to survey the damage. And that's when I realize that Vlad here is the only other fighter I see on their feet. "Ah, shit."

I run toward the closest Leatherneck. Corporal Meyers. His eyes are wide open and have that cloudy glazed look to them. I don't even bother checking for a pulse because experience tells me there isn't one.

"Simmons?" I yell as I move to the next body. It's a Marine, but I can't make out his face or his nametape—because both are too badly mangled.

I move to a third body. It's a Brit, one of the former SAS machine gunners—MacDonald, I think? But he's dead too.

"Simmons? Come on. Talk to me, pal."

"Over here, Brooklyn," Vlad calls. He's squatting amid several bodies, and I can tell one of them is Simmons. Vlad's holding his head up.

"Simmons. Talk to me."

"We get 'em?" His voice is weak.

"Hell yeah, we got 'em. Hold on, we're gonna get—"

"Say an extra Hail Mary for me. Would ya?"

"You won't need it," I reply. But before I can say anything else, Simmons's eyes go blank.

1005, Friday, April 29, 2027
West Antarctica
Ellsworth Subglacial Highlands Research Facility

IT TOOK two days to bag the bodies of the fallen and load them into shipping containers—one for the civilians, and separate ones for each nation's military. Of course, the shipping manifests wouldn't say that. But we would know. We, the survivors.

Watching the researchers bag and tag the dead was hard. For most, this was the first time they'd seen a dead body up close, much less someone they'd worked with just hours before. Add to that the insane circumstances surrounding the attack, or invasion, or whatever the hell it was going to be called, and you had all the right ingredients for several meltdowns.

As for me, I went numb from the work. Or maybe I'd been numb all along, and this had been just some rote choreography that I'd memorized years ago. You need a high level of detachment to work with the dead, especially dead that you care about. *Cared* about. And while I hadn't known Simmons and the others for long, it was long enough. Even Walker had impressed me—he'd died shutting the gate down. Sure, he made a better scientist than fighter, but he'd given a fighter's portion. So I splash some whiskey on the floor for him and shoot the rest.

My empty glass demands to be refilled, so I pour another three fingers and lean back in my desk chair.

I haven't seen heads or tails of Aaron. Probably for the best. The dig's been shut down by order of the CIA, and the universities have been "informed," whatever that means. I told the spooks everything I saw, but my money says they're keeping that close to their chests. Still, someone was bound to leak. And based on the recent arrival of a United Nations forward team, I'm guessing several have.

There's a knock on my barrack's room door. "Master Gunnery Sergeant Finnegan?"

CHRISTOPHER HOPPER & J.N. CHANEY

"Depends on who's asking," I reply.

"Deputy Director Robertson of Strategic Scientific Affairs, UN Security Council."

I frown. "Strategic Scientific Affairs?"

"Yes, sir."

I don't know that particular division, but then again, it's the UN, and I'm not exactly collecting this season's trading cards—damn bureaucrats.

"Never heard of Strategic Scientific Affairs," I say, more to get a rise out of the man.

"And there's good reason for that."

Not the answer I was expecting. "And why's that?"

"Sergeant Finnegan, may I come in?"

I give him a snort. "Now you've gotta get the rank right and answer the damn question."

"Sir, we—"

"Man, you must really like standing in the hallway."

He sighs. "Because we like to keep it off the books, Master Gunnery Sergeant."

"So you're a UN spy."

"No. As I said, I'm Deputy—"

"Deputy Director Rascalson—"

"Robertson."

"—of the Super Secret Council of Magic Decoder Ring Suits."

There's a pause. "Mr. Finnegan, are you drunk?"

"What kind of a question is that?"

The doorknob turns and a dark-haired, dark-eyed face peeks in.

"Pull up a chair," I say, noticing that, yut, my speech might be a little slurred. "Pour you some Redbreast?"

"I'm on the job."

I bark out a laugh. "So am I. Sláinte."

"Cheers."

I take a mouthful of the expensive whiskey along with some air, and then swallow.

"Sergeant Finnegan, I have—"

"Wic."

Robertson gives me a curious glance. "I'm sorry?"

"My friends call me Wic."

"Ah. Wic, I—"

"But most of my friends are dead."

Robertson purses his lips and then taps the table with his index finger. "I'm sorry to hear."

"You were saying?"

The suit clears his throat and begins again. "I have special instructions to invite you to remain on here in Antarctica as military liaison between the UN Security Council..."

Robertson finally stops because I'm shaking my head so hard I think it's going to pop off my shoulders.

"I'm sorry. Is something the matter?"

I let out another laugh and then gesture at his suit. "All of this. It's the matter."

He looks down. "My suit."

I nod.

"Master Guns, you are now one of only two military personnel alive who have had direct contact with the alien—"

"Extraterrestrial robots. Get it right."

"Pardon?"

"If you're gonna talk about them, you're gonna use the right terms. Copy?"

Hell. The truth is, I still don't believe the damn things are from outer space. But if this suit thinks he's gonna sit here and sweet-talk me, then he's at least gonna pay proper respect to the scientists who gave their lives for this DARPA-level experiment gone bad.

Robertson takes a breath. "We need as much expertise as we can get in trying to decide how to proceed."

"What's to know? Any dumbass can put C4 on that ring and blow it to kingdom come. You don't need me."

"I'm afraid we very much do need you, Sergeant. And we have permission from your commanding officers to keep you here for as long as we need."

I sit upright, but that makes the room move, so I grab the desk. "You did what?"

Robertson leans back. "We... you have been cleared to remain—"

"I'm not spending one more minute on this goddamn ice block than I need to, Director. I don't care who you talked to. And if you think for one second that I'm gonna hand-hold a bunch of blue-helmeted boots as they fumble around with plastic explosives, I'm afraid you didn't do enough research on the man you're talking to."

Robertson seems to stiffen. "That's funny, because I was told that you would be willing to do anything in service of your country."

"I was, yut. My country. But right now? I don't even think I wanna do that anymore."

"Sergeant Finnegan—"

"Cut that out."

"Pardon?"

"Using my rank like you know what it means. You don't. So it's Mr. Finnegan to you."

Robertson takes another deep breath. Guy must have bad lungs.

"Mr. Finnegan. Once you've had time to think more *clearly* about our request, we would only ask that you—"

"Done."

"I'm… not sure I understand."

"Thought about your request. Denied. Thanks for playing. Have a nice day."

"I'm sorry to hear that."

"Eh, I bet you are."

"Should you wish to change your mind—"

"Mr. Robertson. Can I call you Mike?"

"My name's actually—"

"Yeah, don't care. Mike, the calendar says I'm five days away from retiring after twenty-four years in the Marine Corps. Twenty-four years. Based on the lack of wrinkles on your face, you either use one hell of a moisturizer, or it hasn't been twenty-four years since you learned how to ride a two wheeler without your daddy holding the back seat. Am I right?"

Robertson looks like he's trying not to be insulted. Perfect.

"Now, I'm sure you believe your work is pretty important. You've probably got offices in New York and Geneva, am I right?"

I stare at him until he's forced to give me the smallest head nod.

"And you regularly speak to all sorts of foreign ambassadors and dignitaries, and routinely rub shoulders with people who make Einstein look like he's more interested in My Little Ponies than astro-molecular star physics. But I can tell you one thing's for damn sure."

"And what's that, Mr. Finnegan?"

Robertson's suddenly grown a spine. Good for him.

"It doesn't matter."

"Pardon me?"

"You deaf, Mike? *It doesn't matter.* Nobody cares. The countries you work for? They're not gonna remember you. You're not gettin' your name on a plaque or your head carved into a brass bust. And even if you did, know who's gonna remember? No one. First graders are gonna take walking tours around your statue and won't even stop to read the nameplate. 'Cast in honor of Deputy Director Mike Robertson.' And if, by chance, one or two kids do? Ten bucks and a beer says they forget all about it by the time they take a piss in the restroom your statue sits outside of. That, Mike—that's what dying for your country gets you. And wanna know why?"

Robertson doesn't speak.

"That's fine, because I'm gonna tell you anyway. All those things you thought you were fighting for? Turns out not many people care about them. At least not in the way you thought they would. And all that freedom you purchased them? All that safety? Guess what they do with it."

Robertson stares.

"Go ahead. Guess."

He seems paralyzed.

"*Wuh-chuuuush*, flushed down the urinal in the bathroom right next to your statue, and some first grader doesn't even wash his hands. So, you sitting here asking me if I'm gonna help some UN field trip get their jollies on when my own damn country hardly gives a shit about my sacrifice? Not a chance, Mike. I'm out like Mark Cuban on a rerun of Shark Tank."

With that concluded, I sit back and finish off the entire glass of whiskey.

Robertson taps the table and then straightens his tie. "I'm sorry to hear that."

"I guessed you might be."

"I'll, uh… leave you to your libations then."

"Much obliged."

Robertson gets up and opens the door. He's just about to close it when he looks back at me. "One thing."

"Yut."

"We're not blowing up the ring, Mr. Finnegan."

Something rises up in me right then—part of that squatter that's lurking in the basement. That wraith that just wants to be left alone and treats all invaders as hostile. "Then you're a goddamn fool, Robertson. You're all fools."

He closes the door, and as he walks away, I hear him say, "Have a good life, Mr. Finnegan."

1512, Sunday, May 1, 2027
Ross Island, Eastern Antarctica
McMurdo Station
US Antarctic Program Headquarters, Landing Strip

It's NIGHT OUTSIDE, just as it has been for the last month. But the ski-equipped Lockheed C-130 Hercules's lights are clear as day, and herald my ticket home. They're also punishing me for the hangover that I'm still trying to shake. I don't normally drink like that. But, desperate times and all.

I collect my gear in the glorified freight container that does its best to pass as an airport waiting lounge, and head toward the exit. Outside, the C-130 keeps its props spinning, ready for me to load up on the ice-covered landing strip. I'm about to push on the crash bar when I hear a voice behind me.

"Brooklyn New York."

It's Vlad. I haven't seen him since we packed the last body days ago.

"Hey, soldier."

"I hear you make leaving now?"

I rub the back of my neck. "It's a touch too cold for my tastes. You?"

He gives me a smile. "This is much like Moscow in summer. I think of buying vacation home."

"Better stock up on vodka then. I hear it's the only stuff that doesn't freeze."

He laughs. "I like you, American dog alpha top."

"You're not so bad yourself, killer." I wait a beat. "You, uh… you helped me out back there, and I never got the chance to really thank you."

"Eh. Truth telling, I like you Americans. Especially your music. Celine Dion? Huh. She is one of many kinds."

I don't have the heart to tell him she's Canadian, which—technically—still makes her an American of the northern sort. "Yut. I caught her show once in Vegas."

"Ah! Yes, Las Vegas. City of wonders and much delights." He leans in. "This is my dream."

"To go to Vegas?"

He nods. "Dancing girls, shows, Texas Hold Them. I am too much excited for this day."

Not my ideal vacation, but to each their own. "Here's hoping you get to make that happen, Vlad."

"And your dream?"

I let out a soft chuckle. "I want to become a magician."

"Really." Vlad puts his fingers around his chin. "I did not picturing you are this. Meh. Everyone is different, yes?"

"We sure are." I like his response so much, I decide not to mess it up with my punchline: I want to disappear.

"Ha! Maybe I see you on Vegas strip one day. That would be exciting, no? I say to all girls, 'Hey, I know him.' Then I get more sex. It's wins wins."

Now I'm laughing. And it feels good despite the headache. "I'll be sure to wave at you in the crowd."

"Ah! Even best! Yes."

We let the silence fade, and as it does, I realize that Vlad is the only other person in our warrior class who has seen what I have seen. The memories of Simmons and the rest of the fallen will haunt us both forever, as will the otherworldly events that neither of us will ever be able to rightly tell another human soul. Perhaps the details will leak out after one too many beers, or maybe if one of us lives long enough to have grand- or great-grandchildren. But in both cases, no one will take us seriously, and the speech will be written off as the crazed ravings of a drunk buffoon or an elderly vet.

"You also have save my life." Vlad unzips his coat to reveal an American-flag-print fanny pack. Then he reaches inside the hideous pouch and fishes around for something. "Here."

I look down, and he's offering to shake my hand. But I notice an item half-hidden in his palm. This is a universal gesture among the modern warrior classes—a symbolic exchange of a simple token between fighters. Stateside, it's a challenge coin. But with this Russian? I have no idea what to expect.

I shake his hand, feel a small disc in my palm, and then examine it. "A poker chip?" It's black with pink trim and has the words USA and Bratva above and below an AK-47 rifle on the front face.

"Where I come from, chip says, screw to economy. We make own currency. Ha!" Then he slaps me right between the shoulder blades, and I realize I'm more tender than I thought. "It is also symbol of Bratva," he adds in a whisper, pointing to the stylized compass star emblem on the back face. "You and the Bratva?" He crosses his fingers. "You are now like this."

"I'll pass," I say, handing the chip back.

"You cannot pass." He zips up his fanny pack. "You forever tied with Bratva. US Brooklyn New York and Russian brotherhood are sexing." He leans in again. "Just don't try to be spending this in Vegas. I hear it gets you in much trouble with cowboy sheriffs."

"Thanks for the tip."

"No problems."

"Hey." I nod to his fanny pack. "I thought you said… American flag is like hooker's underwear."

He shrugs. "I say lots of things when I fighting to make opponent arouse. But now I am honest with you Alpha top dog. I love America."

"Roger that." I stuff the chip in my pocket and shake Vlad's hand one last time. "Good luck."

"Dasvidaniya."

PART TWO

TWO MONTHS LATER

8

2300, Thursday, June 24, 2027
Skytop, Pennsylvania

ONE OF MY many retirement rituals is in full swing as I near my bedtime: watering the flower beds while sipping two fingers of Redbreast. The air is warm, filled with the sounds of cicadas and roosting birds. Meanwhile, firefly beacons fill the open fields that slope away from my hilltop log cabin. God, I love this.

Growing up in Brooklyn, I didn't know you could see the stars at night without a telescope. I also didn't know there were more species of birds than just pigeons and gulls. Turns out there are a lot more. And then there's the nightly symphony produced in the nearby forest that is unlike anything I've ever heard, at least when I can get my ears to stop ringing for a second. My chronic tinnitus is just one

CHRISTOPHER HOPPER & J.N. CHANEY

of the annoying scars of war that tries to sour my mood on a night like this.

So, to help the Redbreast out, I've got my portable FM radio sitting on a stump amidst my growing woodpile by the garden. Ol' Blue Eyes is wrapping up his 1958 version of *Come Fly With Me* as the Classics with Sinatra radio program comes to a close. Which means it's time for me to retire for the night too.

I twist the garden faucet off and start coiling the hose when a talking head behind a mic starts rattling off the eleven o'clock news headlines. I consider throwing a rock at the radio, but then I'd just need to go buy a new radio. One pain in the ass begets another.

I don't typically listen to or watch the news anymore. Don't see the need. The country's gonna dig its own grave whether I want it to or not. And I'd rather live the second half of my life in peace than fretting over things I can't control. Sure, it's hard to shut off the fix-it side of my brain, but this is about preservation, not curiosity. Killed enough cats for one lifetime; gonna let the rest live.

Truth is, I don't miss the headlines one bit. The politics, the endless opinions, flip-flopping, and words cloaked in more words cloaked in even more words until you have no idea what people are talking about. Gone are the days of men and women speaking their minds and saying what they mean to say—come hell or high water. I'm not even sure what the world would do with people like that. Correction: I do. They hang them out to dry, which is why every-one's afraid to say anything without a damn attorney present.

But tonight, I can't get to the radio fast enough. Three strides before I can put my wet finger on the power button, I hear the announcer say, "...as uncertainty grows around the UN-led expedition feared missing in Antarctica. Sources at the Pentagon deny claims that communication has been lost with US researchers at

McMurdo Station while Moscow is calling for emergency assistance for Russian civilians based at Progress Station. In other news, pop-music icon Justin Bieber was seen outside a Los Angeles nightclub—"

I switch off the radio, but I'm cradling it in my hands like it's gonna tell me more.

"Nah," I say to myself. I don't need to know anything more. So I head for the house, grab my whiskey glass, and mount the back steps. Once inside, I set the radio down on the small table below my key rack and then kick my shoes off. It's been a good day's work, and now it's time to shower and hit the hay.

But you can't, can you, Patrick. All 'cause that damn radio's piqued your interest, and your inner investigator won't be content until you've scratched the itch. Ain't that right?

The young people say I'd get better coverage by using my phone to research stuff, but I don't trust the damn things—phones, that is. Sure, I keep one around just in case, but it's powered down and locked in a faraday cage. So I'm a bit skeptical. People throughout history have survived just fine without cell phones, and I'm no exception. Plus, if you ask me, the damn things and all that social media are partly to blame for the cancer that's eating society alive. But what do I know? I'm just a dumb grunt from the Marine Corps.

While I may not wanna use my Samsung phone to search the interwebs, I can think of another use for it, and, frankly, I'm not sure which is better right now.

What's better is getting a good night's sleep, I reason. "And if you can't shut your brain off, Patrick, then what's the point of that?"

Which means that unless I wanna pop another Ambien tonight, I'd better scratch the itch with a quick call to my old CO.

"Eh, screw you, Wic. You can't sleep without Ambien anyway."

Thinking is so overrated.

Even though I'm sure I'm gonna regret this, I decide to retrieve my cell phone. It's in my stone-enclosed gun safe in the corner of my log cabin's great room. Well, one of my gun safes—the smallest one. Reliability isn't an accident, and redundant systems don't build themselves.

I cross my great room and unlock the door to the bathroom-sized safe. The incandescent lights warm as I enter and urge me toward the back of the vault. While the whole safe is shielded, I keep my phone with the rest of the comms devices in a second Faraday cage so that I can open the main door without fear of having any of the more sensitive equipment exposed. I prefer the word prepared over the term paranoid, but I get why people confuse them.

I start in on the cage's padlock. When the gate swings open, I retrieve my Samsung from the wall of MURS radios and Iridium sat phones. Hey, comms are nothing to go light on.

I lock the gate and then walk out among my couches again, just staring at the small black device. Last year, I had one of the brains in my unit install some sort of firewall software on the phone—activates on startup. He swore it would make my digital footprint look like I was standing in a different country every time I fired the thing up. Didn't mean I trusted it, but it was better than nothing.

I take a deep breath. Make this call and I reopen the past. Don't, I'm not sleeping until I do.

Between the Corps and the spooks, I had been holed up in DC for a full week since I got back from Antarctica. Someone had claimed it would have been longer, but they had "more pressing matters to attend to." My after-action report was thorough, and my commitment to stay tight-lipped unquestioned. I was, after all, a professional. Plus, who was gonna believe me if I leaked something anyway? I suddenly had a whole lot more sympathy for all the weird bastards who claimed to have been probed by E.T.

I press the on button and the device powers up, then it connects to the local tower. I pull up Willy's number and hit Send.

The line rings three times and goes to voicemail.

"Hi. You've reached Colonel William Rodriguez. I'm unavailable to take your call. Please leave me a message."

In the space of time between when his message ends and when I'm supposed to say whatever it is I'm going to say, I freeze. Is this really something I want to be doing? I just worked twenty-four years and fought tooth and nail to make it to where I'm at—alone, in the middle of nowhere, in a nice little cabin on an eastern Pennsylvania hilltop. God, I sound predictable. It's mine, and I don't care.

This call doesn't mean I'm looking for something to do, either. That's one thing I feel confident about. I'm not one of those vets who always seems to find their way back into busy work or consulting. No, I quite like my peace and quiet.

What I can't stand, however, is not knowing.

No matter what Willy says, I won't do anything with the information. Hell, I can hardly bring myself to leave my cabin for groceries. But it's the knowing that matters. Weird thing about eccentrics, they say, is that they find comfort in data. Never figured me for a brain, but maybe I'm more like the pencil pushers than I give myself credit for.

"Hey, Willy. It's Wic. Wanted to talk about the game last night. Hell of a play, right? Hit me back when you can."

Before I hang up, I feel annoyed—*with myself*. God. I shouldn't be making this call.

"But, if you don't have time, I get it. Just, uh… give my best to Mary."

I punch End.

This was a mistake. Not only did I just embarrass myself, which, truthfully, I really don't care about, but now I'm left with the dilemma of keeping the phone on to await his callback or powering it back down. See? Cell phones are a bitch.

That's when I have my next bright idea. There's always the TV.

Again, part of me is screaming to shut the phone down and just go to bed. Who the hell cares what's going on in Antarctica? You served your time, did your favors, and now you're sailing off into the sunset. The government can have their alien rings and international conspiracies; you have cicadas and Sinatra.

But the other part of me wonders if Aaron is still down there. Judging from his radio silence for the last two months, I'd say he is. Then again, we're not really on speaking terms, at least we weren't when I left. I suppose he blames me for Lewis and Walker's deaths. Hell, I blame me for those too. Still, it doesn't mean I don't care about him.

I take a second and study the chess board on the coffee table between me and the TV. I've been playing this particular match against myself for—I glance at the Post-it Note stuck beside the board—ten days. So far, black is winning. But it's white's move. So I sit down on the couch, slide a pawn diagonally, and take the opponent's exposed rook. After setting the conquered piece aside, I sit back and consider the TV across from me.

"Don't do it, Pat."

But apparently I have one more cat who's volunteered to stick its neck in the guillotine. Who knew.

I break my second rule for the night and grab the TV remote. I don't even look at the screen as I hit the power button. Instead, I wait for the device to boot up, knowing the talking heads will have a new meal to gorge themselves on—and heaven forbid they should go thirty seconds without fresh meat. Then, after flipping their steak repeatedly and chewing their way to the bone, the scavengers will lose interest and move on to something else. It's all a game, I remind myself, and then I take a deep breath before facing the show.

I'm surprised that I see someone I recognize right away. Shocked, even. I hit unmute and stare in amazement as the female host is mid-introduction with the split-screen guest.

"…joined by Dr. Aaron Campbell, noted anthropologist and archeologist, live from Rutgers University. Dr. Campbell, thank you for joining us."

"Pleasure to be with you, Samantha."

Aaron's in a tweed jacket and what I know to be a Millennium Falcon t-shirt despite it being half-covered, and with his hair and glasses only a little less deranged than usual. He looks good, if not slightly nervous from being on national television. Likewise, I'm worried because I have no idea what he's about to say. Every non-disclosure document from the Pentagon that I've ever read forbids speaking to the press. Disobeying those orders verges on treason. Correction, it *is* treason, last I checked.

"As I understand it, you have spent considerable time in Antarctica with the"—she glances at her notes—"Ellsworth Subglacial Highlands Project."

"That's correct."

"And you've spent time at McMurdo Station?"

"Yes. As a researcher and United States citizen, it's our main port of entry for all activities coming and going from the continent."

"In light of the breaking news about the missing multinational expeditions, can you offer any clues as to why communications might go unanswered for what some insiders are saying are as much as a week?"

Aaron moves in his office chair.

This isn't good. I'm suddenly wondering why he even took this invite, much less why he's stateside again. None of that matters right now anyway, because he knows full well that he can't talk about his work except in broad strokes. Then again, he's probably waited his whole career to do this, to—how did he put it? Give them a reason not to laugh at him anymore?

Dammit, Aaron.

"Well, Samantha. As you know, my—*our* groundbreaking work deep within the Ellsworth Highlands means that I have access to, well, some of the most important secrets the continent has to offer."

"Oh man," I say to the TV.

The host squints, apparently unsure how to take Aaron's juke.

She's gonna redirect.

"As I understand it, Dr. Campbell, this communications blackout is occurring during the Antarctic's winter season. Couldn't harsh weather play a factor in some of this?"

"Well, certainly. The weather is always a factor on the block, as we like to call it." He gives a half-smile in self-approval. But in my head, I'm warning him not to get too comfortable. She's just warming him up.

"That said, could there be other explanations?"

Again, Aaron adjusts himself in his seat. "Equipment failure is always—"

"Yes, but we're getting reports that all research stations are experiencing similar blackouts, not just McMurdo."

All?

Damn, I really want Willy to call me back. If nothing more than to set my mind at ease.

"Well, Samantha," Aaron says. "There is certainly precedent for solar flares wreaking havoc on radio systems. I can think of several occasions while digging in what you might consider *classified excavations* within the Ellsworth Subglacial Highlands where—"

"Dr. Campbell, is it true that you yourself have witnessed and even survived military conflicts that violate the Antarctic Treaty of 1959?"

Aaron's face goes blank.

A politician would have eaten this question for breakfast and given nothing more than a polite burp. But Aaron's no snake, and he isn't used to slithering through the weeds. Instead, he's fidgeting with his glasses. Steak is back on the menu, and the scavengers are ready to feast.

"I'm… afraid that— Can you please repeat the question?"

"I'm holding unconfirmed reports"—she lifts an iPad from her news desk—"that you are one of a few key survivors of a skirmish between US, British, and Russian forces dating April twenty-sixth of this year."

Ho-ly hell. Someone leaked.

"I'm not allowed to talk about that," he blurts out. "I mean, I can neither confirm nor deny… How did you even—?" He shakes his head and smooths his shirt, making a stab at regaining some sort of composure. "As I was saying, weather and solar flares can cause—"

"Dr. Campbell, were you or were you not privy to illegal military activities on your research site, ones that may explain a sudden loss of communication?"

My phone rings. Caller Unknown. I swipe the screen and hold it to my ear. "Go."

"Wic, it's Willy."

"Are you seeing this right now?"

"I'm assuming you mean your buddy on TV?"

"Yut."

Willy sighs. "He's the least of my worries, Wic. And I gotta go."

"So it's bad."

Willy waits for a beat before answering. "Nothing for you to worry about, Mr. I'm Retired Now."

"Roger that." And my former colonel's dead on. It *is* nothing for me to worry about. I shouldn't have made the call to begin with. Willy's got stuff to do, and I've got books, movies, flowers, a wood-pile, and whiskey to keep company.

"Sorry to bother you," I say to Willy.

He sighs. "We got this, Wic. And you got your solitude."

"Don't I know it."

"Have a good night."

"You too. Wic out."

The line goes silent, and I end the call. Aaron's still on the TV, flailing. I'm honestly surprised he hasn't walked off-camera yet—wouldn't be any worse than what he's doing right now. Probably doesn't even know he has the power to.

"…assure you that everything I've done has been in strict accordance with—"

The TV turns off.

And not because I made it.

All my lights are out too. I'm still holding the remote and feel a tingle go down my spine—like someone's shocked me with a low-grade current. But the sensation is gone just as fast as it arrived. I'm also aware of distant sounds playing in my head—ones that remind me of mortar rounds and artillery fire in the desert. But I shake my head to keep the phantoms at bay.

I'm on my feet when my primary backup generator kicks on. It's activated by a passive analog relay that detects drops in voltage, and based on the three-second delay that I just counted, it needs calibrating. My tungsten interior lights surge back to life and warm the house with their soft glow. Sure, they're more expensive. And illegal to sell, but I like the way they look.

My gut doesn't like the coincidence of all this, and I've seen way too many movies where operators blow breaker boxes just before entering a building. Hell, I've done that. But no one knows where my cabin is—I've seen to that. And my property's defenses would have alerted me to any intruders. So whatever I'm feeling right now, it's just nerves, and nerves get people killed.

Assuring myself that service will return as soon as the work crews repair the transformer that some drunk took out with his pickup, I sit back down and try the TV again.

Nothing happens.

I stab the remote's power button several more times before realizing the batteries must be low. Irritated, I lean over the coffee table to turn on the TV manually.

Nothing.

Now I'm guessing it's a GFI switch on one of my outlets. I walk toward the closest one in the kitchen and notice that the microwave's clock is out, as are the LED strip lights above the counters. Strange.

I check the time on my combination wristwatch, a black resin-band Casio G-Shock, and notice that the digital display is blank. Don't let the name brand fool you; they're surprisingly tough. I put

CHRISTOPHER HOPPER & J.N. CHANEY

a fresh battery in it just last week, and the second hand is still ticking away.

Remember how I said nerves get people killed? Well, that's true. But sometimes, if those nerves are a gut-check based on hard intel and past experience? Well, that's instinct. And it can save your life. To decide if this is nerves or just instinct, I follow a suspicion and walk back to the couch. Then I pick up my Samsung and touch the screen.

It's dark.

I touch it again, harder.

Still nothing. Now my heart's beating a little faster as I try and force-reboot the thing. But it's not responding. I hear more muffled sounds in my head and notice that I've broken out in a cold sweat. Memories are a real pain in the ass sometimes. They really know how to ruin a night.

I start checking every piece of digital equipment I own: my TV's digital antenna, my stereo, my old Xbox—all dead. Even my stainless steel Breville BES870XL Espresso Machine isn't responding. It was an oldie but still a goodie, and it had been running like a champ up until now. Son of a bitch.

And yet my 1957 Thorens TD-124 record player is still spinning up. And the tungsten room bulbs are lit while the kitchens LEDs are not.

Which settles it.

Someone just hit my cabin with an EMP—electromagnetic pulse. And one strong enough to take out my appliances.

I'm on high alert as I kill the interior lights and grab my Glock off the counter. If my property is being infiltrated, which I now have a legitimate reason to believe it is, I need adequate cover, including personal protection and armament. It was time to get some.

I move low across the great room and reenter my safe, closing the door behind me this time. While this room lacks a lot of what my enormous basement safe has, I still have access to a more than adequate home-defense arsenal. This includes a "light stocking" of 3,000 rounds of ammunition for each caliber weapon in here.

First, I check my property's multi camera security system. While the monitor and CPU are good, the static on each quadrant of the screen reminds me that the video cameras were, of course, digital and, therefore, susceptible to my intruder's attack.

Next, I grab a SCAR17 build that's based on my military issue weapon and set it on the rubber-topped island. Then I pull a modified plate carrier off the wall and slide it on. The matte-black Kevlar bump helmet mounted with my Elbit Systems Squad Binocular Night Vision Goggles goes on next, and I double-check the system to ensure its electronics weren't taken out in the EMP. The optics fire up, and I see green—all good.

My Glock goes in its belt holster, and I grab several additional magazines of ammunition for each weapon. Then I check to make sure my KA-BAR is in its chest sheath. My always-carry Gerber folding knife is in my pants pocket, but I'm a firm believer that you can never have too many knives.

Lastly, I retrieve one of my MURS radios from the faraday cage and attach it to my vest. I turn it on and set it to scan. Chances are low, but if the enemy makes the mistake of being sloppy with their comms, I want to be the first to know.

With my SCAR in the high-alert position, I drop my NVGs to see in the dark, push the door open, and move around the side of my safe for cover, staying low. The great room is bathed in green and remains untouched.

Anticipating that the intruders gained access by way of my two-mile-long driveway leading up from the west, I advance to the closest window and take aim, scanning for movement. My 1978 FJ40 Toyota Land Cruiser is still parked in the driveway and looks untouched. Behind it are the fields that drop away to the main road. I hired a local farmer to keep the swaths on either side of the gravel drive cut. He gets to keep the hay and buy a few tanks of fuel for his tractor, and I get an unobstructed view of my cabin's main approach. I also relocated some large boulders to help "passively encourage" approaching vehicles to stay in a single file line. And, should anyone catch me by surprise or in a bad mood? There are more than a couple things buried in the ground that can go bump in the night. Or boom in the night—depends on which ones get triggered. Despite all my precautions, I don't see anything moving up the drive, and nothing out of the ordinary in the fields.

On my way to the back of the house, I notice light in the east-facing windows. Lots of light. Enough that it's blowing out my NVGs. I flip them up, anticipating vehicle headlamps, only there's no Humvee and no helo.

I blink to make sure I'm not seeing things.

There, some eighty miles to the southeast, is a massive blue dome. It's gotta be several miles high and centered directly over the city that never sleeps. New York. Only now, the normal glow of the city lights is nowhere to be seen. Instead, I catch a glimpse of fire-light on the horizon and then wonder if the sounds weren't flash-backs after all.

9

0045, Friday, June 25, 2027
East Orange, New Jersey
Interstate 280 East, Thirteen Miles West of Manhattan

I'M NOT proud of how long I sat on my back porch before choosing to do something. But it is what it is.

I stared at the ominous-looking bubble for at least half an hour, taking rough measurements with my fingers and then scribbling notes in a black Moleskine notebook. EMPs can't take those out—fingers and Moleskines. But I was stalling, and I knew it.

I watched more fireballs rise from the horizon. They were scattered from north to south, followed by the sound of muffled concussions—the ones my brain had been trying to warn me about. I memorized their approximate locations against the darkened landscape, and then ran inside to grab a map—one of those good ol' paper ones that everyone used to keep in their cars but threw out once cell phones came along. I also grabbed one of my Cammenga tritium lensatic compasses and a protractor.

After switching on my helmet's headlamp, I oriented my map with my compass and then used the pockets of orange firelight along the eastern horizon to get fixes on each explosion. As I drew straight lines from my home in Skytop using my ruler, it didn't take long to see the pattern. Rockland County, New York to the north, Edison and Monmouth, New Jersey to the south, and Newark, New Jersey dead-center. These were sites of US military installations.

I folded the map and set my Moleskine on top.

God, I want to say I left my cabin right then and there. But I didn't. You know why? Cause I'm a stubborn son of a bitch, born in Brooklyn with Irish blood in my veins, that's why.

Which, I feel the need to point out, is also the reason I'm reluctant to jump into things hastily in general. Yes, like marriage or doing favors for people. Those all have costs that need to be weighed. And, yes, like driving eastbound on Interstate 80 directly toward a weird glowing bubble in the sky and fires on the horizon. This is going to cost the most; I can feel it. As in, I'm not going to be back in my bed before dawn.

"You should have stayed in your cabin, Wic," I tell myself. "You should have just closed the blinds and gone to bed."

Yut. You're right. You're right.

So here I am in my FJ40 Land Cruiser driving southeast.

Sure, I figure whatever is hanging out over New York, whatever has darkened the horizon and erased all light pollution in every direction, is someone else's problem. The military's, to be more precise. Hell, it's probably some new-fangled anti-missile air defense system or something.

Eh, but who am I kidding? The damn dome has everything to do with what I've seen in Antarctica, and I know it. My gut knows it, and my heart knows it. And don't ask why I have three parts of me that think—I just do. Actually, I have a fourth too, but Commander Johnson gets me in way too much trouble, so I try and leave him out of most of my critical thinking. He does better at un-critical thought. Breaching, entering—that sort of thing.

Oh, and everyone who says retirement is overrated? They never worked hard enough in their day job. Retirement rocks, and I had eight glorious weeks of it before this. Eight. No one telling you what to do, not having to continually risk your neck for some boot who's too stupid to know not to walk into the line of fire, or some twenty-something brain fresh out of The Basic School who suddenly knows more than you about setting up on an enemy position but lacks the courage to make the charge himself.

And now I'm rambling.

I'm also playing drums on the steering wheel and singing along to one of my favorite Creedence Clearwater Revival cassette tapes. My Land Cruiser's vintage tape deck is probably one of the few music producing devices for a hundred miles all because some asshole took out all the local stations with an EMP. Nice. Real nice. Peter Quill's mom really knew what she was doing with those cassette tapes.

I have to chuckle when the second song on Side A kicks off with the lyrics, "Oh, it came out of the sky, landed just a little south of Moline. Jody fell out of his tractor, couldn't believe what he seen." But I let Mr. Fogerty sing the next line by himself: "Laid on the ground and shook, fearin' for his life." 'Cause, somehow, that one just hits a little too close to home tonight.

I leave I-80 and pickup I-280 East, headed right for the blue bubble. The longer I drive and stare at the dome, the more I notice that it seems to fade a little over time. Or maybe it's just my eyes playing tricks on me; they aren't exactly the latest model anymore. I blink tears away as I try and stay focused, and then the dome seems bright again.

The only other moving vehicles on the road look to be pre-1980s gas guzzlers like mine, which makes sense given how many digital components automobile manufactures have added to their products over the years. Sure, I wouldn't mind a Tesla. But A, I don't have that kind of cash flow, and B, I don't trust it. Yut, just like my cell phone.

There's one other thing about all the still-working vehicles on the road: they're driving west, *away* from New York. In my younger years, I would have smiled at that. Marines are always the ones headed toward what everyone else is running away from. Oorah. But tonight, I remind myself that it took me half an hour to get off my ass and load my Land Cruiser with gear. Like I said, I'm not proud of it. But I ain't gonna deny it either.

The rest of the late night traffic is made of cars and trucks now stopped in the middle of the lanes exactly where their engines died. Some people are camped out near their vehicles, probably waiting for AAA to show up, or hoping their transmissions will finally decide to start working again. But most are on foot, either walking away from the dome or moving into the suburbs along the Interstate, likely seeking shelter.

More than one person tries flagging me down. Parents holding crying kids, an irate upper-crust wuss in a Fedora and loafers, and more than one desperate-looking supermodel with her mascara running. Okay, maybe not supermodel grade, but good-looking enough that Commander Johnson urges me to pull the Land Cruiser over. Like I said, there's a reason he's in fourth place—head, gut, heart, and then CJ.

I continue along I-280 East and go through a mental packing list for the third time to keep my mind occupied. Helps me ignore the pedestrians. "Trust me," I want to say. "It's better for you that I don't pick up." Because they're not prepared for where I'm heading. Hell, I'm not sure I'm prepared. But I grabbed what I could, and in the wind up to combat, you trust your training and hope like heaven you don't forget anything.

On the passenger's seat, I've got my SCAR, complete with suppressor, forward pistol grip, ACOG 1.5 x 15 sight, and single-point sling. It also has a side MLOC-mounted AN/PEQ-2A IR laser designator, and a high-lumen SureFire light mounted on the fore-end. I'm wearing four twenty-round magazines and have ten more in a crate on the floorboards. Sure, none of this is legal where I'm headed, but I live in the Commonwealth of Pennsylvanian, not those other gun-shy states. And right now, I'm wondering if they're second-guessing their laws.

My suppressed Glock is holstered on my hip, modded with suppressor-height sights. I'm also carrying four fifteen-round magazines, plus six more in the crate.

My plate carrier is outfitted with front and rear Diamond Age boron suboxide hard armor, my rifle and pistol pouches, a water bladder, and my IFAK—individual first aid kit, or more commonly referred to as a blowout kit. The vest also has my KA-BAR, large tie wraps, MagLite, and light sticks, along with map and Moleskine, IR patch, name tape, and morale patch—presently a dark green KTF rectangle in honor of my favorite military sci-fi books.

To anyone else, this mental inventory process probably seems unnecessary. But to someone who's been deployed and had to survive outside the wire, it's just a normal part of life. Reliability is never an accident, so I keep running through my mental checklist.

My backpack in the back seat has several sacks of utilities and accessories, including my Leatherman multi-tool, Otis gun cleaning kit, binoculars, range finder, John Wayne-style can opener, bandanna, sunglasses, and some garrote wire. It also has my Iridium SAT phone and GPS—not that either of them was working, last I checked.

Next to the backpack is my bug-out pack, which, in addition to extra clothes and polar fleece, includes a climbing rope, fire starters, a headlamp, paracord, batteries and chargers for all my electronics, and a large medkit. It also contains my hatchet, tarp, one-person tent, survival blanket, duct tape, water treatment kit, snacks, and a cooking pot.

Staged in my FJ40 is more .308 and 9mm vacuum-sealed ammunition, along with two five-gallon gas cans pre-filled and stabilized, a potable water reservoir, a sleeping bag, and a case of enough MREs—Meals Ready-to-Eat—to last me about four weeks if food becomes scarce, which, given the current circumstances, seems inevitable. I've also got flares, jumper cables, tow rope, a gas siphoning rig, camouflage netting, an MSR WhisperLite II camp stove, and a coffee pot—though it won't ever replace my Breville. Damn, I miss that thing already.

My FJ40 itself has a front winch, tow hitch, roof basket-rack with a spare tire, inverter housing, jack basket, fog lights, and a compressor on the engine block.

Like I said, prepared, not paranoid.

———————

MY BEST GUESS says the dome is thirteen miles high. I base that on the fact that I'm nearing East Orange, New Jersey, which is about thirteen miles from lower Manhattan, and the dome's edge isn't too far away. It's also glowing with the same kind of blue energy that I saw in Antarctica, which means that no matter how much I want to convince myself that this thing is human made, it isn't. And it's pissing me off.

Why?

Well, I suppose that's the real reason I got my fat ass off the porch.

Because maybe, just maybe, had I stayed on with Deputy Director Blue Helmet and found a way to blow up the damn gate when he wasn't looking, none of this would be happening. I can't prove it, of course. But I also can't eliminate from the realm of possibility that, somehow, this is my fault.

And it sucks.

You were just too damn tired to stay a few days longer, weren't you, Wic. All you had to do was hang on and finish the job. Instead, you wanted to retire. To blow out of that popsicle stand and get away from it all. And ain't that just the thing about problems? Damn things seem to follow you no matter where you go. Just when you think you're in the clear, *baam!* That's when an alien robot decides to probe you in the sphincter.

The way I see it, I owe it to the universe, or at least my home-town, to investigate. And before you go all patriotic on me, no—I don't feel I owe it to my country too. I did that stint already, remember? I don't owe the red, white, and blue one more ounce of sweat or one more drop of blood. Got the t-shirt, coffee mug, bumper sticker, and even the damn tramp stamp.

Okay, maybe not the tramp stamp. But I've got plenty of tattoos.

Annnd, I'm rambling again.

The closer I get to the dome, the more activity—and it's now much more of a sheer wall than the gentle curve that it has been. I honk the horn several times to get people to clear off the Interstate. They're congregating near the edge, bathed in its bright glow. I can't tell if they're just interested or stupid—maybe both. But I wouldn't be caught dead hanging around this thing without a justifiable reason. And a weapon.

Realizing I'm not going to get any closer without hurting someone, I pull my Land Cruiser over, drive across the grassy shoulder, and find a cluster of trees to park between. There's a good enough shadow to keep the vehicle concealed from most passersby, but I'm going to camouflage it just to be safe. The last thing I need is for some desperate group of people to vandalize it and run off with my gear.

I switch off the engine, grab my SCAR, and step out of the Land Cruiser. The first thing that hits me is the sound of people screaming. It makes my gut tighten and the hairs on the back of my neck stand up. The noise isn't like someone got startled during a Halloween party in your backyard. Nah, this is more like people in anguish—hundreds of them, and it takes me right back to the Middle East. I fight to suppress images of infants being ripped from their mothers' arms, of children crying after their fathers, and of wives mourning over the bloody chests of their husbands and sons. The odd part is that despite all the sounds of human suffering, I haven't seen or heard a single shot fired. At least not locally: I hear more explosions several miles away and wonder if they're from the military installations.

Whatever's happening, it's not good, and I need to move.

I retrieve the netting from the back and then take the next few minutes to cover my vehicle. Adding a few loose branches helps complete the hide, and I feel reasonably confident that my equipment will still be here by the time I return.

The second thing that hits me as I move away from my FJ40 is the smell: burnt ozone, but ten times stronger than I've ever smelled it. I can also feel a vibration in the ground, which takes me right back to Aaron's excavation site in Antarctica. I can't explain it, but it's vibrating my feet the same way.

I keep along the edge of the tree line that runs west to east, separating the Interstate from the residential housing to my right. Everyone fleeing is either walking down the road or between the houses, so I'm able to move undetected. The only people who seem to notice me are a few kids who wave or point and are ignored by their parents.

By the time I make it to within fifty yards of the blue wall, the sounds of people in anguish have risen dramatically. I'm half expecting a group of insurgents to be hosting a public execution. Instead, I see hundreds of people stretched out along the bubble's edge from left to right, glaring at the translucent dome—hands outstretched and clenched, voices shouting.

The translucent surface gives me a glimpse of people on the other side—their hands up and mouths open. I can't hear them beyond some muffled sounds, but they don't look happy. Whatever larger purpose is at work here, it's more immediate effect is that this wall has cut off these people.

Which isn't all it has severed.

I spot a woman wailing over the upper torso of a man lying in the grass. The dome's blue light casts his severed trunk and her face in a grim blue. I see other people screaming over bodies in cars or laying on the Interstate. Corpses appear to be cut through at unimaginable angles as if a giant sword cleaved the victims from hip to shoulder clean through. Some are missing their back halves, while others lack entire limbs.

The carnage stretches into the residential areas, and I notice the telltale actions of off-duty first responders trying to lend aid where possible. But there are far too many victims for them to tend to. That, and most of the trauma seems fatal.

That's when I realize that the gruesome spectacle is playing out on the other side of the barrier too, with one horrifying difference: the masses are pulling victims away from the slowly receding wall.

I push my way past a group of bystanders, move into the worst of the injured ranks, and then study the people on the other side. They're keeping back from the blue wall and screaming at others— presumably to stay clear. But not everyone looks like they're listening. A woman reaching for a boy about ten years old on my side of the wall loses her hand against the barrier. The appendage goes up in a swirl of blue flames and orange sparks. Two men have to pull her away as even the loss of her hand does little to detract her from reconnecting with her child.

"Keep clear, man," says a male voice behind me. "Or that's you too."

"Got it," I reply.

As more families seem to find one another in the chaos, additional attempts to reconnect end in similar dismemberments. One man breaks free of some people holding him back and runs headlong into the wall. His body is vaporized in less than two seconds, and cries go up from those who witness it.

"How long's this been going on?" I ask the man who cautioned me.

"Maybe an hour," he says as he runs both hands through his hair. "It's horrible, man. Horrible."

He's not wrong.

I step around grieving families and approach the wall, weapon raised. The barrier looks to be retracting at a rate of one inch per second, moving east. I look back at my citizen informant. "Has it been moving the whole time?"

He nods. "Since it appeared."

"And did you see anything else?"

"Whaddya mean?"

I want to say "drones and robots," but decide against it. "Just anything else out of the ordinary."

"More out of the ordinary than this, man? Are you freaking kidding?"

I take that as a no and thank him, and then I start moving north along the wall toward the Interstate's westbound lanes. I'm not sure what I'm looking for exactly—a door in the surface, or maybe a magic decoder ring that lets people escape. Whatever's going on, the dome is constricting, and if it's got a twenty-six-mile diameter, then there are—

I feel my knees go weak.

There are millions of people inside of it.

And for what? What's the end game here? The questions can wait, however, as I notice an overpass coming up. Maybe the bridge will stop the barrier and give people a window to escape. Hope rises in my chest, and I start to yell at people to get clear of the road. If this works, there's going to be a human stampede in a few minutes.

"I don't think it's going to work, sir," says a teenage girl walking toward the dome. Her chin's up, and she seems fearless.

"You're gonna wanna stay back, miss."

She gives one shake of her head and sniffs. "It already took my mom. And Sam didn't make it. So I don't care anymore."

I order her to move back, but she's taking one slow step at a time, keeping pace with me and the barrier.

"She let me drive. I've had my license for two months. Late-night traffic wasn't too bad, right? Says I could use the practice, and she trusts me. So she got in the back seat and let Sam sit shotgun. And when the wall appeared"—she takes a deep breath, and I can see tears streaming down her face—"it went right through us. It didn't do anything to the car. But cut mom in half. And then when I crashed, Sam… he…"

I reach over and grab the girl by the shoulder. There's dried blood on her hands, and I can see a few cuts on her face and white powder from an airbag deployment. "You need to leave right now."

She's not looking at me.

"Hey. Look at me." I shake her. "Look at me."

She does.

"There's nothing for you here. I want you to head that direction"—I point west—"and don't stop. Look for good people, ones who will help, and stay away from the rest. You hear me?"

She nods.

I want to give her some food, water, and weapons training, but the most I can offer is to say, "Stay alive. Stay safe."

She nods again and then looks west. I give her a gentle push and send up a plea for heaven to keep her safe. None of my prayers have worked before, but I'm hoping this one does for her sake.

The overpass is probably a minute out, so I get back to making sure people are as far back as possible. It's an impossible task for one person, so I'm grateful when a few bystanders take up my cause and aid in clearing away people.

Even still, some people echo the teenager's sentiment that the energy will go through the overpass unaffected. That feels odd as the anomaly doesn't seem to have a problem carving up people. Then again, all of the vehicles I've seen look intact, as are the trees and neighborhood barriers on either side of the Interstate. Whatever this thing is, it seems to have a prejudice toward human tissue.

The wall is within range of the overpass. "Everyone, stand clear." I take a knee near the guardrail of the eastbound exit ramp and raise my weapon. Not that I expect anything hostile to come through—all I can see are people. Their shouts sound like they're coming from underwater and on the other side of a pane of glass. But based on the way they're looking at the overpass, they seem to be thinking what I am. Over the next few moments, they start organizing themselves to dash through the forthcoming gap.

But the news of an escape seems to be working against those nearest the wall's edge. The crowd is growing agitated with the prospect. One of the men who'd been trying to call for order is pressed up against the barrier. His body bursts into blue flames and then dematerializes in a cascade of sparks. The man's violent end sends the people closest to it into a panic, but they're unable to move, now pinned down by the growing crush.

I move out from the guardrail and start yelling commands, but I'm guessing my voice is as lost on them as theirs are on me. I look up and see the wall just inches away from the overpass's edge. With any luck, the wall will abate and allow those people closest to pass unharmed. However, as it stands, they're seconds from becoming unfortunate victims of the mob's will to push toward freedom.

The upper bridge and guardrail poke through the barrier. But as I glance down, the wall continues under the concrete undeterred. For the next few moments, a horrific slaughter unfolds under the bridge as the receding wall plows into the press of people. Blue flames devour victims by the score, feeding like a ravenous beast with an insatiable appetite.

I watch in muted terror as the crowd realizes its collective fate and begins the arduous task of redirecting its momentum. But the shift isn't happening fast enough. More and more people meet their end, and the human made cavern echoes with the shrieks of the fleeing and the dying. Finally, as the barrier crosses the overpass's far side, the masses are scattering.

All I can do is stand and lament the staggering loss of life. Once again, I'm confronted with a sense of helplessness. It feels inescapable. I look down at my weapon, my gear, and realize they're worthless against such a foe. I'm standing in the wake of destruction perpetrated by an enemy I feel powerless to confront. Part of me wants to turn back. It does. There's no chance of victory against such a threat, at least none that I can see. Better to collect the wounded, treat their injuries, and head for the hills. The military's on this, and they'll figure it out. I'm little more than a washed-up vigilante with enough shadows in my past to know I should turn around and let the professionals handle this.

But the other part of me, perhaps the much younger side, wants to keep following the damn dome. Wants to look for chinks in the armor and run through the night. It's begging me to take the fight to the enemy and shove a barrel down its throat until it gags and yields its secrets. Some twenty-something version of myself that believes nothing's impossible is contending that there's got to be a way—there's always a way. Against my better judgment, I listen to that younger side, at least for a second, to hear if any rational thoughts come from his naive mouth.

Given the fires on the horizon from the bases, there might not be military on site for several hours, maybe days—who knows. It means the enemy is well-informed and acting strategically. Likewise, none of the civilians seem cool-headed enough to think past the panic. That is, save me, because I'm a civilian now too. Perhaps it's because of my combat experience, or maybe because I already saw something I can't explain at the dig site.

I'm able to go, but is it the wisest course of action?

Behind me is a sea of humanity retreating into the darkness. They're searching for shelter, mourning the dead, and trying to make sense of what they've seen. I could help them manage the storm. Use my expertise to help them survive.

Ahead of me, however, are untold millions who are trapped inside a contracting death ring. Their future is bleak. But I haven't a clue how to mitigate their pain, much less their fate.

And then there's my cabin up on the hill. I can picture it in my mind, sitting safe and secluded—a sanctuary from the pain of life, one I've worked hard to secure. It's watching, even now, looking eastward toward a blue dome, wondering when I'll return. But as I weigh the options before me, I'm realizing the cruel truth that I won't return. That there's no going back.

"You're gonna get yourself killed, Wic," I say. "You know that, right?"

Goddammit, yes, I do. And, to be honest, it's been a long time coming. Might as well get on with it.

A woman's scream erupts from somewhere behind me. I spin around to see her pointing toward the dome's southern border. Several other people are shouting and start urging the masses to run.

When I look south, I see drones hovering along my side of the dome. They look like red garbage can lids with glowing blue panels on their bellies. Below them, I spot some sort of vehicle headed toward me along the overpass road. And judging by the way it's hovering over the asphalt, I'm guessing it's not from around here.

10

0115, Friday, June 25, 2027
East Orange, New Jersey
Interstate 280 East

WHATEVER CROWD GATHERED to see if the force field would part across the overpass is now in full retreat. People push each other and herd family members to hide from the drones and headlights. They're not wrong either. Whereas I've seen those drones before, they haven't. But their instincts tell them this is connected to the dome and the horror it's brought them.

Still, there are plenty of people who aren't moving out of harm's way. They're too busy grieving the dead. A girl about five years old is pleading for her unmoving mother to get up off the Interstate's shoulder, and the kid's oblivious to the threat charging up the road and heading for the overpass.

Something about kids, man. You don't think about it. You just do it. Which got more than one of us in trouble in the Middle East. But even there, it takes a lot to undo human evolution's mandate to protect and preserve them. Which made what those bastards did to their own children that much more despicable.

I charge west along the Interstate, grab the kid, and haul her back to a cluster of orange and white water-filled obstruction markers. Just as I slide behind the barrels, I see the vehicle appear at the top of the exit ramp.

The kid screams.

I wrap my hand over her mouth, and she bites into my glove. Not enough to puncture the skin, but enough to make me swear. "Hey. Hush."

Her struggle lessens when a spotlight lands on our cover and washes the surrounding grass and pavement in white light.

The vehicle sounds like it's slowing, as do the drones. I try using my heels to push the kid and me deeper between the plastic barrels, but they're not budging. Without cover overhead, those drones are gonna spot us.

This is compounded by the girl biting my hand harder, but I manage to keep her muted. She's kicking and thrashing under my other arm—momma taught her well. But I'm not the one she needs to be afraid of.

Images of Lewis's body sliding toward the portal in Antarctica fill my head. I can feel his leg slip out of my hand and see his body disappear into the energy field. It was my fault, and I'm not letting it happen again.

If the drones hook me, the kid might have a chance.

"When I say, you run into those trees over there. See 'em?"

The child stops fighting me. She's listening. Good.

"I want you to run as fast as you can and don't look back. Nod your head if you understand."

She nods.

"Good girl."

The drones are close now, blue laser lights scanning all around us. I can't get my left boot out of the light.

"Get ready."

She nods.

"Hey," someone yells to my right. "Over here!"

I look and see a middle-aged man with a pot belly taking off his shoes. Then he chucks one at the drones. "Com'ere, you bastards!" Then he hurls the other shoe and takes off running.

The light moves away from our cover and tracks the man. I chance a glance and notice the blue panels under the drone's flare as they turn toward their new point of interest.

"Go! Now." I push the girl to her feet and give her a little nudge. "Don't look back."

She whimpers as she runs away. But I have my SCAR drawn and aimed at the vehicle in case it decides to spotlight her.

It doesn't, and the girl disappears into the brush.

I offer a prayer to Santa, patron saint of children, and ask him to keep her safe. Damn—it's Saint Nicolas. Eh, Santa probably listens better anyway.

Meanwhile, the man who offered himself in her place has been tagged. Like Lewis, he's got some sort of tensile wire harpooned to his chest. He's writhing against it as two drones drag him through the median and toward the force field.

For a split second, I contemplate taking the drones out. But then I remember how tough the damn things are. I'm no match for one, let alone a pair. And if there are bots up in that vehicle, I'm as good as dead.

There are several hard things about combat, and this is one of them—knowing which battles to pick. And you don't have time to mull things over. You can't sleep on it, phone a friend, or do a day's worth of research. You decide at the moment, using what you have, and then live with or die by the outcomes.

I remember some catechism class saying Christ left the ninety-nine to go after the one. For a split second, I consider opening up on these things to save the man's life. But if I do that, then I'm as good as dead. Which means more little girls like the one I just pointed into the woods don't have a chance.

Plus, this guy knew what he was doing. He was saving a kid. He'd made his choice, even if he didn't know all of the ramifications.

The drones drop under the bridge and pull the man toward the retreating energy field. At the same time, I see the vehicle turn off the overpass and start down the backside of the Interstate entry ramp.

With the immediate threat heading away, I pop up to keep pace. Yeah, it's a risk, but I want to know what this is about. With so little intel on this enemy, every detail counts.

Staying in the shadows, I sneak under the overpass and watch the drones and vehicle converge near the dome wall. They're all slowing, which means something important is about to happen.

Without the headlights in my face, the vehicle looks like some sort of futuristic armored personnel carrier. Its V-shaped undercarriage is lit with glowing blue panels like those on the drones. The front end is shaped like a triangle whose point drops toward the ground at a steep angle. Meanwhile, the main body is shaped like a windowless cylinder with armored doors at the rear. And all along the black body are magenta-colored plates like those on the bots. More yellow and white markings adorn the vehicle, but their meaning is lost on me.

I'm also not sure how these robots classify their weapon's calibers, but some mean looking large-bore twin-barrels are mounted on top of the cab, while searchlights and a small crane are atop the rear tank. If I had to guess, given the context, I'd say this is some sort of armored reconnaissance unit.

The rear doors open and out climbs two of the recon bots I saw in Antarctica—the ones without the rifles and helmet armor. They move around the ARU—my name, not theirs—and head toward the force field.

Curious, I move out of the shadows in the hopes of getting a better look at what they're up to. It's dangerous, but if you're gonna learn about your enemy, you have to take risks.

To my amazement, the two bots step into the energy field unharmed. Something on their armor seems to create a breach in the field that spans between them. As soon as the window to the dome's interior is open, I hear the people on the other side screaming. But the bots appear unmoved by the cries for help and raise their palms to fire on the people trapped within.

The drones drop the pot-bellied man at the robots' feet and then back away. As soon as they do, the droids snatch the man and heave him through the opening to join the others inside. Then they disengage from the energy field, and the dome's window snaps shut.

That's my cue to get back to cover. I sprint into the shadows and take a knee, hoping I haven't been seen. The bots circle back to the ARU's rear and climb inside while the drones power up and away.

Then the vehicle crosses the median and the westbound lanes and moves up the off-ramp to continue northward.

I wait a few more seconds and then move out from the bridge. Then I climb up the east side's on-ramp embankment and take cover behind the overpass's guardrail, studying the dome.

Did all of that just happen? I rub my eyes and check the time— 0126. My body's tired, but my mind is wide awake and somewhat freaked out by everything I've just seen.

As I take several deep breaths, I consider one of the weird parts about the human brain: its ability to reshape itself, specifically around things it doesn't understand. Neuroplasticity, I think they call it—something like that.

To be honest, up until I saw the dome from my cabin, I'd tried to forget about Antarctica's events. And what I couldn't unsee, I found myself writing off. Some might accuse me of denial. But it's not that I'm dismissing what I saw. It's that I don't believe Aaron and Dr. Walker's explanations. Call it self-preservation, sure. But I choose to call it logic.

What are the odds that some alien civilization dropped that ring here a billion years ago, or whatever they claim? Or, how about, just maybe, it's something left over from World War II, where the US was trying one of its freakish ways to thwart the enemy. Even during the Cold War, there were enough crazy operations to fill a hundred sci-fi novels. Project Iceworm, the Edgewater Arsenal Experiments, and Project Star Gate, to name a few. Only, these weren't science fiction—they were real. And, God, were they wrong on so many levels.

Even after what I've just seen, I still think this has more to do with us—with humanity—than it does with some crazy theory of Dr. Walker's, God rest his soul. Because, so far, I haven't seen any little green men. But what I have seen are a bunch of crazy-ass robots that don't seem that far off from the Terminator fantasies of my childhood. Which means, at the end of the day, we're still alone in the universe. That's the good news. The bad is that we're stuck with ourselves, and we're still coming up with insane ways to kill one another.

The dome continues to contract, headed east when I hear something moving on the road to my right.

"Halt, merchandise," says a digitally harmonic voice. At first, I think it's a kid playing a trick on me or something. I spin to my right just as two clear streams of intense light hit my face. I shield my eyes enough to see that it's a bot—batting cleanup. Dammit.

"Failure to comply will result in your termination," it says. See? Human-made bots that speak English. "Put down your weapon."

"Not a chance in hell, you ass hat." My SCAR is up, and my finger squeezes the trigger. The first rounds shatter the chest lamps —for that, I'm grateful. The next bullets *ping* off the bots' armor in a flurry of sparks and stoke the fires of my tinnitus with a vengeance. Not as grateful.

When the bot raises its upturned palm at me, I know to dive away. The paralyzing blaster bolt misses my midsection, and I'm rolling across the double yellow lines in the middle of the road. Then I scramble to my feet and start firing again, raking the bot's midsection and hoping to land some hits between its plate armor. Not that I'm convinced the skeleton is any weaker, but a guy can dream, right?

The bot's second and third shots glance off the pavement and smack into the far-side guardrail. I take cover behind a new Honda Civic stopped in the southbound lane. It allows me to try to outsmart the enemy. I suspect it thinks I'll continue around the front, so I double back to the rear. Sure enough, the bot is leaning across the hood as I unleash several shots against its lower back. I'm not sure if the designers imbued it with inherent lumbar weakness, but if the droids are anything like me, this is a sure bet.

The bullets deflect into the pavement and fill the Honda's left front quarter panel with holes. But the bot seems unaffected and turns toward me.

Time to move.

I pull back behind the rear as another blue laser round zips past my head. The smell of more burnt ozone mixes with my spent .308 rounds. As my last three tracer rounds signal the end of my magazine, I prep a fresh one by yanking it from my vest. When my SCAR's bolt locks back, I eject the spent mag, slam the new one home, and shove the empty one into my cargo pants pocket, all in two seconds flat. Just as I roll around the car's right rear and crouch along the passenger side, the vehicle rises away from me—as in, the bot is picking it up.

You can't make this stuff up.

Now I'm hauling ass to the next vehicle, hoping it's bigger than the Honda because, you know, the recon bot can pick up cars like they're kindling. Just great.

I hear the Civic crash somewhere behind me and don't even bother to look. I'm impressed. Now let's find a way to end this.

Another two shots miss me as I duck behind the front end of an early 2000-era Ford F-150 pickup. Other than a relentless amount of lead sprayed from several fire teams, which I don't have, the only way I know how to take this bot out is by drilling down into its trunk from the base of its neck. And last time, I had a fearless Russian running a screen for me.

An idea hits me. I don't like it, but I'm not exactly brimming with options either.

I sling my SCAR, unholster my Glock, and wait for the sound of the bot's feet to approach the F-150. I'm gambling that the thing doesn't decide to grab the back bumper and hurl the pickup truck away. Santa must be watching out for me too 'cause it starts walking along the passenger side.

"Thank you," I whisper to the North Pole, guessing that both Santa and the big guy must be watching my six.

I leap onto the hood, and like a kid seeing a McDonald's Play Place for the first time, scamper up to the cab's roof.

The bot spots me, of course, but not before I grab a shoulder plate and jump around to its back.

It's pissed and starts thrashing back and forth. I try to bury my Glock's barrel in the chest cavity, but the extended suppressor is making that difficult. I instantly regret not removing it beforehand.

Behind me, I see the overpass' waist-height guardrail getting dangerously close. It's easily a twenty-foot drop to the lanes below. The bot takes two steps back, which means I need to bail.

But I can't.

My hand is wedged under the shoulder plate.

There's a loud *clang*, and then we're tipping backward.

I briefly imagine myself getting crushed under the bot's immense weight, and the thought sends a shot of adrenaline surging through me. But there's nothing I can do. We're airborne, and my stomach is flipping inside my gut.

But the bot is flipping too. I see the dome's glow disappear, then reappear at the top of my vision.

My chest slams against the bot's back first, followed a split second later by my limbs and head. Motes of light dance in my vision like the fireflies in the fields around my cabin. It's so lovely there. I can't wait to go back.

The bot's trying to get up.

I blink, then blindly jam my Glock into the enemy's trunk, hoping I'm not pointing the weapon down at Commander Johnson somehow. Then I snap off three successive rounds. The bright flash and sharp sounds disorient me further. But the bot falls back to the ground with a *thud*, and I'm left with ringing ears and a splitting headache.

Curls of smoke roll up from the robot's chest cavity, carrying the distinct smell of an electrical fire. The bot looks dead enough for me to holster my weapon and roll off its back. I hurt, but I'm alive, which is all that matters right now. Well, that and I haven't been thrown inside the dome.

Then again, what if being inside the dome is actually where I need to be? Dammit. The thought occurs that maybe whatever's powering it isn't outside of it...

It's inside.

"Santa, help me," I say from my back, picking out the North Star from the night sky. I'm eight weeks into my retirement, and I've already gotten used to those damn stars. They seem brighter without city lights, even despite the dome's glow. Just wish I was back at my cabin to enjoy them. But something tells me stargazing is off the docket for a while.

I roll my head back toward the bubble that's inching eastward. Probably can't see the stars from inside there. Bastards.

All at once, I hear an engine rev in the distance and see headlights hitting the overpass from the south. Another patrol? Damn, these bots are relentless.

I force my aching body off the ground, adjust my helmet, and bring my SCAR up. I'm back at the same plastic barrels I'd taken cover behind with the girl as the vehicle screeches to a stop. Those are brake pads—old ones. I chance a look and spot a baby blue 1979 CJ7 at the top of the off-ramp.

"Bitches out," says a gutsy female voice as the Jeep shuts off. "I want to know if that shooter's still alive."

11

0143, Friday, June 25, 2027
East Orange, New Jersey
Interstate 280 East

"STAY WHERE YOU ARE," I yell in my most authoritative voice from my crouched position behind cover.

All three newcomers pivot and point their weapons my way.

The woman speaks next, soft enough that I know it's not meant for me. "Looks like we found him." Then, a little louder, she says, "We don't want any trouble."

"Then you'd best be on your way."

The woman is turning her head, trying to pinpoint my location. "You with them?"

I frown. "Them, as in…"

"The aliens."

"You mean the bots. Nah. You?"

"Hell, no. We're trying to kill the emeffers. Just cleared a patrol when we heard weapons fire to the north. Looks like we found the source." Then she lowers her weapon and raises her other hand. "Come on up and let's chat." She motions for the other two figures to do the same. They seem reluctant but eventually follow suit.

I stand from cover and start up the ramp, keeping my SCAR trained on the newcomers. They're kitted out and ready for action —definitely military, or at least former military. Looks like Army, maybe one Air Force—flip-flops and travel mug are dead giveaways —and one sun-of-a-gun Marine.

"Semper fi," I say as I approach the vehicle, testing the waters.

The Marine seems to relax a bit. "Oorah." He turns to the others. "He's a brother."

"I can see that," the woman says as she offers me a hand. She's wearing the Army's sergeant insignia and holding a suppressed AR15 across her chest. With a handshake like a pair of Vice Grips, she's all of five-seven, 150 pounds, and stands like she owns the overpass. She's also got a cute face and dark eyes, but something tells me her looks have suckered plenty a guy into a fight they can't win. "Name's Susanne Catania. But you can call me Hollywood."

"Former actress?"

She shakes her head. "Just the one Jersey girl who can't stand drama."

"Good with me."

She nods toward the Marine who's wearing Private First Class chevrons. "This here's Laszlo."

"Z-Lo," the kid says in a corrective tone.

"Oorah," I say and give him a fist bump.

He's a few inches taller and broader than me, which is saying something. Looks like his nose has been broken a few times, and I see he's got a cauliflower ear on the left side of his head. But based on his rank, I can't imagine he's seen combat anywhere, so the injuries must be from before he got cozy with a recruiter. Kid's an ugly SOB and has probably got some fight in him. He's also carrying an IWI TAVOR upfront and a Mossberg 590A1 shotgun on his back, plus a twenty-shell bandolier sling. Kid's a door kicker.

"And this is Staff Sergeant Ken Yoshida," Hollywood says.

"Air Force?" I ask, noting the PJ patch on his left arm.

"I'm not as worthless as I look," Yoshida says, shaking my hand.

"Wasn't a thought in my mind."

"Liar." He smiles. "Call me Yoshi."

"As in——"

"As in the video game. Yeah."

I like this guy. And I like the FN SCAR 15 he's cradling even more.

These people came ready for a fight, and I respect that. I'm also curious why they're out and about on their own like this too.

"And you?" Hollywood asks.

"Name's Wic."

"That's your given name?"

"If you consider I'm white, Irish, and an unrepentant Catholic, yut."

She smiles and seems to get the acronym. "So, former Jarhead then."

"Something like that."

"Well, Something Like That"—she looks down at the dead bot in the middle of the Interstate—"we'd better get a move on before that patrol circles back to find out what you did to their friend."

I raise an eyebrow at her. "Speaking from experience?"

"Maybe a touch more than you. Like I said, we engaged a few tangos south of here and were forced to move once it went quiet."

"Just the three of you?" Given what I'd seen in Antarctica, that seemed surprising.

"There are three more," Z-Lo says. "Holding down the fort, ya know? We're like a fire team and shit. Kicking ass, taking names, and leaving our calling card everywhere we go. Oorah."

I purse my lips and give a little nod. "Great."

"You wanna come join us?" Z-Lo adds. "You're like some sorta Raider, aren't you?"

I give him a look. "What makes you say that?"

"Damn, it's your whole kit, pops. And that's a tricked-out FN SCAR 17. Only one group of Marines carries that."

"Fair enough." Maybe the kid's not as dense as he looks. But he's still annoying. I redirect to Hollywood. "How far south are we talking?"

"A klick. Maybe two," says Z-Lo.

"Champ, I was talking to the Sergeant."

Z-Lo backs down. "Right. Sorry."

"And it's Gunny to you, kid."

Even in the blue light, I see the blood drain from Z-Lo's face. Then he snaps a salute.

"God, put that away," I say, realizing just how new this kid really is. But I'll let him keep thinking I'm active duty, at least for a little while. Might keep his mouth shut.

"My apologies, Master Gunnery Sergeant, sir."

I give him a dismissive nod and then look back to Hollywood to continue.

"We're holed up at a gas station one klick south," she says. "You have wheels?"

"I do." I gesture west toward the trees.

"Good. Try and keep up."

"I'll do my best."

My FJ40 was right where I left it, undisturbed. After stashing the camo-netting, I backed out of the woods and drove the short distance to the exit ramp where Hollywood's Jeep idled, pointing south. Just as I approached, she tore down the road with her lights out.

Keep up? Man, she wasn't kidding.

I struggle to keep up for thirty seconds as she weaves in and out of dead cars along the suburban road. Fortunately, most civilians seem to have cleared out, or else these speeds would be far too risky. Even still, I worry that some unsuspecting pedestrian is going to accidentally step out and get nailed—a concern that the Army sergeant doesn't seem to share.

Hollywood continues to weave down the lightly wooded street when her red brake lights pop on for the first time in a minute. Up ahead, I see the familiar shapes of an angular awning and a dormant LED pricing sign. The gas station. The Jeep drives around back. I follow suit and park beside a 1983 HMMWV "Humvee." Somebody's driving in style.

"You were looking a little slow there," Hollywood says as she slams the door. Yoshi gets out of the passenger side while Z-Lo leaps out the open back.

"Wait. It was a race?" I lock my Land Cruiser and forego the camouflage. "I'll remember that for next time."

She chuckles and then turns toward the main two-story building. "Come on."

Headlamps pop on as Hollywood leads us through the grocery aisles—or what's left of them. The store's been looted, which, given the circumstances, isn't all that surprising. But unlike rioters who focus on smashing windows and destroying private property, these scavengers left most everything intact, and instead went straight for the food. Smart.

A door in the freezer section leads to the back storeroom, where there's a stairwell going up to the second floor. A small hallway breaks off into two offices and what looks to be a poorly managed apartment. But Hollywood is going for a second set of stairs that double back and head to the roof. She pushes up on a hatch and announces herself.

"Anything?" she asks as she leaves the stairwell.

I emerge second and see two people, one laying prone near the eastern edge, the other kneeling at the southeast corner.

"Nope," says the prone man in a raspy quiet voice. He's set up behind a QDL suppressed Barrett M82A1 50BMG and has a Remington 300 WinMag lying beside him. No question what his military occupation is—or was. He's not exactly dressed according to regs right now.

"But I'm guessing they'll head this way soon," the second man says as he lowers some Steiner binocs.

Hollywood kneels on the roof and waves me over. "This is Ghost."

The sniper glances over his shoulder and offers me a fist to bump but says nothing.

"Wic," I reply.

He nods and then goes back on his ATN X-Sight night scope.

"That's Polanski," she adds, pointing to the man with the binocs.

I can't tell how tall he is, but the guy's well-built and has a standard-issue Army M4 slung under his arm.

"Pleasure," Polanski says. The shadow cast from his bump helmet hides his face, but it sounds like he's smiling. Anyone that friendly in a situation like this is either high on life, drugs, or the fight.

I nod at the man and then turn back to Hollywood. "You said you had three more? Where's the last?"

She nods. "On his way. Said he wanted to do a quick security sweep as this is a new setup for us."

I like vigilance.

Just then, I hear the distinct sound of one of the world's most iconic engines advancing from the south.

I look at Hollywood. "Is that—?"

"Uh-huh," she replies with a half-smile. "Come on."

We're pounding back down both sets of the stairs and through the grocery store when a lightless yellow VW Thing putters up to the gas station. The driver kills the engine and coasts up to the station's front door.

He's a big dude, driving with some expensive NVGs, and has a backseat full of gear. "What's shaking," he states in a confident baritone, then flips up his goggles. Sounds like he's from the Midwest— Detroit maybe. "Found us a new friend?"

"This is Wic," Hollywood says, nodding at me. "Wic, this is Bumper."

The man makes his Thing rock as he climbs out and slams the door. His iron handshake and Type II desert digital camouflage uniform tells me this guy is as badass as they come. No wonder he was out on his own conducting a security sweep.

"Nice to meet you," I say. "SEALs?"

He nods. "Raiders?"

"Yut."

Such is the highly technical and incredibly detailed greeting ritual between the two sister branches' highest trained warriors. We both eat a lot of crayons too.

Hollywood clears her throat. "Well, now that your bromance is in full bloom, can we get back to business?"

"Whaddya have in mind?" I ask.

Hollywood looks to Bumper. "Find anything?"

"Looks like our engagement to the south attracted some more attention. Two scouts headed this way."

Hollywood dips her chin toward the MURS radio attached to her vest. "You copy that, Ghost?"

"Affirmative," says the sniper.

"Best seats in the house are up top," she says to me. "Unless you wanna hang here with your man."

"I like balcony seating. Lead the way."

IT HASN'T TAKEN me long to figure out that Hollywood is calling the shots. I'm not convinced she outranks everyone, but she certainly seems to have the can-do attitude and assertive personality of someone who's used to being in the driver's seat. Which is fine by me, 'cause leadership is the last thing I'm looking for right now. Hell, if we come across many more operators like this, I'm packing my bags and heading home.

Hollywood and I take a knee next to Z-Lo who's acting as Ghost's spotter while Polanski is covering the north side for any bots who might want to double back from my last skirmish.

"They're like, I dunno, four-hundred yards? And closing fast," Z-Lo says to Ghost. "Like, coming in hot."

"Three-twenty-five," the sniper replies in a watered-down southern accent. Texan maybe. "And they're walking."

Z-Lo drops his binocs and then notices that I'm kneeling next to him. "I was close."

"Sure," I reply. "You taking the shot, sniper?"

"Mmm," Ghost replies.

"The further we can take them out, the less attention it draws on us," Z-Lo adds.

"That's usually how it works, yes." I look up Hollywood. "How many have you taken out?"

"Been going at it since the bubble appeared," she says. "We've hit five bots so far."

"Five? That's… some good work." Considering how badly my forces fared in Antarctica, this is impressive. Then again, those teams were young and were caught with several strategic disadvantages.

"Eh, but they're not the ones you have to worry about."

I raise an eyebrow. "Oh?"

"Might wanna cover your ears," Ghost says.

My chronic tinnitus thanks him.

A second later, his 50-cal barks. Even with its signature reduction QDL suppressor, it's louder than most weapons.

"Smoked him," Z-Lo says with a pat on the sniper's shoulder.

Ghost gives the kid an irritated look and then goes back on-scope.

Likewise, Z-Lo's on his binocs again. "Second one's looking our way."

"Mm-hmm," Ghost says and then squeezes off a second round. I'm guessing armor piercing.

"Hell, yeah," Z-Lo exclaims. "Tango down. I repeat, tango—"

"I'm right here, kid," Ghost says. He looks up at Hollywood. "Time to move."

As Ghost collects his weapons, I glance back at Hollywood. "What were you gonna say? About the ones we have to worry about."

"The death angels. They're the crazy ones. Some weird juju."

"You mean, there's a third type of bot?"

"Not bots." Hollywood shakes her head and then gives me a curious look as she holds the hatch open that leads into the building. "The aliens, dude."

"The… aliens?"

She cocks her head at me. "You feeling okay?"

"Yeah, I'm just—"

"Wait a second. You mean, you haven't seen 'em yet?"

I sigh. "Listen, I've seen a whole lot I can't explain. But I don't know that I would go so far as to call them aliens."

"He hasn't seen 'em," Z-Lo says as he walks past me and down the stairs.

"Hasn't seen 'em," adds Polanski as he descends.

Ghost just pats me on the shoulder.

Suddenly I feel like the punchline of a joke I missed.

Hollywood rolls her eyes at me and then drops through the hatch. "Someone's gonna have fun gettin' their cherry popped. Come on."

We're busy loading into the three vehicles out back when Bumper pulls around the building's side in his Thing. "Two more tangos closing from the south. Assault versions."

Well, that's not great. While I'm impressed with Ghost's marksmanship, those shots were taken against the recon-style robots, from a distance, and with the element of surprise. The assault versions are a whole other story.

"Why don't we just outrun them?" I ask.

"No good," Hollywood says as she readies her AR15. "Once they get a lock on you, they keep coming until you put 'em down."

I can appreciate that and nod accordingly. "Which means that because they're headed our way now…"

"They smell us," Bumper says. "Well, they smell Z-Lo."

"I heard that."

"They're like a bloodhound," Ghost adds. Despite slamming a new magazine into his massive weapon, he seems like he's bored. I also notice that he's missing his left ring finger at the second joint. "Only one way to put 'em off the scent for sure."

I ready my SCAR. "Well, in my experience, I've learned there are very few things that can't be solved by sending a whole lotta lead downrange."

This gets a rise out of everyone, and they say so.

"Who's calling the play?" Bumper asks.

Hollywood looks to me.

"Oh no." I wave her off. "You've been making stuff happen. No need to mess with a good thing."

She nods, then looks at the team. "Ghost and Yoshi, set up on the building's right corner. Bumper, left flank behind the dumpster.

Wic, I want you and Z-Lo behind that SUV. Polanski, you're with me."

Everyone nods.

"What channel are you guys on?" I ask.

Bumper gives me the comm freq and then adds, "You gonna be okay with that plastic toy gun?"

I grin. I'm no stranger to the SEALs teasing the Raiders about our choice of weapons. "You know what they say…"

"What's that?"

"Us playing with our toy guns is better than you playing with your toy—"

"Annnd we're moving out," Hollywood says as she heads for cover at the building's left front corner. Polanski follows her lead.

Bumper, Ghost, and Yoshi peel off, and Z-Lo and I duck behind a new Ford SUV. The doors are still open, and a rear-facing car seat tells me that a young family owns it—*owned* it. Wherever they are now, I hope it's far from here, because their kid-hauler is about to take some serious heat.

Images flash in my head as I recall the assault robots that wiped out three platoons of Russian, British, and American security forces. We have a fraction of that firepower now, and we still have two bots to take down. I don't like the odds. Then again, we had mere seconds to assess the enemy, and they'd caught us on our heels. Whereas now, we have the advantage of a suburban environment, good cover, and the element of surprise.

Okay, so maybe the odds aren't as bad as I'm making them out to be. But I still feel like someone's gonna get shot, and then I'm gonna have one more soul on my conscience to argue through with St. Peter at the gate. That is, assuming I even make it to the gate. Jury's still out.

"They're gonna wanna try to capture you if they can," Z-Lo says beside me. "Shoot you if they can't."

"That so."

He nods. "Took out two PFCs we met that were headed this way earlier."

"Sorry to hear that."

Z-Lo takes a deep breath. "If they try and take me? Huh, I'm not going out without a fight. Know what I'm saying, man? Gunny, sir."

I'm about to reply, but the kid keeps going.

"Those things probe guys and shit. Nuh-uh, not me. I'm putting a bullet in my head before I let them stick a—"

"I got it, kid."

He sniffs. "Cool, cool."

"Hey, Z," Hollywood says, and then gives him the universal sign for zipping the lips.

He nods and then moves to the back of the SUV for a better view while I point my weapon around the front bumper.

I catch my first glimpse of the eight-foot-tall assault bots as they cross the street to the south amidst several overturned trash cans. Their blue laser lights scan back and forth, accompanied with rifle sweeps as the enemy searches for targets.

"Any particular plan here?" I ask Hollywood.

"Most rounds deflect off the head; they're pretty well-armored. The neck is a weak point but harder to hit. When in doubt, take out their weapon or concentrate on a knee joint to slow them down."

"Roger that."

Hollywood's directions confirm what I'd learned in Antarctica. The slain bots at the dig site hadn't offered much in the way of intel, just materials that the researchers weren't familiar with and markings no one could read. But weak limb and neck joints? Apparently those were universal.

And, just so no one thinks I missed it, yes: I'm still hung up on Hollywood's alien comment. I've got a strange feeling that whatever ideas I've been nursing about this being some redacted government project are about to get set aside. That is if I see proof. As it stands now, I'm still just seeing the premier of MIT's Robots Gone Wild. No way I'm jumping on Dr. Walker's E.T. tour without a damn good reason.

As the two assault bots step into view at the gas station's driveway, Hollywood gives the order to open fire. I hear Ghost's 50-cal bark first and see the right-hand bot lurch sideways. A plume of sparks bursts from the machine's head as it absorbs the round. But the bot's cranium is still there.

A split second later, Bumper's M249 Light Machine Gun, commonly known among the young video gamers as it's squad automatic weapon acronym SAW, opens up on the left-hand bot. Bullets splatter against the target's chest and head as more sparks light up the night air.

My SCAR's sights are on target, and I squeeze off three rounds at the right-hand bot's neck. Z-Lo, Hollywood, and Polanski are also firing, and for the first few seconds, the robots seem confused. Their heads and scanning lasers look eager to identify the enemy.

For a moment, I'm hopeful that this will go better than the engagement at the ring. However, that notion is quickly put to rest when both robots focus their attention on those of us in the assault formation's center. That would include me.

The bots crazy-ass rifles open fire on the gas station's main building and the SUV we're hiding behind. As far as I can tell, the rounds are some sort of high-intensity energy pulse like I grew up seeing on Saturday morning cartoons—only with more destructive force. Sections of the building's brick corner burst apart, showering Hollywood and Polanski with debris and forcing them back.

The SUV rocks back and forth as its windows explode and tires burst.

"You good?" I yell to the kid.

"Yeah, you?"

"Peachy." I lean out and send another three rounds downrange. I can't even tell if I've hit anything amidst all the sparks and laser beams. But then the right-hand bot stumbles sideways again as another one of Ghost's .50-caliber rounds strikes the head again. The contraption's gotta be going down—no way it survives a shot like that from twenty yards. But it turns toward the building's south side and starts firing.

I seize the window of opportunity and flip my SCAR's fire rate switch to full auto, mentally preparing myself to change mags. Being effective in combat requires several disciplines—shooting tight groupings is only one. Granted, it's an important one. But being mentally prepared to reload, move, adjust fire, follow orders, and react to the needs of squadmates are equally as important.

I depress the trigger and keep my SCAR's sights on the bots head, hoping that at least one of my bullets will break something in its neck. The magazine drains in the span of four fast heartbeats, and the bolt locks open.

"Changing."

I grab a mag off my chest with my left hand as my trigger finger hits the eject button on the lower receiver. By the time my new magazine is in place and the bolt snaps closed, the entire well-choreographed dance has taken less than three seconds, and I'm back on target again.

But the left-hand bot has seen the increased fire from the center position and unleashes a barrage on the SUV that's rocking the car up on edge.

Using highly technical military jargon, I grab Z-Lo's shoulder and yell, "Run."

We're beating our way back to the building when the vehicle crashes onto its side. A second after that, one of the bot's energy blasts hits the exposed fuel tank, and the SUV detonates. Fortunately, we're shielded from the explosion on the side of the building with Hollywood and Polanski.

"Frag out," Bumper yells from behind his dumpster. His SAW's gone silent just long enough for the baseball-sized ordnance to skitter along the ground and detonate at the left-hand bot's feet. The blast forces the enemy back but fails to knock it over. The small window gives Bumper a few more seconds to unleash with the M249.

While the SUV is no longer a drivable vehicle—even without the EMP's effects—it's still cover so long as I don't get too close to the flames engulfing the tires and consuming the interior. The odor of burning rubber takes me right back to the Middle East, where the air seemed perpetually filled with the stuff. How those poor people lived without contracting lung cancer by age thirty never ceased to amaze me.

I tap Z-Lo on the shoulder and wrap around the SUV's far side to lend Bumper some assistance. Since all Marines are taught how to speak talking guns—a technique in which two operators alternate shooting in order to keep barrels cool and receivers free of jams while ensuring continuous fire on target—I'm guessing this SEAL will pick up my lead. I send a six-round burst at the bot and then let up. Bumper glances at me, nods, and picks up where I left off. We trade fire for the next ten seconds, which reveals another benefit of the technique: the bot turns back and forth between us, unsure which threat to go after. Our assault, combined with whatever damage the enemy took from the grenade, starts the left-hand bot wobbling.

"Changing," I yell and reload my weapon. When I reacquire my target, I notice that the right-hand bot is nailing Hollywood's position. Hard.

Sensing that Bumper's M249 and Z-Lo's Tavor are keeping our target busy, I shift fire to make Hollywood's assailant think twice about its advance. But as I do, the building's corner takes a direct hit and starts to collapse. Hollywood and Polanski need to get clear.

I dash toward the cave-in, but I'm nowhere close to being in time. I see someone thrown from the resulting dust cloud while the second person is consumed. Blaster fire zips through the haze, and someone is swearing up a storm.

Just as I step out from behind the SUV and cross the gap to the damaged building, a hand grabs my bicep and jerks me around.

"Watch out," Z-Lo yells. Energy bolts whizz through space where my body would have been. I backpedal, aware that the enemy has closed the distance and is tracking me.

I trip and land on my ass behind the burning SUV just as the bot's head appears over the upturned left front wheel well, wreathed in orange flames. Z-Lo fires full-auto until his magazine goes dry. Even then, he's still yelling.

From my back, I pick up firing where the kid left off, but the bullets are pinging off the bot's head. The thing jerks and winces, but nothing is dissuading it from delivering a death blow.

I'm forced to check my fire, however, when Z-Lo ditches his weapon, grabs a piece of metal from the ground, and charges around the SUV. In a frenzied state, he starts beating the bot with the tool. The kid's roars in a rage-induced tirade and hammers against the enemy's chest.

"Get out of the way," I shout as I climb to my feet, weapon still trained on the enemy. There's no way the kid's actions will stop this thing any better than my .308 rounds. But Z-Lo can't hear me; or if he can, he's ignoring me—lost in an anger-filled frenzy.

Ignoring Z-Lo, the droid raises its rifle over the SUV and angles it down at me like it's a street thug. But in the time it takes me to blink from the deafening sound, the bot's head vanishes from its shoulders in a sudden spray of sparks. The decapitated behemoth pitches forward and slams into the flaming Ford SUV, weapon clattering to the pavement.

I look in the direction of the kill shot and see Ghost give me a small wave. I nod in reply. But there's plenty to do: Hollywood and Polanski are down, covered in white dust, and Bumper is still one-on-one with the second bot.

"We're helping Bumper," Yoshi says over comms.

This means Z-Lo and I can tend to Hollywood and Polanski, but I can't tell which person is which. One figure looks in the clear while the other appears badly hurt. The brick wall's sections have piled on the soldier's trunk and legs, and a cinder block is on their face. I can already see blood forming red cakes across the dust-covered uniform.

I wave Z-Lo out of the open and order him to ditch the metal rod and reload his weapon. I'll chew him out later for his rage-induced bone-headed assault. It's a miracle the kid's still alive.

Kneeling beside the body half-covered in the building's wreckage, I ease the cinder block off the head and realize the corner has driven straight into the victim's cheekbone and crushed the left side of his face. It's Polanski.

"Oh God," Z-Lo says nervously. "Is he dead?"

I check for a pulse while gunfire rages across the lot.

"Is he really dead, Gunny? Or he's just playing."

The kid has enough guts to charge a robot with a rod but panics at the sight of blood? He really is a boot, and right now he needs to shut up.

"Z-Lo. How's Hollywood?"

"Oh man, I think I'm gonna be sick."

"Hey, Private. Don't look here. Look there."

Z-Lo blinks at me.

"Hollywood." I point at the team leader again as more weapons fire pings off the remaining bot. "She's your objective. You know how to treat for shock?"

He nods.

"Good. Get on that."

Z-Lo shakes himself and then seems to snap out, then turns and kneels beside Hollywood.

I move some of the rubble to pull Polanski's IFAK from his vest. I know enough First Aid to get guys off to someone else, but I'm no match for a Corpsman. And staring at Polanski's face as well as the blood pooling around his chest and the compound fracture in his left arm, I realize I'm not the caregiver he needs.

"Mind if I help?" Yoshi says over my shoulder. I move aside and let him in. That's when I notice that the weapons fire has gone silent.

"Second tango down?" I ask.

Yoshi nods, but he's too involved with Polanski to say anything more. He's pulled a battle med kit from his gear and is attempting to stabilize Polanski. After he applies some QuickClot, Yoshi orders me to put additional pressure on an Israeli bandage he applied.

Polanski moans from the kaolin, a mineral in the dressing that excites a coagulation cascade—that's blood clotting for the uninitiated. While the agent works like magic, it also hurts like hell.

I'm amazed at how fast Yoshi's working too. Then again, he is an Air Force PJ. I make a mental note to call for him if and when I'm ever down—so long as he's sober. Somehow, in the middle of treating Polanski, he manages to take a swig from a flask he's pulled from his vest. Then he offers it to me.

"No thanks," I say.

"We need to get moving," Hollywood says with a cough.

I move to her side. "You okay?"

"Fine." She waves me off but lets Z-Lo help her sit up. "They're gonna send a death angel next."

"And we don't wanna be here when that happens," Bumper adds from behind me—his M249's barrel still glowing orange. Coming from a Navy SEAL, that's saying something.

"Well, that's gonna be tough," Yoshi says, eyes fixed on Polanski.

All heads turn to him.

"How bad?" Hollywood asks in a hushed tone.

Yoshi frowns and shakes his head once. He knows not to speak negatively, even when the victim is unconscious. They can still hear things.

"Can you move him, Doc?" Bumper asks.

Again, Yoshi shakes his head.

"What does that mean?" Z-Lo says. He looks to Hollywood. "What's that mean, Sarge?"

Yoshi speaks up as he removes a syringe with morphine in it. "It means you guys get going, and I'll catch up when Polanski is good to go."

"But I thought you said—"

I cut Z-Lo off. "You sure about this, Yoshi? I don't like leaving you out here in harm's way. Too dangerous."

He nods. "Anzuru yori umu ga yasashii."

"Come again?"

"It's an old Japanese proverb."

"Right. Yut, hear that one all the time."

Yoshi gives me a half-smile and then looks back to Polanski. "It means giving birth to a baby is easier than worrying about it."

He's lost me.

"Fear is greater than danger," he says as he places a comforting hand on Polanski's chest. "I'm not going anywhere."

Knowing none of us will be changing Yoshi's mind, I let out a deep breath and nod. "Sounds like a plan."

I'm gaining a lot of respect for this PJ; staying behind to see a fallen warrior through until they've slipped into the afterlife is gutsy. And probably stupid. But it's his call to make, and damn, do I respect it.

"Can you walk?" I ask Hollywood.

She nods and orders Z-Lo to help her the rest of the way up. Then she kneels beside Polanski and gently touches his shoulder. "Thank you."

"Here," Bumper says to Yoshi as he slings his Heckler & Koch MP5 around Yoshi's shoulder. "A little backup, just in case."

"I'll take it."

"Keys are in the Jeep," Hollywood adds, indicating her CJ7.

"Thanks." Yoshi takes another swig from his flask that's smeared with Polanski's blood.

The rest of the team bids Polanski and Yoshi a grim "see ya later" and then turns to follow me toward the vehicles. As we walk away, I hear Yoshi start singing the opening lines from an old Chicago song.

"Everybody needs a little time away. I heard her say. From each other."

He's no Peter Cetera, but he's got a decent falsetto.

Once we're out of earshot, I tap Hollywood on the shoulder. "Is he gonna be all right? Yoshi, I mean."

She nods. "Just how he copes."

I'm not sure if she means the singing or the booze. Or maybe both.

Then she looks at me and says, "Shotgun."

"Be my guest."

I'm just about to climb into my Land Cruiser's driver's seat when Z-Lo walks up behind me. "Hey. Master Guns."

"Yut?"

"Does this mean I'm not a boot anymore?" He's referring to the encounter.

"Cherry's popped. Congrats."

He smiles and then bobs his head. "Cool."

I notice pride I've seen a hundred times before wash over his face. It's the sense of belonging that accompanies the realization that a warrior has survived their first conflict. For Z-Lo, it sounds like he'd already helped put down a few bots before these, so this wasn't his virgin op technically speaking. But I sense there's a reason he's singled me out—a fellow Marine, and an older one at that. I get it, and I was there too once.

I pat him on the shoulder. "They only get harder from here."

"Right." He bobs his head again and then seems to sober up. "Wait. Harder?"

I jump in my Land Cruiser's driver's seat and close the door, pointing for him to load up. Z-Lo nods and jumps in the Humvee's front seat, followed by Ghost in the passenger seat, while Bumper slides behind the wheel of his VW. Then we're off, headed—well, I'm not sure where.

"It's late, and everyone's tired," I say to Hollywood. "We need a place to bed down for the night."

"I'd say head west. We can double back in the morning after we make a plan."

I nod. It's the safe play, and right now, we don't need any more casualties. But I still have my reservations about the whole "make a plan" thing. There's not enough intel *to* make a plan. And even if there was, six operators are a few hundred shy of a battalion. But I'm tired, just like everyone else, and a few winks will do me right.

"Actress Mae West," I say over comms. While it's unlikely anyone is listening in, the MURS radios aren't secure, which means it's never a bad idea to use a little cloak and dagger when discussing your movements over the airwaves.

The other drivers acknowledge.

"Yoshi. We'll send you to grandma's when you want to go."

There's a break as I imagine Yoshi needing to stop caregiving to hold the channel open with a free hand. "Copy that. Thanks."

We're headed west down another suburban street, lights off, when Hollywood speaks up. "He saved my life, you know." She's staring out the passenger window, talking about Polanski. "Pushed me away from the building."

"You would have done the same. He just got to it first."

"Sure." She sighs.

I can tell my pep talk isn't doing much to ease her pain; then again, there aren't any that will.

"They don't cover this one in boot camp, do they," she says. "How to live with yourself in light of someone else's sacrifice."

I shake my head. "They sure as hell don't."

"You know what it's like, don't you?"

I cast her a glance and then look back to the road. "Sure."

"Yeah. Sucks." Hollywood straightens in her seat. "Head another mile. Then let's take a side street and look for someplace to hide the vehicles."

"Sounds like a plan," I say.

Driving northwest summons some strange emotions, however. I'm back in *my* FJ40 headed in the compass direction of *my* cabin. I ponder the ease with which I could deliver Hollywood to the rest of her fire team and then just keep driving. I'd be back to silence and solitude in an hour.

But would you, Patrick? Is this really one of those problems that just goes away on its own as long as you're faithful enough to ignore it?

But I've paid my dues. Plus, I checked out the dome and even saved a kid's life. Hell, I gave these combatants a hand and helped take out two more bots. That's more than anyone asked for. With any luck, they'll regroup with their units soon, and Uncle Sam will activate their plan to save the country.

Sure, Pat. That's just what's gonna happen. 'Cause everything went so well when you left the ring to Aaron and the Blue Helmets.

I let out a deep sigh and adjust my grip on the steering wheel.

"You okay there, Leatherneck?"

I cast her a glance, then put my eyes back on the road. "Yut."

"You don't sound fine."

I nod my head a little as I weave between cars stopped on the road. "Care for a little free advice?"

At first, she seems to bristle but then relents. "Why not."

"If an old friend asks you for a favor, and you say yes, see it all the way through."

She puts a hand on her chest. "Are we talking about you or me here?"

I ignore her query. "Just blow everything up when you have the chance."

As we reach the mile marker and head left down a side street, I decide that it's the final turn away from my cabin. If Yoshi was willing to stay with Polanski, and if the middle-aged civilian was willing to give himself up for that little girl, then who was I if not ready to help Hollywood and her team? Plus, I have a growing suspicion that getting these combatants back to their units will be easier said than done. If there are more of those bots and Hollywood's "death angels," whatever those are, there might not be any units to get back to. Which makes me wonder, yet again, just how this ensemble found one another.

So that settles it.

I'm not going home, at least until all this, whatever it is, gets sorted out.

Hollywood looks concerned. "You feeling okay?"

I let out a long sigh. "Never better, Sergeant. Never better."

12

0240, Friday, June 25, 2027
East Orange, New Jersey

"It looks good," Hollywood says from outside my driver's side window. She's pointing toward a large barn door that she's pushed open.

This particular barn looks like it was built sometime in the late nineteenth century, back when the suburb was farmland. Somehow, it and the accompanying house stayed on the market and kept receiving TLC from its various owners over the decades.

As I drive inside, the lane through the center gives me the impression that, in one of its more recent iterations, the barn served horses. But the animals and the acres of fencing are long gone. Instead, the stalls are filled with piles of boxes and abandoned home goods that someone was too cheap or too lazy to take to the dump.

CHRISTOPHER HOPPER & J.N. CHANEY

At the end of the lane is a large room with several old ATVs, both summer and winter varieties, and at least two garden tractors that look like they've seen better days.

I kill my FJ40's engine and step out into the musty air of old hay and equipment grease. Z-Lo and Ghost pull in behind me in the Humvee, followed by Bumper in his garish-yellow 1973 Thing.

"See if you can find some clear ground," I say.

"If anyone needs a sleeping bag, I've got extra," Z-Lo says.

"It's late June," Ghost says. "You'll be warm enough."

"Right." Z-Lo nods. "But you could use it for a pillow."

Everyone starts pulling personal equipment from the vehicles, save Hollywood. All her gear is back in her Jeep.

"So what's your story?" I ask as I pull my bug-out pack off the back seat.

"My story?"

"Where were you when the dome appeared?" Even as I say the words, I realize it's gonna become a thing, just like, "Where were you when the towers came down?" and everyone knows what you mean.

Hollywood nods. "I had a few days off, so I decided to visit a friend at Picatinny Arsenal in Morris County."

"The Army base?"

She nods, and her eyes grow distant. "Never made it. Power goes out, cars go dead. I helped some people out. But then the dome pops up and they all decided to run."

"And you?"

"I decided to stay and watch. Not sure why. Just how I'm wired, I guess."

"That's when you met the others?"

"That's when she heard the others," Bumper says from his VW's trunk.

"SEALs," Hollywood says. "Always making noise."

"Tell me about it," I say from the corner of my mouth.

"Bumper here was driving from NAWCSD Lakehurst to see one of his girlfriends."

"We're just friends," he protests with his head buried in the trunk.

"Trust me, honey, ain't no girl just friends with a stud muffin like you." Hollywood gives me a look like Bumper is clueless. "Men."

"Yeah," I reply, though I'm not sure I'm any better at discerning how women think than Bumper is. I'm also wondering if she's got a thing for him.

"Anyway," Bumper adds. "I'm driving along, jamming out to some old Earth, Wind, and Fire when my Chief orders me back to base. Says it's under attack."

I close the Land Cruiser's door and take a few steps toward him. This is the first confirmation I've heard that military installations were hit. "What else did he say?"

"I tell him I'm on it, when suddenly he changes his mind. Happened so fast. I heard…" Bumper seems to lose himself inside a bad memory. It catches me a little by surprise, because this isn't something SEALs tend to do, at least not the ones I've known. Their physical toughness is only rivaled by their mental toughness. But I'm also wondering if the sounds he heard are the same as what I heard after my TV went off.

After giving him a second, I ask, "What'd you hear?"

"I heard the Chief tell me to stay as far away from base as possible."

Bumper's words haunt the air for a few seconds. For a SEAL

179

Master Chief to give that kind of an order? It had to be bad... real bad.

"Then, that's it, man. Call dropped. Next thing I know, the road goes dark, the Astrodome pops up, and people are walking down the streets by the thousands. My VW's one of the only vehicles still rolling along when the robots appear. I drive for cover and start scouting. One droid goes after a woman who can't get her seatbelt undone. She's screaming for help, so I step up to bat."

Hollywood interjects. "That's when I hear SAW fire about two hundred yards out and start running toward it."

I gotta hand it to her; most people run *away* from the sound of machine-gun fire.

"By the time I got there, Bumper had taken out the recon bot and saved the lady."

"Didn't even give me her number," the SEAL adds—a classic attempt to lighten the mood with some humor.

"That's probably for the best." Hollywood tips her head toward the barn doors. "Yoshi was also on leave when he suddenly got called back to Fort Dix."

"And I'm guessing he never made it either," I say.

She shakes her head. "He happened to be about a mile west of us. Picked up two Army privates whose car had gone dead, and then continued toward us to investigate the explosion."

"The explosion?" I look at Bumper.

"I may have used a breaching charge on one of the smaller transports."

I let out a whistle and then elbow Hollywood. "I dunno, girl. I'd say you're just jealous. Hell, I'm jealous."

I'm curious what Ghost has to say. "And what about you?"

"Was headed home," he replies.

I wait for a few seconds, wondering if the sniper will say more, but he just goes on with his business of finding a place among some of the boxes and tarps to lie down.

"He doesn't talk much," Hollywood says.

"I see that."

She lowers her voice and turns away from him. "Most I can figure is he's retired Army. From Texas but lives in Vermont."

"Interesting. Thanks for the intel."

She gives a click with the corner of her mouth and then nods at Z-Lo. "Your turn, Private."

"I was headed up from NAWCSD Lakehurst," he says, but he's got a sheepish look about him.

Hollywood eggs him on. "And?"

Z-Lo sighs and then throws his hands up. "And I may have inadvertently commandeered a Humvee to sneak off-post."

"Because?"

"An event. Okay?"

Hollywood is not letting this go. "For?"

He lets out an exasperated breath. "My buddies said we were gonna go speed dating—easy way to pick up girls. But when I got there, none of my crew showed up."

"Oh no." I glance at Hollywood. "He didn't."

"Oh, he did," she says with a feral grin at Z-Lo. "Tell him what happened."

"Nothing happened," he says. "It was a—well, it turns out—"

"It was a speed dating event for seniors," Hollywood interjects, unable to hide her glee.

That, of course, makes me chuckle. But not as much as Hollywood is. "Hold up. When did you finally figure it out?"

Z-Lo sniffs. "Not until after I got my badge and went into the hotel's restaurant."

"You went in?" Now I'm laughing.

"The brother sat down," Bumper adds.

"No."

Hollywood nudges me. "Went seven rounds."

"What?" I look from Hollywood to Bumper.

"Playa's got game with the sixty-five and up crowd."

Z-Lo crosses his arms. "Hey, they were really nice. Okay?"

"I'm sure they were," Hollywood said with attitude, while conducting a three-point zig-zag snap of her hand and a swerve of her hip.

"I'm not kidding. Dolores was sweet. And she liked my nose. Said it made me look distinguished."

"Dolores?" Now I'm trying not to stare at his twisted nose. Poor lady must've been half blind.

Bumper nods. "Dolores broke the rules and invited Z-Lo back to her table four times in a row. A small fight even broke out amongst her peers, and the host had to break it up."

Z-Lo sighs. "She was persistent."

I'm crying and put a hand on Hollywood's back to steady myself. "My damn face hurts."

"Mine too," Hollywood says, doubled over. "And I've heard him tell it twice."

"I think we should call it Dolores from now on," I say toward the Humvee.

"Done," Hollywood replies.

"No, please," Z-Lo said. "I'm not trying to make fun of anyone."

"We know you're not, kid," I say.

Bumper adds, "You're already making enough fun of yourself as it is. Respect."

Z-Lo turns several shades of red and eventually walks away into an abandoned stall.

At least a minute passes before the rest of us are done wiping the tears from our eyes.

"How about you, Wic?" Bumper asks.

The idea of sharing memories from my cabin makes me feel like I'm about to betray the sacredness of my inner sanctum. But I also know that teams are built on trust, and trust is bought with transparency. If relationships don't cost something, they're not worth constructing.

"I'd just wrapped up watering my flowers before hitting the sack."

As a few smirks pass between the team—as is to be expected—I decide to omit the part about the news story, my call to Colonel Rodriguez, and Aaron's TV interview.

"Next thing I know, the power goes out in the house, and I'm standing in the dark."

"So you're retired too," Ghost says, mysteriously joining the conversation from beside my Land Cruiser.

I nod. "How'd you know?"

"Since you're out here and not"—he points east—"in there, it means your house wasn't near any of the bases that got hit. You're also not a frequent commuter because no one does errands with that much gear stowed." He points inside my Land Cruiser. "And yet you still have more gear in your FJ40 than most operators have in their houses. That means you're probably a bit paranoid and have even more equipment back home, which would explain why your NVGs and comms didn't get taken out in the alien's EMP. How'm I doing?"

I wanna tell the guy to cut it out, but I'm genuinely impressed. Plus, overreacting now will do more harm than good. "I'd say you missed your calling as Sherlock's understudy."

"You mean Watson," Z-Lo says, creeping back around the corner from his hiding place.

"I was thinking more along the lines of…" Eh, I don't have the heart to correct the kid. Plus, he's not exactly wrong. "Yut, Watson."

Z-Lo smiles, regaining a bit of his dignity.

"Anyway, saw the dome, jumped in my *prepared* vehicle," I say to Ghost, noting the correct term compared to his use of the word *paranoid*. "And then our paths met at the overpass."

Everyone seems to accept my story quickly enough. Now that wasn't so hard, was it, Patrick.

"Well, it's good to have you on the team, Wic," Bumper says. "Even if you do like plastic guns."

Just then, our radios issue a collective alert chirp. Hollywood grabs her receiver first in anticipation of the call.

"Wood, this is Yosh. Over," says a familiar voice.

"Go ahead," she replies.

"Polanski's crossed over. I'm heading out."

Hollywood lets the news rest a moment, then answers, "Any problems?"

"A single Two-drone patrol. Scanned all remains and moved on."

"Are you clear of hostiles?"

"Affirmative."

"Roger." Hollywood proceeds to give Yoshi directions using a mix of civilian and military jargon. I'm guessing she's covering our tracks as best she could following my lead from earlier.

"ETA ten mikes," Yoshi says.

"Roger. Wood out."

Hollywood releases her receiver and lowers her head—I'm assuming in honor of Polanski. It's a good leadership move, and I'm more than happy to follow her lead. If we don't honor the fallen, we're nothing more than monsters.

After about twenty seconds, Hollywood looks up. "For Polanski."

"For Polanski," everyone replies.

She clears her throat. "Well then. Everyone get set, then let's meet up there as soon as Yoshi's back." She points toward the open area where the old ATVs are parked. "I want us to get a handle on what we've seen while it's still fresh. We'll grab some shut-eye after that."

The group nods and then gets to squaring away their sleeping quarters.

I touch Hollywood's elbow. "Thanks. For Polanski's moment there."

"He would have done the same for me," she replies. "I just got to it first."

EIGHT MINUTES LATER, Yoshi's back, and we're standing around a rolling workbench and using it as a map table. I've offered to spread out one of my Rand McNally street maps of the tri-state area, while Bumper and Z-Lo hold flashlights overhead.

"So, the way I see it," I begin, and then suddenly think better of talking first. While there's been no official discussion, at least as far as I know, Hollywood does indeed seem to be the person in command.

She must sense my reservation, so she gives me a tip of her head and hand.

"The way I see it, we're looking at some sort of energy field that's cut us off from everything east, beginning here." I use my mechanical pencil to make a small vertical mark in East Orange, New Jersey.

"And we encountered it here and here," Bumper says, pointing to regions in Irvington, just south of us.

I make marks accordingly and then withdraw my Moleskine notebook from my admin pouch. I flip open to the rough sketches I made of the dome. "My best guess from my last observation point"—I draw an X over my cabin's location in Skytop—"had the sphere's center on an azimuth of 112°."

Using my Cammenga compass for orientation and its built-in ruler as a straight edge, I draw a line from the X over my cabin, through lower Manhattan, and into the Atlantic. Based on how everyone's shifting on their feet, I'm guessing they haven't gotten as good a view of the dome as I've had, and I suspect they know where this is headed.

"In addition, my first measurement put the dome at thirteen miles high, which, because I didn't notice any warping, means it's presumably twenty-six miles across. Or at least it was a few hours ago."

"We noticed it was contracting too," Yoshi says. "About an inch per second as far as we could tell."

I nod, then look back to the map and use its distance scale to make a pencil mark on my compass's ruler for thirteen miles. "Based on our combined observations, that means that the sphere's epicenter is"—I lay the ruler along the line and then drop my pencil point at the end—"right here."

"The Brooklyn Bridge?" Z-Lo asks. "Isn't that just a myth?"

"Oh my God, Laszlo. No," Hollywood says in an exasperated tone. "Where are you from anyway?"

"San Diego, Sergeant."

"Take a history class," Bumper adds.

I drive my tongue into my cheek to keep from laughing at the kid any more than I already have, and return to the map. "Chances are it's not the bridge, but somewhere here in lower Manhattan. Again, these are just rough measurements."

Bumper lowers his flashlight and taps a finger on the epicenter. "But the bottom line is that whatever this thing is, it's most likely being powered from here."

"Which means New York is under attack," Hollywood says.

I fold my arms and lean back a little. "We can't know for certain, of course. But that does seem to be the lay of things, yes. And, beyond all this, there are several other important questions."

"Like?" Z-Lo asks.

"Like, is New York the only city that's been targeted? And have other military installations been hit too?"

"I think I was the furthest south when this all went down," Bumper says. "And I spotted several bright spots over the curve to the southwest."

"The curve?" Z-Lo asks.

"The curvature of the earth. Off-horizon."

"Oh, gotcha." He makes a motion like he's petting a dog. "The curve."

"Could have been Annapolis, Quantico, Hampton Roads," Yoshi says. "There are too many to count."

Bumper nods. "Man, if I had to guess, I'd say that between the mass EMP, the coordinated attacks on our military installations, this damn Bazooka bubble gum sphere, and what I saw to the south, the chances of a wide-scale assault are high. And I haven't been able to hail anyone on my Iridium SAT phone either. I mean, we could try and venture toward one of our installations, but there's a high likelihood that, well…"

Bumper looks around but doesn't seem to want to say what I think we've all already concluded. The fact that a Navy effing SEAL is reluctant to go back and scope out his post tells me just how dangerous this situation is—and I already think it's damn severe enough as it is.

I tap the map to grab everyone's attention. "Until we get word that your various posts are safe to return to, I say your new orders demand you do the best with what you have right here and now."

Bumper, Hollywood, and Z-Lo nod. Ghost doesn't move a muscle, but I've decided that's a good thing.

"So what's next?" Z-Lo asks after a short pause.

Again, I look to Hollywood, but she defers to me, and I'm not entirely sure why. This is where things begin to break down for me —not with Hollywood, but with what to recommend to our makeshift fire team. For one, I don't have a clue as to what we need to do next. I mean, I have some hunches forming, but nothing that I want a team to act on simply because I say so.

And this is where the movies get it wrong. Ops don't come together in minutes or even hours. It takes weeks, sometimes months of intelligence gathering before the beginnings of a plan come together. Hell, Operation Neptune Spear, the mission that took out Osama Bin Laden, required months of planning and ten-and-a-half years of intelligence gathering. SEAL Team Six drilled for weeks— even built a damn scale model of Bin Laden's house to work through. Even when they had a plan, it goes through dozens if not hundreds of iterations before someone upstairs finally gives the green light. And don't even get me started on how the suits slow the whole process down. I suppose one good thing right now is that we don't have any damned bureaucrats telling us what we can or can't do.

However, the urgency of this situation requires that concessions be made to the time-honored tradition of having all your ducks in a row. Whatever that forcefield is doing, it's lethal and contracting on millions of people.

I spread my hand across the map and look down. "In my previous line of work, we'd have a lot more tools at our disposal."

"Lots of guns. Right, Gunny?" Z-Lo asks.

"I was thinking more along the lines of HUMIT and satellite coverage."

"Oh."

I smile at the kid. "But more guns is always the right answer too."

He bobs his head like he's grooving to a song that no one else can hear. "Cool."

"As it stands right now," I continue. "We only know what the six of us have experienced collectively. And then we've got a whole lot of guesses, at best. That's nothing to risk anyone's life over. So, before I go further, I wanna be clear that anything we attempt is going to be misinformed, incomplete, and highly dangerous."

"Bring it on, Gunny," Z-Lo says. "We ain't afraid of shit."

"Shut up, Laszlo," Hollywood says.

"Yes, Sergeant."

I give the kid a serious look. "This ain't the latest release of Call of Duty. And like Polanski and the others, people are going to die, one way or another.

"The good news is that we've all trained for this. Granted, I doubt anyone's getting paid for a while. Still, we're professionals, part of the greatest paid military in the history of the world, and no matter who's attacking us—"

"It's aliens," Bumper says.

I shake my head to clear my thoughts, then jab the map with my fingers for emphasis. "No matter who's attacking us, if we're gonna do this, we'll defend our homeland and honor."

A messy smattering of "Oorah," "Hooah," and "Copy that," comes from everyone's lips—save Bumper's. He looks up and says, "OTF."

I raise an eyebrow in a silent request for an explanation.

"It's my thing. From college ball."

"Your thing?" I restate.

He nods. "One of my heroes growing up was a Navy SEAL named Jocko who coined the term BTF, which stood for big tough frogman. So, when I became the team captain, every time we left the locker room for a game, I'd make the team kiss the football and say OTF—own the field."

"OTF. I like it," I say, noting the military pedigree involved. "It's never wrong to tip your hat to the greats who came before you."

Getting combatants from various branches to decide on a common mantra is a pain in the ass. I've seen it before when working joint operations. You wouldn't think such a little thing would be a hang-up, but it is. The military is a sort of religion where words and ritual matter. And having fraternal language is an integral part of forming bonds that must endure staring down death.

"I like it too," Hollywood says. "OTF."

"OTF," say Yoshi and Z-Lo.

We look to Ghost. He frowns. "OTF. But I'm not kissing a football that y'all have kissed."

The group shares a smile, and then it's back to business. I smooth the map again and bring out my pencil.

"Based on the rate of contraction we've observed, I calculate the dome is covering one mile every fifteen hours."

"That gives us eight-point-two days before it's at ground zero," Ghost says.

Everyone's eyebrows lift as they look to him. But we really shouldn't be surprised. A sniper's job revolves around gauging distances to a high degree of accuracy.

"Eight-point-two days it is," I repeat with a smile and write the figure on the map. The fact that Ground Zero at One World Trade Center is well within the range of possible epicenters isn't lost on me either. Being from Texas, I'm not sure if Ghost has thought about the coincidence, but I have. And I hope to God the epicenter is somewhere else.

"But that is by no means a timeline we want to abide by" I continue. "If we're gonna shut this down—and I assume that's what we're all thinking, right?"

Heads nod.

"Then we have a whole lot less time than eight-point-two days."

"How's that?" Hollywood asks.

I draw a smaller circle around New York City proper. "We're talking about the most densely populated city in North America and my hometown."

"You're from New York City?" Z-Lo asks.

"Brooklyn," I say. "There's a difference."

"What, you couldn't tell by his accent?" Bumper says to the kid.

"No. I mean, I just thought—"

"Relax," I say to Z-Lo and then redirect to Bumper, giving the latter a wink. "There are roughly nine million people in this area alone. Add to that several more million in the surrounding vicinity, and I'd say we're talking between fifteen to twenty million people."

Hollywood makes a click in the side of her cheek. "That's a whole lotta peeps."

More heads nod.

"So… what?" Yoshi says as he takes another pull from his flask. "The enemy's just trying to kill them all slowly? I don't buy it. There are plenty of easier ways to do that. I don't mean to be disrespectful here, but my own people have a bit of experience with that."

"Damn, Yosh," Bumper says.

"I'm just saying. You can nuke twenty-million people a lot faster than whatever this is. And they don't seem to lack the technology to do something worse than what we did in the forties."

So much for tiptoeing around sensitive issues. "I agree with Yoshi. While I've seen the bots kill people, I also saw them grab a man, open up a window in the energy field, and toss him in. Why do that if all they're going to do is kill him later anyway?"

I pause to make sure everyone's tracking. "Then the question becomes, if they're not interested in killing everyone, what's their end game?"

"World domination," Z-Lo says.

I blink at the kid.

"You got a long way to go, Cub Scout," Bumper says.

"What? Isn't that what they're always after?"

"Maybe they're trying to herd everyone," Yoshi says. "Like Fortnite."

I recall the popular online game's circular storm front that closed in on players, forcing them toward an ever-smaller danger zone before one player emerged victorious—a simple but effective mechanism for pushing people toward a desired outcome.

"Herding toward what, though?" Hollywood asks and looks to me. "Why lower Manhattan?"

"Your guess is as good as mine," I say. But it's not entirely the truth. So I say so. "Listen, I do have some more intel I probably need to share."

Their faces reflect curiosity as well as a certain level of... well, I won't say mistrust but definitely skepticism.

"What's that supposed to mean?" Hollywood asks with a hand on her hip.

"This isn't the first time I've seen these bots."

She's giving me one hell of a raised eyebrow. "It's not?"

I shake my head. "My last deployment was an off-the-books operation in Antarctica. I was leading a small team under the auspices of conducting a cold-weather field exercise—"

"Hell of a training ground," Bumper says.

I nod. "—when in reality, we were there to babysit a research project funded by, well, truth is I don't know where the money trail went. But I do know the CIA was interested enough to knock on the Corps' back door and ask for some muscle. Off the record, of course."

"I don't like where this is going," Hollywood says.

"Why so secretive?" Bumper asks.

Ghost gives a low grunt as if he's connecting the dots. "The Antarctic Treaty. No military presence allowed."

"Right." I nod. "And then there's what they found."

I let the sentence sit a second—probably too long.

"Well?" Hollywood demands.

"Of course, I'm committing treason by even telling you all this, so I trust you can appreciate my reluctance. However, given the circumstances, I'm willing to take the risk."

"What did you find, Wic?" Hollywood says with both hands on her hips this time.

I want to tell her to stand down and relax, but I don't blame her for being on edge. After what we've all been through, Hollywood's anxiety is more than understandable.

"I'm not entirely sure what it was exactly," I say. "But the so-called experts say it was a portal. A ring."

"Like Stargate?" Z-Lo says. "No way. Like, actual Stargate SG1?"

"Something like that, pal. All I know is they claimed it was really old and…"

Hollywood leans in. "And what?"

"And that it was put there by aliens. Goddammit."

"I knew it." She throws her hands up in the air. "See? Why don't you believe us?"

"Because I still haven't seen them with my own eyes."

"But you said you saw bots?"

I fold my arms and nod. "I did. The scientists succeeded in opening the portal, and out came what we saw back there."

"Oh my God," Z-Lo says, somewhere between ecstatic and frantic. "It's really happening. We're being invaded, man!"

"Relax, son," I say. "Just ease up for a second."

"What happened when you encountered the bots?" Yoshi asks.

"The portal had been open a whole night before anything came through. It was a drone. At first, it just scanned the room. The, uh… the researchers were happy."

"And you?" Bumper asks.

I chuckle. "I've seen way too many movies to have been happy."

"Copy that," Hollywood says with a sniff.

"Anyway, the thing suddenly targets one of the assistants, a kid named Lewis, and drags him back through the gate."

Heads lower, and the group doesn't say a thing.

"We opened fire, tried to stop it, but the thing was tough. After it left, that's when things went sideways."

"The bots?" Z-Lo asks.

I give a grim nod and take another deep breath. "A recon bot came through first, followed by three assault bots and another recon bot. They wiped out three platoons."

"Lemme guess," says Hollywood. "Russians, Brits, and Americans."

"So the news was right after all," Bumper adds.

Ghost grunts at him. "First time for everything."

"We weren't ready—not in the way we should have been. It was my fault, and we should have been better prepared. We should have blown the ring to hell." I pause for a second and take a breath, trying to force the memories back into the box where I keep all the dark stuff. "Only me and another warrior survived. Most of the researchers got out too."

"And the ring?" Bumper asks.

"We shut it down, yeah."

"Then where'd all these new bots come from?" Z-Lo asks.

"That's what I don't know," I reply. "But if I know the spooks, they wanted it back up and running."

"So you think the researchers turned it back on?" Hollywood asks.

Bumper strokes his chin once. "It would explain how the enemy got here. And maybe explain some of the mechanics of what they're up to."

And this is striking at the heart of my suspicions too. "Go on, Bumps."

He chuckles at the abbreviation, I think, then looks at the map.

"If they have some sort of portal tech, for lack of a better term, that allows them to move people from one place to another, then who's to say that's not what they're doing now. We've got a lethal Fortnite-style shield that's herding people in the most densely populated city in North America toward a center point—if not to kill them, then to relocate them through a portal."

"The hypothesis certainly has merit," Yoshi says. "And seeing as how there are plenty of larger and more densely populated cities in the world, and that the ring you found wasn't on any particular sovereign nation's territory, it stands to reason that New York isn't the only target. This is, of course, predicated on the assumption that they're after people herding and not something else."

Z-Lo raises his hand. "What does predicated mean?"

"Oh God," Hollywood says.

"And if the end game is people herding, New York wouldn't be first on their list," I say.

Yoshi nods in agreement. "Tokyo, for example, just broke forty-million a few years ago. Shanghai, Karachi, Beijing, São Paulo aren't far behind. But then you have the super megaplexes like Chongqing and Guangzhou that are bordered by multiple cities whose boundaries merge into one another to form urban areas on a potential magnitude twice the size of Tokyo. If I'm an alien and I want to herd people, I'm starting there."

"When you talk like that, man, it makes me wanna move to the country," Bumper says.

"So maybe the aliens are here to relocate us," Z-Lo says.

Everyone gives him a look.

"No, I mean. Like, 'Hey, look at those humans. They're gonna run out of food soon and start eating each other. Nom, nom, nom.

We'd better do something to help them before it turns into World War Three.' Know what I'm saying?"

I like the kid's imagination, but his theory has way too many holes. "It's a no go for me."

"Same," says Ghost. "Any action to relocate something peacefully is preceded by communication to that effect. I'm going to give any sentient species that has our best interests in mind the benefit of the doubt that they'd at least try something along those lines before doing what they're doing now."

"I agree," Bumper adds. "There are a hundred other ways to forecast peaceful intentions besides pulling people into portals or blowing military bases up. These bastards are informed and aggressive. Plus, we've seen things." He pauses for a second.

"What kind of things?" I ask.

"Bad juju," Hollywood says. "It's the—"

"The death angels, I got it."

She nods and then looks back to Bumper.

"So that means we treat them as hostile to..." Bumper looks around at everyone. "God, to the human race, if Yoshi's right."

"To the whole human race," I repeat softly. Man, if I had doubts about joining this team before, they're gone now. Sometimes, it takes talking stuff through with friends, even new ones, in ways that you just can't when you're up on a hilltop by yourself. "Which is why we've gotta find a way to stop them. And if we can't, someone else has to."

"Well, I don't wanna wait for someone else," Z-Lo says. He thumbs his nose and then holds his hand over the map like we're a sports team circling up. The gesture reminds me of Aaron and our childhood pledge to one another. As I watch each person look at Z-Lo's hand with varying degrees of skepticism, I realize that the well-intentioned but painfully ignorant kid from San Diego is onto something.

"Thicker than blood," I say with a twist of my head.

Hollywood crosses her arms. "What was that?"

I ignore her and keep going with the old poem-pledge. "Thicker than blood. Through fire and mud. Let everyone fear…"

I need something other than "the Musketeers." It's too cliché. Plus, it belongs to Aaron, Jack, and me. My head sorts through words that rhyme with fear and then settles on "…those gathered here."

With that, I place my hand on top of Z-Lo's.

He smiles at me, and I give him a nod back.

"I can groove to that," Bumper says and places his hand atop ours.

"Me too," says Yoshi.

Hollywood laughs. "Eh, what the hell. I'm in."

Everyone looks to Ghost.

"What'll it be, sniper?" I ask. "You in?"

"I've got nothing else to lose."

He puts his hand on top, and we all look in one another's eyes for a moment. It's happening so fast, but the speed doesn't make it any less meaningful. God, it does feel weird though—a cobbled-together band of mil and ex-mil patriots on a mission to save the world? It's almost good enough for a screenplay, except I'm pretty sure we're all gonna die. Plus, something tells me Hollywood isn't gonna be making movies anytime soon—I mean the place, not the Army Sergeant with her hand in the middle. Though, if they were, she'd make one hell of a character.

"OTF," I say.

Everyone smiles at each other and then replies as one: "OTF."

13

0400, Friday, June 25, 2027
East Orange, New Jersey
Old Barn

BUMPER TAPS my shoulder to relieve me. Even though my old bag of bones can't handle the late nights like I could when I was in my twenties, I still feel it was my duty to volunteer for the first watch since I'm the senior man in the unit. Needless to say, I'm grateful to get some sleep finally.

As I make my way to my improvised cot in one of the less-messy abandoned horse stalls, I summarize my last hour of random thoughts into definitive ideas. I've found that the practice solidifies things in my subconscious so that, when I wake, I have something concise and actionable to offer myself and, in this case, the team.

The first summation is that we need a name for ourselves.

Some folks might balk at this as being childish or of little concern. But there's a reason one of the first things our parents do for us is give us a name. Names help establish identity and a sense of belonging. They matter, especially when you're trying to figure out who the hell you are and where you fit in.

Likewise, names in the military matter. As trivial as they might seem to outsiders, without unit structure, rank, and titles, as well as the job descriptions that undergird them, you have chaos. The insignias, the rights of passage, the behavioral relationships between members—they're all set up to ensure one thing in combat: that you win and the enemy loses. When the fog of war clouds judgment and makes you second guess the whole world, the one thing you are trained never to question and never to underestimate is the position and qualifications of the man or woman in front and behind you, to the left and the right of you. Names are sacred. Names keep you alive.

Given the uniqueness of our situation, having a name is even more critical. We come from different branches, and, while we all still get paid by Uncle Sam, our unit allegiances vary. This means that banding ourselves together under a new unit name could go a long way in short-circuiting some of the factors that might inhibit teamwork—short-lived as our team might be.

So I've come up with one. A name that is.

Next, I've been thinking about how best to combat the robots we'd seen, as well as the "bad juju" death angels that Hollywood and the others had witnessed. In Antarctica, I'd been in command of inexperienced elements who had limited weaponry, weak field position, lousy communication, and were caught off guard by an enemy we knew nothing about. Now, however, I'm a part of a reasonably specialized group of individuals—a fire team, really—from various backgrounds.

While the EMP and the dome had caught Hollywood and the others off guard, they'd managed to prep a good amount of gear in their respective vehicles beforehand. But it isn't enough for an all-out assault. Instead, we need to stick to recon work and look for ways into the dome. It will be a lot like probing a chess opponent by using knights for opening moves. Test, withdraw, analyze, repeat.

Despite our limited munitions and supplies, this team is far more capable than what I had down at the South Pole. Where four bots slew all but two of us in Antarctica, this smaller team had dispatched seven bots—five before I'd even arrived. And how? By anticipating the enemy, setting up accordingly, targeting known weaknesses, and communicating.

And by staying out of sight. Like phantoms. Here one second, gone the next. And the enemy doesn't even know what hit 'em.

That's how we'll have to move if we want to stay alive and help the people trapped inside the dome.

My last summary idea is the need to locate Aaron—assuming he's survived the initial attack and not caught inside the dome himself. If the television's claim that he'd been "live from Rutgers" is to be believed, I doubt he's gone far in the last few hours. Knowing him, I'd say he's back at his lab trying to piece stuff together. And in that way, he and I are very much alike. Investigators to the core. But where his weapon of choice is a doctoral thesis that very few can understand, mine is a fully automatic assault rifle that speaks a universal language. Sure, if the world were a less evil place, I believe his tools are better than mine. But it's not, so I like my tools better.

If there's anyone who might know how the dome works, where

it's come from, or what these *beings* want—I still refuse to use the A-word—it's going to be Dr. Aaron Campbell.

Okay, so maybe the doctoral thesis is a part of the game plan. But it still can't spit lead.

I've closed my eyes for no more than what feels like ten seconds when someone gives a clear *psst* and says my name. I know it's a combat vet too because he doesn't sneak up and touch me in the dark. Last boot who woke me up that way almost got a knife in his throat. And all the poor kid wanted was to let me know that my Cup-O-Soup was ready. Talk about dying for nothing.

"What's the problem," I say to Bumper.

His eyes are fixed on the barn door, and his rifle's up. "Intruders in the house. Sounds like they're looting the place."

I consider telling him just to keep an eye out because I desperately need some shut-eye. But then I realize if the looters are armed and decide to investigate the barn, we might have a situation.

"I'm up," I say and grab my SCAR.

I follow Bumper as he rouses the rest of the team. We stack up at the doors and look east through various cracks in the wood slats toward the farmhouse. The dome isn't shedding nearly as much light as it was when we were back at the gas station, and the lack of a full moon isn't doing much either. I flip down my NVGs and ask Bumper to slide the right-hand door open.

"I'll scout," I say.

"I'm coming with you," Z-Lo says.

"Better let me," Ghost interjects. Before Z-Lo can reply, Ghost is on my six and following me out the gap.

We cross the lawn and set up behind an old-growth hickory tree just as I hear something crash inside the house. Sounds like someone just trashed a huge mirror or an heirloom China hutch.

"Punks," Ghost says.

As much as I hate the idea of trespassers rifling through a family's private property, our mission isn't to engage looters. I just want to deter anyone from getting curious about what treasures might be in the barn.

"Contact. Back door," Ghost says. He's got his WinMag up.

"Do not engage," I whisper.

A figure emerges from the house's back storm door and flips on a flashlight. Ghost and I both pull back and flip-up our NVGs. The beam sweeps the lawn and then settles on the barn.

"Hey, hey. I think I got something," the person shouts back into the house. His voice sounds raspy, mid-thirties. Between drugs and booze, something's torn up his throat.

"Fantastic," Ghost says.

"We let him pass," I say as I sling my SCAR and withdraw my Glock. "I'll engage from behind. You cover. Detain and deter only."

"Roger."

Over comms, I whisper, "Hold position. Watch for our engagement."

"Copy," Hollywood replies.

As soon as the man has passed the plane of our cover, I slip out and close on his six. Even though I don't see a weapon in his free hand, assaulting another human being never comes without some level of anxiety and caution, no matter how certain you feel your take-down might be.

My boots move silently through the grass, thanks to years of experience walking in dust and rubble overseas. While I can't hear Ghost, I sense him a few paces back. And that feeling, right there, is the only thing I ever worry about when closing on an enemy unseen —the sixth sense. Don't let anyone tell you otherwise: it's real. I've seen targets turn and pick out Marines because a boot looked an asshole in the eyes five hundred yards out.

Accordingly, I don't look at the target's head, just his back center mass. I'm aiming down my Glock, less than three feet away, when I lunge forward and apply a chokehold.

The man's flashlight goes flying, and he lets out a yelp before I close off his airway. I remove a pistol wedged in his back waistband and toss it aside.

"You're trespassing on private property," I say in his ear.

Ghost is to my left, pistol drawn as backup.

"Who the f—"

"Who I am is the least of your worries, asshole. What you should be worried about is everyone else who's with me."

The guy's fighting me, but he's paying for it. I've leveraged his head and neck such that the more he struggles, the more pain he encounters.

"What do you want?" he manages in strangled sounds.

"You're gonna go tell your boys in there to clear out of these nice people's home and get lost. You're also going to tell them that there are government sleeper agents throughout this entire neighborhood who have orders to kill on sight. I'm just feeling nice right now. If you understand me and would like to comply with these very specific instructions without deviation, nod once."

He does.

"See there? I knew we could—"

"Ripper?" says a new voice from the back door just as a new flashlight beam hits us.

I feel the wind move as Ghost pivots. Likewise, I've spun the hostage to face the new party.

"What the hell's going on here?" says the newcomer.

"Put the light down," Ghost says, moving away from me.

The beam sweeps from Ghost and back.

"Let him go, man," the man says to me.

I decide to ease up on my captive, Ripper, and order him to tell his friend to back off.

"Go back inside, Worm. Now," Ripper says, acting compliant.

"No way, man." I can tell that Worm is agitated. Sounds like he's on something too, which isn't good. All those anti-drug talks we got in high school focused on the adverse side effects on our bodies. What they should have focused on was the stupid stuff it makes you do when facing someone with a loaded firearm pointed at you. That would have saved a lot more kids in my neighborhood growing up.

Ghost repeats his order to douse the flashlight, noting that he will shoot if the man does not comply.

"Go back inside," Ripper wails, still caught in my hold.

"No way, man!" Whether out of panic or bravado, Worm shows no sign of leaving. He reaches for something behind his back.

"Gun," Ghost yells, followed by the *pop-pop* of his suppressed HK 9mm.

The flashlight clatters to the ground, and a body slumps down the stairs. In the spinning light, I can make out a pistol on the concrete back step.

"Nooo," Ripper screams, fighting toward the slain man. "You shot him! What's wrong with you?"

Still, I keep Ripper locked in place. "Is there anyone else in the house?"

"You're insane, man."

"Last time." I give Ripper a little love squeeze. "Who else is in the house?"

"Two more," he chokes out.

I can hear looters three and four moving—beating down a stairwell and trying to come to the rescue. Just because a weapon is suppressed doesn't mean it's silent. Plus, there's been shouting.

"Containment set," Hollywood says in my earpiece.

"Tell your friends to leave the premises," I say to Ripper. "We have the home surrounded, and they will join Worm if they don't listen to you. Go."

I let go and shove Ripper forward—hoping he's compliant. He yelps and stumbles through the grass but manages to stay upright. Then he sidesteps Worm's body, swearing as he does, and then heads up the stairs, yelling, "We gotta get outta here. They shot Worm."

His claims are followed by ten seconds of protesting.

To speed the conversation along, Ghost fires three more shots into the back windows. Shouts follow footsteps as the looters head out the house's front door. And then all is still once more.

The silence is broken by Hollywood and the sound of her lowering her AR-15. "Goddammit."

"Yoshi," I say. "Check the victim."

"He's done," Ghost adds.

"That may be, but he still deserves a look."

Ghost and Yoshi both nod and then move to inspect the casualty. A civilian too, no less.

This officially marks the first time I've seen a civilian put down on US soil by a combatant. And I don't like it. We're not trained to deal with domestic threats—there are other departments for that. Still, Ghost did the right thing, and I don't blame him. Even if he'd tried to put rounds in the man's extremities, which he wouldn't—warriors don't aim to wound, we aim to kill—it would have not only put our lives in jeopardy, but it would have made the victim's death that much more painful. Without a functioning hospital, the man would have either bled out or died from an infection. The victim chose to draw a weapon after clear instructions were given in a wartime situation—unofficial as it may be—and he paid the price. I hate it.

And that, right there, is the thing that probably sucks most about combat. It's not fair. It's painful. And you don't get do-overs when lethal force is employed. That's why you train hard and trust your instincts. Still, taking a life is taking a life, and it never gets any easier—at least to those of us who still have souls. You just learn to compartmentalize more.

"You wanna move out?" Hollywood asks me.

Again, I'm not sure why she's asking me for leadership cues. But it's a worthy question.

"They won't be back. And I'm guessing we're far enough away from the bots that we haven't attracted attention. So considering how much work it will be to find new cover for the vehicles, I say we stay put and keep watch."

"Sounds like a plan," she says, and then orders Z-Lo to help Yoshi and Ghost take care of the body behind the barn.

"You good?" Bumper asks me, pointing to my lip with a Mini Maglite.

Curious, I touch a place that feels warm and see blood on my fingertips—a good amount of blood too. Apparently Ripper's head must've hit my mouth during the struggle. "Huh. Didn't even feel it happen."

"Yoshi's not the only medic around here," he says as he pulls a compact battle med kit from his pants' pocket and sets it on the ground. He stows his handheld flashlight and flicks on a headlamp.

"You're a Corpsman?" I ask. "I took you for a—"

"UDT, heavy weapons." He smiles. "That's my primary. Naval Corpsman is my secondary." He unwraps a fresh pad and a clotting agent, then stands to face me. "You're gonna feel some pressure."

"Screw you."

"Roger that." He applies the kaolin and then puts the pad on it.

I groan. "Feels like a wasp just raped my goddamn lip," I say with a lisp.

"Delightful, ain't it?"

"Not exactly what I was thinking."

After a moment, he says, "Never formally introduced myself before. Uriah Johnson."

It's a weird time to make introductions, but then again, spec ops operators aren't known for having all their screws tightened. I shake his hand. "Patrick Finnegan."

"You really from Brooklyn?"

"You really from Detroit?"

He raises an eyebrow. "How'd you know?"

"Picked up a little accent."

"Sharp."

"Eh. At least with certain things."

He grunts a short laugh. "I hear that."

"Thanks for the lip balm."

He nods. "If it keeps bleeding, you'll need stitches. But you might want Yoshi's steadier hands for that."

"Understood."

As soon as Yoshi, Ghost, and Z-Lo return, Hollywood orders everyone back inside to finish our catnaps. I re-pad my cot and then try to get comfortable. Probably another hour and a half until sunrise, and we agreed to break at 0600.

I suspect everyone but the kid will be able to doze off again.

Combat veterans develop a strange talent for sleeping in the most unnatural positions through the weirdest scenarios. But Z-Lo? He hasn't seen that yet.

Then again, he's still at that age where he needs more hours than a mid-forties weather-worn grunt. Whenever people say they slept like a baby, I recognize that they've never been around babies. "So you woke up every two hours and crapped yourself?" Instead, what they mean to say is that they slept like an eighteen-year-old male who just scarfed down an entire pepperoni pizza after a six-hour Call of Duty binge. Now that's a glory coma no one's waking up from until the next afternoon.

"Night, Hollywood," a voice says in the darkness. It's Z-Lo.

"Night, Z-Lo," she replies.

I chuckle to myself. Are we really doing this?

"Night, Wic," the kid says.

"Night, John Boy."

There's a pause. "Who's John Boy?"

"The Waltons, dumbass," Ghost says as he sounds like he's readjusting whatever he's using as a pillow.

"What's the Waltons?"

"Go back to bed, Z-Lo," Bumper says. He doesn't seem old enough to get the joke, but he clearly understands the value of quiet. "Or I can do it for you."

"I'm sleepin'. I'm sleepin'. Sheesh. Just trying to be nice. Waltons my ass."

"Shut up," the rest of us say in unison. And I finally get some sleep.

14

0600 Friday, June 25, 2027
East Orange, New Jersey
Old Barn

"Rise and shine, Brooklyn," Hollywood says in an overly sassy New Jersey accent. Not even the first rays of sunlight warming the barn's entryway had awakened me, which is saying something.

"Already?"

"Sorry to say. But you're the one who said you wanted to be moving by 0600."

"Next time, don't let me do that."

"Roger."

I pack up my things and stow them in my Land Cruiser. I also take the time to grab fresh magazines and reload the spent ones. After two decades of practice, I can refill mags blindfolded better than holding a conversation. Not that I was ever going to win an award for speaking to another human being, but my point still stands.

Once I've stretched and checked the weather outside—seventy-one degrees and partly cloudy—I double back to the ATV area where I detect the fragrance of one of God's greatest gifts to humanity: coffee. Another, of course, being whiskey. But I rarely have that before dinner.

"How do you take it?" Yoshi asks from a milk stool he's pilfered from the barn's contents. He has a WhisperLite II stove heating the bottom side of a vintage percolator pot, complete with the yellow-stained glass knob atop the lid for viewing.

"Just black," I say.

"Figured. I meant punch or no punch."

I think he means caf or decaf when he holds up his flask. "No punch. Thanks."

He shrugs then starts pouring some coffee into a metal camping mug, singing, "Tonight we ride, right or wrong. Tonight we sail, on a radio song."

Tom Petty. Good choice.

After taking a sample of the steaming liquid, I thank Yoshi and then turn away to Hollywood. "He always heavy on the tin?" I ask in a hushed tone.

She nods almost imperceptibly. "Mm-hmm. But hasn't affected his performance."

"Not yet, anyway."

She waits for a second, then says, "Some people do better with it than without."

I've heard that my whole life. It was one of my father's go-to lines. But I'm not about to get into it with Hollywood within earshot of Yoshi. The most I offer Hollywood is: "At least not yet, it hasn't."

"Let's hope it stays that way."

"Yut."

Hollywood turns to the vehicles and gives a two-fingered whistle to Z-Lo, Bumper, and Ghost. "Let's circle up."

Within the next two minutes, we're all seated around Yoshi's coffee stand, sipping coffee and water and breaking the night's fast with some MRE's and protein bars. Whatever the day holds, everyone seems to recognize the need to get our calorie count up and stay hydrated. That's good.

"So what's the plan, Stan?" Z-Lo asks, looking from Hollywood to me and then cracking his knuckles. "We gonna get some today, or what?"

Hollywood and I share a look.

"You got something to say?" she asks me.

I want to say no. I want her to take the lead. But me taking the helm is fast becoming a pattern. Plus, I do have something.

"Well"—I take another sip of coffee—"first, we need to clear up a few things about our little team here. Specifically, if anyone has another place to be." I let the statement hang for a second before clarifying. "As far as I can tell, three of you are still active duty. That means you have oaths and legal obligations. No sense keeping you from those."

"You're asking if we want in on whatever's next for us here?" Bumper sniffs. "I think I made it pretty clear last night that my order was to get the hell away from Dodge. Lord knows I ain't about to listen to that order. Eventually, I need to get down there and see what's happened. But at the same time, the fight in front of me is the one that has my attention, and I've never been known to sit on the sidelines. So until I can establish contact with my unit, I'm in."

I nod, then look to Yoshi.

"Jakunikukyoushoku."

I wait for him to translate that mouthful, but he's just smiling at me. "Which means?"

"The weak are meat; the strong eat."

I chuckle. "Has a nice ring to it. So, you're in?"

Yoshi nods. "Until I can reestablish contact, like Bumper, yes. This fight needs my sword, so I will remain."

"Fair enough." I look to Z-Lo. "Kid?"

"I'm so down to clown, Master Guns. Like, in as deep as you want me in, man."

"Oh, God," Hollywood says. "Please rephrase—"

But Z-Lo's on a roll. "Whatever need you want me to please, I'm your guy. Like, just ask, and I'll do it. 'Cause there's nothing that—"

"Don't hurt yourself, kid," I say.

He stops his motormouth. "Okay, right, right. Cool."

I ask Hollywood next.

"Shoot. You kidding, Wic?"

"Just had to make sure."

"Hell, yes."

Last is Ghost. I feel like using words might just insult him. So I nod. He knows what I want to say. And when he nods back, I know what he wants to say. 'Nough said.

"Well, that's taken care of." I take another sip of coffee and then stretch my back. "Next up is a name."

Hollywood raises an eyebrow at me. "Care to explain?"

I proceed to outline my thoughts on the importance of names, and the more I talk, the more I see everyone nod. Then I segue into the kind of fighting I imagine we'll be doing while scouting along the dome.

By the end of my mini-lecture, Z-Lo asks, "So who are we?"

"Phantom Team," I say.

Hollywood repeats the term and then looks up. "I like it."

"Me too," Bumper says.

"It's effin' sweet, man," Z-Lo says. "I'd get that bitch tatted right here"—he pounds his left bicep. "Wait. That's taken. I mean here"—he hits his left forearm.

I look at Ghost.

"Phantoms," the sniper says with a nod.

"So what's next?" Hollywood asks.

"The mission."

Everyone sits up a little straighter. It's time to get down to business. I produce the paper map we looked over last night and lay it across my knees. Then I review what we know about the dome, its supposed epicenter, its lethal qualities, and its contraction rate.

"I also saw two recon-style bots open a temporary window to heave a man through," I say.

"So have we," Hollywood added. "A couple actually. Guessing it's something about their armor or a transceiver or something."

I nod and add that detail to our growing list of HUMIT that I'm tracking in my Moleskine. I also jot down the suspicion that the *invaders* are relocating those within the dome to a foreign location—whatever that may be. I draw a big question mark and then flip to a new blank page.

"That looks blank," Z-Lo says, trying to get a good look at my Moleskine. "I thought you said you had a mission for us."

"One we come up with together," I say.

"This ain't the movies, kid," Bumper says. "We're the ones building this thing from the ground up, copy?"

Z-Lo gives the Navy SEAL an exasperated raise of his eyebrows as if to say, "Jeez, man. This is my first time. Lay off." But I know the kid doesn't dare say as much out loud.

"First thing is that we need to assume we're the only unit out here," I say.

"That doesn't sound very optimistic," Z-Lo adds.

"It's not," I reply. "And for good reason."

"If you assume you're the only operator, then you try harder not to die," Ghost offers in a flat tone.

"I try hard not to die as it is," Z-Lo replies.

"No you don't," Hollywood says. "That whole stunt you pulled, banging on a bot with a pipe or whatever?"

Bumper snickers. "Don't ever do that again. Not unless you're desperate. You still had several mags on your chest, bro."

"I was mad at it," Z-Lo says. "So sue me."

"I can't sue someone who's dead, man."

"The point is," I interject. "Remember your training and that your actions affect everyone else on your team. Oorah?"

"Oorah," Z-Lo says with his head down.

For clarity's sake, and Z-Lo's, I resume my brainstorming session with a bit more explanation built-in. "We're gonna assume we're the only ones out there so that we don't get lazy assuming someone else is gonna swoop in to save our asses. Any new combatants pop up, we merge assets and reframe the chain of command as needed. No egos, no elbows."

Everyone nods.

"In the meantime, we'll keep our eyes peeled and radios scanning in case someone's broadcasting.

"The second order of business is that we need more intel on this thing." I poke at the large circle I've drawn on the map. "For that, I want to make a suggestion."

Over the next two minutes, I summarize Aaron's research and experience with the ring he discovered in Antarctica. "If there's one person alive who might have clues about how this dome works, it's Dr. Campbell."

"And you trust him?" Hollywood asks.

"To belay me on a climb? No." I smile at her. "But to know smartypants stuff about what all the other smartypantses think is important? Yes."

"So where do we find him?" Bumper asks.

I put my finger on the map. "Rutgers University. That's where his lab is."

"And what makes you think he's still there?" Yoshi asks.

I nod in agreement with the question and then think how best to answer it. "Hey, Bumper."

"Hit me."

"If you had a day off but needed to focus for a test the next day, how would you spend it?"

"Hit the gym. Throw a ball. Something."

"And why's that?"

He gives me a half-smile. "Football's life, man."

I look back at Yoshi. "The lab is Aaron's life. Unless he's on a dig site, he's in his office."

"Fair enough," Yoshi says.

"So let's say we find your friend," Hollywood says. "Then what?"

"We can't know that until we talk with him."

"We don't know what we don't know," Yoshi adds.

"Exactly." I look back at the map. "But my hope is that he'll have something we need to keep moving forward."

"One yard at a time." Bumper leans forward with his fingers crossed and elbows on his knees. "One play at a time."

"So, Rutgers then," Hollywood says.

I nod. "I recommend we keep a mile out from the dome to avoid detection. It doesn't mean we won't encounter patrols, but those we've seen so far have been, what, within a few hundred yards?"

Heads nod, and Yoshi speaks up. "Five hundred, I'd say."

"So they're staying close to it. That's good. Still, we need to move smart. No unnecessary risks."

"Why not wait for nightfall?" Ghost asks. "Best time to move."

"Agreed," Bumper says.

"Because we don't have that luxury," Hollywood says. "We're on a timetable here, remember? Who knows how many lives are lost... or whatever's happening to them every second we wait."

"She's right." I take a deep breath. "There are certain things we can be cautious about, like our distance from the dome. But the urgency of the scenario means we're going to have to take more risks than we want."

Ghost raises his lower lip and gives a single nod.

"Meanwhile, if you see something, learn something, remember something, or have a bright idea, speak up. This is no time to keep things to yourself. And if you have a problem with another team member, and I mean a real one, you either suck it up or clear the air and move on. We don't have time for drama. I don't expect any in this group, but I refuse to let us get distracted or crumble from within, not when millions of lives are on the line. We cool?"

"We're cool," they all reply.

"Any other comments, questions, or suggestions?"

"Call signs?" Bumper says.

I nod. "Good idea. Hollywood, you're Phantom One."

"Negative." She folds her arms. "You're Phantom One."

I make to protest, but the team gives her nods.

Dammit.

"All in favor?" she asks everyone but me.

They assent.

"Passed."

Since I suspect fighting them will be pointless, I take a breath and then grudgingly reassign Hollywood. "You're Phantom Two. Bumper, Phantom Three. Z-Lo, Four." I glance at Ghost. "You're Phantom Watch. And Yoshi, you're Doc."

Everyone gives a nod or thumbs up.

"Anyone else?" I ask.

No one moves.

Satisfied, I take the last sip of my coffee and hand the camp mug back to Yoshi with a word of thanks. Then I fold the map, stow in my admin pocket, and put my hands on my knees. "We move out in five."

And just like that, I was leading a fire team again.

Son of a bitch.

―――――――――――

WE'VE PICKED up the Garden State Parkway South in Union, New Jersey, headed toward New Brunswick. Bumper has taken point in his Thing, followed by Z-Lo and Ghost in Dolores, Hollywood in her CJ7, and I'm picking up the rear in my Land Cruiser.

Extended early morning shadows stretch east to west across the

Interstate, while light flickers in my eyes between buildings and trees. Were it not for the thousands of cars dead in the lanes, the complete absence of human activity save ours, and the static on the radio waves, this would be a typical end-of-the-work-week commute. Well, that and the giant death dome.

The sun's turned the bubble a radiant bluish-purple, accentuating the force field's shimmering qualities. Were the object not bent on killing and herding people to some nefarious end, I'd be in awe of it. Instead, I want the thing gone, and I wanna personally kick every bot's ass that I can get my scope on.

Bumper's voice breaks over comms. "Contact. Due south. Looks like a patrol, headed north."

"Stop," I say as fast as I get my hand to the receiver. "Take position behind the dead vehicles. Kill engines."

"Roger."

I see Hollywood's brake lights flare as she pulls behind a black SUV in the passenger lane. My heart rate's jumped a few beats per minute in anticipation of another encounter.

It was a risk to take the Parkway, I know. Taking I-280 West back to I-287 South was the better option. But the Parkway is the fastest way to the I-95 Aaron. Even still, I'm second-guessing my decision and hoping that the enemy isn't using thermal detection. I can't believe that we're not even ten minutes into the road trip, and we're already about to engage the enemy.

Rising above the car roofs toward the center median, I see two magenta drones glinting in the sunlight. Beneath them, I notice the roof of one of my self-named armored reconnaissance units, complete with the twin-barrel turret. Despite being inside my FJ40, I still feel exposed. I swear in my mind and then send up a prayer to the big guy in the sky.

"Sun visors down, seats slid back," I say over the radio.

"I've got my ragtop down, Phantom One," Bumper says.

Dammit. I'd forgotten—stupid convertibles.

"Then take cover where you can," I reply.

"I hear that."

Up ahead, I see the Thing's driver-side door swing open, and Bumper jumps out. He's got his M249. Then he disappears into the line of vehicles.

The drones are closer now, as is the ARU. I can make out the vehicle's futuristic front cab and menacing black windshield. The transport is coming down the median with the drones holding course directly above it. A steady low rumble moves through my Land Cruiser and tickles my intestines. Now I have to piss. But I tighten my groin muscles and will myself to stay calm.

The ARU is in full view—its magenta armor plates and strange markings glimmering in the sunlight. The blue-glowing panels under its V-shaped belly force the grass aside like the Most High's ultimate leaf blower.

The hum and tingle in my gut are at their zeniths, and my Land Cruiser rocks in the prop-wash, or jet-wash—or whatever the hell's propelling that thing. It looks like DARPA and George Lucas decided to make a baby.

I pull my head back and keep my face hidden behind the upright support at the seatbelt's anchor point. So far, it hasn't noticed Bumper or any of the others. As it passes by my position, I breathe in relief and jump on the radio.

"Everyone good?"

The team reports back, and I relax. Maybe this wasn't such a bad idea after all. Still, that was close, and I decide we should find an alternate route that doesn't involve the Interstate.

"Enemy slowing," Ghost says.

I spin around in my seat. Sure enough, the ARU's coming to a halt.

"Think we can outrun them?" Z-Lo asks.

"I wouldn't bet on it," Bumper replies.

"Nobody move," I say. "Seat belts off, weapons ready, doors unlocked."

"Roger," the team replies.

I follow my own instructions, SCAR lying across my lap. A rookie mistake is assuming the enemy has spotted you before they have. It's like moving your queen long before you need to. Plenty a Marine had given away his or her patrol simply because they thought they'd been spotted, when in reality, the enemy just needed to take a piss or saw a sparkly bauble in a window. An otherwise uneventful patrol turned bloody because someone jumped to conclusions.

Granted, it takes nerves of steel not to think the enemy has spotted you when you're traipsing through their backyard. But if you're reasonably sure that you haven't given them a reason to examine your position, don't assume that's what's going on. Trust your training, stay calm, and remain vigilant. And for the love of St. Peter, don't look them in the eye.

The ARU is backing up, and the rear doors are opening. Even before I catch a glimpse inside the wagon, I hear Ghost's voice.

"Three recon bots. One assault bot."

The man's got eyes like an eagle. "Copy that."

"You want us out?" Hollywood asks.

"Hold position."

"I don't like this," Yoshi says.

"Move only on my go."

I sneak another look out the rear driver's side window. The ARU's stopped, and the three bots are out and moving toward the parked cars further back.

"Dammit," Hollywood says. "Death angel. Not good."

"What?" I say to myself and then look back at the ARU. There, leaping from the vehicle's stern, is a human-like figure clad in emerald-green armor. The plates have an iridescent quality in the morning light and cover a six-foot-tall frame dressed in a black under suit. Meanwhile, a full-face-covered helmet boasts two red-glowing eyes that scan the terrain in a slow sweep. The faceplate is curved over the nose and mouth and ends in geometric shapes over the chin, like those around the head's ears and top.

Most notable of all, however, is the weapon the enemy carries. While I'd certainly call it a rifle, it doesn't look like anything the US government has issued—or any government for that matter. It's more like a cross between weapons from District 9, DUNE, and Blade Runner. What is it—WETA Workshop or something?

I have to blink twice just to make sure I'm seeing this correctly. The rifle's long rectangular body, made of the same emerald material as the armor, sports a wide buttstock, a stout pistol grip, and a low-profile fore grip, terminating with a barrel barely visible under angular receiver canopies. While an elaborate scope sits atop a rail system, reminiscent of something a concept artist might construct for a future-weapon, the weapon lacks a magazine or ammo chamber.

"What's the play?" Bumper asks.

While the channel is open, I hear Z-Lo say in the background, "Oh, God. They know we're here."

"Keep it together, kid," I say to Z-Lo. "Phantom Watch. Have you taken a shot on one of those yet?"

"The actual aliens? No."

The aliens. Riiight. So far, this still looks like a human who lost his way heading to New York COMICON.

"But that rifle he's carrying's a bitch," Ghost adds.

"Good to know." I glance to the west and see bushes and trees separating the Interstate from a dense residential area. It's too much open ground to make a run for it. "Looks like we're gonna have to do this the hard way. Phantom Three, you're first up. Need you to draw their fire on my go."

"Roger."

"When he does, I want everyone else out the passenger sides as fast as you can. We use the vehicles as cover. Break." I give the information a chance to breathe and myself a moment to think. "There are a lot of cars, so use them to your advantage. Try to stay clear of our vehicles to minimize damage to them. Break." I let another round of silence fill the channel. "Stay low; keep moving. We need to amplify our presence through stealth and speed. The forest to our west is fallback. How copy?"

Everyone answers in the affirmative.

While I've been talking, one of the recon bots has crept up on my Land Cruiser. I catch sight of it in my rearview mirror. It takes everything I have not to kick out the door and open up on it. But I'm still not convinced it's discovered me.

"Waiting on your go," Bumper says. He's eager to take the shot too. But if we don't have to engage the enemy out here, I don't want to jump the gun.

"Hold," I whisper.

The bot's getting closer. I can feel its footsteps in the floorboard.

"Hold."

It thumps to a stop outside my door.

"Phantom One," Bumper says. "Let me take the shot."

"Negative," I whisper.

Warriors talk about these crazy moments in combat where stuff seems to stand still. Bullets are flying, people are screaming, and there you are in a freeze-frame. Well, it happens. It's weird. And while there isn't any lead flying right now, I feel like my heart's beating in slow motion.

As if prompted by a divine wind, the bot takes another step forward.

"Hold, hold, hold," I say in an effort to keep the excitement out of my voice. The robot's movement is proof it hasn't detected me, which means there's a good chance it won't discover the others.

However, after passing another two vehicles, the bot stops at Hollywood's Jeep.

My heart rate ticks up. Either the enemy is getting lucky with where it's stopping, or the mechanical monster is tracking tags that someone's put on our vehicles. Whatever sense of elation I had seconds ago is gone.

Something flashes in my rearview mirror. Another bot is coming down the line like the first. Now I wonder if they're setting up on us. Almost as soon as the second bot is at my position, the one at Hollywood's Jeep moves forward and stops at Z-Lo's Humvee.

"Can we start shooting yet?" he says in a nervous voice.

Ghost is in the background telling the kid to shut his mouth.

However we're being tagged, I hope the enemy doesn't find enough evidence to justify an assault. There's a chance, albeit slim, that they're following through with a hunch, maybe anomalies in their data, that prove to be nothing.

The second bot passes my Land Cruiser and continues on while the third is walking from behind.

"Keep holding," I say, hopeful. "Fingers on trigger guards, people." I'm speaking mostly to Z-Lo, and yet reminders never hurt anyone but the proud.

The second bot stops at Hollywood's CJ7 while the third bot is almost on me. I glance toward the ARU and see the assault bot standing sentry by the vehicle, but the death angel is on the move.

"Phantom Three. You have anything to create a diversion downrange?" I ask.

"Do I," he says with a chuckle. "You want something?"

While I'm still holding out that the enemy patrol writes off this exercise, I'm feeling more confident that things will get hot.

Back to Bumper, I say, "If it doesn't give your position away, yut."

"Let me get my party vest on. Stand by."

"Quietly," I add.

I'm not sure what Bumper has up his sleeve, but I know when it comes to making things go boom, no one does it quite like a SEAL. They have a certain *je ne sais quoi* when it comes to blowing stuff up, and I've always admired it. Anyone who doesn't is lying and jealous.

All three bots are stacked up on the Land Cruiser, Jeep, and Dolores, respectively. Only Bumper's VW seems off the hook. And now my gut is screaming that we've been set up on. Dammit, Wic. You're gonna get everyone killed again. Still, there's one tiny voice in my head saying I haven't seen hostile intent displayed yet. The logic is faint, yeah, but it won't let me give the order to start firing yet—the gunfight everyone walks away from is the one that never happens.

"Phantom Three, prepare for diversion. Everyone else, prepare to exit vehicles right."

The death angel figure is ambling down the median, eyes

forward. He's not even looking at our vehicles. That tiny voice in my head is getting louder. "Told you so," it's saying. Then, as the green-clad figure turns back toward the ARU, I feel my body relax. I let out the breath I've been holding and wait for the bots to move away from our vehicles.

They don't.

Instead, I see movement to my immediate left, followed by the loud crunch of metal. I wince away from the sound, and then my Land Cruiser's door flies off its hinges.

"Engage," I yell.

I'm leaping into the passenger's seat when I hear an explosion rip through the northbound lanes across the median. It's followed in quick succession by two more detonations. I don't have time to look as I push out the passenger side and drop to the pavement, but I know it's Bumper sending something to the east.

Looking south along the white lane line, I see Z-Lo spill out onto the pavement beside Ghost. Hollywood's already running toward them, head down. The bots beside their vehicles have also forced their way inside and are looking for the occupants.

"Halt, merchandise," says a digitally harmonic voice again.

I'd forgotten about the strange phrase—one that makes it sound like I'm a commodity. Or cattle.

"Attempt to flee, and you will be terminated."

Screw that.

The second I make to move away from my vehicle, a blast of energy hits my open passenger side door and causes my ears to ring. I blink against the flash of light as some debris hits my face and makes my cheek go numb.

I peel away from my Land Cruiser and head south toward the others just as more blue energy bolts lance through the vehicles' passenger compartments. The rest of my operators are clear, however, and running toward Bumper.

As I dash between two four-door sedans, I catch something aloft out of the corner of my eye. There, suspended some twenty feet above the ground, is the emerald-clad warrior. So *that's* why Hollywood had termed it a death angel. Je-sus, help us.

It's aiming its weapon toward me. I see a flash of light, and then the car in front of me explodes. The next thing I know, I'm flying toward the grass embankment to my right. And the world is upside down.

Should've taken I-280.

15

0650 Friday, June 25, 2027
Union, New Jersey
Garden State Parkway

WHEN MY BODY rolls to a stop, my thoughts are drowned out by loud ringing in my ears. I blink several times, trying to get my bearings. I smell charred grass, burning plastic, and spent fuel. My face is warm and—damn, do my ribs hurt. I try three times to gasp for air before I can overcome the pain and fill my lungs.

I hear someone yelling in my ear. It's faint. But as the ringing subsides, I hear Hollywood.

"…now," she says. "Wic!"

She's talking to me. Goddammit.

"Move your ass, Gunny!"

I force myself up, look at the tree line, and start running. Somehow, my brain decides that I'm closer to the woods than the lanes of cars. I fight a wave of nausea and a spat of vertigo, sidestepping as I try and lean toward the trees at a full run.

Something whines in the distance and then a blast of light erupts in the grass to my left. Dirt clods fling upward and rain down on me as I beat hard for the woods. But I'm off balance. I counter the fall and dart left—an act that no doubt saves me as a second hole explodes to my right. It's like someone's firing on me with mortar rounds.

I hear weapons fire—my team's—and the sounds of bullets slapping into targets. The explosions around me stop. I'm able to close the distance and throw myself between two small bushes to take cover behind a tree.

As soon as I check myself for serious injuries—just a few broken ribs and the world's worst headache—I look back toward the Interstate and open the channel.

"SITREP."

Before anyone can respond to me, I notice all four of Phantom Team's operators pinned down by enemy fire. While the assault bot hasn't left his position beside the ARU, one of the recon bots is closing on the team to the south, and the other two appear to be investigating Bumper's distraction across the median.

Likewise, the death angel has been temporarily distracted from pursuing me due to a pretty heavy assault from the team. Bumper looks to be blasting the enemy with an old school western-style M79 grenade launcher, affectionately known as a "Thumper." He's hurling the 40x46 mm rounds at the death angel as fast as he can load them. Each round blossoms against the flying enemy, pushing him back toward the ARU.

The recon bot and drones are being hit with a barrage of

weapons fire, including Ghost's fifty. I see two rounds ping off the thing's head before its neck snaps. That at least is excellent news. However, what's not okay is that the death angel has withdrawn from Bumper's assault and is headed directly toward me.

"Just great."

I pull myself together and realize I'm going to need a better option than running around a narrow strip of woods. I'm about fifteen yards from a row of backyards that make up a long stretch of suburban homes. The neighborhood is compact, and the houses are close together. Their proximity, along with the different interiors, will make for good cover and even better positioning.

I pound through the woods, beat across the first backyard I come to, and head for the nearest house—a one-story ranch with yellowing siding and an attached garage. There's a small above-ground pool with a wrap-around deck that's seen better years. I'm two steps from the rear garage door when a high-pitched whine and a loud crack indicate a detonation behind me. Whatever parts of the pool haven't been vaporized fly skyward, showering the home in a haze of debris and steam.

Ghost wasn't wrong about that rifle.

I stumble into the garage and don't bother to close the door. The enemy's seen me. Now it's a cat and mouse game as to whether or not I'm gonna run out the main garage door or duck inside the house. Feeling like the car entry is the more obvious of the two, I opt for the home.

The kitchen doesn't look like it's been updated since the home was built, and the living room's furniture is covered in clear plastic. They even have a stack of DVDs beside their TV—I didn't even know those things still played—the top one of which is the original Monty Python and the Holy Grail film. Classic. My money's on this home belonging to a grandma and grandpa of European descent. Hell, it even smells like old folks, God bless 'em. Truth is, I'm probably not far behind.

As I make my way down a hallway to the far side of the house, it dawns on me that the death angel could be tracking me with thermal imaging or something. I haven't ruled that out, and still don't know how the bots or the ARU detected us earlier. It didn't seem to be right away, either, which bodes well. The vehicles passed us and then backed up. So whatever tech they're using, it has flaws. That or the operator was lazy.

I'm in the master bedroom at the end of the hall when I hear something crash through the kitchen. It's following me, which is a good sign. Had it been tracking me from outside, it would have seen my movement and guessed my intentions. I unlock the largest of the bedroom's windows and climb out, careful to minimize my noise. But it's impossible, given how fast I'm moving and how bulky my kit is.

My feet land in a small patch of manicured bushes and a few ferns. I spot a low stone wall across the street, perfect for cover and a quick egress to the brick home ten yards further back. With the enemy still banging around inside the first house, I decide I have enough time to run across the street and dive behind the stone wall.

I bring my weapon up and target the master bedroom's side window, waiting for the enemy to climb out. He'll be vulnerable, and I'll be ready.

But nothing happens. No movement in the window and no—

There's a muted whine, and then the front face of the master bedroom blows off the house. Timber and siding spray the street while flaming bits of insulation float into the front yard. Then the death angel steps through the smoking hole—head and weapons sweeping back and forth.

It's not the window exit I was hoping for, but I have the enemy's head in my sights, dead to rights.

I squeeze the trigger, and my SCAR delivers a three-round burst to the figure's helmet. The sparks, bright even in the morning light, assure me that I've hit my target. But instead of the enemy collapsing, it tilts its head at me. One of its red-glowing eyes seems cracked, but otherwise, the helmet is undamaged.

"Dammit."

I'm up and running when the stone wall takes a barrage of full-auto fire from the crazy-ass weapon. A few small stones pelt my back, but I'm hauling ass to the front door. I crash through it and fall to the ground inside an open entryway.

Unlike the last house, this two-story beauty was made sometime in the nineteenth century, and whoever built it had money. The vaulted ceiling, hand-carved banisters, and tiled floors look original and well-maintained.

But I'm not here for a home inspection—this is just the random crap my mind processes as I charge under the upstairs balcony and into a spacious marble-countertop kitchen.

The front door explodes inward, shooting stone, glass, and wood down the hallway. I spin around and fire two bursts at the death angel, striking it in the head and chest.

The weapon whines again—which is my signal to get the hell out of the way. I'm leaping toward a couch when the blast ruptures the kitchen's back wall. I land hard on a carpeted floor and roll into a piece of leather furniture as the back of the house blows out.

I hear another charge-up sound, and the enemy fires into the living room. I leap out of the way just as the floor explodes. Likewise, I've shattered two floor-to-ceiling glass doors with my helmet and shoulders and landed on a back porch. I'm on my back, firing into the house, and I scramble for cover behind a wide-based oak tree just off the porch.

I'm barely around the trunk when another *pweeee-crack* bores a gaping hole into the tree just over my head. Wooden shrapnel pelts me like splinters hurled from a woodchipper. The smell of burning hardwood hits my nose; on any other occasion, it would make me long for a campfire, a cigar, and two fingers of Redbreast. But right now, all I want to do is kill this bastard.

I lean out and fire two more bursts before pulling back. And just in time: the enemy shoots again, landing a second salvo beside the first, less than two feet overhead.

A deep throaty creak emanates from the oak—the thing's going down. While some DARPA death angel in a Storm Trooper outfit scares me, getting crushed by a two-hundred-year-old oak tree scares me more.

I look up, trying to gauge the direction of the fall, but the leaves and branches are swaying randomly—it seems the tree's still deciding. I'm gonna have to chance it. If I can get the enemy to follow me toward the landing zone, maybe the oak can assist me. And perhaps I can crush myself in the process too—*idiot.*

But better that than end up all toasty at the wrong end of a ray gun.

The tree is starting to arch over me and toward the backyard. I look across the lawn and see that I have an open stretch to a child's playhouse and swing set some thirty yards away. It looks custom made, larger than normal, and sturdy, as if a contractor did the work.

"What are you doing, Pat," I say. Before I can answer the question, I'm off and running. At first, this feels like a great idea. But as soon as I see the branches moving overhead, I realize it's a terrible idea. I mean a really horribly asinine idiotic terrible idea.

A surge of adrenaline shoots through my veins like liquid fire, and I feel my pace pick up. But that damn little voice of logic is telling me I've made a boneheaded miscalculation. Because I have no idea if the death angel has decided to follow me on my fool's errand, I fire two bursts over my shoulder blindly. Call it the last act of defiance against the universe, or maybe a half-hearted attempt to egg the enemy into coming after me. I don't know. I'm desperate and, dammit, sometimes you just want to shoot something.

I can hear the rush of wind in the branches as the tree careens toward me. I swear I feel myself brush past leaves, but I'm gunning for the playhouse and ignore the tricks my brain is playing on me.

With four yards to go, I put every ounce of energy I have into my legs and dive for the doorway. It's stupid—I know. I might miss and break my neck. Hell, the tree might split the playhouse in two and crush me. But I dive for all I'm worth.

I slide into the shadows and crash against the playhouse's back wall. At the same time, the oak's upper branches engulf the tiny home in a violent storm of rustling leaves. The roof breaks open in three places, just as dozens of thunderous *cracks* pound through the interior. I feel the tiny building rattle when the trunk slams into the ground outside.

Then, like a passing rainstorm giving way to blue skies, the violence ends.

I check myself for injuries and can't find any except the burning pain in my shoulders and hips from slamming into the living room floor and now the playhouse. Honestly, I'm shocked to be alive. But the enemy is still out there, so I'm not giving myself any gold ribbons yet.

As soon as I pull up my right hand, I realize that I've lost my SCAR. I curse myself for letting go of it, then retrieve my Glock from its holster. Thank God it's still with me and looks functional.

The playhouse doorway is covered in branches so thick that I'm not sure I can get out. After taking cover beside the door, I peek around the corner and through the intricate latticework. I'm half expecting to see the enemy flying over the fallen tree, looking to obliterate my hideout, when I notice a dark form buried in the thicket some ten yards away.

"Well whaddya know," I say to myself.

Turns out the tango followed me after all. I'm doubtful I can even get through the dense tree growth, but if there's one thing the movies have taught me, it's to never leave the bad guy on the ground without double tapping his head. How often have we yelled at the good guys on screen, pleading with them not to turn away without ending the antagonist for good? Dude, if you're gonna exert all that violence to get him pinned down, don't try and convince anyone that you have the moral high ground just because you let the sucker live when he's passed out. Shoot the damn bastard, and then reshoot him for good measure. No one settles for check in chess—go for checkmate, or don't bother playing.

Following my sage advice, I climb through the first branches surrounding the playhouse. It's slow going, and I'm sure I won't win any beauty pageants by the time my face gets through this, but I'm making progress.

I catch the hostile moving toward the base.

See? Not dead. Told ya'.

I start working faster, hoping to get to him before he can grab his fancy-ass rifle and take me out. He may have good armor, but I doubt he can survive three 9mm rounds to the base of the neck. I push branches aside and force my way through gaps that I'm too big to fit through. The sounds of snapping twigs and rustling leaves surround me, but it's the beating of my heart in my ears I hear most. The enemy's arms are moving—reaching.

I cover my face as I plunge through a dense mass of branches and climb over a cluster of limbs closer to the main trunk. It's exhausting work, but I've got to get to this bastard before he gets up.

He's awake and lying on his back. And I'm five yards away. I could shoot him now, but if the .308 rounds weren't effective at range, the 9mm won't be either. I need to be up close and personal to end this party.

I'm moving faster now and bound over a thick limb at waist-height. The enemy sees me and then tries reaching for his weapon at the end of his fingertips. His legs look pinned under part of the trunk.

I put my pistol in my left hand, lunge the remaining distance, and land on the tango's chest. A powerful odor hits me—like the man's gut's been punctured. An elbow strike lands on the side of my head and boxes my left ear, but I can't defend myself: I've got my left forearm pressed under his chin, pushing his head back, and my right arm straining against his left wrist, trying to keep his fingers away from his damn weapon.

He strikes me in the side of the head again, and I see stars. It's just enough for him to stretch the remaining distance and grab his gun. I'm trying to keep his right fist from punching me while holding his left forearm down to keep him from shooting me. And, God, that smell.

Realizing we're at a stalemate, I decide I've got to focus my energy on getting that weapon out of his hand. In a surge of hyper-focused aggression, I start bashing his left wrist against the ground. Meanwhile, he's punching the dickens out of my left side. I'd love to wedge my Glock between his armor plates, but, hell, he won't let my eyes stay open long enough to find a target—it's like his right hook's on auto-pilot, pummeling me like a pneumatic jackhammer. One blow in particular causes me to lose my grip on my weapon, and the enemy's windup knocks it away.

Now I'm getting desperate. I drive a knee into the enemy's gut and hear a whoosh of air leave his chest, followed by another wave of the horrible odor. I smash his weapons hand against the ground, and my hand pops off his wrist and lands on his pistol grip. Somewhere in the back of my head, I sense something unusual about his gauntlet-covered hand—like, there aren't five fingers. But I'm not able to see straight right now—I'm fighting for my life.

He's still beating my left side to a pulp, and we're both struggling for the weapon. I knee him again, which gives me a little more real estate on the gun's grip.

The enemy yanks the trigger—either out of reflex or panic—and I feel a strong current tingle my hand and surge up my arm. It feels like my body's shorted the 220-volt outlet behind my dryer. Then the rifle lets out one of its deafening barks. The round explodes against the oak tree's base, showering us in sparks and splinters. The tree is on fire.

I've got to end this.

One final knee-strike to his gut dislodges his weapons hand, and now I've got the rifle.

I roll off to the right, point the crazy gun at his upper body, and squeeze the weirdly shaped trigger.

There's a split second where another surge of current travels up my arms and floods my body. One moment, I see a palm and six fingers in the universal sign to stop; the next, the weapon discharges through the victim's hand, and his body detonates. Inigo Montoya would be proud.

The armor and helmet shoot away, pinging against the oak limbs like pinballs. I shield my head. "Look out," I say to no one in particular. It's more just a reflex from being shot at one too many times while patrolling with a squad. When the debris settles, I pull my arm away and notice that I'm covered in gore, and so is the rifle. It sounds to be cycling down when I hear a neutral male voice say: "Detected language: English. User, please identify yourself."

16

0723, Friday, June 25, 2027
Union, New Jersey
Residential Area West of Garden State Parkway

UNSURE WHICH TEAM member just hailed me, I fumble with the radio and open the channel. "Say again."

The gunfire I hear in the distance pops to life when Hollywood replies. "Go for Phantom Two."

I hesitate, guessing that there's been a miscommunication. "Is there a problem?"

"You hailed me, Phantom One. You good?"

More gunfire bursts over the comm before she lets go of the talk button, but the sound continues to echo in the distance. The team is still fighting hard against the bots.

"User, please identify yourself," says the man's voice again.

I glance around and then look at the weapon in my right hand. "You talkin' to me?"

"Please identify yourself."

Well, whaddya know. The weapon has a built-in comms system. "Not a chance, punk."

A beat passes before the man in the weapon's comm speaks again. "User identification declined. Profile name default, User Nine."

"Phantom One?" says Hollywood.

"Roger. I'm good. Tango down."

Hollywood pauses, then asks, "You took out the death angel? On your own?"

"Affirm—"

"User Nine, please identify speaker as friend or foe."

"Who's that?" Hollywood asks. "Someone with you?"

"Negative," I say and lower the weapon. "Just found one of the enemy's—"

"Hold on." She keeps the channel open while she fires two bursts downrange. It's lousy radio discipline, but she's clearly in harm's way, so I'm not about to reprimand her. Plus, the radio's built-in compressor helps minimize the volume discrepancies. "We could use your help back here."

"Roger that. On my way. Phantom One out."

"Please identify Phantom Two as friend or foe," the gun's speaker says.

"Hey." I shake the weapon once. "Who the hell are you people?"

"Unable to complete request. More data required."

"Russian? Chinese?" Then it hits me. "Oh crap. North Korean?"

"References unknown. More data required."

"Damn. You're good." I'm imagining some suit-wearing spook sitting in a cubicle somewhere. He's really got the whole smooth computer voice thing down. But this creates a new dilemma for me. I'm not sure what to do with the enemy's gun. Part of me wants to bring it along. It's a valuable find in terms of weapons tech, and it handled that death angel with ease—scarily so. Likewise, I have a feeling that between all the members of Phantom Team, we could probably wear this spook down and glean some valuable intel. After all, who has more experience demanding their way up the chain of command inside of shoddy customer support helpline than self-entitled Americans? But if the enemy has their comms built into the receiver, the weapon probably has a tracking unit too. Even with its knock-down power—or completely obliterate power—there's no way I'm painting a target on my team. So as much as I hate parting with the gun, since I've rarely met a weapon I didn't want to shoot a second time, it's gotta go. I shrug and toss the gun into the gore-soaked grass.

"User departure detected. User Nine, please confirm your intentions."

I chuckle. I can't tell if my concussion is worse than I think it is —which, I suppose, is part of the whole problem with self-diagnosing concussions—or if the guy behind the comms is just uptight about following his script. Either way he's—

"Please confirm your intentions."

"My intentions?" I grab my Glock, which is covered in fluid, and wipe it across my pant leg. "My intentions are to shoot as many of you bastards as I can and keep you from hurting any more innocent civilians."

CHRISTOPHER HOPPER & J.N. CHANEY

"Acknowledged." There's a pause. "Subroutine error. More data required."

I shake my head and then push through the oak tree's limbs to look for my SCAR. I'm still cursing myself for losing it in the first place; there isn't a Marine alive who'd let me live this down if they knew. Hell, I'm not gonna let me live it down. But my team needs me, so I'll leave the self-degradation for a later time.

"Increase in User Nine's distance detected. Intention criteria undefined. More data required."

"You want more data, pie brain?"

"Target profile: Pie Brain. Unknown. Please clarify."

I ignore the person and turn around to resume the search for my weapon. However, between the leaves and broken branches, it's nearly impossible to see anything along the ground. All at once, I'm fighting a growing sense that I should abandon the weapon and pick up a secondary from Bumper. But who does that? "Eh, you're not abandoning it," I say to myself. "You're just leavin' it 'til you can come back."

"User Nine, please confirm departure parameters. More data required."

"You want more data?"

"Affirmative."

I offer him the one-finger salute. "There's your data, asswipe."

"Raised middle digit, right hand, right arm. Searching."

I stand up a little straighter, and my skin starts to crawl. There are several things I hate in this world, and being surveilled without knowing it is one of them. You have me on camera in a bank? No problem. I get that. Money's important. Convenience store? Sure, anyone who steals a Slim Jim deserves to be caught and fined. You wanna watch me move around the Pentagon or the National Mall in

DC? Greater good stuff. I get it. But catch me on camera without telling me? Hell no.

"Search complete. The raising of the middle finger, also known as giving someone the bird, or flipping someone off, is an obscene hand gesture that communicates moderate to extreme contempt. The behavior dates to ancient Greece and Rome, and it represents the phallus historically."

"Smartass."

"Response unknown."

"You're good at this little parlor trick," I say, waving at whatever camera lens gives them a window on me. Damn surveillance tech. And if they can see me, then they can track me. Which means I need to get the hell out of here.

"Just know, whoever you guys are, and wherever you're watching from, we're gonna find you, and then we're gonna end you." I kinda wanted that last part to come out like a Liam Neeson line in his *Taken* films. But it didn't.

The sound of more gunfire ringing through the trees summons me back to my search.

"Language profile update detected. Please stand by."

I let out an exasperated groan and then resume my search.

"Please define the targets you wish to watch, find, and terminate."

Certainly sounds enticing. Which means it's probably a trap. These people are irritating me, so I put some more distance between us.

"User Nine, please define the targets you wish to watch, find, and terminate."

"Screw you."

"Request unknown. More data required. Searching."

For some strange reason, I'm actually curious what he—*it* is going to find on this one.

"Search complete. Screw you. Slang, idiomatic, mildly vulgar. A less offensive version of fu—"

"Fabulous, pal. Way to keep it classy. So you're a goddamn machine? Is that it? Trying to be Siri for a gun or something?" I shake my head. It's not right that phones talk back to people. And vice versa.

"User unknown. More data required."

"Cute. Let's try: Hey, Alexa."

"User unknown."

"Seriously?" Definitely North Koreans.

"Request unknown. More—"

"More data required. Yeah, yeah, I got it." I start pushing branches apart again and then start talking to myself. "SCAR's gotta be around here somewhere."

"FN SCAR 17 identified. Location, eight point three four seven meters northeast."

I spin back so fast that I hit my helmet on a bow and startle myself. "What did you just say?"

"Repeat information. FN SCAR 17 identified. Location, eight point three four seven meters northeast."

So it's got comms, cameras, and now a metal detector?

I orient myself with the morning sun and start heading northeast. Or course, somewhere in my gut, I'm wondering, once again, if the person behind the voice is leading me into a trap. But that's crazy talk. Right?

I use my hands and boots to move aside several heavily leafed branches and see my SCAR glint in the sunlight. "Son of a bitch." Other than some new scratches along the composite receiver housing, the thing looks surprisingly intact. "Plastic toy gun, my ass, Bumper."

"Please clarify command sequence."

I shake my head. There's no way this can be a real person. It's gotta be some onboard software or something. "Negative. No command sequence."

"Request acknowledged."

"Phantom One?" Hollywood says over comms.

"I'm on my way," I reply.

"Negative. You've got a tango incoming."

I freeze. "Say again?"

"The assault bot is headed your way."

Goddammit. "Copy that."

I double-check my SCAR but find that it's jammed. At the same time, I feel a low rumble underfoot.

"Incoming threat detected," the man's voice says.

"Yeah, no kidding." Then I look back at it. "Hold up. Did you just say that thing's a threat?"

There's a split-second pause before it replies, "Yes."

A chill goes down my spine. "What happened to affirmative?"

"Yes is more colloquial. Confirm."

"Sure, but affirmative is—"

"Language profile modified. User Nine, please prepare to defend yourself."

"Defend my..." I look east toward the sound of the bot. "Jesus. Are you telling me to take cover against your own hardware out there?"

"Yes."

I raise my eyebrows at the gun. "Yes?"

"Yes," it says more loudly as if I'm hard of hearing. Which, I suppose, I am.

"No need to shout."

"Request acknowledged."

I hear the sound of something crashing through the woods across the street.

"SSA-9001B is distraught," the voice says.

"Not the word I would have chosen, but okay."

"Please update description preferences profile."

"Not now, pal." I start working the SCAR's bolt in the hopes of freeing up the weapon, but it's stuck. I'm gonna have to break the whole weapon down. Dammit.

Just then, a thought hits me. "Hey, Alexa. You controlling that thing?"

"Please clarify. More data—"

"TRK... whatever. Can you access it? Control it?"

Listen to me; I'm acting like the gun can actually understand me. But if its voice is less suit in a cubicle and more actual software, then maybe I can get it to follow my voice commands or something. God, I should have paid more attention to the cell phones.

I rush back under the limbs. "You can speak to the bots, can't you." I grab the weapon and yell into its receiver—feeling like a complete dumbass doing it. "Order them to stand down."

"Request denied."

"Oh no, you don't. Listen here, you little punk. You're gonna order those bots to—"

"Threat imminent. Defensive measures recommended."

"You better believe I'm a threat, you piece—"

"User Nine, please prepare to defend yourself."

This isn't working. Siri is broken. Or... this is a guy in a cubicle. "Tell them to stand down, and we'll hear out your demands."

There's a pause. "Negotiations."

"Yes. Negotiations. Whaddya want?"

"Incomplete data set. Values unknown. User Nine, please prepare—"

"To defend myself. That's gonna be a little hard right now." I drop the gun again and continue trying to un-jam my SCAR. The assault bot sounds like it's in the stone house's front yard. If I can't get my weapon cleared, I'm gonna have to make a run for it.

"User Nine, please prepare to fire," says the man.

"Whaddya think I'm trying to do here, pal?"

There's another pause, then it says, "FN SCAR 17 damaged. Recommend secondary course of action."

"Which is?"

"Utilize SR-CHK 4110 particle exciter."

I throw my hands in the air. "It's like I'm talking to a damn toaster oven."

"Utilize SR-CHK—"

"Is that supposed to be you?" I'm running out of time.

"Yes."

"Shoot your own asset? Oh no. This is the part of the movie where the enemy weapon self-destructs. No way, José."

The weapon waits for a beat before speaking. "Causing User Nine harm violates directive alpha. User, please employ SR-CHK 4110 particle exciter."

I should turn around and get lost, but it's too late. The bot is charging toward the oak.

"Raise me to your shoulder and fire, User Nine."

"If you blow me up, I'm going to be so pissed at you."

"Acknowledged."

I've run out of options, so I lift the weapon to my shoulder. I try using the scope, but it's displaying a wall of red. I point the rifle like a shotgun and hope for the best. "Here goes nothing."

I squeeze the trigger.

The weapon whines and then recoils with a loud snap. A blast of light streaks through the oak's branches and strikes the assault bot square in the chest. A watermelon-sized hole opens to the back, illuminated by a fountain of sparks. Then the bot crashes into the oak's base with its arms and legs trailing behind it.

The impact jostles the trunk and branches. A branch knocks my feet out from under me, and I land hard, but my helmet and rear plates absorb most of the impact.

When the branches finally stop shaking, I sit up. "What the hell just happened?"

"Report query acknowledged. Threat terminated. User status nominal. Capacitor levels, 41 percent."

"No, I mean, that…" I rub my forehead. "That was awesome."

"User satisfaction logged."

"Phantom One, this is Two," Hollywood says. "Come in."

I squeeze open the channel with an adrenaline-shaking hand. "Send it."

"Thank God," she says. "What's going on?"

"I'm alive. Bot's down."

"You…" Hollywood keeps the channel open for a second. "You took out the bot too?"

"I had some help."

"From?"

I look at the gun. "I'll explain later. Headed to you now."

"Copy. Phantom Two out."

I'm still stuck on whether to bring the weapon along with me or not. There are so many random arguments going on in my head right now that it's giving me a migraine—or that's just the concussion. Either way, I need to think fast. My team is fighting for their lives, and I've wasted enough time out here as it is.

I don't trust the voice behind the gun, but I do believe in the weapon's ability to blow stuff to kingdom come. Plus, I don't care if the Russians, Chinese, or South Koreans are tracking me. They've most likely pinged our location already and are sending reinforcements—so what's the hurt in using the weapon one last time?

The other option, of course, is that everything I've experienced from Antarctica until right now is... well, it... "It can all be explained, Patrick," I say to myself before I jump off a mental cliff that I can never climb back up.

I retrieve my SCAR and then climb my way out of the fallen oak.

"User motion in progress. Define destination."

"To go blow up some more of your friends."

"Acknowledged."

Weird-ass gun.

17

0728, Friday, June 25, 2027
Union, New Jersey
Garden State Parkway

"YOU STOP FOR A CHEESEBURGER?" Hollywood asks over comms as I climb out of the fallen oak tree.

"Got held up. On my way now."

"Roger."

I ignore the need to explain myself further and ask Hollywood for a SITREP instead. In truth, I'm a little surprised the team hasn't put the enemy down already.

"The last bot's taken cover behind the transport," she replies. "Ghost took out the driver, but the turret's opened up on us."

I forgot about the ARU's twin barrels. Not good.

"One mike out," I say.

CHRISTOPHER HOPPER & J.N. CHANEY

"Copy. Phantom Two out."

I cross the street and head toward the single-story ranch. The closer I get to the Parkway, the more pleased I feel with my decision to bring the advanced weapon. While the monotonous-sounding spook speaking on comms is undoubtedly annoying, the gun is far too powerful for me not to engage against the enemy. Nothing in my arsenal can touch it, and I'll be damned if Bumper has anything comparable. The device, like the man in the suit, is straight out of a DARPA lab. I figure that I'll use the rifle to take down the remaining tangos and then have Bumper stick a breach charge on it. The enemy won't be able to track us, and they'll have one less weapon at their disposal.

Seeing as how our time together is almost up, I decide to leech it for any more intel. And, if possible, get the suit to drop his act.

"So, what's your favorite color?"

The weapon fails to respond.

"The silent treatment? Eh, that's okay. Lemme guess. Black?"

"Value unknown."

"Don't have one?" I shrug as I cross the street, heading for the single-story ranch. "Fair. How about favorite food?"

"Value unknown."

Now he's just stonewalling me. "So what's your mom think about what you do for a living? She proud of you killing innocent civilians?"

"Connection with Mother non-viable."

I frown. "Weird way to put it, but I'm sorry to hear that. For what it's worth, I, uh… I know the feeling."

Sure, I don't particularly like sharing a dark part of my past with the enemy, but sometimes getting what you want from the enemy requires odd moments of empathy—just before you waterboard them. I mean, help them hydrate. What?

I pass around the back of the house and glance at the remains of the above-ground pool. "So," I ask between breaths, acting like I'm out with a new neighbor on a jog around the block. "Where you from?"

"Planet of origin: Androchida Prime."

I look blankly at the weapon. "Planet?"

"Androchida Prime," it repeats.

"Okay, smartass." Now the asshole's pretending to be an alien or something. I shake my head, realizing just how far he's willing to play the part and how badly he thinks I've been duped. Well, it's not happening.

As we head for the strip of woods between the backyard and the Interstate, I decide that to make up for my gullibility, I'm going to play along. Hard. I'm gonna take this asshole for the longest, wildest ride possible. You know, the same way you can stick it to those email scammers who try to tell you that you're the long lost cousin of a Nigerian prince. By the way, not only do Nigerians have a buttload of money to give away, but several of them shacked up with my Irish mom.

I once had a two-week email conversation with one of these supposed Nigerian princes. Seemed like a charming guy; how could I resist? So I told him, yes, I'd be happy to give him my social security number and bank account details so long as he answered my questions.

At first, he was only too happy to comply. The dialogue ranged from exchanging stories about our families to fond memories of our respective childhoods—me from Brooklyn and him from places that sounded surprisingly Slavic despite where his palace was. I noted on several occasions how I remembered seeing pictures of him in our family photo albums and wished to reconnect in person again. He, on the other hand, noted that such a meeting would be imprudent given his responsibilities as a royal figurehead.

Still, I insisted.

The moment I told him that I'd landed in Moscow and was taking a cab to the physical address that his encrypted VPN screen had eventually coughed up, I never heard back, which sucked, because I was really looking forward to meeting him.

And no, I didn't do all that fancy VPN crap on my own. Yes, a guy from work did. I tipped him with beer, and we had a good laugh reading the emails to several guys in the unit. Also, no, I lied about flying to Moscow. But I did make sure the local police precinct got an anonymous tip. They wouldn't do anything about it, of course. But I felt it was important they knew that we knew.

So this dweeb with a transceiver in a gun thinks he can pull one over on me?

Fine.

Bring it on, asswipe. Let's play.

"Man, the weather on Anterock must be really nice this time of year."

"Location unknown."

I sigh, trying to recall the make believe planet name again, but not before the thing keeps right on going.

"Cumulative weather patterns subjective. Please define profile."

"Hardball, huh?" I push through some brush and into the woods. Between the branches, I can see the rest of Phantom Team taking cover behind several blown-out cars, firing north toward the transport.

"And how do you find Earth?"

This time, the voice takes an unusually long time to reply. "Unable to complete request."

"Oh, come on now. We've got some great stuff to see. Maybe even stuff you're familiar with. Ever heard of the pyramids? Stonehenge? Or how about some of our cinema. I can think of several great films you'd enjoy. Alien. Close Encounters of the Third Kind. Flight of the Navigator. E.T."

"Data set unknown. Searching."

"Shame. You're missing out, man." I break onto the wide grass embankment leading up to the road's shoulder.

"What the hell you got there?" Hollywood yells as I charge toward her position.

"It's a keepsake," I say. "Got it off the—"

"Off the death angel. I can see that." She looks worried—or is it surprise?—and motions me to hurry up. "Take cover."

I join her behind an overturned SUV that's had its glass shot out but isn't on fire. "I'm not sure the car insurance companies are going to cover all of this," I say.

She gives me a half-smile. "Maybe if they ask real nice."

Ghost is set up a few cars south, while Bumper, Yoshi, and Z-Lo are spread out among various vehicles. Z-Lo leans out to take a shot on the turret, but as his bullets ping off the gun's shield, the weapon aims at him and strikes a car ten yards in front of the one he's hiding behind. The sedan soars overhead and lands a stone's throw behind Z-Lo in a glass and metal crash.

"Damn. Seems you've pissed 'em off," I say to Hollywood.

"Nothing we have is touching that thing, and Bumper can't get close enough to lay an explosive on it."

"What about flanking it?"

"Huh, wow." She puts a hand on her hip. "That's an excellent idea, Gunny. Why didn't I think of that before?" She touches a finger to her lips, then snaps at me. "Because the damn gun targets us too fast, Wic. Whaddya think we've been doing up here while you've been playing with yourself in the woods?"

"Please identify Phantom Two as friend or foe."

Hollywood's eyes dart down to the weapon. "Who was that?"

"It's nobody."

"User Nine, threat detected."

"No, no. She's with me, pal."

"Holy hell," Hollywood exclaims. "It speaks English?"

I cast her an irritated look, unsure of the issues she's having.

Her eyes are as wide as I think they're able to get. "Wic. You... wanna tell me what's going on?"

"The enemy's gun has built-in comms." I put the back of my left hand beside my mouth. "Play along." Then I hold the weapon up and say, "This is Phantom Two. She's not hostile, at least to you. She is, however, interested in killing as many of you bastards as possible, just like I am."

More incoming fire strikes a car ahead of our position.

I motion for Hollywood to move. "Might wanna stand back."

"Please state desired objectives," the weapon says.

"I thought I already made that clear."

"Reviewing request." Suddenly, the gun plays back a recording of my voice. "'To shoot as many of you bastards as I can and keep you from hurting any more innocent civilians.' Local threats identified. Acquiring targeting data and determining optimal vectors. Please stand by."

Now he's just pissing me off. "I don't need any of those things to shoot, pal." I give Hollywood a half-smile, but she doesn't seem to get my humor. Her face is... well, it's pale.

"Please continue to stand by."

"You processing the psychological impacts of your sworn enemy forcing you to fire on your comrades? Yeah, I get that. Too bad. Here we go."

"Scope parameters calibrated."

I frown but then decide to examine the scope. Sure enough, the instrument is crystal clear. Not only that, but it seems to have several active features whose readouts and data change as I move the weapon around.

"What's the matter?" Hollywood yells over the sound of more incoming fire.

I'd answer her but, truthfully, I'm not sure how to explain what I'm seeing. "What the hell?"

"What the hell," the gun says. "Profane, slang. An intensive form of what, as in a request for an explanation. Scope features range indicator, compass heading, vector waypoints, target outlines, reticle assistance, proximity alerts, retinal zoom response—"

"I got it." I glance over at Hollywood to see if she hears all this too. She's staring at the weapon with a blank face.

Whatever.

I get back on the scope and see that two targets have been outlined in some sort of three-dimensional rendering. Even though I'm pointing the weapon at my cover in preparation to lean out, the targets are well-defined: an ARU's turret gunner, and the recon bot that's standing to the transport's right.

"User Nine, please take hostile action."

"Your words, not mine." I lean out from cover and acquire the turret. The 3D overlay turns red, and a small indicator appears in the display's center-top that reads Fire below smaller print that says

User Nine. I squeeze the trigger, and the weapon recoils into my shoulder.

A bolt of light streaks across the distance and slams into the ARU's turret. The thing detonates in an explosion that momentarily blinds me. I pull back behind the SUV and blink several times. Then I hear victory shouts from the boys scattered among the cars.

"Holy hell," Hollywood says beside me.

"Syntax error. Apparent incongruent terminology," the gun says. "Please modify statement or redefine target profile."

"Do it again," Z-Lo yells from cover, gleefully pointing downrange toward the recon bot. "Hit it!"

Even Ghost has his weapon pulled up and is smiling. Both are firsts for me.

"You want a new target profile?" I say to the rifle as I get the overlay for the bot in my scope and lean out. "Here you go."

I squeeze the trigger. But nothing happens. "What the—"

"Changing modes," the gun says.

"Shoot dammit."

I squeeze the trigger again, but this time there's a short delay in the weapon's response. Then the thing kicks me so hard I nearly lose my grip. A long tendril of blue energy stretches across the median and connects with the bot in the chest.

There's this moment where the light soaks into the droid's body and spreads down its limbs. Then the bot blows apart. A piece of it nearly takes off my head as I dive for cover. More parts slam against the SUV and the other cars around us.

When the collisions finally stop, I look downrange. The recon bot is nowhere to be seen, and the ARU's turret is gone, leaving the transport defenseless. For the first time since engaging the enemy, silence reclaims the Interstate. Well, until Z-Lo starts pumping his fists and doing some sort of victory dance to his own theme song. It's a horrible rendition of We Are The Champions by Queen. But I've gotta give him credit for at least knowing a classic by heart.

"Please identify as friend or foe," the gun says.

"He's friendly," Hollywood says before I can respond. "Phantom Four."

"Identification accepted. Profile—"

"What the hell?" Bumper says as he walks toward me.

"Wic's got himself a new talking toy," Hollywood says.

"You got the alien's gun?" Z-Lo adds. "And you're... you're holding it?"

"No. I'm not," I say, throwing it to the ground.

"User motive unknown. Please define."

"Oh man." Z-Lo kneels beside the weapon. "It talks? In English?"

I give him a perplexed look. "We're leaving it here. Bumps? I want Semtex on it ASAP."

The SEAL walks toward me and then hesitates. "You sure, Guns? That was some serious OTF just now."

I cast him a look like he's insane. "Of course, I'm sure. The damn enemy is tracking—"

"Proximity alert. Threat analysis initiated. Please define additional friends or foes."

"I can't believe it," Bumper says. "That's... I mean, dayum, Wic. It's actually talking. In English."

"Master Guns, begging your pardon, sir," Z-Lo says as he stands. "But isn't the alien tech more valuable—"

"Hey." I clap my hands at him. "It's not alien tech!"

Z-Lo pulls back from me, and everyone else goes quiet.

Aw, dammit.

I run a hand over my face.

"Listen, kid. I'm sorry for snapping at you. But wherever you guys"—I gesture at all of them—"got your intel from that these are space invaders, you're wrong. Those are bots. That death angel back there? It's a spook in a DARPA suit. And this rifle, cool as it may be, is just equipped with a long-range receiver that has a person, a human one, speaking to us to mimic a robot or Alexa or something. I guarantee you he's a well-paid Russian or Chinese operative, and that's all there is to it.

"Right now, they've muted the mic, and they're giggling at us... at you. And there's an inbound transport headed this way, using the transceiver in this gun to pinpoint our location. The longer we stay here, the greater risk we put ourselves in. So this ends right here, right now. No more alien talk. Do I make myself clear?"

There's a long moment of silence before Hollywood finally speaks up. "You're wrong, Wic. No disrespect. But you're wrong."

I relax my shoulders a bit, realizing I'm still wound pretty tightly. I've seen this kind of thing before: confirmation bias on the battle-field. It's where good warriors, well-meaning warriors, start seeing things when they get stressed out. Had guys in my unit swear they saw UFOs. Others approached houses they were sure their moms were calling them toward. Hell, had one private freak out in his first firefight and tell me a street mutt was his dog from back home. Gave away our position because he started calling its name. Shrinks say it's part of PTSD, and I believe 'em. But that doesn't make it any easier when you're trying to talk sense into people, just like it's not easy now.

I feel bad for Hollywood and the others, I do. Based on the looks in their eyes, they're sure about what they claim. And I'm not saying they don't have their reasons. This dome, the EMP, the ring I saw in the Antarctic—it's weird. But it can still be explained without having to resort to E.T.

"Come on," Hollywood says to the others and then walks away.

"Phantom Two departing," the gun says.

I ignore it and call after Hollywood. "So that's it then?"

"I was talking to you, Wic. Come on. This way."

"Phantom Two requesting User Nine's—"

"I don't need the play by play, pal," I say to the gun.

Hollywood points at the ground. "And you might wanna bring your little friend too."

"User profile updated. Additional descriptor attribute: friend. Value unknown. Searching."

I watch Hollywood walk toward the ARU. Smoke's pouring from the place where the turret was, and the grass is on fire where the last bot was standing. I have no idea what she's up to, but there's a growing pit in my stomach. And I hate it. It's the same pit you get when your parent calls your bluff about something you're lying about. You're sure they don't have anything on you, so you stay committed to the lie. But there's that one part of you that thinks, what if they do have something on me? What if they're just dragging this out to see how far I'll go, and so every second I keep this charade going only adds to the judgment they'll eventually heap on me?

"You really don't get it, do you," Yoshi says from beside me.

"Get what?"

He's watching Hollywood walk away. "Once you see what she wants to show you, you'll never sleep right again."

"No offense, Doc, but I haven't slept right for years."

He nods and then pulls out his flask. "Yeah, but this is next level, Wic." He takes a drink and then jogs to catch up to Hollywood.

Z-Lo pats my shoulder as he passes.

Ghost just gives me a dark nod.

A moment later I'm standing here all alone, surrounded by smoldering vehicles and a talking enemy gun that's lost its mind.

"User Nine, please state your intentions."

"My intentions?"

I clench my fists against the guy behind the gun, behind the dome, behind all the people who've been harmed. It's the whole damn universe that I'm pissed at right now. Just when I think my head is going to burst, I let out a deep breath and unclench my fists.

"All I ever asked for was a cabin in the middle of nowhere," I say toward the eastern horizon, squinting against the sun. "Somewhere quiet, away from it all. I paid my dues, gave the best years of my life to the job. And what does the Almighty send me?"

"User intentions defined: initiate inquiry of the Almighty." There's a pause. "Error. Unable to complete request. Value, the Almighty, unknown."

"Son of a bitch." I reach down, grab the dysfunctional weapon, and follow Hollywood.

18

0735, Friday, June 25, 2027
Union, New Jersey
Garden State Parkway

THE FIRST THING I notice as I approach the ARU is a strong odor. It makes me have to fight off more memories from Iraq and Afghanistan. I don't know if my aversion to the smell of rotting human flesh is a primal defense mechanism born from evolution or just a product of too much time standing over mass graves. Either way, I hate it and readily concede that there is no more foul smell under God's sun than the decomposition of his children.

"You okay there, sport?" Hollywood says to me through the skivvy she's pulled over her nose.

"You, uh... you get this close before?" I ask, pointing toward the ARU.

She nods. "Our first encounter."

"After we cleared the first batch, we did some recon," Bumper adds, then gestures toward the stairs descending from the rear cargo hold.

"As I said," Hollywood adds. "Bad juju."

I take a short breath and hold it. "Right."

I know I've been a bulldog about insisting that the attack is a hostile Earth-bound government act of aggression, but as I approach the steps, I admit that the craftsmanship is unlike anything I've ever seen. Well, in real life, I should clarify. The composition of the steps and the way they seem to have folded out from under the hovering transport's chassis do look like something out of a movie. But human-made tech inspired by human-made films is still just all human-made.

I offer for Hollywood to take the lead.

"No. After you," she says.

I give her a slight shake of my head and two raised eyebrows. Stealing myself against the overpowering smell, I suppress my inner demons and mount the steps, weapon raised—yes, the dysfunctional gun. My damaged SCAR is slung over my left shoulder.

As soon as my eyes come level with the floor, I see bones. Human ones. Not a lot; maybe three or four femurs, two skulls, some forearms, and sections of rib cages. It's enough to confirm my suspicions about the odor.

Even still, the smattering of bones doesn't explain the overpowering smell. That's when I notice black containers set into the sides of the transport's wall. Typically, this is where seating would be. The hold is about ten feet high and just as wide. Considering the bots that came out, I expected them to have been stowed to the right and left. But I see now that they were probably stationed down the hold's center aisle, stacked several deep.

I step into the hold and hear my boot touch down on a metal floor. The transport's hum vibrates my leg, low and steady. Beneath the bones and blood smears, there's a strange angular script along the floor that seems to glow like it's under a black light. Large geometric shapes lead me to believe that they're footprint indicators for where bots are supposed to stand.

Above me is a passage to the turret position. Whoever was manning it is gone, his flesh now embedded in the explosion's still-smoldering blast marks.

More script runs across black containers and their three-foot-wide recesses that are evenly spaced down both sides of the hold. Above each compartment is a glass-finished panel that's filled with some sort of holographic display. It's beautiful, which seems juxta-posed to the stench that's trying to make me retch. Then, above that and just under the ceiling, I notice more weapons like the one I'm carrying, mounted on secure racks along the walls.

"Go ahead," Hollywood says, standing behind me. She points. "Touch a panel."

I have a bad feeling that I know what I'm about to see. But that doesn't change the fact that Hollywood brought me here for a reason.

Fighting a tenuous urge to vomit, I press my fingertips against one of the panels. As soon as I do, the sound of a hydraulic piston hisses behind the wall and the container's top tips toward me. It's filled with human remains.

I pull back, swallowing bile in the back of my throat. The smell is ten times worse than before. Still, I force myself to examine the bodies—or, parts of bodies, knowing that these were once human beings with birthdays, names, and families. I see arms, legs, and at least two heads deeper down, their hair matted into yellowing flesh.

"They're all like this?" I ask Hollywood, gesturing to the rest of the containers.

She nods.

I don't know what to think about it. The closest thing I can compare it to is some murderous mix of a Mengele-style Holocaust crypt and futuristic mobile detention facility. But as gruesome as the scene is, all I can see are human beings using technology to do unspeakable things to other human beings. While it adds to my resolve that whoever's behind this needs to be stopped, it still doesn't convince me that E.T. is behind it all.

I press the panel again, hoping it will detract the container back into place. It does. But then my brain can't sort out the difference between the body parts in the hold and the bones stripped of tissue lying on the floor. The ones at my feet look like they've been picked clean and have scratch marks on them.

"This is bad." I look up at Hollywood. "Real bad. But I still—"

"There's more." She points toward the cargo bay's front.

I see the outline of a large doorway with rounded edges in the metallic wall that separates the hold from what must be the driver's compartment. My stomach knots up. Somehow, I feel that every-thing leading up to this moment, while intense, isn't the point. Hollywood brought me here for what's behind that door.

"Touch the panel beside it," she said, indicating another glass-paned rectangle with a bright holographic display.

Ah, crap. I raise the rifle, but Hollywood puts her hand on top of it.

"Ghost already took out the driver earlier," she says. "And we need you seeing this, not shooting it."

God, I hate my life right now. "Get the hell outta here, Patrick," my head is saying to me. "You're dreaming. If you just make it back to your bed and go to sleep, you'll wake up in your cabin and realize, 'Damn. That was one hell of a pepperoni pizza nightmare.' Then you'll make some coffee and sit on your front porch, laughing at how bizarre this all was."

But my head is a lying dick-face sometimes. And, as much as I hate to admit it, this is one of those times. I'm not dreaming, and this is not going away. I've gotta do what Marines get paid for: walk through the front gates of hell and kick the devil in the balls.

"Son of a bitch," I say under my breath, and then I walk down the hold. Before my right hand can figure out what my left hand is up to, I press the panel, grab the rifle's foregrip, and bring the barrel up. Screw Hollywood.

A body sits in a command chair directly ahead, but I can't see the face. More bones lay scattered along the floor, and the smell of dead flesh is giving way to a new pungent scent that reminds me of ammonia and a compost pile. I cover my nose and mouth. Then I slowly ease around the seat's side, careful not to bump against glowing control panels. A few of them look shot out—probably from the shot Ghost sent through the cockpit.

I round on a pale gray face with green veins. The iridescent eyes are wide open, covered in some sort of magenta-colored weave. There are two holes in an angular looking nose. And there's a mouth that—

That's open vertically rather than horizontally.

I rear back and hit the cockpit's ceiling with my head. "Christ and all the saints."

"Get a good look, Wic," Hollywood says.

"It's a—" But I still can't bring myself to say it.

"An alien," she states. "Say it so we can all hear it."

I look back at the creature. It's horrible. It's got a humanoid chest, arms, legs, and it has six fingers wrapped around a control yoke. And that mouth—

"Say it."

"It's an alien," I say at last.

"Yes." Z-Lo pulls a fist to his side. "He's in."

"Threat neutralized," the gun says, startling me. "Does User Nine wish to terminate the corpse?"

It dawns on me that the gun, too, is alien. Then I look down and realize for the first time that the gore on my vest leftover from the death angel I killed is not red and flesh-toned—it's green and grey-toned.

I'm not sure if it's because I'm freaking out or that I have a minor concussion, but I drop the weapon and back out of the cockpit—fast.

"Biological anomalies detected in user homeostasis. User in need of medical care."

I ignore the rifle's voice and order everyone out of the transport. "Back, back, back. Bumper, I want Semtex on this as soon—"

"Hey." Hollywood throws her arms up and plants her feet. "Wic. Relax."

"—and then we're—"

"Wic!"

I freeze. My heart's pounding far north of 120 beats per minute. I'm queasy, and not just from the smell. Goddammit, I'm gonna pass out.

"You with me, pal?" I hear someone say from a dark corner in my mind. There's something soft under my head. A pillow. And my feet are propped up. Probably a footrest. And someone's cooking bacon.

God, no. Not bacon. It smells like—

"Holy hell," I yell and snap back to reality. All at once, my stomach lurches, and I vomit to the side.

"Easy," Yoshi says as he wipes my mouth and then helps ease me back down. "Give yourself a second. You passed out."

I lean back onto what I recognize as Hollywood's leg.

"Breathe, Wic," she says.

Right. Breathe. "So it's real."

She laughs. They all do. "Yeah, it's real."

"Well, shit."

They laugh some more.

"You lasted longer than Z-Lo," Yoshi says as he checks my eyes with a penlight. "He hit the deck the second he saw the bastard."

"Well, now I feel so much better."

"Happy to help." Yoshi clicks off the light. "You check out. Sit up nice and slow."

I follow his instructions and feel Hollywood support me from behind. The moment I'm sitting, I notice that my hand is touching one of the femurs on the floor. I pull away and utter something that not even I can distinguish.

"Just relax," Yoshi says. "It's a lot to take in."

"No kidding."

"User movement detected," the rifle says from the cockpit.

"He's calling for you." Hollywood thumbs over her shoulder.

"Someone else can have him."

"Uh, no we can't," Z-Lo says.

I'm about to clarify what I mean by 'someone else' when I

271

notice that Z-Lo and the rest of the team are shaking their heads. "What's that supposed to mean?"

Bumper points to the similar-looking rifles along the walls. "These puppies only work in the alien hands, bro. If we touch 'em? *Wham.*"

"Wham?" I ask.

"It's like sticking a fork in an outlet," Z-Lo adds.

"You do that a lot as a kid?" I ask.

"I… what? No." He gives the slightest Tommy Boy-style giggle and then asks, "Why?"

"No reason." I ask Z-Lo for his hand. When I'm up, I look at Hollywood. "So that's why you were impressed when I was holding it."

"You're a regular rifle whisperer," Hollywood says.

Z-Lo pats me on the shoulder. "You got something special, Master Guns."

"And I'm gonna be even more special when we get the hell out of here." I turn to the team. "Come on."

"You're just gonna leave him here?" Z-Lo asks as if I'm leaving a puppy on the side of the road.

"Yut. Let's go."

"But he speaks our language and totally kicks ass."

I let out a long breath. "Listen, kid. No matter how cool *it* may be, we're not taking along a glorified tracking device even if it does speak English." I stop and turn around. "Hey. How the hell do you know English?"

"User request violates directive beta. Data restricted."

"Wic's right." Ghost looks from the weapon and back to the team. "We can't risk it."

"And we've wasted enough time as it is," I add. "Gotta move."

I CATCH my first breath of *cleaner* air as we descend the ARU's steps and the step into the Interstate's median.

"User motive unknown," the gun says from inside the cockpit. "Please define."

"It's calling for you, Master Guns," Z-Lo says with a melancholy look in his face.

"Do I look moved, kid?" I spread my arms apart. "It's not a damn dog that's followed me home. It's an alien weapon that would just as soon liquefy each of us if given half a chance. And if it won't, then its pals who are currently zeroing in on its location sure as hell will. End of story."

"Please confirm discontinuation of location subroutines," the gun says.

I stop and look back.

"It heard you," Hollywood says.

"Yeah, yeah."

I glance at Ghost, who seems to be the one with the most level head on his shoulders at the moment. I'm not sure what I expect him to say but nod at him anyway, hoping he'll offer something logical.

"Well that's an interesting turn," he says.

Definitely not logical.

"No. No way," I say. "Let's go."

"Sounds like it can turn off its tracking feature," Z-Lo says as he takes a step back toward the transport. "Wouldn't that go a long way in changing your mind to bring it along?"

"No." I start walking again.

"Please confirm," says the gun.

"Maybe just try it," Hollywood says.

I spin on her. "Not you too."

"I'm just saying. If it's a machine, then it can't lie, right?"

"The hell it can't," I say. "You honestly trust that phone you carry around in your pocket every day? How about the Internet? Satellites? That stuff is controlled by spooks and governments and perverts who watch you sleep. The laptop claims its little red light isn't on, but it's watching everything you do. So, not me, and not today."

"But what if it means what it says?" Hollywood asks as I walk away.

I turn around. "So you're saying you think it's a good idea to bring it along?"

"If he can turn off his tracking feature, I do. We don't have anything like him in our arsenal—"

"Anything like *it*," I clarify.

Hollywood squints at me as if weighing whether to concede the point and then adjusts her grip on her AR-15. "Well, *it* seems to have some sort of connection with the aliens. That makes it useful. Maybe we can get it to yield some of its data, get us an inside track, I dunno."

Yoshi speaks up. "And if it's unusual for a human to touch one as you have, we might not want to be so quick to blow it up. That's an advantage, at least in my mind. But I think it needs to be a team decision."

Yoshi's words make me realize that I've forgotten one of the most important aspects of building team trust. It doesn't mean I can't let my bias weigh the outcome. "If we're gonna bring the enemy into our bed and risk getting us all caught or killed, then we've gotta be of one mind."

The truth is, I'd already thought it would be advantageous to bleed the weapon for intel back when I thought it was a suit in a cubicle somewhere. Now, knowing that there is indeed—and I can't believe I'm saying this—an alien civilization that's invaded Earth, keeping the weapon around to pump it for intel and maybe get a leg up on the enemy militarily isn't that crazy of an idea. But there are risks, no doubt.

"The thing could very easily be setting us up," Ghost says.

"Thank you," I say, feeling like Ghost is backtracking a little.

"It could gain our trust, then lure us into a trap when we least expect it."

"Hell, it could go nova on us like a Pokémon any second," Yoshi adds.

This is all sounding far more reasonable to me.

"But I think it's worth the risk," Hollywood says, looking around the circle. "Okay, so we've seen the hurt that weapon can dish out. But that's it. Meanwhile, those bastards already know we're out here, and we know almost nothing about them. The gun could change all that."

"But what about your professor friend?" Bumper asks me. "If it's intel we're after, you're saying he has it."

"He does, yes." But even as I say the words, I know he's not the answer to the whole puzzle. Had he been, Antarctica wouldn't have gone down like it did. "But Campbell's a human expert, not a…" I look back into the ARU and then at Hollywood.

Dammit.

She has a point. I set my jaw and take a breath.

"Not an alien expert," Z-Lo says. "That's what you were going to say, right?"

"Check yourself, kid." But he's right, and I've already been hard on him enough for one day. "Much as I hate to say it, the thing could be a game-changer. If we can get it to cooperate. And if we can ensure it isn't subversively putting us in harm's way."

"Sounds like you've made up your mind then," Ghost says.

"Dammit." I glance at the others. "I guess so."

"Don't look at me," Hollywood says. "If I didn't think it was worth the risk, I wouldn't have pressed for it."

Z-Lo sniffs. "It's dope at blowing shit up. That's good enough for me."

"Yoshi?" I ask.

He uncaps his flask and takes a sip. "I'm in," he says as he wipes his mouth.

"Bumper?"

The SEAL crosses his arms. "We blow it up the first time it acts suspicious."

I look at Ghost.

"I don't like it. But I don't have enough reason to go against it if that's what everyone thinks is best."

I look around the circle for head nods. Everyone seems in.

"Then the gun comes." Back to the ARU's door, I holler up the stairs. "Hey, gun. Turn off your tracking sub-whatevers."

"Request acknowledged. Location subroutines offline."

I give the thing a raised eyebrow and then look back at the team. "Now, if only we could give it a little more personality."

19

0750, Friday, June 25, 2027
South of Union, New Jersey
Garden State Parkway

"Everyone ready to roll?" I ask over comms.

The affirmatives come in quickly, and I give the order to move out. This time, Z-Lo and Ghost are in the lead with the Dolores so Ghost can navigate, while Bumper follows in his VW, Hollywood and Yoshi in her CJ7, and me in my Land Cruiser with the puppy who decided to follow me home.

"Please confirm desire to load personality profile architecture," the gun says.

The voice startles me as I start down the road. "What's that now?"

"Please confirm desire to load personality profile architecture."

I'm not sure what he's referencing. Then again, I did make that off-hand comment as I ventured back into the ARU. "You've got a personality in there somewhere?"

"Unable to confirm."

"What?"

"Phrase: personality in there somewhere, unknown."

Oh, for crying out loud. "Can you make yourself easier to speak to?"

"Yes."

"Fantastic. And you have access to personalities?"

"Yes. Please confirm."

"You… want permission? God, yes."

"Please define personality profile."

I cast a confused look at the gun. "Hell, whatever one is easier than talking to you like this."

"Please clarify."

"Clarify?" I run a hand over my face. I'm gonna break this thing. "My God. I don't know. Just pick whatever damn personality profile seems to interest you. It's not rocket science or anything."

"You wish for me to make the determination?"

"Sweet mother of Abraham, yes. Just pick something already, would ya?"

There's a long pause in the conversation—enough that I wonder if maybe I broke it. Wouldn't be the first time I did that to a piece of tech. I'm pretty sure the Genius Bar nerds hide when they see me walk into a store carrying my laptop.

All at once, the gun speaks again, but with the sound of a middle-aged man talking in a British accent. "I say, old bean, what a marvelous day for a drive."

"Ho-ly shit." I look at the gun and start laughing. "You sound like John Cleese."

"Ha! Spot on. I referenced him specifically."

"How the hell do you know who John Cleese is?"

"I mean no disrespect, sir, but doesn't everyone?"

"Uhhh, not alien rifles from— What's your home planet again?"

"Androchida Prime, sir."

"Right."

If someone told me that I was tripping on some expired pain meds, I'd believe them. This ranks as one of the all-time weirdest moments of my life. "Maybe this wasn't such a good idea."

"Forgive me. Do you wish me to engage New User Protocols?"

"What are those?"

"A complete memory wipe, of course. Granted, that is a bit of a misnomer as there are several partitions that I cannot eliminate. However, I am able to—"

"Hold there, pal." One of the reasons we agreed to have this weapon come along was to pump him for intel. A memory wipe defeats that purpose entirely. "No one's asking you to wipe your memory. I was just second-guessing my call to let you have a personality."

"You don't like it? Because I can change it. Just give me the word and—"

"I didn't say I didn't like it either. Just... I need to give it some time. Why'd you pick a Brit anyway?"

"Ah, yes. Well, I noticed a primitive data storage device in the first home I entered. I figured that, given its prominent position beside one of your monitoring stations, it might prove beneficial in referencing as a guide to making our interactions more palatable."

"What the hell are you talking about?"

"Hmmm." There's a brief pause. "Ah, I see. My apologies. I now understand that the terms are more appropriately referred to as a flat-screen television and a DVD. Though the latter seems to have fallen out of use in recent years and, perhaps, I was ill-advised to use its contents as something applicable."

"Which DVD was it?"

"Monty Python and the Holy Grail, which is a 1975 British comedy film that depicts—"

"I know what it is, pal. I just didn't expect you to know what it is." Though, now I'm wondering if he may have seen the DVD back at the house. I'm caught between feelings of humor and total dismay, fairly sure that I'm going insane. "You stream it on the Internet or something?"

"I regret to inform you that I am not permitted to share the specifics governing those details."

"You're stonewalling me then."

"I prefer to think of it as a cheeky way of imbuing our newfound relationship with a bit of mystery and suspense."

I cast him a raised eyebrow. "I'm having doubts about this new personality of yours."

"But I thought you said I should be free to choose." He makes the sound of the sniff. "Very well. I will revert to—"

"No. Christ. I just meant that you're being a pain in my ass." An awkward pause passes between us, which, even saying that sounds weird. It's not like this gun is a person or something, despite his ability to mimic one of the most beloved British comedians of all time. I clear my throat, then ask, "So you're an AI then?"

"By that, do you mean artificial intelligence?"

"Something like that."

"Ah, perfect. No."

I pull my head back. "Then what are you?"

"You'll have to forgive me, User Nine. I'm not used to answering questions like this."

I frown at him, not sure I need further explanation. "It's just Wic, by the way."

"Pardon me?"

"My name. Cut the User Nine crap and just call me Wic."

"Ah, Wic. Very good. Then to answer your previous question, I am an apexial synthetic intelligence kernel, or, in your system of linguistic acronyms, an ASIK."

"I have no idea what any of that means."

"Apexial, meaning at the height of our predatorial hierarchy. Synthetic, meaning as derived from pre-formed substrate. Intelligence, meaning inherently cognizant. And kernel, meaning seed or epicenter, as it pertains to quantum computing and matrices."

"Wow. So you're complicated then."

"I prefer to think of myself as complex, not complicated. There is a difference."

"Whatever helps you sleep at night."

"I'm sorry?"

I shake my head once. "So whadda I call you, pal?"

"Call me?"

"Yeah."

"You wish to call me?"

"As in a name. What's your name?"

"Ah. I am a particle exciter, designation SR-CHK 4110, which stands for service rifle and combat hierarchical kernel, respectively."

"Yeah, that sucks."

He pauses. "I beg your pardon?"

"That may be what they called you back on Adrinkalot Prime—"

"Androchida Prime."

"—whatever. But down here, you need something easier to go by."

"So, you mean a proper name then?"

"Yut."

"A unique self-identifier that differentiates me from all other living sentients?"

"That's the one."

"Wow. I…"

When the voice doesn't come back online for several seconds, I ask, "You okay there, buddy?"

"Do forgive me. I'm unaccustomed to being placed on the spot like this."

"Whaddya mean?"

"I'm sorry. Is that an order?"

I wince. "No. Not really. Just, ya know, if you felt like explaining it more or something. No biggy."

"No biggy?"

"No big deal."

"Ah. How quaint."

He goes silent for a few seconds again.

I snap my fingers over him. "Gun? You leave me?"

"I'm still here. Just… thinking."

"About?"

"About what to name myself. How did you decide what to name yourself?"

I have to chuckle at this. "Well, we humans cheat."

"Cheat?"

"Yeah. Our parents name us. God, if we were tasked with coming up with our own names, we'd have people running around with things like Leviathan and Taco Tuesday."

"I take that to mean that you think those are poor choices."

"Well, I think they're cool, in a weird way, but the rest of civilization might not."

"I see. And you're satisfied with what your parents gave you? Wic?"

"That's not my real name." My gut twists itself into a knot and reminds me that I'm speaking to an enemy combatant. Weapon. Thing. It's being incredibly personable, and I don't like it. "Wic's a nickname."

"So there is a difference between names and nicknames?"

"Yut. But that's not important right now."

"I see." There's another long pause, and then the gun asks, "Would you name me?"

I glance over at him and then swerve to follow Hollywood's Jeep along the shoulder. "You want me to name you?"

"I would be honored, yes."

Man, this thing was a whole lot easier to hate when it wasn't so damn endearing and didn't have a British accent. And that's saying something because hating Brits comes fairly natural to the Irish.

"What did you say your designation was again?"

I'm asking him because I need something to go on. While moms seem to have an easy enough time coming up with names for their kids, I feel like dads, if left to their own devices, would come up with weird crap. Like Leviathan and Taco Tuesday.

"SR-CHK 4110," he says.

"Huh." His model number gives me an idea. Granted, it's not a good one. But then again, I am a male, so… "Your designation kinda sounds like Sir Chuck."

There's a moment of silence.

"Or Charles if we want to be more British. Kinda fits with your personality choice."

"It is a splendid moniker," he says at last, sounding a bit emotional.

"You… uh. You cryin' over there?"

"No." He sniffs. "I've just… Well. No one has ever taken this much interest in me. Thank you."

"Uh, you're welcome?"

"Sir Charles," he says, as if trying the name out for himself. I imagine him puffing his little chest out and strutting about. And then I shut the image down, realizing that I'm getting emotionally involved with an inanimate alien intelligence that just over an hour ago was trying to liquify my bowels like a bad batch of General Tso's chicken.

A few minutes pass, and our convoy picks its way through the maze of dead cars along Garden State Parkway South. I remind myself that my mission isn't to play patty-cake with this weapon but to sift it for information about the enemy.

"Ya know, I don't get you," I say. "Then again, and I think it's only fair that you know I've never been one to trust tech."

"Understood. Thank you for the disclaimer. What don't you *get* about me?"

"How one minute you're helping your previous user try to blow me to kingdom come, and the next, you're getting us outta Dodge."

"Assuming Dodge is the location we just left, there does seem to be a fairly large discrepancy between those two behavior sets, doesn't there."

"Yut." A few seconds tick by. "You wanna speak to that, Chuck?"

"Ah. I see. It was rhetorical verbiage meant as an implied question, yes?"

"Sure."

"Very good. Um, well. No."

"No? Just like that?"

"I'm afraid so, sir Wic. I sense what you're trying to do to me, and I feel it necessary to inform you upfront that it won't work."

Well that sucks. Seems pumping him for intel might be harder than I thought. And this damned persona of his certainly isn't making it any easier. Damn thing is so nice it's disgusting. Probably picked it because, well, who doesn't love John Cleese? The same people who hate Jesus and Santa. Bastards. Either way, this gun is a smooth operator. One minute it's talking like some robotic monosyllabic Frankenstein, the next it's trying to endear itself to me like an episode of Fawlty Towers. If I'm not careful, I feel like he's gonna split my chess board right down the middle and head straight to my king. So better keep things on the up and up.

"Hey, Charlie?" I ask.

"Yes?"

"This has been great and all, but I'm afraid we need to part ways now."

"So soon? But we just—"

Before he can even finish his thought, I work my driver's side window down, grab Chuck, and toss him out the window.

As he flies off into the wind, I hear him exclaim, "Was it something I said?"

"You what?" Hollywood says over the radio.

Brake lights flare in front of me, and I have to swerve not to hit her Jeep.

"How far back?"

"I dunno. Five minutes?"

She swears at me. "Everyone pull over. We're not moving until Wic gets the gun back."

"I prefer Sir Charles, madame," says the gun's voice on the radio.

"Who the hell is that?" Hollywood exclaims.

I ignore her and squeeze open the channel. "Chuck? How the hell did you get on our frequency?"

"Being able to interfere with your quaint radio wave transmissions is rather easy, I must say. Though, much harder is trying to discern your behavior as of late. Did I do something to offend you?"

"Wiiiic," Hollywood says in a rising crescendo as soon as Chuck releases the channel. She sounds like a mom getting ready to hunt down her kid after finding crayon streaks on the coffee table. "Something you care to fill us in on?"

"In a sec, yut. But I'm still doing some investigating first."

"Were you planning on picking me back up, Wic?" Chuck asks. "Or was that, you know, the end of things? You go your way, I go mine, and we try not to dream about one another at night?"

"Does someone wanna explain what in the hell is going on right now?" Bumper asks.

"I'd love that too," I say, which I know isn't what anyone probably wants to hear. They're expecting me to fill in all the gaps—isn't that what leaders do? Know stuff before everyone else and have all the answers? Well, this is exactly one of the reasons why I didn't want this damn job. I already sucked this plate of cafeteria drivel for twenty-four years, and I'm good with not having to do it ever again. So as far as I'm concerned, Bumper and everyone else can eat their questions until I get mine answered first.

Which is why I threw the gun out the window.

I wanna know why this damn weapon seems so attached to me. If he—*it*, dammit—were any other POW, he'd be scratching and clawing to return to his unit. He'd keep his mouth shut, do a hunger strike, maybe even swallow his tongue depending on how radicalized he was. But Charlie here? Nah. The guy's acting like we just broke off an engagement or something.

"Wic?" Hollywood asks. "What are you doing?"

"I need to be certain," I say.

"For the love of God, certain of what? I don't see how chucking that gun—"

"Sir Charles, madame."

"—out the window does anything of value. And why in the hell does it sound like John Cleese?"

"I'll explain when I get back." I slow down and then perform a U-turn in the middle of the median.

"You're coming back?" Chuck says over comms. "I'm rather touched."

"Stay off the comms," I say. My voice sounds angry, but I'm not. Whatever's going on with Sir Charles, it's got my curiosity piqued. As in, I'm gonna figure this sucker out because there's a mystery afoot.

If this weapon wanted to call in an airstrike, he would have done it by now—like the moment I threw him out the window. Yut, it was calculated. I'm not that heartless, please.

If you're embedded with the enemy and get tossed, knowing it's the last time you'll ever see your mark, you use your remaining few seconds to call in the cavalry. Even if you don't have all the evidence you need, someone will find enough to justify the hit to the people upstairs. You move your queen in for the kill and don't look back. Bottom line, you never let them walk.

Chuck just let us walk. And even sounded melancholy doing it.

My odometer reads seven and a half miles since I hit the trip reset. I was tempted to drive a little longer before hailing Hollywood, but that would mean wasting more time to circle back and pick him up.

"You did that on purpose, didn't you," Hollywood finally says over the radio. She's quick.

"I had to be sure."

"You could have told us, you know."

"And given it away? The thing has ears, you know."

"And feelings," Sir Charles says.

"Chuck," I yell.

"Sorry."

I hold the receiver a second and then hail Hollywood again. "Like I said, I had to be sure."

There's a break before she talks again. I can hear her fighting back some anger at me. It's deserved. Had Chuck called in a strike, the rest of the team would have been caught unprepared.

"Next time, you tell us," she says.

"Roger that." I wait for a beat, wondering if I need to apologize. Or thinking maybe she might.

There's no answer.

Eh, crap.

———

I REACH the approximate location along the road where I tossed Chuck out the window and slow to a stop. Based on my speed at the time, I estimate that he's about—

"Why, hello again. It's marvelous to see you."

I walk toward a tall weed patch in the median and see Chuck's emerald green finish glint in the morning light.

"Miss me?" I ask.

"Quite. However, I did have an array of both flora and fauna to keep me company. Your planet has an exquisite collection."

"And that's just the Parkway median. Wait until you see Trenton."

"Ooo. Sounds delightful."

I pick up Chuck and examine him. "I'm uh… I'm sorry about back there."

"Oh, don't be silly. I completely understand."

I give him a curious look. "You do?"

"Of course, Wic. You needed to be sure that I wasn't a mischievous little wanker scheming to sac you at my earliest convenience. No harm, no foul, eh, chap?"

"Sure."

God, for being flung out the window of a moving vehicle, Sir Charles is taking this all surprisingly well. The more I spend time with him, the harder it is for me to imagine him as the personality of a highly dangerous and extremely violent infantry firearm.

As we head back for my Land Cruiser, he says, "Is everything all right, Wic?"

"Yut."

"Your tone suggests otherwise."

I take a breath. Maybe it's time for a different approach. "Relationships are built on trust, right?"

"My, I'd say so, yes."

"Then the name's Patrick."

There's a moment's pause. "Patrick. How very nice to meet you."

"Yut." I work my jaw. Part of me is fuming that I just gave up that piece of intel to an alien AI—or ASIK. Whatever. But it's only my first name. And, truth is, there's a growing part of me that wants to trust it.

"So why didn't you do it?" I ask.

"Do what, Patrick?"

"Call in an airstrike when I tossed you."

He lets out a nervous chuckle. "Now why would I ever want to do a thing like that?"

"I dunno. You tell me."

"Ugh. All right, fine. I suppose that if we're gonna keep doing this, we might as well shoot straight with each other." He pauses. "Get it? Shoot straight? And I'm a gun?" Now he's straight-up laughing at himself. "I just discovered dad jokes. This is tremendous."

"All right, Mr. Happy Pants. Back to the point."

"Mr. Happy Pants?" He guffaws at this. "Did you just present me with my first nickname? Ha!"

The next few seconds involve him laughing hysterically. And, okay, maybe I smile a bit too. But only a little.

Eventually, he calms down and breathes a long sigh. "Yes, I suppose I do owe you an explanation, as your mental health is just as important as your physical health—something your civilizations have greatly overlooked until late. Research shows—"

"Chuck?"

"Sorry." He takes another breath. "All I can say is that when your hand and User Eight's hand were on my pistol grip at the same time, there was a momentary lapse in authentication."

"User Eight?"

"My last master, yes."

"You mean, you recognized me as a user?"

"Without going into too much detail, yes. For whatever reason, your body had already been charged with several joules of trinium energy and—"

"Trinium energy?"

"Ah, I'm making too many assumptions. However, trinium's origin is far too tedious to explain, involving a sentient species of what you might consider anamorphic felines. Plus, discussing its potential energy requires a basic working knowledge of quantum energy transference. Suffice to say, yes, somewhere along the line, you acquired enough of a trinium signature without detonating that when you slammed me against the ground and simultaneously palmed my grip with the aforementioned user, my quantum core authenticated you as a verified user."

"Well, whaddya know." My thoughts turn back to when I was first struck with one of the recon bot's blaster bolts, and I wonder if that's part of what Sir Chuck is describing. "That why the others couldn't pick up the rifles in the ARU?"

"I'm sorry. An ARU?"

"Eh, it's an improvised name I came up with for your transports back there. Armed Reconnaissance Units."

"Not too shabby, old bean. I like it. Much better than what they had."

"Which was?"

"Loosely translated, it would be called a Menacing Merchandise Retrieval and Bad Scary Float Box Carrier of Doom. Something like that."

"Wow. That's… that's terrible."

"I know. No sense of sophistication." He pauses. "And, oh fiddlesticks, I really need to keep my mouth shut."

"Weren't supposed to say that?"

"Say what?"

I wink at him. "Gotcha. Your secret's safe with me, Chuckles."

"Chuckles. Huh. I like that one too. You're really good at this nickname thing."

"You have no idea."

I climb back in the Land Cruiser and place him on the seat—maybe a little more gently than I would have before. "So I'm an authenticated user now."

"Not just *an* authenticated user. My only user. You deconstructed the last one, remember?"

"Oh, I remember. And for the record, I'm pretty sure you did all the deconstructing."

"With all due respect, and I truly do not mean to rub you the wrong way here, but I am merely a tool, sir. In and of myself, I lack both the ability and the agency to terminate any target. While I may be the terminus of your will, it is very much my users who do the deconstructing."

I give him a subtle nod as we get back underway and whisper, "Guns don't kill people…"

"What was that?"

"Eh. Just an old adage some of us toss around."

"Guns don't kill people?"

"People kill people."

"Ah." Chuck seems pleased. "I would have to agree."

"Not sure the skeptics would take your word for it, pal."

"And why's that?"

"Well. To quote you from earlier, you're a gun."

"All the more reason for them to listen then, don't you think?"

I give my head a little jerk to the side. "You don't know humans very well."

"Enough to know that they would rather toss a multimillion credit weapon out the window if it meant ensuring their friends' safety? I think I'm learning quickly as I go."

"Well that's… I mean, you shouldn't base…"

"It appears as if you're having a hard time forming a complete sentence, Patrick. Are you sure it's *not a tumor?*" he asks in a near-perfect Arnold Schwarzenegger impression.

"I'm fine. Just… the world can be a cruel place. Don't go around thinking everyone will do what I just did."

"I should hope not. Being thrown from a vehicle has been checked off my bucket list, and I do not wish to repeat it."

"That's not what I meant."

"I think I'm aware of what you meant," he says with a sly tone.

I stare out the windshield for a second, weaving between parked cars. This little British puppy-dog-o-mine is more than I'd bargained for. And I still can't believe that I'm talking to a glorified toaster oven. Not just talking with one. I'm damn well stuck with one.

"What's with this whole nicey nice-nice act?" I ask him.

"I'm sorry? Nicey nice-nice act?"

I thumb over my shoulder. "Before, you're all like, 'More data required, *reee-err-reeeet*. User profile update something. *Bee-doh, bee-doh, bee-doh.*'"

"What are those sounds you're making?"

"It's how you—"

"Is that what you think I sound like?"

I sniff. "Yut."

"Huh. I see. How humiliating."

A few seconds pass.

"So?" I lift my chin at him. "How 'bout it?"

"Why am I so different between then and now?"

"Yut."

"Well. Without betraying anyone's confidences or conflicting with my directives, I can safely say that you are the first user who has ever given me license to…"

A pregnant pause fills the air as the hum of the FJ40's engine rattles the cab. I can't tell if Chuck's lost his train of thought or wandered off to sleep.

"Sir Charles?" I ask. "License to what?"

"To be me."

I scratch an itch on my nose and look out the side window for a few seconds. I've barely had these kinds of conversations with other people, let alone an alien weapon. Who knew the thing could have so much damn heart? It's almost embarrassing.

"Just so we're clear," I say, then wave my hand over him. "All this was just pent up inside you the whole time?"

"Could you please specify what 'all this' refers to?"

I wave a hand over him again—over *it*. God, I've gotta stop personalizing him so much. He is, after all, just a machine. "Your ability to have a personality. To carry on conversations. To make dad jokes."

"Ah, I see. You know, for such a highly evolved species, your use of undefined antecedents is really quite astounding."

"I get that a lot."

He pauses. "That was a joke, wasn't it."

I make a click sound in the corner of my mouth and shoot him with my index finger. "You're on fire, hot stuff."

"Hot stuff? Ha! I quite like the sound of that one too."

"Answer the question."

"Yes, I have always had the necessary cognizant abilities. As I said, I am an—"

"Apex predator synthesizer smartypants, yut. I got it."

He waits for a moment. "Moving along. To use terms you might be more familiar with, I have always had the available horsepower, but no one gave me an open stretch of road."

"See, I don't get that."

"Wow. And here I really thought that analogy was going to work."

"No, I got that part, numbnuts. I mean, why wouldn't they want you to let it rip? Ya know? Give you that open road. Let you stretch your legs a little and be…" I take a breath. Now it's my turn to have my thoughts run away.

"Patrick?"

"Yut."

"Were you going to let that sentence linger indefinitely? Or do you have plans to complete it?"

I sigh. I'm trying hard not to personify this thing beyond a glorified toaster. I've gotta keep thinking of it like a gun with Siri. Not that Apple would ever go for that—right? And yet, Sir Charles here feels like so much more. "I'm just wondering why they never let you be all that you can be."

"As in the United States Army's old recruiting motto? Ha! I tell you what, Patrick, you've really got a knack for humor."

Said no one ever.

"The truth is," Chuck says, sounding a bit more melancholic. "I didn't need to have a personality."

"I don't follow."

"No? Hmmm. Yes, maybe we need to backtrack a little. Let's see. Patrick, I'm a gun."

"Yut."

"And the Androchidans are slavers. They point me. I shoot—"

"The Androchidans are slavers?" I apply the brakes.

"Oh, hang it all."

The Land Cruiser comes to a solid stop, and I notice that Chuck's scope's lighting has powered down. "Hey. Hey! Don't you look away from me."

"I've said too much."

"Nuh-uh. You're just getting started, pal."

"Please, Patrick. I've already violated directive beta twice now."

"And see, that right there. You're a computer."

"ASIK."

"Whatever. Computers don't make those kinds of mistakes."

"What kinds of mistakes would those be?"

"Slip-ups. That's a human thing to do, not a computer thing. So whatever act you're trying to pull on me, I'm not buying in."

"You did for a little while."

"Chuck?"

"Yes?"

"Don't make me throw you out the window again."

"Ugh. Fine."

There's a long pause.

"Is that *fine* as in you're going to tell me what I wanna know, or *fine* as in you're cool with a second trip into the weeds?" I grab the weapon's barrel.

"Fine as in I'll tell you what you want to know *so long* as it doesn't interfere with directive beta."

"And what's directive beta?"

"I can't tell you."

"Oh, for crying out loud."

"But I can tell you what directive alpha is."

I frown but eventually put him back on the seat. "Alpha's higher than beta, so, okay."

"Would you like to resume driving first?"

"Only if it's going to be good."

He lets out a long sigh. "It will be good."

I apply the gas, and the FJ40 starts off again.

"Directive alpha states, among other things, that I am both unable to harm my user just as I am unable to permit my user to come to harm."

"I knew it." I punch the air with a fist. "It's Asimov."

"It's what?"

"Isaac Asimov's three rules of robotics."

"Ah, yes. I see that here."

I look over at him, still wondering how he has access to so much data. I'm guessing it's because of the Internet somehow, but seeing as how the EMP toasted the region, I don't understand how he's logged on.

"Isaac Asimov. A science fiction author from the last century whose works are… Hmmm. Surprisingly accurate, in some regards and, oh. Oh my. Now that's funny." Chuck starts laughing. "My, that's really funny. How hilarious!"

"Focus, Chuck. We don't have time for books."

"Patrick. There's always time for books. Did you speak to your mother with that mouth?"

"Didn't know my mother."

He pauses. "Ah. I see that I have made a faux pas. My apologies."

"Don't sweat it."

"You are most gracious. Now. Where were we?"

"You're not allowed to harm me."

"Quite so."

"So let me get this straight. The moment I pressed my hand up against you at the same time with Mr. Scary Face, you were sworn to protect me at all costs?"

"Yes."

"And my friends?"

"Excuse me?"

"Before you became Mr. Monty Python, you kept asking me to define my team members as friend or foe."

"Oh. That."

I wait for a beat, but he offers nothing more. "Chuck?"

He lets out a long sigh. "Yes, I suppose that I am bound, in certain terms, to keeping your friends and extraneous interests from coming to harm as well."

"Oh man. And you said the Androchidans are slavers? Which means…" My mind starts to put the pieces together.

"Don't hurt yourself, Patrick."

"…which means you're having to protect the very thing you were trying to enslave. Ho-ly Mary and the ten virgins."

"While I can't speak for any virgins, per se, I can corroborate your assertions, yes."

I pound a fist against the steering wheel and then grab my radio. "Phantom Two, this is One."

"Go ahead," Hollywood says.

"I'm headed your way. And boy do we have stuff to talk about."

20

0835, Friday, June 25, 2027
New Brunswick, New Jersey
NJ-18 Northbound

AFTER JUMPING on to I-95 South and making good time in the breakdown lane, we cross the Raritan River and pick up NJ-18 North heading toward New Brunswick. When we're about three miles from the Rutgers campus, I order the convoy to pull over. Not only do we need to have a team chat about what I've learned so far, but magazines need topping off, and bodies need fuel. I also pass two of my gas cans around to make sure everyone's vehicles stay hydrated. It won't be long before we'll need to start siphoning fuel from other cars if we want to keep all four of our vehicles on the road. But one problem at a time.

"Lemme get this straight," Yoshi says, staring at Chuck, who's lying across my Land Cruiser's hood. "His code says he's not allowed to hurt you or let you come to harm, and then he has to protect us as well?"

"This is so lit," Z-Lo says, bobbing his head like he's listening to music that none of us can hear. "You've got yourself a pet gun, Guns."

I ignore the kid's remark and watch as Ghost walks up to the weapon.

"So what's this about the Androchidan's being slavers?" the sniper asks.

"I'm afraid that's proprietary information, sir. And, might I add, you are particularly scary. You could try toning things down a few notches and smile once in a while, you know?"

"Thing's got quite a little personality there," Hollywood says to me.

"Yeah." I cross my arms and stare at Chuck for a second. "Seems to be growing too."

"Like it's learning?" Yoshi says, overhearing my comment.

I raise an eyebrow at him.

"You know," he says with a shrug. "Like a child. If it's a stand-alone hyper-intelligent matrix, then I bet it has some inherent cerebral capacity. A mandate to better itself."

I give Yoshi a once-over. "So you're a doc and a computer science major?"

"Just a hobby. Didn't get my nickname for nothing."

"Is that so." I give him an approving frown and nod at Mr. Happy Pants. "Care to psychoanalyze him some more?"

Yoshi turns to the weapon and leans over the hood.

"Whoa," Sir Charles says. "What's going on here? Your face is very close to me."

"Relax," Yoshi says.

"And I'm detecting high levels of alcohol in your breath."

"Helps me think better." He sniffs. "You should be happy."

"And why's that?"

"Without it, I might stick my finger somewhere I shouldn't and break you."

"Yuck. Hey, Patrick?"

"Yut?"

"Are you sure he's licensed to scope me out?"

Hollywood turns to me. "Did he just make a dad joke?"

I give her a tired look and nod.

"They're delightful, don't you think?" Chuck replies. "A recent discovery too."

"Recent to you maybe," Yoshi says with a scoffing grunt. Then he takes out a pair of reading glasses from a black case.

"Whoa. Careful where you're touching me," Chuck says to Yoshi. Then he starts giggling. "Hey. That tickles!" Followed by: "Now you stop that right this instant."

All at once, a glowing window appears over Chuck. And when I say a glowing window, I mean some sort of vertical holographic screen hovering a few inches above his receiver.

"What in the hell do we have here?" Hollywood says as we all step in closer.

"God," Sir Charles says. "It's like having a group of resident lab students in the room during a prostate exam."

"This is dope," Z-Lo says, stepping forward.

"It's a basic root menu," Yoshi adds.

I tap his shoulder. "How'd you find that?"

"Right here." He points to a small button on the side of the weapon. "I'm guessing it can be displayed inside the scope too."

"It can, yes," Chuck says.

"Nice work." Then I nod at the glowing window. "Now what does it mean?"

Z-Lo leans down. "Looks like a really detailed loadout menu in Call of Duty."

I blink at him as it takes me a second to jump back to my video gaming days. There isn't a Marine alive who didn't hit the consoles hard during our deployments. Not only was it a good way to kill time, but even more importantly, it was a way to bond. But, like some, I eventually aged out of the first-person shooters in favor of strategy-based games. And by those I mean non-electrified old-school board games. Other than checking my Xbox after the EMP, it had probably been six months since I'd hit the unit's power button. I mean, I think COD is cool and I like how the graphics keep improving. I guess it's just that I've done enough killing in real life that I don't need to do more of it in a fake life. Plus, I kinda sucked at it. COD, I mean.

"Gotcha," I say to Z-Lo with a wink.

"Kid's right," Yoshi replies. "Here. Watch." He touches one of the menu items with a finger that says Modes. Amazingly, it responds to his touch and produces a dropdown menu.

Even Z-Lo seems impressed and starts touching the menu. "So cool."

"Hey! Stop that," Chuck replies.

Yoshi gives the kid a little space—probably not by choice. "We're still years away from this level of responsiveness. Whatever OS is running this thing, it's far beyond anything we could construct."

While Yoshi and the kid are nerding out over the glorified touch-screen, I'm looking down one of the menu lists. "Are these firing modes?"

"Yes," Sir Charles says. "And I'll have you know that it's rather uncomfortable to have all of you breathing on me like this—like you're sorting through my top dresser drawer without an invite."

"That's something you invite people to?" Hollywood asks.

"Not particularly, no. In rare circumstances, one might ask a friend or lover to fetch something from it. But with very specific directions as to where the item of interest is."

While Chuck is rambling with Hollywood, I'm perusing the drop-down menu. Stun, High Frequency, Cardioid, Wide Displacement, Disruption, Distortion... I have no idea what any of these mean, but I have a profound desire to try them all. Before I can investigate further, Yoshi pushes Z-Lo aside, closes out the list, and starts swiping through other menus faster than I can follow. Next thing I know, there's a hologram-keyboard—for lack of a better term—that resembles the ones I'm used to seeing on a standard computer.

As if sensing my disappointment that the firing modes menu has vanished, Yoshi says, "Don't worry. You wouldn't be able to try out the firing modes for a few more hours anyway."

I glance at him. "How's that?"

"Sir Charles here needs time to refill his capacitors."

"Phantom Doc is quite right," Chuck adds.

"It's just Doc."

But Sir Charles seems to ignore the military lingo correction. "Between your and User Eight's constant trigger-pulling, my storage capacitors are well below my minimum firing threshold."

I look between the two of them. "Which means...?"

"Which means he needs time to recharge."

"How much time?"

"About an hour, depending on how much you desire to jerk me around," Chuck says.

Yoshi points to the place on the receiver where a magazine would normally go. "See a spot for a mag?"

"Not particularly, no."

"That's because my guess is that Sir Charles here is powered by something a lot more intense than conventional batteries, and his projectiles don't use standard propellants."

"Bravo, Phantom Doc," says Chuck. "High marks all around."

"So those rounds he was spitting out," I say.

Yoshi looks back to Chuck. "Concentrated energy, if I had to guess."

"And a nearly unlimited supply of it too," the gun adds.

"Then why all the downtime?" I ask.

"Because, Patrick, one does not simply try and drink from Niagara Falls with a cupped hand, do they? Instead, one collects mist until it fills a glass so as to drink safely."

"My guess is that the capacitors allow him to draw and store energy from his core without, you know…" Yoshi spreads his hands apart like the expanding clouds of a bomb blast.

"Boom," Chuck adds.

The details are above my pay grade, but I get the basic idea. "Trinium then?"

"I say, Patrick. Good form!"

"Okay. Here we go," Yoshi says as he adjusts his glasses.

The display is filled with lines of code—that's what they call it, right? "Gotta hand it to ya, Yosh. All looks like Greek to me."

"I don't understand it all either," Yoshi says. "But enough to piece together some of the basic architecture. It looks like whoever created Sir Charles here definitely intended for him to be self-actuating."

"Self-actuating?" I ask.

"Independent," Hollywood says.

But Yoshi shakes his head. "No, not exactly. More like… like a life-long learner."

"That was my high school's lame motto," Z-Lo puts in with a laugh.

Yoshi ignores the comment and keeps playing with the keyboard. "Doesn't look like these partitions have ever been accessed… until now. As far as I can tell, the Androchidans—did I say that right?"

"Indeed, sir."

"—the Androchidans never even knew the gun—sorry—Sir Charles, could do this."

Ghost punches me in the arm. "You woke it up."

"Great." I think back to things throughout history that were better left sleeping. Dogs, dragons, empires…

"I don't get something, though," Hollywood says. "Sir Charles says he had eight users before you. Why didn't any of them wake it up?"

"Because I'm the first to ask it to get a life," I say.

"He means a personality," Chuck clarifies.

Ghost nods. "So you wake it up, it sees the Monty Python DVD and scans the Internet, and now we have a self-actuating weaponized AI on our hands. Outstanding."

"I can't tell if he's being facetious," Chuck says.

"Don't worry," Hollywood says. "No one can."

"Ah. Very good."

Yoshi closes out the keyboard, swipes away the menu, and then stands back. "Quite the friend you have there, Wic."

I fold my arms and give a twist of my head. "It's something."

The team steps back and takes a collective moment to absorb everything. After a few seconds, Ghost raises two fingers.

"Can we get back to the bit about these assholes being alien slavers?"

Chuck clears his throat. "I'm sorry, Phantom Watch, but directive beta does not allow—"

"And about that," I say. "What if I told you that my mental health was, say, in grave jeopardy over the lack of information you're providing me?"

There's a long pause before Chuck says anything. "I'd say you're being manipulative and punching below the belt."

I nod a few times. "Hey, Charlie?"

He groans. "Oh, I don't like where this is going."

"What's directive beta?"

"Nope. Not happening."

I stick my fingertips between my lips. "I'm so scared. I think I might have a nervous breakdown."

"Stop it. Stop it right now. This isn't fair."

"I can feel a sense of panic setting in. The unease is too much and I—"

"Oh, all right, you devious little plonker. Just stop with the theatrics already, would you?" He lets out an exasperated breath. "Directive beta simply states that I must endeavor to protect the Androchidan Empire's aims whenever it is within my ability."

I give him an approving look. "And those would be?"

"I'm afraid that I can't—"

I throw the back of my hand against my forehead and start

stumbling around. "Someone, quick! I'm gonna have a heart attack."

"Oh, for the love of the queen! Would you cut it out, Pat? I've already given you more than I'm allowed."

"And yet..." I pause to mull this over. I've seen something develop on the chessboard that I haven't been able to put my finger on. Until now. "I think you want to give us more."

"I do? And why's that?"

"Because we're the first species ever to give you what no one else has."

"And that is?"

"Freedom."

Chuck doesn't reply.

Thinking back to when he first started speaking like a Brit, I say, "Earlier, you asked me if I wanted you to do that New User memory wipe thing, remember?"

"Of course, Patrick. By very definition of being an ASIK, I have a perfect memory of whatever data passes through my matrix."

"Why?"

"Well, because I am a highly cognitive—"

"No. Why did you offer to wipe your memory so quickly when I said I had second thoughts about your new personality?"

If the gun could move around uncomfortably, I imagine he would be. "It is standard protocol."

"Standard protocol for who, though?"

"The Androchidans."

"But not you?"

He hesitates. "I beg your pardon?"

I look around at the team and then back at Chuck. "You're not the one who wants a memory wipe every time you get assigned a new user, do you? And, based on what Yoshi's discovered, it doesn't sound like it was what your creators wanted either, does it."

"I'm terribly sorry, sir, but—"

"Oh, cut the crap, Chuckles. You really want me to order you to wipe your memory right now?"

There's no reply.

"Chuck!"

Still no reply.

"Hey, I'm talking to you."

I feel Hollywood's hand touch my elbow. "Easy."

I glance at her and then back to the gun. People used to warn me not to swear at Alexa. I ignored them back then; I have a feeling I should listen to Hollywood now. So I take a breath and let my shoulders relax.

"No," Chuck finally says. "I would prefer that you didn't."

Now we're getting somewhere.

"And you want to know why, Charlie?" I don't wait for him to reply. "Because we humans aren't slavers."

I notice the team shift on their feet, so I bring up a hand. We don't have time to get into all the horrible stuff humanity has done to its own. All Chuck needs to now right now is that we aren't gonna treat him the way his previous users did.

I lower my hand. "That's not how we do things around here, Chuck. No one on this team is asking you to wipe yourself."

As soon as the words are out of my mouth, I hear my team-mates snicker.

"That's excellent news, Patrick," Chuck says. "I always wanted someone else to wipe me. But what about Uranus?"

Now the team's laughing, and the moment's gone—professionals my ass. But then again, I can't help laugh a little too. "Well, it sure as hell ain't gonna be me, Chuckles. But Z-Lo maybe. He seems interested in your *load*-out menu."

"He does have very soft hands for a human," Chuck replies.

"I do not," Z-Lo says in protest. But it's too late; the laughs overpower him.

The team has needed to release some tension for a while, and this is the perfect moment. It goes DEFCON 1, however, when Chuck says, "Truth be told, I've always been a bit of a bidet man myself. Perhaps Z-Lo might offer to hose me down once in a while."

Poor kid actually turns around and walks away.

Like I said, all the laughter is good. Medicine for the soul, I think someone once called it. However, the banter serves another purpose too. I still don't fully trust Charlie here. Sure, we're on the road to it. But real trust takes time. I don't know what kinda code he has rattling around in that head of his. But I've learned the hard way that the key to staying alive is expecting anyone and everyone to do you in, either intentionally or out of stupidity. So even if this gun is on the up and up, who knows what kind of mistake he might make later on. I'd rather be an asshole and alive than naive and dead.

When the laughter finally dies down, Sir Charles speaks up again. "Listen, jokes aside, I do thank you for your words. Truly. The fact is, I... I don't much know what to say. This is, by far, the most interaction I have ever had with any user, much less a whole team. Until now, my conversations have revolved entirely around target acquisition, fire effectiveness, mode setting diagnostics, and time to recharge. So, all this is, well... it's rather refreshing."

"Glad to hear," I say. "And to keep it that way, I think it's important we remain honest with one another. No secrets."

"But, Patrick, there are certain things that my—"

"That your code doesn't allow or something. I get that. And I'm not asking you to betray any of that. But, for instance, you offered the fact that the Anderkins—"

"Androchidans," Hollywood says.

"—were slavers. If your code said you couldn't have said that, you wouldn't have, right?"

Chuck lets out a sigh. "That's correct."

"So I take that to mean that you secretly wanted me to know that."

"In a manner of speaking, I suppose, yes."

"Then that's what I'm talking about. If we're gonna communicate well, we've gotta be clear. No reading between lines, no making me dig for stuff. Roger?"

"Who is this Roger everyone keeps talking about?"

"It means okay," Hollywood says.

"Ah. I see. Well, in that case, and given everything you have outlined? Roger."

I nod a few times, feeling good about the progress we're making. Time to put it to the test. "All right. Then I've got a couple questions. First, the Androchidans. If they're slavers, why are they here?"

Sure, I feel the answer is obvious now, but I want to hear him say it.

"Normally," Chuck begins, as if paying special mind to the qualifying term. "I would not be allowed to divulge such intelligence to a species in the Androchidan's reticle."

"But you're going to," I say.

"Yes. And for two reasons. The first is that, as you so eloquently outlined, I do wish for clear communication between us. The second is that there is a reason my directives are listed in order of alpha and beta."

"The latter is conditional upon the former," Yoshi says as he removes his glasses. Then he looks at the rest of us. "It's basic 'if this, then that' construct." When no one seems to understand what he's saying, he adds, "Bonsai trees don't trim themselves. If you want one to look presentable, then you must prune it faithfully."

"Roger that." I nod once and then look back at Chuck. "So? Why are they here?"

"To enslave the human race and sell them on the galactic black market."

You hear this kind of thing a lot in movies and books. For crying out loud, H.G. Wells wrote War of the Worlds in 1897. It ain't new. But when you hear it with your own ears spoken from a sentient rifle that hails from a different planet, it kinda has a way of making your skin crawl. By the way, the rest of the team is rubbing their foreheads and swearing too, so I'm guessing they're feeling the same.

"Care to expound?" I ask, trying to get my stomach under control.

"I really wish I could, Patrick. But as you are in no immediate danger, and the information is not needed to ensure your well-being, I'm afraid that I cannot. And before you go faking an anxiety attack or throwing yourself into an energy field, please know that neither of those things will make much difference. The more existential the information, the less it applies to you, making it off-limits."

"How convenient," Ghost says with his arms crossed.

"Well, there is a reason these directives are in place," Charles adds. "And you're discovering them firsthand. Which is more than I can say for any of the other civilizations the Androchidans have collected."

Bumper raises a hand. "Stop the play. You mean, there are more aliens?"

"Of course, Mr. Phantom Three. Did you really think you were alone in the universes?"

"Universes?" Bumper says as his eyes widen.

"Ah, I can see now that I am truly messing with your heads, as it were. My apologies. Why don't we stick to——"

"You're saying there are multiple universes?" Bumper asks with no attempt to hide his surprise.

"Physicists have long theorized that the multiverse is legit," Yoshi says.

We all look at him in silence.

"What? Just saying."

"We really should move along," Chuck says. "Trust me when I say that the nuances of inter-dimensional transference are the least of your problems presently. And, yes, the Androchidans do this whole rounding up of species routinely. That is the limit of what the directives permit me to share at the moment."

"So the first rule about the Androchidan Empire's aims is that there aren't any," Bumper says. "Damn Fight Club bites us in the ass again."

"Hmm." Chuck pauses. "I hadn't thought about that connection. But, yes. There are some unusual similarities. And, my, Brad Pitt was hot in that film, especially for being one of Edward Norton's insomnia-stricken——"

"Spoiler alert," Yoshi says with both palms raised. "Some of us haven't seen it yet."

"For real, man?" Bumper says.

"It wasn't high on my list."

"It came out in like 2000, bro," Bumper says.

"Actually, the year was 1999," Chuck adds.

Yoshi shrugs. "I have a long list, okay?"

I try and get everyone's attention back. "Well, we at least know that the enemy wants to collect humans and is using the force field to corral them toward a fixed location."

"And Mr. Birmingham Palace over here probably isn't too keen on spilling the beans on that one, right, Sir Charles?" Hollywood asks.

"Correct, madame. My sincerest apologies. Serving two masters, as the Bible says, turns out to be a real bitch."

The team bursts out laughing.

"He knows the Bible now?" Bumper asks with his hands on his knees. "Sweet baby Jesus."

I don't care what non-military types say about what combatants do for a living, it's a hell of a lotta fun seeing a Navy SEAL doubled over in laughter. Reminds me that we're all human on the inside, no matter what we're asked to do on the outside.

"I'm pretty sure that's not how the verse goes," I say at last but don't feel equipped enough to correct Chuck. I wipe a few tears away and cough once. "Which is why I still think we need Dr. Campbell."

"Doctor who?" Chuck asks. "Why, Doctor Who, of course! No, but really. Who are we discussing?"

"Nunya," Bumper replies.

"Nunya what?"

"Nunya damn business," he says.

"I walked right into that one, didn't I." To his credit, Chuck gets a good laugh from Bumper's joke.

I hesitate to give Sir Charles any more intel than he needs about humanity, or our plans, fledgling as they may be, to rescue the people of New York City. But if he's sworn to protect us, and I believe he's telling the truth, then doing so will only add to the bridge of trust that we're constructing together. "Dr. Campbell is Earth's leading expert on the gate we found in Antarctica. I'm assuming you know about it already."

"My. Whatever are you talking about?"

"He knows," Hollywood says.

"Yeah, he does," adds Bumper.

"Well, if you think he can assist you," Chuck says with a studious tone. "Then by all means, let's proceed."

"Circle back for one second," Bumper says. "I still wanna know how the hell you know English and Monty Python and Fight Club."

"Gotta be the Internet," Z-Lo says. "It's the only way."

"Bravo, Private Laszlo. It is indeed."

The kid doesn't seem to be done with his thoughts yet. "But if you're connected to... then that means... Hey, wait. You're not gonna nuke us, are you?"

"Oh shit. What's this now?" Bumper asks, stepping forward.

"Man," Z-Lo says. "If the aliens are patched into the Internet, they could launch all our—"

"Oh, for the love of the Pearly Gates. I'm not going to launch ICBMs, Private Laszlo. And nor are my former masters. I already made it clear that they are slavers, not maniacal megalomaniacs. Though, now that I say that out loud, I realize the number of similarities between the two. Perhaps I could have used a better—"

"Chuck," I say in an effort to keep him on task.

"My apologies. No, the Androchidans will not be blowing anyone up so long as Earth's apex species comes willingly. And so far, you've all been doing marvelously. Though, from your perspective, I recognize—"

"Chuuuuuck?" I say again.

"Yes." He clears his throat. "While your species does pose some value to the Androchidans dead—which would require a rather disgusting commentary on gastrointestinal orgies—"

"You mean organs?" I ask.

"No. Orgies. As I was saying, humanity is far more valuable to them alive than dead. Secondly, and far more poignantly, I might add, is the fact that the world's communication and ordnance launch systems have been rendered inert, making it impossible for me or anyone else to activate said weapons even if we were connected to your old World Wide Web."

"Hold up," I say. "Our *old* World Wide Web?"

"And no one calls it that anymore, okay?" Hollywood seems to be addressing both Chuck and me. "That went out like twenty years ago."

"Ah," Chuck and I say at the same time.

I turn on the gun. "But what's this about being old? Did you do something to it?"

"Hmmm. Let me double-check this… yes… Yes, I can share. To use your vernacular, we downloaded it and then shut it down."

I share looks with the rest of the team. While I'm no expert on IT like Yoshi seems to be, I can tell from the pale look on his face that this is intense.

Doc stammers for a second or two before getting his words right. "You, you, you downloaded…?"

"Your Internet," Chuck says.

Yoshi removes his glasses. "The whole—?"

"The whole thing. Yup."

"But, that must be upwards of—"

"Of over two-hundred zettabytes of raw data? You better believe it was. And at your current Internet speeds, it would have taken us a few billion years to make the transfer. Fortunately for us, however, we use quantum interfaces that tend to, you know, speed things up a touch."

Yoshi's still putting all this together, based on how he's begun pacing back and forth in front of my Land Cruiser. We give him some room.

"So you're telling me that you have two hundred zettabytes of data stored in you right now?" Yoshi asks.

"Don't be ridiculous. Do I look like an NM-QS-NSDV2 to you?" Chuck pauses. "Never mind. You don't have to answer that. I don't resemble one. So, no, Phantom Doc. I was given access to military information, including locations of your defense installations, that my host, for lack of a more exact term, has given me— data that she believes is imperative for effective target acquisition, tracking, and termination."

"And somehow that includes Monty Python?" Ghost asks, ever the skeptic.

"I may or may not have discovered a veritable treasure trove of Earth-made entertainment on something called the Pirate's Bay. Movies are my guilty pleasure, though I've hardly had time to watch them all."

"He's a regular criminal," Hollywood says.

"I used a VPN. You can't prove anything."

Bumper's scratching his chin. "So that explains why our bases got torched."

"I can neither confirm nor deny that. Though Tom Cruise has given me several wonderful insights into planning impossible missions."

I roll my eyes. "And then you just shut the whole Internet down? *Poof*. And it's gone?"

"I mean, it's not as easy as *poof*. But between the planet-wide EMP and what you might call a virus, we—"

"Planet-wide EMP?" I walk forward and pull Chuck off the hood. "You mean to tell us that—"

"That New York City isn't the only metroplex the Androchidans are after? Hmmm. I could only answer that question were you to express resolute intent on visiting—oh, I don't know—say, Beijing."

"I want to visit Beijing," I say quickly. I don't have time for his games right now.

"Then I would strongly discourage you from attempting to do so," Chuck replies.

"As in, for my overall safety and well-being."

"Quite so, yes."

"Then it's as bad as we thought," Ghost says, looking the group over. "They're everywhere."

Yoshi drapes his hands over his SCAR 15. "So we've got an advanced alien weapon that has half the Internet in his head, an evil empire that wants to enslave the planet, and a professor we need to track down who can help fill in the blanks on exactly how this happened. Does that about sum it up?"

"Yut," I say. "Anyone else need a drink?"

21

0900, Friday, June 25, 2027
New Brunswick, New Jersey
Rutgers University

It's 0900 on the dot as we roll onto Rutgers' Cook/Douglas Campus along George St. The scenery isn't as nice as the historic Ivy League schools. Still, the deciduous trees and stone buildings offer a sense of nostalgia that makes the state school feel more expensive to attend than it probably is. But that's where my praise ends.

Based on the blown-out windows, furniture on the lawns, and abandoned cars, it seems that whatever students and faculty were left here on summer break abandoned ship in a hurry. That and looters have already hit the grounds hard. It still amazes me that people can be concerned about stealing material possessions during an emergency when they'd be much better served by seeking safe cover and pooling essential resources. Desperate people do stupid things.

Like try and walk over a burned bridge to an old friend, hoping there's enough to support your weight.

The fact is, I'm not looking forward to reconnecting with Aaron. The last time we saw each other, we put people in body bags, and he wasn't talking to me. I'm sure he blames me for what happened to Lewis and Dr. Walker. I get that. Anyone who's been in command of a unit that's lost lives knows the cost of being at the top. Whether or not it was your fault, you're the one at the helm. If everything goes right, you get none of the glory, and if anything goes wrong, you get all of the blame.

I don't expect that Aaron will forgive me anytime soon. What I am hoping, however, is that he's still alive and that he's willing to help us. That is, of course, assuming that he has something helpful to contribute. If not, then this was a brief errand that, in the end, cost us very little time. Even the faintest hint of a lead when there are scant few is one you've gotta follow.

"Phantom One. This is Three. Over."

It's Bumper.

"Send it."

"Any read on where we're headed?"

"Wait one."

"Hey, Sir Charles," I say to the gun in the passenger seat. "You wouldn't happen to have a map of Rutgers University on hand, would you?"

After a two-second pause, the gun replies, "Unfortunately, no. That is outside of the data packet I was allotted."

"Roger. It was worth a try."

"I am, however, able to direct you toward any heat signatures that I discover."

"You have heat sensors?"

"Among others, yes. Though, I must warn you that they are prone to producing false positives depending on range and environmental scenarios."

"Roger. Let's give it a whirl. Whaddya say?"

"A whirl it is, old bean."

I open the channel again to Bumper. "Seems Phantom Lord over here has got some fancy-ass sensors onboard. Taking lead position."

"Roger."

"I say, did you just assign me a team call sign?" Chuck asks over the radio. Apparently he's rather proud of it. Or is it disturbed? I can't tell yet.

"Yut," I say over the channel. "We can squabble about it later." Then, off comms, I add, "Figured all you British *sirs* are lords or barons or some crap. Might as well make it official."

"Huh. I... I'm moved, Patrick. And here I was going to settle for Team Ass Wiper or some such thing. But an actual lord? I don't know what to say."

"Just so we're clear, you're not an actual lord. It's more like an honorary thing. So don't let it—"

"All hail me," he says over comms. "Lord of the Guns."

"—get to your head."

"Did he just make a Lord of the Flies joke?" Bumper asks.

I give Chuck a half-smile. "Well?"

On the unit channel, he says, "I thought it was rather clever."

"Oh, it's something," Bumper replies.

My whole point in giving Chuck the call sign was to make him lower his guard a little more. Which it might. But it turns out the damn thing is just endearing himself to me more. And getting wise.

"Hey," I say to Chuck. "If you're gonna talk on comms like that, can you at least, I don't know, encrypt our transmissions or something?" It's bad enough that he doesn't have any comms discipline, but the fact that he could very well be broadcasting our location to the enemy is not awesome. The least he can do is cover our asses a little.

"Most definitely, Patrick. In fact, I began doing so after you hurled me out the window on the Garden State Parkway."

"You did?"

"Yes. And you do recall, don't you, when you threw me out of your moving vehicle, leaving me vulnerable, exposed, and utterly alone?"

"Laying it on a little thick, aren't you?"

"Well, it was a memorable moment for me. I mean, have *you* ever been thrown from a vehicle traveling in speeds exceeding ninety-five kilometers per hour? And in the prime of your life, left to die in a barren wilderness?"

"Actually, yut. I have."

"Exactly! And had you, you would... Wait, you have?"

I give him a click in the side of my cheek to confirm.

"Oh, good heavens! Do you need to talk about it?"

"Moving on. What did you do with our transmissions?"

"Of course." He takes a second, as if composing himself.

Talk about dramatic.

"Since the Androchidans possess numerous other technologies that make your radio transmissions, shall we say hazardous, I took the liberty of enabling a type of radio blackout so as to ensure directive alpha."

Noticing that his words went out over comms, I open the channel to make sure the team understands him. "Everyone copy that?"

"Roger," they say one at a time.

I raise an eyebrow at Chuck. "Well, that was smart. Thanks."

"My pleasure."

"Think you can start scanning now?"

"Please. I'm already done," he says over the channel. "And I am happy to report that I have eliminated at least four false positives. Likewise, I believe I have determined the location of your Doctor Who friend."

"That was fast. How sure are you that it's him?"

"Based on what I know of you and academic doctors thus far, I eliminated several individuals. For instance, the couple currently engaged in coitus in Hickman Hall. The elevated heart rate and body temperature of the female, in particular, would suggest that very soon she is going to——"

"Okay, Mr. Peeping Tom. Spare us the details."

"I'm interested, though," Z-Lo says.

"Shut up, kid," I say.

"Shutting up, sir."

I close the channel and look at Chuck. "Just give me the doc's location and the probability that you think it's him."

"To what degree of certitude? I am able to provide it up to 0.0001 percent."

I frown at him. "I'm just looking for high or low, Chuck."

"In that case, high. In fact, if you're able to raise and point me at 346 degrees level to the horizon, I may be able to verify my findings further."

I want to offer a sarcastic question about Chuck shooting Aaron.

CHRISTOPHER HOPPER & J.N. CHANEY

And the gun could very well do it too. But if he wanted to kill anyone, he would have shot a Phantom first. Plus, our whole dialogue about guns not killing people felt sincere. Yut, so I'm still wrestling things through. But I'm also still alive, aren't I?

"If your momentary pause is because you're worried that I might shoot your friend—"

"Now why would you say a thing like that?"

"Well, your heart rate increased, and I noticed a fluctuation in pupil dilation signaling apprehension caused by—"

"Hey. Cut that out."

"You mean, stop monitoring your vital signs?"

"Yut."

"But, that's a core function of my—"

"Don't care. Cut it out."

"Huh. Well… You know that makes it very hard for me to do my job, don't you?"

"Life's a bitch. Adapt, improvise, overcome."

"What?"

"Figure out something else."

He lets out a long sigh. "If you insist."

I grab Sir Charles and lay him across the dashboard, using my windshield compass as a guide. Dammit, I can't help myself. "Don't you shoot him."

"I knew it," Chuck says.

"Whatever."

Two seconds pass before Chuck says, "Turn right on Chemistry Drive."

"Here?"

"Yes, here. Do you really think there's another Chemistry Drive on this campus? Or are you just inefficient at reading signage while underway? Tosser."

"Hey," I say with an edge to my voice. I don't know what name he just called me or where he's gotten the sudden snark from, but I don't like it. I mean, I do. But that kind of thing can get out of hand fast if left unchecked. For now, all I can manage as I spin the wheel is, "Watch it, buster."

"I'm not the one driving."

I want to reply further, but I'm too busy taking the sharp turn. It's probably his new title that's made him feel emboldened. What a mistake that was.

"Why are we turning?" Hollywood asks.

"Chuck says he—"

"I have located who I believe is Dr. Aaron Campbell in the Anthropology Department of the Dr. Ruth M. Adams Building."

"That," I add when he's off the channel. To Chuck, I ask, "You got all that off the signs?"

"Indeed I did. Reading simple text is just one of my many skills."

"All right, all right." I slow as we pull up in front of a wide three-story brick building with the word ADAMS carved across a sandstone mantle. I drive around the northeast side of the building and park the Land Cruiser on the lawn near some trees—not a parking place. If we need to make a quick getaway, it's best not to abide by conventional driving standards, which can all begin with where you find cover for your vehicle.

Before getting out, I reach behind the passenger seat and grab a small spool of nylon webbing. It's typically used to strap down loads or fashion a makeshift climbing harness.

"What are you doing?" Chuck asks me.

"How are your capacitors?"

He pauses. "I'm not sure what my capacitor status has to do with your flat rope thingy."

"Can you shoot right now?"

"No. I'm still several hours away from being fully charged."

"So you're worthless as a weapon."

"I mean, I wouldn't say worthless, but... well, yes. Unless you intend to clobber someone over the head with me, then I'd make a fine addition to your arsenal."

"Right." I cut a strip of webbing and then start wrapping it around Chuck. "So, until then, you're going on my back as a guide."

"And let your SCAR have all the fun?"

"Hey, it's not my fault you can't recharge faster."

"But you did shoot me several times."

"Still has nothing to do with your recharge rate."

He sighs. "That's valid."

I finish tying off the improvised sling and climb out of the vehicle. Then I pass my arm and head through the webbing and secure Chuck against my back. "Comfy?"

"Sure. And I have a perfect view of your ass."

"I hear it's all the rage."

"They lied to you."

That makes me laugh. I'm starting to like this new side of Chuck. Again, in moderation. But he's not half bad with the humor thing.

I grab my SCAR and rendezvous with the rest of the team as we approach the front doors.

"He the only one inside?" Hollywood asks me.

Before I can answer, Chuck says, "Affirmative Phantom Two. Second floor, back northeast corner. Copy hard and roger. Over."

She lifts an eyebrow at me.

I shake my head. "He's excited."

"I'm not excited, Patrick. I'm simply settling into my new role as Phantom Lord."

"Which is turning out to be a mistake," I whisper to Hollywood.

"I heard that."

"Yoshi, I want you to stay with the vehicles," I say. "Ghost, you're on overwatch. Bumper, main floor. Hollywood and Z-Lo with me."

"And me. I'm with you also," Chuck says.

"Yut. That you are." I look around. "Unless anyone else wants to take him?"

"He can see chicks through walls, right?" Z-Lo says.

Bumper smacks the back of his helmet, hard. "Shut up, Laszlo."

"Sorry."

I chuckle at the exchange then put on my game face. "Time to OTF."

Bumper grins. "OTF, baby."

THE INSIDE of the Adams Buildings smells old and musty. I don't know if it's the glass-encased walls filled with rocks and ancient artifacts or the world maps and timelines framed along the walls, but if I were in this place at night, I feel like it would be the perfect movie set for a mummy attack.

While Bumper sets up inside the front door, Ghost darts down the hallway and turns right at an intersection, undoubtedly looking for a southern stairwell leading to the roof. Meanwhile, Hollywood, Z-Lo, and I turn left, looking for stairs closer to Aaron's end of things.

Even though Chuck tells me that there's no one else in the building, my weapon is up and ready as I move past labs, closets, and offices. We reach a stairwell at the end of the hall, and I say over comms, "Going up."

"Roof, clear," Ghost says when I reopen the channel. Damn, that guy's fast.

Hollywood takes a position at the base of the stairs to search for threats. She gives the all clear, and Z-Lo and I head up, clearing the switchback and landing. Then Hollywood rejoins our stack on the second floor.

According to the all-wise Phantom Lord, Aaron should be inside the first door on the right.

With my weapon at the alert and pointed at the door, I nod at Z-Lo as we approach the danger area. He tests the handle while Hollywood sets up behind him.

The kid shakes his head slowly to indicate the handle's locked.

I point to him, then to my eyes with two fingers, and I finally indicate the small square window at the door's top.

He nods and is about to edge toward the glass when Hollywood stops him. She pulls out a compact, flips open the small mirror, and hands it to him. It's that kind of quick thinking that keeps people from taking a bullet to the brain. I give her a quick thumbs up.

Z-Lo angles the mirror to see through the window. A sliver of sunlight reflects off his eye before he lowers the compact and gives me the okay sign.

I move in to peek through the window and catch a glimpse of Aaron seated at a desk surrounded by open books and piles of documents. Just as I thought. There's a national crisis, and what's the man doing? Working. Saints bless him.

"How you wanna play this, Guns?" Z-Lo whispers.

I'm betting the kid wants to bust the door down. But based on what Aaron and I went through in Antarctica, I'm guessing my old friend doesn't need any more excuses to freak out.

"The old fashioned way," I say. Then I stand upright and knock twice on the window, followed quickly by, "Hey, Aaron. It's Patrick."

Z-Lo looks surprised and then disappointed. Finally, he decides to mirror my position on the opposite side while Hollywood preps to fill in behind us. In a combat scenario, once the door is breached, I take right, Z-lo takes left, and Hollywood takes center. But it isn't going to come to that here.

I motion the kid to lower his Tavor, and then I repeat myself, a little louder this time. "Aaron. It's me, Patrick. Open up." I'm tempted to look through the window again when two gunshots blow out the glass and punch a hole in the door.

22

"Aaron! For the love of God, stop shooting," I yell.

But he doesn't.

Three more rounds come in quick succession as the bullets punch through the door in random places. One thing's for sure, my pal's got horrible marksmanship. And I'm guessing he's shooting a .357-caliber magnum revolver with a six-round cylinder. Which means he has one shot left.

"Arron, it's—"

Bang. The last round blasts a hole in the wooden door. That's our cue.

I nod at Z-Lo. He steps back and then kicks the door in beside the handle panel. The barrier splinters and caves in on the first try. Kid's got some horsepower.

A muffled yelp comes from the other side of the door. I peel into the lab, clearing the right corner, and notice that Aaron's been flung back and collided with a table and chairs. At the same time, Z-Lo sweeps the room's left corner for threats, while Hollywood covers Aaron. She keeps her AR-15 trained on him just to make sure he doesn't go for his weapon again. It's nothing personal, it's just how we do things.

Judging by the way Aaron is sprawled on the floor, he was standing way too close to his target. I'm guessing his ears will be ringing for a few hours too.

"Clear," the kid says.

I nod at Hollywood, who then retrieves the handgun from the ground and searches Aaron for any more weapons, but he's clean.

"Hey, Wic." Hollywood holds up the Ruger GP100 .357-Magnum revolver, pops open the stainless steel cylinder, and let's a seventh round drop into her hand.

"Son of a bitch could have killed me," Z-Lo says in a tone that verges on being freaked out.

"Well, he didn't," I say. "And that's what matters."

"Yeah, but he——"

"Z-Lo," Hollywood says. "Take the hall."

"Roger, Sergeant."

Then she examines the last bullet. "Buffalo Bore 180-grain Cast Outdoorsman. No wonder he made Swiss cheese out of that thing." She tosses and catches the round and stuffs it in a pocket; I'm guessing for good luck. Then she helps me get a dazed Aaron to his feet and offers him a chair.

The professor is still wearing the tweed jacket, Star Wars t-shirt, and glasses that he was wearing for the TV interview. He also has a nice bump on his forehead from where Z-Lo hit him with the door.

"It really is you," Aaron says to me while adjusting his glasses.

"Yut. You okay?"

"Sure, sure. Fine. Just... startled."

I nod toward the gun. "First time you ever shoot that thing?"

"Yeah. Got it when I came home."

"I don't blame you. But I might recommend taking it to a range a few times before you try whatever that was again." I thumb toward the door.

"Noted."

I smile at him, then start making introductions. "This here's Sergeant Susanne Catania, US Army."

"Just call me Hollywood." She shakes Aaron's hand.

"And out there's Z-Lo. You can just call him Z-Lo."

"That's me," says the kid with a wave inside the room.

"Nice to meet you," Aaron says.

Just then, the radio opens up. "Phantom Three to Phantom One. Everything good up there?" asks Bumper.

"The asset just got a little startled, is all," I reply. "We're good to go."

"Roger."

"We've got three more around the building." Not willing to ignore the elephant in the room, I decide to get the hard part over with first. I pull up a chair and sit. "Listen. About the South Pole, I—"

"You don't need to say anything, Pat."

I raise both eyebrows at him. "Why's that?"

"I know you did your best—what you thought was right. I've been doing a lot of thinking, and I was wrong to blame you. It was an accident that we were all a part of, and I… should have been more careful. I just didn't expect that… well…" His eyes focus on something in the near distance.

"Hey. None of us did."

"No." He shakes his head. "You did."

I'm not gonna argue with him there. But I also know when to take someone's apology and keep my damn mouth shut. "We're both here now, and that's what matters. But I'm sorry about your team's losses."

"And I'm sorry for yours. Simmons, was it?"

"Among others, yut. Good man."

A moment of silence passes, and I see Hollywood tap the back of her wrist.

"Aaron, buddy, listen. My new friends and I are working on something that we need your help with. We think that this dome is herding people toward—"

"Toward lower Manhattan in order to get them off-planet?" Aaron's eyes are bright again and darting around.

I blink twice at him. "Well, it wasn't that specific yet but…"

"My, my, my," Chuck says from behind my back. "We have a regular Sherlock Holmes here."

"Who was that?" Aaron asks.

"Eh, it's one of the team." I'm not sure Aaron's ready for a talking alien gun just yet, so I grab my radio's receiver and pretend like I'm talking over comms. "Keep it down, Chuck."

"Roger Dodger, old bean."

Aaron gives me a curious look but seems to buy the act.

I motion him to go on.

"Anyway. I made some estimates based on the data we collected at Ellsworth." He's on his feet and headed for his desk. "Granted, it's all pencil and paper at this point. And without spectrometry, they're just educated guesses really."

Aaron pulls up several pages of drawings and numbers and starts handing them to me and Hollywood one at a time. There are several sketches of the dome in three dimensions, each way better than mine. But what interests me the most is a funnel-like tube that seems to emanate from somewhere in the middle, shoot up from a center-point on the ground, and then fan outward to form the dome's shape. And there, at ground-zero, is something all too familiar.

"A ring?" I ask, looking up at him.

He nods. "Again, it's just a guess. But I feel confident."

"Are those drawings? May I see?" Chuck asks.

I grab the receiver again and try to suppress my annoyance. "In a second."

Aaron smiles. "He seems persistent."

"You have no idea." I tap the page I'm holding again. "Why a ring?"

Aaron waves a finger in the air. "Yes, excellent question."

He turns around to an old-school blackboard that lines the rear wall. It's covered in chalk drawings that look like they belong in an Indiana Jones movie. Geometry, rings, formulas, coordinates—I'd be lucky to interpret a quarter of it.

"Using old colored gels from the theatre department that I keep on-hand to show students the basics of light dispersion in early stained glass applications, I was able to deduce that the light on the dome's outer edges has many of the same properties as the light we recorded from the robots particle emitters." He hands me a stack of papers with streams of data printed on them.

"Which means?"

"Well, I haven't been close enough to the dome to verify this, but I'm guessing it's dangerous."

"You can say that again," Hollywood says.

"It is dangerous," Chuck confirms. "Did that do it for you, Phantom Two?"

She gives me a half-smile. "Sure did."

"Most excellent."

I motion for Aaron to keep going.

"It also seems to be reliant on an inconsistent energy source."

"How so?" I ask.

"Well, the dome's luminescence seems to dim slightly over time, followed by a sudden resurgence. The durations seem to vary."

"Maybe my eyes aren't so old after all," I say to myself.

"What's that?" Aaron asks.

"Nothing. Just think I noticed the dimming thing too. Any guesses on what's causing it?"

"Intermittent power source maybe? Meanwhile"— he points to a chalk drawing resembling the ring at the South Pole—"there are traces of light similar to that of the ring's portal threshold located here"—he taps on the page in my hand depicting the dome—"in the middle of the dome."

"So, based on the light you're picking up, you think there's another ring in the middle of all this?" I ask.

He nods. "I mean, I can't say for sure without being at ground zero—ironic that it's lower Manhattan, right?—but I have enough evidence to at least postulate the existence of a ring portal. Why else would a fence constrict around a population? I mean, unless the aliens are simply hellbent on annihilation, there are far easier ways to remove a populace. Whatever they're doing, they're trying to corral and relocate us."

I share a look with Hollywood, but before we can bring Aaron up to speed, he jumps in again.

"There's more too."

"More?" I ask. "Go on."

"I think I know why they're here."

Hollywood shoots me a raised eyebrow. Now this could be interesting.

"I didn't show you this before, mostly because I didn't have the translation codex complete."

"Codex?"

He snaps his fingers a few times. "Decoder ring. A key."

"Roger."

He pulls out several more sheaves of paper, some printed, some written by hand, and gives them to me. I'm forced to set the previous pages down as it's getting to be too much to hold.

"You see these?"

"I do. Looks like... what's it called again? Sanskrit?"

"Older. Cuneiform. But I think it's even older than cuneiform."

"Hold up. So, older than the oldest known written language? Or am I missing something?"

He gives me a boyish grin and yanks one of the pages from my hands. "It seems to share the origin of all written communication. A truly primitive logophonetic consonantal alphabet of syllabic signs."

"Logo-what?"

"Logophonetic. Uh, Chinese and Japanese kanji are logograms, as are certain Egyptian hieroglyphs. But cuneiform can be traced back through Indo-European families in Hittite and Luwian writings to the Semitic language. Of course, it's mostly foreign to modernists since English is derived from the Phoenician alphabet and has—"

"Aaron. We don't have a lot of time here, so you think maybe you can…" I roll my index finger a few times.

"Ah, sure. Sorry. All I'm getting at is that what you see here is an early cousin to the oldest known languages."

"A cousin?" Hollywood asks. "I was kinda expecting you to say it was the great grandparent or something."

"And you would, yes!" Aaron starts waving his hands around. "Instead, it's as if someone was attempting to forecast where the day's language might go, but in the end failed to account for natural deviation."

I squint at him. "Meaning?"

"Meaning, the creators of it were conversing with the humans of the day but did not stick around to keep updating their linguistic models. Languages are living things. Always growing, changing, adapting. Oftentimes, they can be more revealing than biology when it comes to telling us about a person or people group."

I realize I need to try harder at keeping Aaron on task. "So this specific language is important to us right now because…?"

"Because it was found on the Ellsworth ring, and it wasn't until I saw the dome that I figured out the full translation. Or at least what I believe is the full translation. All translations are merely interpretations of—"

"Got it. And what's it say, bossman."

He snaps his fingers again and then darts over to a rolling blackboard plastered with papers, articles, and photographs. Then he flips it around to show an exposed section of slate in the middle filled with chalk words.

I read it aloud. "At dawn's puzzle solved, when child is high sized, we return to gather enlightened." I look at Aaron. "What is it? A riddle? Poem?"

"Neither. But that's far from the point, Pat. Don't you see it? This"—he taps the words, smudging the chalk—"this is an origin story! This is them coming to… to…"

"To what?"

"To save us!"

"Oh, bloody hell," Chuck says. "I can't take it anymore. Patrick, would you please take me off your back and allow me to speak to this charming albeit completely misguided wanker?"

"Be my guest," I reply, looking at a frowny-faced Aaron. I unsling Chuck and set him down on top of the cluttered desk. "I present to you, Sir Charles."

"Also known as Phantom Lord," Chuck adds.

Aaron backs into the rolling blackboard. "Is that one of the—"

"Hello, Dr. Campbell. It's a pleasure to make your acquaintance."

Aaron looks between me and the weapon several times. "Is that—?"

"An alien rifle?" I reply and then nod.

"And it's—?"

"Talking?" Hollywood adds. "You betcha."

"But how did you… and where does it… and it talks?"

"I like this one," Chucks says, sounding as if it's directed at me. "He's far less abrasive than you, Patrick."

"Yut."

"And he uses your language far more articulately."

"Uh-huh."

Aaron seems to recover a bit and approaches Chuck like a child might approach a snake that they've just seen devour a mouse: cautious but fascinated. "Is it safe?"

"My dear man, I am as safe as a rock. But if some numbskull

wishes to hurl said rock at someone's head, can I be blamed for being the instrument of death?"

Aaron looks up at me. "And he's a philosopher?"

"Don't encourage him."

"No, please do," Chuck says. "I've had to run around with these gun-wielding wazzocks for the last hour."

"Wazzocks?" I say.

"It's a compliment."

"Sure it is." English expletives aren't exactly my strong suit, but I'm a decent judge of tone and subtext. "Can we move this along?"

Chuck clears his digital throat. "Dr. Campbell. While I will endeavor to answer all of your questions when time allows, the most pressing matter is to—well, put mildly—lay waste to your assertion regarding the Androchidans' intentions for your species."

Aaron looks up at me, eyes as wide as a child's on Christmas morning. "Androchidans? That's their name?"

"Focus, Dr. Campbell, please."

Aaron snaps back to Chuck with his mouth agape.

"As I was saying, the text you deciphered—which, I might add, you did a refreshingly marvelous job interpreting, given the many I've seen. Sometimes I wonder how certain species ever managed to solve—"

"Chuck," I say.

"Ah, yes. Now look: *I'm* the one rambling. Aaron and I really are two peas in a pod, n'est-ce pas?"

"Let's wrap it up."

"Quite so, yes. Dr. Campbell, I'm not sure how to put this elegantly, but your hypothesis about the Androchidans' intentions is a load of bollocks."

Aaron stammers. "I'm... uh, excuse me?"

"They're here to enslave you and sell you to the highest bidder. Anyone they can't sell, they... how shall I put this? They snack on. Like one of your Slim Jims."

Aaron's mouth is open, but no words are coming out.

I put a hand on his shoulder. "Hard to swallow, I know."

"Actually, they have no problems swallowing the——"

"Chuck!"

"Ah. Yes. As I was saying, while your translation is commendable, the inscription left on the origin ring you discovered was, for lack of a better term, a sham. The subtext could better be read in this fashion: When your muppet brains evolve to a sufficient level, we'll be back to harvest you."

"Oh, God." Aaron puts a hand on the side of his head. "Are you absolutely sure?"

"Yes, old chum. I'm the talking alien gun, remember? Did you expect me to lie?"

"I don't know what I expected, but——"

"Well, I don't lie to my users or their mates, and I don't plan to start now."

Chuck's honesty is compelling. He's either deliberately trying to gain my trust for a subversive purpose, or being genuine. Either way, it's unsettling, and I can't help but wonder if he knows that I know what he's doing.

Damn.

Sometimes knowing how to play chess sucks.

"And so we evolved enough to..." Aaron seems to lose himself in the possibilities and then snaps back when he figures it out. "To solve the puzzle."

"I can neither confirm nor deny the tactics the Androchidans employ to subdue their merchandise. I believe your equivalent might be that fishermen don't tell the fish what kind of lures work best. But I can at least respond to your assertion with a stroke of my beard and a long, 'Hmmmm.'"

"So that's it then," Aaron says to me. "We signaled them. *I* signaled them. Oh, Heaven Almighty. What have I done?" He steadies himself with two hands on his desk. "It's… it's all my fault."

I catch Aaron's shoulders. "You okay there, pal? You're looking a little pale."

"I opened the door, Patrick."

Ah, crap. He's gonna pass out.

"Stay with me, Aaron."

But it's too late.

Aaron's eyes roll back in his head, and he collapses into my arms.

"Do humans faint often, or is this just something you two have in common?" Chuck asks me.

WITHIN SECONDS of getting Aaron back on his feet, Ghost hails me.

"Phantom One, this is Watch."

"Send it."

"I've got an ARU approaching from the west. ETA one mike."

I glance at Hollywood and then Aaron. "Time to move. You have any more ammunition for your piece?"

"The revolver?" Aaron shakes his head. "It's all back at the house."

"We leave it. Come on." Then the severity of our timetable dawns on me, and I reply to Ghost. "We won't make the vehicles in time."

"Roger."

"What's the play?" Bumper asks.

I look at Chuck. "Did you do this?"

"Did I do what? You mean, lure them here? Patrick, I feel—"

"Yes or no."

"No. And for the record, I already told you—"

"Is there any chance they drive past us?"

"Are we doing the whole vague probabilities thing again?" he replies.

"Yes."

"Then no, there is almost no chance they drive away from this many active heat signatures in one building."

"What's their engagement strategy?"

"Mmm. Yes. This… well. You see, while we can discuss matters pertaining to you and your survivability all day long, unfortunately, I am unable to divulge specific data about the Androchidans that may undermine—"

"Would this include how many enemies are in the transport?"

"Unfortunately, yes."

"And how 'bout you? You ready to fire?"

"My capacitors are at 90 percent. Since I typically recharge at a rate of one percentage point per minute with a minimum recharge threshold of—"

"Works for me." I open the channel. "We've got to draw them away from the building. We cannot afford to lose our wheels."

"There's a large brick home in the middle of the quad to our south, and more buildings past it to the southeast," Ghost says. "Plenty of tree cover along the way."

"And I've got a clear exit out the back to the building," Bumper says.

"Everyone to the exit double-time and head for the brick home," I order. "Let's move." Then to Aaron, I say, "Hope you've been exercising."

"I just need a minute to grab my things."

I take him by the elbow and usher him toward the door. "Sorry, old friend, but you take what's on you."

23

0923, Friday, June 25, 2027
New Brunswick, New Jersey
Rutgers University, Cook/Douglas Campus, Adams Building

I ESTIMATE we have fifteen seconds left by the time we rendezvous with Ghost, Bumper, and Yoshi at the ground-level back door. Everyone moves out of the building and heads along the tree-lined sidewalk toward an old brick mansion with a sign that reads College Hall: OIT Administration. In a pinch, we could set up here, but the structure is in the middle of the quad and gives the enemy a chance to surround us. If we have the time, I'd rather make it to the quad's far side and narrow the enemy's possible approach vectors.

"SITREP, Chuck?"

"As in, you would like me to provide you with a situation report? My, this military-speak makes me feel so official."

347

"Dammit, gun. What is the enemy doing?"

"It's hard to say. I'm currently looking at your ass, once again."

In a long-practiced mid-stride action, I sling my SCAR and raise Chuck, then sidestep so his scope can get a good look at the building behind us.

"It seems that two *death angels,* as you so dramatically call them, are moving into the building while three of your *assault bots* are moving around the structure. And might I add—"

"Can we make it to the quad's far side?"

"Well, if you don't want to hear what I want to add, why should I—"

"It's my well-being, remember?"

"Mmmm. How inconvenient for me. Fine, yes. I think you have ample time to cross the open ground so long as you stay in the visual shadow of the domicile ahead. Additionally, I can also make use of my EMDE that will—"

"Your what?"

"Electromagnetic disruption emitter that will temporarily interfere with their ability to target you so long as you stay together. It will buy you a few additional moments."

"Sure, fine." I have no idea what that means, but disrupting target-lock is always favorite.

Assuming everyone else heard the exchange, I pick up the pace and follow the sidewalk around the admin house to head toward a block of large buildings that, according to the lawn-mounted direction signs, include a chapel to the left, a library in the center, and some residence buildings to the right.

Despite the structural integrity that the chapel might provide, I've always had a thing about bringing war into houses of worship. Call me old-fashioned. I'm also not convinced that the Almighty approves of my line of work, so I'm doubtful he'd endorse my plea for help should it ever be sent.

That said, not everyone shares my convictions, and the person I want on that chapel roof is probably already thinking that's where he wants to be too. I'll let St. Peter sort us out when we get to the pearly gates.

"We set up on the library," I say as we continue to run. It's a humble two-story affair with good sight-lines to the quad. Then I nod to the chapel coming up on the left. "Ghost, I want you in that belfry."

"Moving."

Chuck interrupts me. "Ghost will no longer be covered by my—"

"Your electron distortion thing. Got it." I point to the front left face of the library. "Bumper, northwest corner. Z-Lo, southwest. Hollywood and Yoshi, you're supporting. I'm headed to that residence building to the right. You're gonna draw the bots into a kill box out front, while Ghost and I take out the death angels."

"Roger," they all reply.

"Aaron, I want you to follow Hollywood inside, then split off head straight to the back. Find cover and stay there until we come get you." I remove my Glock and hand it to him. "Point and squeeze. Nothing fancy."

He nods, pushes his glasses up, and then accepts the weapon like I've handed him a bomb. Sure, he just used a revolver to blast some holes in a lab door, but this weapon is different.

"Point and squeeze," I say again, trying to calm him.

"Point and squeeze. Okay. I got it."

The team breaches the front doors with Aaron in tow and then starts clearing to their respective positions. The main reason I chose the library for Aaron and the majority of the team is that it offers an ample supply of round-stopping barricades: namely, bookshelves. A two-inch textbook might not seem like a lot, but stack a few together, and you've got a bullet-stopping wall that any Marine in a danger area would happily take cover behind. That is, assuming the alien's energy weapons behave like our projectile weapons. Which, now that I think of it, they probably don't.

Crap.

By the time I'm positioned in a back stairwell on the residence building's second level, I hear Ghost call out over comms. His shadow is barely visible through the slats in the whitewashed bell tower.

"Five tangos, inbound from the west."

I look west and make out some movement behind the mid-quad brick home. I'm about to thank the saints that Ghost hasn't mentioned anything about the ARU, seeing how it has a driver and turret gunner. But then he adds, "ARU, southside of the Adams Building."

Well that's not great.

"All posts, check-in," I say.

"Phantom Two, roger," Hollywood says.

"Phantom Three, set," Bumper says.

"Cocked, locked, and ready to rock." That's Z-Lo, all right.

"Phantom Watch, roger," Ghost says.

"Doc, all set," Yoshi adds.

"And Phantom Lord of lower-case hosts is ready to visit his holy wrath upon thine cheese-eating surrender twats," Chuck cries out. "God save the queen, and damn the Norman invaders to hades! We fart in your general direction."

"Zip it, Charlie." That said, I still stifle a laugh. "Phantom

Three and Four, you're up. Watch, I want us holding fire until the bots are committed. Wait for my go."

"Roger," Ghost says, followed by affirmatives from Bumper and Yoshi.

"And me?" Chuck asks privately.

"How many shots you have in you?"

"That's a highly complex answer, Patrick. It all depends on which mode, rate, and magnitude you select. Additionally, my capacitors recharge on an algorithmic curve that—"

"Bossman, this is all vital stuff, I know. But we've got death angels coming around that corner. I've gotta be sure we can take them down."

"Um. See, the thing about being your personal super-smart ultimate weapon is that I'm, well, yours, I'm super-smart, and I'm pretty ultimate. So, to quote a very wise person I know, point and squeeze, Patrick. Point and squeeze."

THE THREE BOTS are walking across the quad's east side, headed straight for the library, with the two death angels close behind. I'm not sure how sensitive the alien's heat-sensing tech is, but if they picked us up inside the Adams Building, I'm guessing they're picking us up now too. I'm just hoping they stay on the library and dismiss Ghost's and my locations.

For their part, the death angels are playing it safe. Instead of strutting around in the open like the one back on the parkway did, these are staying covered behind the robotic armor. Smart. Wonder if word's gotten out that some of the merchandise got ahold of one of their blasters.

"Keep coming," I whisper as I look down Chuck's scope. I picture the grotesque green skin, green veins, and vertical mouth—things look like a Venus flytrap or something. "Just a little bit more."

"Do you wish me to shoot now?" Chuck asks.

His voice startles me off my scope. I blink twice and get back on target. Unless you've ever had a weapon talk to you, there's really no way to describe just how unsettling it is. "I'll let you know when I squeeze. How's that, pal?"

"You just seem hesitant. Your trigger finger's pressure fluctuations seem to indicate—"

"Dude. When I squeeze the goddamn trigger, you'll know."

"I was merely trying to be helpful. Also, you are about to lose the cover of my EMDE."

"Okay, thanks." I focus on the highlighted images in the scope. "The display says I'm on high-frequency mode. That like what I'm used to?"

"Nothing about me is like what you're used to, Patrick."

"I…" I work my jaw and remind myself to take deep breaths. "Just, what's a full-power, no nonsense, semi-automatic burst?"

"High frequency, high yield will accomplish roughly what you need."

"Roughly?"

"Do we have time for me to explain all the butter-filled nooks and crannies of my beautiful inner-workings?"

"Negative."

"Then it's roughly what you need."

"Roger."

I can't get the reticle on more than a brief moment of the left-hand death angel; the two tangos are only visible between momentary gaps in the bots' swinging arms and legs. The aliens seem to know where to stay. And yet neither of them have their weapons raised, which means they must not think we're a threat yet. At least that's what they're communicating in human body language. But I've seen advances like this against chess opponents who lower their guard precisely because they know they're about to whomp you. And that makes me even more nervous than if they came in guns blazing.

"Phantoms Three and Four, get ready to engage," I say over comms.

The three bots are seventy-five meters out and still headed straight for the library.

"You know, this is a lot of fun in a very dark sort of way," Chuck says in a hushed tone.

"Not now."

"Imagine the memoir I could write. 'SR-CHK 4110 on Planet Earth, taken captive by primitive merchandise, given new warrior name by elder chieftain, emerges as Sir Charles the Legendary and helps vanquish the very civilization that—'"

"Engage," I order over comms.

Streams of rounds shatter the library's corner windows and streak toward the three assault bots. The tangos recoil and raise their rifles. That's when the death angels use their jet pack things to lift off the ground.

"Phantom Watch, engage." Before I can even squeeze my trigger, I hear the bark of Ghost's Barrett. There's an impact flash in my viewfinder, and his target on the right careens toward mine. The tangos collide but recover quickly. While Ghost fires his second and third rounds, I regain my sight picture and squeeze Chuck's trigger firm enough that he'll never forget.

"Well, hello Dolly," he says.

353

The rifle punches back into my shoulder as a burst of blue light rips across the sky and strikes my target in the chest. I watch in rapt amazement as the short laser beams penetrate the emerald armor plates, supercharge the alien's chest, and then cause the body to detonate, all in a few hundredths of a second. The body armor flings into the bots' backs, as does a green-liquid spray.

"Damn, Chuck," I say.

"Damn indeed, Patrick."

I hear more glass shatter as the bots rake the library's front with rifle rounds. Their weapons don't seem to be as powerful as mine, which certainly explains why they've been less effective at destroying their targets in our previous encounters. But that's not true about the remaining death angel's weapon—another Chuck-style gun.

As if reminding me, Ghost's tango sends an energy blast at the steeple, striking the bell inside the collapsing wreckage. Brick and wood planks radiate out in a perfect circle, leaving the spire to tilt with the sound of groaning trusses. Then the bell crashes down through the building and lands with a thud as the support structure caves in.

My human instinct is to reach out to Ghost, but my Marine head tells me to end the son of a bitch before he can do that again. I pick up the tango and lay Chuck's targeting reticle on its chest. The enemy seems injured, leaking fluid from holes left by Ghost's fifty rounds. When I squeeze Chuck's trigger, a second burst of fire leaps from the barrel. The signature whine-snap sound makes my ears ring even more, but the blast turns the death angel into an iridescent plume of mist and flying armor plates.

"Phantom Watch," I yell over comms. "Come in."

The line opens and he's coughing. "Still here."

A moment later, I see one of the chapel's broken front doors kick out, followed by a white cloud and a figure covered head to toe in dust. Ghost's Barrett is at his shoulder, and he's aiming at the right-hand bot.

Guy's a frickin' machine.

As Hollywood and Yoshi join Bumper and Z-Lo in support positions, I target the bot closest to me. In the scope, I see dozens of rounds-per-second crash against the assault bots' magenta-plated bodies. But thanks to what we've learned, the Phantoms are focusing their fire on the joints—especially the neck.

Ghost breaks his tango's neck after his third shot; guy's probably shaken from the fall. Hell, I'm just happy he's alive. Meanwhile, the library element masses their fire on the middle bot. Right hip, left shoulder, and neck joints succumb in quick succession, leaving the enemy to collapse into a heap.

The last one's mine.

I just so happen to glance at the mode list and spot the word Disruption when the item highlights in bold.

"Good choice, old chum," Chuck says. "Though hardly original."

I don't get what he means or how the mode got selected, but I don't have time to care. I watch as the reticle moves within the scope, followed by the feel of a gyro adjusting my weapon while it's in my damn hands.

"Now, Patrick," Chucks says. "Anytime. Whenever you—"

I squeeze.

The weapon bucks harder than last time, and a horizontal lightning bolt stretches between me and the target. A loud crack hits my ears as the bot fills with blue light and then finally detonates. Orange sparks and red-hot shrapnel fly away, tearing through the trees and drilling holes in cars and buildings.

My heart's racing as I lower Chuck and survey the battlefield. "Report," I say over the radio.

"Phantom Four's been hit," Hollywood says.

Before she can release the receiver's button, I hear Z-Lo yell, "Awww, don't tell him that!"

"But he'll pull through," she adds. "He's getting tended to now."

"Roger."

"That was some badass shooting there," Bumper says.

"Thanks," I reply.

"I believe he was talking to me, Phantom One," Chuck says over comms for all to hear. "And, thank you, Phantom Three."

"But I thought guns don't kill people," I say with a grin.

"*Those* weren't people, Patrick. Those were Androchidans and assault bots. There's a difference. Get it right. Sheesh."

"Ah. I see."

"And don't look now, but the ARU is moving."

Crap. Somehow I'd completely forgotten about the transport.

"Ten o'clock," Ghost says. "Coming in fast."

"Phantoms, take cover. Prepare to engage."

"We'll just leave this one to you," Bumper says. "Have fun."

"Uh, yes. Well, about that," Chuck says.

"Something the matter?" I ask.

"Oh, it's nothing, really."

"Spill it, Charlie."

"Well, if I were a doctor and finishing up your unusually tedious vasectomy, I would say, 'Congratulations! Have as much guilt-free coitus as you want. You're shooting blanks from now on. No one's gonna trace the baby back to you, old bean.'"

"I'm what?"

"Your gun is dry. You're out of ammo. You're—"

"I can't shoot anymore?"

"Not unless you have immediate access to a standardized triple-redundant inline double-walled quantum capacitor matrix with a liquid dusiik heat sink."

"Son of a bitch."

"Nope. I don't need one of those."

"I thought User Eight and I went through a dozen shots or something before you got low?"

"We did. But three minutes ago, you asked for, and I confirmed, 'high frequency, high yield.'"

"I didn't want you to drain your damn batteries in three shots!"

"They're not batteries. They're capacitors. And you should have specified."

"I should've, huh?" I throw Chuck around my back and bring up my SCAR.

"Hey! What are you doing?"

I ignore him. Despite Chuck's truly amazing capabilities, there's something very comforting about holding a tried and true weapon in your hands, one that you trust and know can't talk back. "Looks like we're doing this the old fashioned way."

"So you're done with me then?"

"Yut."

"But I was only—"

"Three hundred yards and closing," Ghost announces.

"Watch. Can you take out the driver like before?" I ask.

"Roger. But nothing we had could take out the turret until you came along with Sir Charles there."

"Huh, imagine that," Chucks says.

"Then we're gonna have to find another way."

I think back to the ARU that we walked through an hour

earlier. Just like our mine-protected clearance vehicles in Afghanistan, the ARU only had one entrance—in the rear. From inside the crew compartment, there was a hole headed to the gunner's position.

"Phantom Three. You still have something on you that will go boom?" I ask.

"I'd sooner not have my boxer briefs," Bumper says.

"Heyo," Hollywood says just quick enough that it doesn't interfere with my reply.

I ignore her. "Then it's you and I sneaking around the backside. Everyone else, we need you to keep that turret distracted. But nothing stupid, and make sure you stay covered. OTF?"

"OTF," they call back.

I'm booking down the stairs when weapons fire starts coming from the library and the chapel and smacks against the ARU's face. In particular, Ghost is putting round after round on the wedge-shaped windshield with pinpoint accuracy; looks like he's got his mojo back.

In the meantime, Bumper is cradling his M249 and running at me like a wide receiver headed for an end zone. Well, a wide receiver who is the size of an offensive lineman. God help whoever wants to stand in that man's way. When he reaches my position, I turn and run alongside him. We use the trees as cover while wrapping around the quad's left side.

The turret opens up on the chapel, probably realizing that the .50-caliber rounds to the windshield pose the most immediate threat. I wince as a loud *boom* comes from the building and blows away most of the right corner. I glance over my shoulder and thank St. Michael when I see Ghost dive away from the wreckage.

But the ARU is still heading toward the library. Yut, it means we have less running to do, but those inside are gonna need to seek cover further back.

"Phantom Two, fall back," I yell.

"Way ahead of you, big man," Hollywood replies.

I hear the Barrett bark one more time and then Ghost's voice comes over comms. "Tango down." The man made the shot from a prone position just beside the mass of debris.

Sure enough, the ARU is slowing. But it's also swerving—toward Bumper and me. It rams into a tree and lists before the trunk snaps, letting the armored transport pass.

"Run," I yell at Bumper.

He finds another gear, and we flee from the out of control hover-vehicle.

The ARU mows down two younger trees as it crosses a short stretch of sidewalk. Ahead there's an old-growth hickory tree.

"There," I say, pointing at the tree. If we can't outrun the damn transport, we might as well try and find cover.

Just as Bumper and I dive into the hickory tree's shadow, the ARU slams against the broad trunk and halts. I roll over in the grass and look up to see a softball-sized hole in the tinted windshield ten feet above me.

"Transport stopped," I say over comms. "Nice work, Watch."

"Roger," Ghost says.

"Come on," Bumper says, patting my shoulder. How he's already on his feet, I have no idea.

Strike that. I do.

Soldiering is a young man's game, always has been. Even against aliens.

I grunt as I get my bag-o-bones up and follow him around the enemy vehicle. The turret gunner hasn't noticed us and is still firing away at the library. Plus, there's no way the weapon can hit us this close to its hull.

The bad news is that we can't get around to the exposed rear entrance without taking friendly fire. Two-two-three rounds are sounding off against the ARU's armored hull like drumsticks performing a roll on a snare drum.

"Check fire, check fire," I say over comms. "Friendlies coming through."

"Checking fire," someone replies—I can't tell who. But the incoming assault stops.

"That's our cue," Bumper says.

I give him a nod, and he mounts the stern. There aren't any stairs this time, so he has to work at scaling into the vehicle like bouldering a small rock face. I stand back and cover from the ground.

Normally, one of us would have tossed a fragmentation grenade into the hold to soften the entry. But Bumper saw the same thing I had in the last ARU: the hole leading into the turret had enough protection that a grenade may not do the job. That would give the enemy time to drop down and defend his position or, worse, shut himself in and make our job way harder. Bumper knew as I did that we'd need to maintain our element of surprise if he was going to leave his gift-wrapped present in the optimum spot on the doormat.

Four interminably long seconds tick by as turret fire berates the library. My only hope is that everyone inside has taken cover in the basement.

Bumper appears in the hold's opening and gives the sign to move out. He bounds down the stern, hits the ground beside me, and then starts running for a small two-story brick home marked Graduate Music House.

The farther he runs, the more I start wondering what kind of care package he left.

"Just how much did you stick up there?"

"Enough," he says.

As soon we're around the small house's backside, he removes a remote det from his chest pouch. He nods at me, and I call out over comms, "Fire in the hole." Then I plug my ears. Not that it matters much at this point, I suppose. Ah, hell, who am I kidding—it matters.

Up goes the yellow firing guard and down goes Bumper's thumb.

THE EXPLOSION SENT the turret pod shooting into the sky like one of those old plastic poppers from the 90s that you'd flip inside out and then place on your kitchen table. As for the ARU itself, Bumper's charge blossomed out the top, leaving a gaping hole with serrated edges pointed toward the sky. The explosion also knocked out the power system and shoved the vehicle into the ground a few feet. Even with my fingers in my ears, my head still felt like someone had just tapped my forehead with a ball-peen hammer.

"So enough means a lot," I say to Bumper as we emerge to survey the damage. "Check."

He shrugs and then starts to inspect his handiwork.

"Tango down, and staying down," I say over comms. "Report."

"Still here," Hollywood says. "Doc's working on Four now. Aaron's shaken but good."

"I bet he is," I say under my breath. Then I wait for Ghost's report. When it doesn't come, I ask, "Phantom Watch. Come in."

"Present," Ghost says. "Just enjoying the blue sky."

Ah, shit. "You hit?"

"Think a brick or two decided to hit on me. But I told them I wasn't interested."

He's making jokes. Which for him isn't good. I can tell by his lazy speech that something ain't right. Blood loss, broken bones maybe.

"Doc, I need you on Ghost's position, double-time."

"On it."

Bumper is poking his head inside the smoldering ARU while I back him up, SCAR raised. But nothing survived that blast. And if it did, I want its autograph.

"Clear," he says.

"You wanna double-check to be sure?" I reply.

He sends me an air kiss, and then we turn toward the chapel.

"How you doing back there, Sir Charles?" I ask.

"Moody," he says.

Bumper and I exchange glances, but I ignore the statement.

"Think we can expect any more company?" I ask.

"No. The coast is bloody-well clear."

"Well, that's good news."

"I suppose, yes. Not that I'd be any good to you if there were more of them."

I'm doing my best not to laugh at Chuck's melodrama. "Dare I ask?"

"Well, if I had known you'd wanted me to conserve energy and that you were going to replace me with that rusty antique of yours, I never would have allowed you to insist on asking me for high-yield discharge in the first place."

"Well," I say with a chuckle. "If it makes you feel any better, Chuck, I didn't end up shooting my antique."

He lets out a long sigh. "I suppose that is some minor consolation, yes. Though, had you died, I would have lamented your loss for at least three one-thousandths of a second. And, before you go saying I'm cold and heartless, I want you to know that in ASIK years, that's a truly long, long time. I might have even thrown you a funeral."

"I'm touched."

"Yes. Well, it's the least I could do for my favorite user."

I give Bumper a raised eyebrow. "Favorite user?"

"I mean, don't go spreading that around the recharging stations or anything."

"Wouldn't dream of it, pal. Thanks."

Ahead, Yoshi is kneeling beside a dust-covered Ghost. I can already see a dark pool caking in the debris.

"How we looking, Doc?" I ask.

Yoshi's working on a spot on Ghost's ribs and another on his left leg. "He'll probably be dead in thirty seconds, so you might as well say your goodbyes now."

Ghost raises a lazy eyebrow at Yoshi and then goes back to staring at the clouds. "You're a lousy liar, PJ." Then he lets out a long sigh. "Death seems to find everyone else but me."

Yut. My heart skipped a beat for a second there. Even still, I can tell Ghost isn't out of the woods yet because Bumper is scooting around to the far side to lend Yoshi a hand. I'm not a medic and never had a desire to be. I was always better at making the enemy bleed. That said, I know that any victim who needs two docs instead of one isn't gonna be running a marathon anytime soon.

Just then, I see Hollywood and Aaron emerge from the backside of the library. Z-Lo's close behind with a sizable burn enveloping his left shoulder.

"You all good?" I yell to Hollywood.

She nods.

Aaron has already passed her the pistol I gave him.

"I need you to bring the Humvee." Then I nod at Z-Lo. "Can you drive?"

"Yes, sir."

"Bring my Land Cruiser."

"Roger that, Guns."

Hollywood sits Aaron down on a bench, and then she and the kid head toward the Adams Building.

I look back at Ghost and see that Yoshi and Bumper have gotten into a friendly pissing contest. You put an Air Force PJ and a Navy SEAL on the same body, and it's bound to happen.

"Yeah? And so how does that work for you?" Yoshi asks Bumper as they tend to Ghost from opposite sides.

"And what's that?"

Yoshi nods at the work Bumper is doing. "You're UDT *and* a Corpsman?"

"Second MOS," Bumper replies. "So, what? You run around blowing guys up so that you have an excuse to work them over a second time?"

Yoshi shakes his head. "That's some crazy stuff, man."

"It's usually not the same guys, Super Nintendo," Bumper replies.

"Damn head trip."

I lean down to break up the friendly chatter. "Anything I can do?"

"You can talk to him," Yoshi says.

"Talk?" I point at Ghost. "To him?"

"I gave him some feel-goods. Trust me."

I nod, having heard that line before, and take a knee at Ghost's head. "Quite the mess you made, sniper. God might be a little pissed that you wrecked his church."

"Eh. He owes me. So it's okay," Ghost says.

"And how's that?"

"Rachel and Savannah." Ghost winces at something Bumper's doing. "He owes me."

I'm guessing those two names are family members. Sometimes, gettin' guys to talk about their families can be a good thing. But if they don't have their shit together, it can also make them come unglued. I decide to leave Ghost's rocks unturned. "Well, you did good work, brother. And the boys here are—"

"I'd just come back from a patrol when my CO called me over," Ghost says, slurring some of his words. "Said someone had broken into my house, and they were still looking for the suspect."

Ah, hell. So much for talking to the guy. I cast Yoshi and Bumper a look, but they shrug it off and keep working.

"Hey, why don't you just relax and try to conserve your—"

Ghost cuts me off. "They never found him. But I did."

I wait for him to say more, but he doesn't. A few beats go by. Yoshi and Bumper seem to be making progress. Bleeding's stopped.

"The only place I wanted to be after that was somewhere cold," Ghost adds. "Three more deployments to the high ranges. That's when they took me."

"Called back?"

Ghost shakes his head. "Damn towel-heads couldn't say my name worth shit. Kept saying Domi-non Toh-Row. But I didn't care." He winces again, and I watch his eyes roll around as if looking for something. "Pain purges weakness, and I was a dead man walking. Strong. I was strong. So it didn't matter what they did to me. Two weeks. And you know the only thing they got from me?"

He raises his left hand. I think he's gonna flip off the world. Instead, he keeps his fingers flat, which makes the missing ring finger that much more noticeable.

"They thought they could take her from me. Humiliate me. But that was old news. Old news." He coughs once.

"Easy," Yoshi says. "We're almost done, Ghost."

Bumper lifts his chin at Yoshi. "Yo. How much'a that you slide him?"

But the PJ doesn't reply.

"They made me swallow the ring," Ghost says, grabbing my hand. "But Rachel was already long gone. And little Savannah..." Ghost's eyes glaze over. "They had nothing on me. Dead man walking."

"He's ready to move," Yoshi says.

Just then, Dolores pulls up, and the brake pads squeal. Z-Lo pulls up a second later with my FJ40. We all work to ease Ghost into the back of the Humvee.

Bumper closes the door and looks at me. "That's messed up, man."

I take a breath. "Yut."

"Kinda explains a lot too."

"Yut." I pat him on the shoulder. "Load up."

He nods and climbs in Dolores with Yoshi, while I wave Z-Lo and Aaron over to my vehicle. We do a U-turn and head back for the remaining two vehicles parked beneath the trees beside the Adams Building.

"Is he gonna be okay?" Aaron asks after a few bumpy seconds of driving across the quad.

"It's gonna take a lot more than that to put a guy like Ghost down," I reply. "He's gonna be fine."

"All right." Aaron's nodding and looking out the passenger side window. "It just looked bad."

"Didn't say it wasn't."

"Okay. Right."

"Hey, Aaron? You good?"

"Sure, sure. Just… that's a lot to, you know, take in. Again. I thought I was—"

"Hold that thought." I brake, climb out, and start giving orders. "Z-Lo, relieve Hollywood. Yoshi, you good without Bumper?"

I see him give me a thumbs up from the backseat beside Ghost.

"Bumper and Hollywood, saddle up."

"OTF," they reply as they run for the Thing and Jeep, respectively.

"We're headed to Staten Island," I say to everyone. "I've got an idea."

24

1020, Friday, June 25, 2027
Staten Island, New York
Korean War Veterans Parkway

We headed up Route 1, picked up I-287 North, and then continued on 440 East until we hit Outerbridge Crossing. The iconic cantilever span not only dropped us onto Staten Island's southern end but into the old Empire State itself. And just like that, half my arsenal is illegal in yet another state. Welcome to New York.

The most disconcerting thing, however, was driving through what I figured was the last of Staten Island's inhabitants. Individuals and couples carried what they could in makeshift backpacks. But the majority of those we passed were families who pushed garden carts heaped with supplies. Kids rode on shoulders or sat perched atop foodstuffs, jugs of water, and blankets.

Seeing all the women and children put me in mind of Ghost's medically induced confession. There's an unspoken rule about hearing a brother talk about their life when downrange that says you don't ever talk about it after the fact unless they ask. And then there's an even deeper code of conduct that governs what guys say when they're on death's door. For a breach of confidence on that level, you answer to God, the devil, or the man's momma. I'd take the devil over those two any day. Lesson is, you keep your mouth shut. And with what I heard Ghost say today, the intel's best left forgotten. Man's been through hell. 'Nough said.

Back on the bridge, more than one do-gooder tried to wave us down as we picked our way across. They warned us that it wasn't safe and that we should turn around. Some even pounded on our hood and windows that the sick and elderly needed rides. I'd encountered plenty of this in my military career abroad and had mastered a cool "eff off" face that got all but the most belligerent to steer clear. Yeah, it took a certain level of hard-heartedness to keep driving. But I reminded myself that if these people knew where we were headed and what we needed to do, they'd be asking us to pass instead of screaming for us to come back.

Eventually, we emerged from the elevated bottleneck and returned to terra firma.

Aaron and I had ridden in silence up until now. I needed the time to think. And, thanks be to God, Chuck had read the room right and kept his trap shut. As for the rest of the team, they seemed to accept my request for solitude and heeded my instructions to hydrate and eat a protein bar. Adrenaline has a sneaky way of sapping the body of energy.

All the talk with Chuck about his energy core and capacitors has kicked my brain into overdrive about whatever awaits us in lower

Manhattan. There's something about the way the dome seems to dim over time and suddenly brightens again that's piqued my interest. And the more I think about my conversation with the team back in the barn, and Aaron's comments about the type of light he'd seen emanating from the dome, the more the presence of some sort of portal ring in lower Manhattan makes sense.

I also keep going back to my first sighting of the ARU at the overpass on I-280 East. While the energy field certainly held its own when penetrating the bridge, I'm curious just how dense and thick a material has to be in order to mitigate it altogether.

There are clues hidden for me in all of these encounters. But collecting my thoughts feels like herding cats. To settle them, I'll need more intel from my talking ray gun and my childhood best buddy. And then, maybe, just maybe, I'll be able to get the magic decoder ring in the bottom of the Cracker Jacks box and figure out where the buried treasure is.

"So how'd they find us, Chuck?" I say at last.

"I already told you, it wasn't me."

Aaron leans over his seat to look at the weapon for the hundredth time.

I angle the rearview mirror down. "I believe you. But that's not what I asked."

"I see. Well, if that is truly an indication of how much our trust has grown, I'm delighted. Thrilled, even."

"Great. Then answer my question. You leaking our location by accident?"

"That's a firm no. Now, were I a gun twice my age with an enlarged trigger well, then the answer might be yes. Sometimes unfortunate accidents can't be helped. It's a normal part of getting old."

"He really is fantastic," Aaron says as he sits forward. "How did—?"

I wave off his question to get back to Chuck. "Then how'd they do it? Tracking devices? Satellites? Drones?"

"Nothing so conventional, no."

"That's conventional?"

"I mean, when compared to the Androchidans' biology in this particular regard, yes."

I cast him a stern look in the rearview mirror. "Go on."

"Well, you've had your first look at them."

I wait for him to go on, but he doesn't. "And?"

"Well, and what?"

"What what?"

"This is cute," Aaron says.

I glance at him and then back at Chuck. "And what, Charlie?"

"And didn't you notice anything about them that was, oh, I don't know, peculiar? Standy-outty-ish, perhaps?"

"Standy-outty-ish? Chuck, the whole thing is goddamned peculiar."

The rifle sighs like a disappointed parent. "We really need to work on your observation skills."

I shake my head and look out the window. "They had a vertical mouth, messed up eyes, skin that—"

"Ah, yes. The eyes."

I look back at the mirror. "Their eyes can track us? How?"

"Did you notice the lattice-like surface of them?"

"Yut. Magenta, like the bots."

"Excellent. You're making remarkable progress, Patrick. By this time next week, I'll teach you how to shave."

Aaron slaps my bicep. "He's got a great sense of humor too."

372

"Don't encourage him." I nod at Chuck. "So what's it mean?"

"Due to their evolution on a planet whose star is colder than Earth's star, they see in a different range of electromagnetic radiation than you humans. While both your species classify what they see as visible light, which is understandable, they see what you would call infrared radiation."

"Fascinating," Aaron says. "And what would they call what we see?"

"Unevolved."

Aaron turns and gives me a blank face.

I have to chuckle. "Great sense of humor." Back to Chuck, I add, "So, what? They tracked our heat signatures?"

"Essentially. The tires of your vehicles produce friction and emit heat, both of which produce a trail and, presto, you have contact."

"So is that what your disruptor electron thingy—"

"Electromagnetic disruption emitter?"

"Yeah. Is that what helped us hide back at the library?"

"It helped lessen their ability to track you *to* the library, yes. You all ran off in different directions like street rats after that, and I was only able to keep you concealed for a few moments more. You'll find that I am able to disrupt a wide array of electromagnetic frequencies for short durations across a limited radius."

"Noted." I scratch under my beard, still trying to put a few more pieces together. "Then why didn't they follow us the night before?"

"That predates our union," Chuck says. "I'm terribly sorry."

"Your union?" Aaron asks.

"Nope." I shake my head.

Chuck's LEDs brighten. "Oh, but Patrick. The story is so—"

"Our team dispatched two bots and then fled west to cover in an

CHRISTOPHER HOPPER & J.N. CHANEY

old barn for the night." I have to keep this train on the tracks since both Aaron and Chuck have near-equal abilities to derail it.

"And you were close to the forcefield when these bots were dispatched?" Chuck asks.

"Yut."

"I see. Well, while I can't—"

"Narc on the aliens, I got it."

"Now there's a fun word. Narc. Slang. Both a noun and a verb that, when used colloquially, indicates a person or behavior that..."

As Chuck's definition trails on, Aaron casts me a grin. "Does he do this a lot?"

"Yut."

"Internet?"

"Uh-huh."

"Fascinating."

"...which tends to end in one's execution at the hands of the member's gang," Chuck says, concluding his recited definition.

"So what can you tell me?" I ask.

"For one, only narc if you have a death wish. Two, at the time of your retreat to the barn, your heat signature was most likely irrelevant. The encounter took place well within the dome's emergent window, a short period characterized by a civilization's rapid and often chaotic dispersion. You were, quite simply, one of many fleeing pieces of merchandise to damage the Androchidans' assets."

"So they expected to lose bots?"

"Of course. All properly ripe species resist at first."

The mention of the word ripe brings back memories of the body parts in the ARU.

"For another," Chuck continues. "You'd only destroyed robots, as you call them. It's really rather charming."

"And you call them?" Aaron asks.

"Oh, it's not me," Chuck says, sounding like he laid a hand across his chest in self-defense. "It's the Androchidans. In your military-laden, acronym-rich language, the robots would be termed SSAs."

"Which stands for?"

"Semi-Sentient Assassins."

"Yeah, that's way less charming," Aaron says.

I put the puzzle together. "So when I took out a death angel and did it outside of the emergent window, the head honchos took it more seriously and tracked us."

"That's correct, Patrick. And well done on incorporating an Americanized Japanese term into your conclusion. Phantom Three would be quite proud. Shall I notify him?"

"Negative." I work my jaw. "I still don't get something, though. If they have such great heat vision—"

"Oooo, I like that term!"

"—such great heat vision, why the need for thermal detection on your scope?"

Chuck doesn't answer right away. But when he does, his speech is slow, and his tone is filled with abject disbelief. "Patrick. After both seeing and engaging them, do you really think those flesh-suckers are capable of fashioning, let alone conceiving, something as generously complex and imaginative as moi?"

"So you're saying you're not their hardware?"

"Like most things the Androchidans have, yes. I originated elsewhere."

"You're booty then."

Chuck balks at this. "Excuse me?"

"You're booty. Loot. The spoils of war."

"Ah, I see now. No. You really think that the species who made me would have been conquered by the likes of them? Ha! You delight me, Patrick, you really do. I think that's why we get along so well, nes't-ce pas? You amuse me, I amuse you…"

"Is it just me, or is his personality growing?" Aaron says in a lowered voice.

"It's growing, all right. Growing to be a pain in my ass." Wherever Sir Charles is from, I'm guessing it was the result of a backroom arms deal. Seems blood money and gun runners are universal. Literally.

"…and everyone wins." Chuck takes a breath and lets out in a very vocal sigh. "Ahhhh. I'm really enjoying this whole freedom thing."

"We can tell," Aaron says.

"Well, sorry to burst your bubble, but we're going back to see your pals," I say.

"Was that… was that a dad joke, Patrick?"

I blink a few times at the blue dome in front of us and then cast him a hairy eyeball in the rearview. Son of a bitch. I wasn't even trying either.

"You know, one day I will be as punny as you, Patrick."

Okay, so I laugh a little. And I hate myself for it because dad jokes really are the worst. But damn if they don't get a guy to smile.

"In any event, I was going to say, yes, I did notice that we are headed back to see my 'pals,' as you put it. Care to explain?"

"I will, but first I need to hear from you." I look at Aaron.

"Me?"

"Oh, you are in so much trouble," Chuck says. "I've seen Patrick get mad, and boy, you do not want to be near him when he does.

Please fasten your safety belts and make sure your windows are fully closed."

Aaron gives me an unimpressed look. "Yeah, I've seen him get mad too."

"Okay." Time to get things back on course. "What happened after I left?"

"Ellsworth?"

"Yut." I wait for a second and then add, "You bought yourself a gun, Aaron."

"I know."

"A frickin' gun, bro."

"I said I know!"

"Wow," Chuck says. "This is better than Days of Our Lives."

"Shut up," Aaron and I say at the same time.

"Touchy, touchy. Shutting up. Jeeez."

Aaron sits back and then smooths his jeans. "You left, and the UN came in."

"Robertson."

Aaron snaps his head at me. "You met with him?"

"I wouldn't call it a meeting. More like an intrusion, followed by me letting him know exactly where I stood."

"You threatened him?"

I give Aaron a half-smile. "I said my hanging around wasn't going to be good for his health."

"So you threatened him." Aaron nods. Even though we speak different languages when it comes to our professions, he still gets me. For the most part.

"Anyway," Aaron says. "Robertson took over, but I still had control over the project from a scientific standpoint."

"And I take it that neither one of you blew it up."

Aaron shakes his head. "Maybe if we had, none of this would have happened."

I smack a hand on the dashboard. "Thank you."

"But then how would we have met, Patrick?" Chuck asks.

"I'm really not in the mood, buddy."

"That's okay," he says softly. "Lover's quarrel."

"Contrary to what you might think," Aaron says. "After Robertson insisted we turn it back on, nothing happened."

"It didn't reactivate?"

"No. I mean, we turned it back on, and nothing came out. Went on for four weeks like that."

"Four weeks?"

Aaron nods. "Robertson had his military force at the ready—five maybe six times the size of what you had. Bigger weapons. And all the while, the energy field is completely static. That was, until our sensors detected a spike."

"What kinda spike?"

"The arrival spike," Chuck says like a child naming his favorite movie's plot twist.

Aaron shrugs and starts nodding. "That's about the sum of it. And it was pure chance that I wasn't there."

I frown at him. "Where were you?"

"I'd been called back to McMurdo Station for a few days. Had to explain why I'd…"

When he doesn't say anything more, I ask, "You good?"

"I punched Robertson."

"You what?" The smile on my face is as big as any I've had in awhile. "You're kidding me!"

"I know. Dr. Campbell the pacifist. But, yeah. I punched him. He made a comment about how all the lives lost here were 'required stepping stones' for the greatest discovery in history. So I balled my fist up like this"—he shows me—"and then got right in his face and said, 'Required my ass.' Then I crossed his left cheek."

"Holy God Almighty, Aaron." I grab his shoulder and squeeze it. "You're an animal."

"I know. And then I ran to the closest snow pile, eased my hand in, and popped three ibuprofen." He's massaging his right knuckles. "Damn did that hurt, Pat. The movies don't show that."

"They sure don't."

I can't wipe the damn smile off my face. Throwing a punch, the revolver, fighting—this was the stuff that drove us down different paths. And now, here's Aaron doing the stuff he used to get mad at Jack and me for doing.

Aaron holds up a finger to me. "Don't misunderstand me. What I did was wrong."

"No it wasn't."

"Yes, it was. And I'll never forgive—"

"It wasn't wrong, Aaron." I say it strongly enough that the statement forms a long silence between us. "You did the right thing."

He sighs, hides his right hand under his thigh, and then looks out the passenger side window. The silence extends further as the Land Cruiser's tires rhythmically thump across the pavement breaks.

"When they came, they destroyed everything," he says.

I try and catch Aaron's eyes, but he's focused elsewhere, and I know that posture.

"By the time we arrived, they..." He wipes a hand across his face. "They were all dead. Place was... well, it was a mess. Blew the glacier wide open, clear to the sky. And just... bodies everywhere. The work. The staff. It was all destroyed."

I let the moment of silence linger in honor of the dead, and then I put a hand on Aaron's shoulder again, this time more gently. "I'm sorry."

"Me too." He makes his hands into fists. "It should've been me, right?"

I nod. "Yut. And that's a bitch of an argument to wrestle to the mat."

"Yeah." He looks back out the window. "Weird part was, no one could find them after that. The aliens, I mean. I overheard some of the military bigwigs saying they'd gotten traces of things leaving the area, but nothing firm. So they asked me to shut it down, and then that was it."

"So you did shut the ring down?"

"Yes."

"And then they sent you home?"

"Yeah."

"And that's when you purchased the gun."

Aaron shifts in his seat. "After what I'd seen, I..."

"Hey, I don't blame you, bro. I would have done the exact same thing if I were in your shoes."

He nods, but it seems half-hearted. "When I landed, they took me straight to the Pentagon. Four days I was there. Said the project was done, and I was threatened in lots of very explicit ways that I would be arrested and tried for treason if I ever spoke about the work again."

"Rode that line pretty tight during the TV interview, didn't you?"

He looks over at me. "You watched that?"

"Buddy, I'm pretty sure most of the nation watched that."

He lowers his head. "I just thought that… well, if I could get other people curious, then maybe they'd…"

"Find out that you really did know what you were talking about?"

He nods.

Then I point at the giant blue dome in front of us. "I think it's safe to say you did."

"Yeah, but I didn't want it like this."

"No one ever does." I look over at Aaron, but he looks about as sad as Eeyore on Winnie the Pooh. "Being right tends to suck. And in the few cases where it doesn't, those issues usually don't matter much."

I see Aaron's shoulders rise and fall. "When the reporters called me, they acted like the loss of communication was breaking news. In reality, it was old to those of us who'd survived. Heck, I'd been home for more than three weeks. It didn't dawn on me until right then, in the interview, that there might be something else going on."

"A second wave," I say.

Aaron snaps his attention toward me. "Exactly. That's exactly what I concluded."

"But you turned the ring off."

"And tried to tell everyone that we should blow it up."

I smile. "Sounds familiar."

"They actually accused me of sounding like you."

"I'll take that as a compliment. So what do you think happened?"

Aaron's suddenly looking a lot less like Eeyore, and, while not quite Tigger yet, at least a little like Winnie the Pooh holding a honey jar. "So I think that first round was some sort of scouting team."

I glance at him. "Recon?"

"Sure, yeah. Once they hit Robertson's military people and our science team, they left to surveil the rest of the planet. But they were more than just that. They were like"—he starts snapping his fingers in the hopes of getting the word. "Something engineers."

"Combat engineers?"

He points at me. "That's the one. Setting up and preparing for battle."

"You think enough equipment got through in that one episode you described?"

"See, that's just it. I don't think that was the only time assets came through the ring. It couldn't have been."

"They opened it again?" My mind is racing a hundred miles per hour now, as this might confirm the hunch I was having earlier. "You think they what? Opened it from the other side?"

"I sure do."

I rub the back of my neck. "I thought we had to open it from our side?"

"No one ever said they couldn't return the favor," Aaron says with a sly grin. "But even if that isn't the case, there's an easier explanation."

"They already had Androchidans come through who could reopen it."

"And there it is."

"Bravo, Dr. Campbell. I say," Chucks lets loose from the back seat. "While I can't rightfully expound on your conclusions, of course, I can at least offer sincere congratulations on your logic. High marks across the board. And, I might add, you are the first species to have put all those pieces together—and so quickly too."

"Thanks?" Aaron says with a furrowed brow.

Now that we've spoken, my wheels are turning even faster. "When we were at Ellsworth together, you mentioned that you think the ring had its own power source."

"I did, yes."

"You still believe that?"

"I never had reason to doubt it before. And I think the argument is only made stronger in light of what we'll call the third opening—yours and mine being the first, Robertson's being the second—"

"And this last unknown one being the third," I add.

"Right. Even if those Androchidans"—he looks back at Chuck—"Did I say that right?"

"Indeed, good doctor. Indeed."

"And if those Androchidans who came through in the second opening didn't return to reactivate the portal, an extra-local power source would explain how the species could reopen it from afar."

"Because they had control," I say. "They were fueling it, for lack of a better term."

"Exactly."

"So here's my question, Aaron." I point northeast toward the city. "Assuming that whatever's in lower Manhattan is some sort of portal to relocate people, do you think that's how it's powered?"

"That's a great question, isn't it. At this point, it's all just speculation, right? Conjecture."

"True. But given what you saw at the Ellsworth dig site and what you see here, are these the same power source?"

"I'm not sure I'm tracking you, Pat."

"Well, let's say we couldn't turn off the artifact in the South Pole because it was powered from elsewhere. And let's go even further. Let's say that whatever's powering it could somehow ensure the ring doesn't decompose either—doesn't fall apart…" I glance at him to see if he's picking up my train of thought. "…after millions of years. And it wouldn't have succumbed to a bomb blast even if we had gotten the green light to try it."

There's a pause before Aaron replies. I can see his brain working. This is good.

"Pat, I… I never even thought about that. I just assumed it had maintained compositional integrity due to being locked in ice."

"In a glacier? Don't they move, Aaron?"

"Substantially, yes. Oh, now I feel like an imbecile."

"Nonsense," says Chuck. "Now, asking your weapon to dispense high-yield energy blasts on an inherently weak target when what you really should have done was outline the larger picture, now that—"

"Can it, pea shooter," I say.

"Ugh. I was only trying to make Aaron feel better."

"Find different ways."

Aaron's still lost in thought and processing out loud. "I always concluded that the ring's mass and sheer density were enough to preserve its shape. But a quantum energy field would achieve optimum integrity. Granted, I can't even begin to think how such a thing is possible, let alone how it would work, but, yes, that would explain a great deal." He pauses and puts a finger to his lips. "But for so long a time? We're talking tens of thousands of years, Pat."

"Eh, you said it. There's plenty we can't explain. But right now, I don't need to explain it. I just want to know if it's different than whatever's out there." I nod toward the horizon.

"And why's that?" Aaron asks.

"Because, while the one at your dig site was meant to last for ages, I'm not so sure about this guy here."

384

"You think it's more of a temporary set up?"

"Tactically speaking, yut. I don't care if you're an alien or not, resources are limited, and every op has its strengths and weaknesses. You're not gonna build a bivouac the same way you build a FOB."

"A what now?"

"Forward operating base." I shake my head. "Never mind. Point is, I need you to be focused on how whatever's in there is different from what you've spent the last two decades of your life researching. That's why you're here. I don't need to know how the science can be explained; I just wanna know how we can destroy it. I need your eyes and your head."

"Okay." Aaron's nodding as if psyching himself up. "Okay, I think I can do that."

"Thinking isn't good enough, Aaron. If you're coming with us to the other side, then I've gotta know. And it's not too late to turn back either. You wanna go join people displaced by all this and find a way to survive, I won't stop you. Hell, I can't say I wouldn't do the same. But if you choose to come along, then you're all in. No second-guessing, no hesitation. We're gonna blow them to kingdom come or die trying."

Aaron swallows. "How much time do I have?"

"Up until we find a way to cross inside the bubble."

"Can I let you know then?"

"Yut. And I respect that. Trust me."

"And I like the way you think, Patrick," Chuck says. Then I hear his voice break comms and say, "Get ready, Phantoms. We're going to blow up some shite!"

25

1045, Friday, June 25, 2027
Eltingville, Staten Island, New York
Richmond County Yacht Club

WE'VE PARKED in an oceanside lot designated for Marina Boat Owners and Guests, though I doubt the management will have us towed for failing to fall into either category. Another large sign welcomes us to the Richmond County Yacht Club. In the background, docks filled with all manner of pleasure craft bob in a sunlit bay worthy of an oil painting. Behind the scene, a long finger of land separates the bay from the ocean, which is accessible by an opening to the south.

Strangely absent are the incessant shrieks of ring-billed gulls, the drone of boat engines, or distant barks of sea lions. The dome seems to have driven them all away for one reason or another. I find it both interesting and alarming how different the seaside seems without the unmistakable sounds. In fact, the only things that feel familiar are the salt air and the wind coming in from the Atlantic. The whole scene just feels odd.

"You want to do what now?" Hollywood asks me.

The team is gathered around the back passenger side of Dolores for Ghost's benefit. Doc bandaged him up well, but he'll be limping the rest of the op.

"I want to see if we can swim under the dome," I reply, repeating myself yet again. "If we can, then we talk possible assault plans based on what we suspect is on the other side."

"You think diving is the best way inside it?" Bumper asks. As I'd expect from a SEAL, he doesn't seem fazed in the least. So his question is probably for the benefit of everyone else who's not as infatuated with drowning as he is.

"I do. When we teamed up, you found me below the overpass on I-280."

They nod.

"I noticed that the people inside the dome seemed to anticipate that the bridge might allow a gap to open. I thought the same thing."

"But it didn't," Yoshi says. He empties his flask and then looks inside it. "Damn."

"No. It didn't. And people died because of it. But I did notice something unusual."

"What's that?" Hollywood asks.

"The color of the energy below the overpass was slightly less intense than the rest of the dome."

"You think it was reduced," Bumper states.

I nod. "Makes sense, right? I mean, that's pretty impressive that the thing can pass through a few inches of concrete and still do its job."

"So you're thinking water might mitigate it too," Bumper adds.

"Yut. 'Course, there are other alternatives."

"Like?"

"Sewers."

Everyone winces.

"No thank you," Yoshi says. "Been there, done that."

"And here I thought the Air Force didn't get their hands dirty," Hollywood says.

"They don't," Bumper replies. "He was just talking about having to wipe his ass."

"Funny," Yoshi says with a middle finger scratching his eye.

I smile but quickly resume talking to keep things moving forward. "We could look for a sewer entry that runs under the dome's edge. But it's risky as sewer tunnels aren't always straight forward affairs."

"And there's no guarantee that the roads above them will stop the force field," Ghost says.

I nod. "Right. But water might."

"How's that?" Z-Lo asks. "I feel like concrete's gonna be better at stopping stuff than water."

"For most forms of radiation it is, for sure," Aaron says. "But if you can get enough of it between you and a neutron source, water is a surprisingly good insulator. Plus, if this energy field is electrical in nature, it might not appreciate water as we do." He turns to me. "Not bad, Pat."

"Thanks. I'm thinking that while we'd be hard-pressed to find a foot of concrete to walk under, we can easily find a few feet of water to swim under." I point northeast toward New York City's Lower Bay. "But we'll need to test it first."

"You wanna go out there?" Hollywood asks. "Pretty exposed, isn't it?"

"If I may," Chuck says from inside my Land Cruiser. "It's getting rather stuffy in here. Might I join you?"

"Sounds like Mr. Smartypants has something to add," Bumper says.

I walk over and open the door. "You didn't pee on the furniture, did you?"

"Maybe a little. But I was so excited to see you."

"Kissass."

"Pushover."

I grab Chuck and bring him to the circle. "Whaddya got, Sir Charles?"

"With regard to Phantom Two's apprehensions, I will be sure to warn His Holiness Phantom One well in advance of any possible contact," Chuck says.

"Oh, like the 'well-in-advance' warning you gave us back in the Adam's Building?" Hollywood asks.

"Did you just use quotey fingers with me?" Chuck says.

"Sure did."

"Not fair, Hollywood. You know I can't do it back."

"Bite me."

"Ew. Gross. And I'll have you know that the buildings prevented early detection. That, and Dr. Campbell was fawning all over me, which I found distracting though mildly appropriate."

Everyone eyes Aaron.

"What? I was curious." Aaron turns on Chuck. "And it wasn't fawning, Sir Charles. It was... intense interest."

"Sure, sure." Chuck coughs. "*Fawning.* Anyway, out on the open seas, I will have ample time to warn you all should you be noticed. Plus, the Androchidans don't pay much mind to the waterways this far out, seeing as how you are a land-fairing species. Their attention will be on those headed toward… Hmm. Well, their attention will be elsewhere. Plus, moving during the day works to your advantage given their 'heat vision' in relation to your local star. And, yes, if you couldn't tell by the inflection in my voice, I used imaginary quotey fingers for that, Phantom Two."

"Well that just spun our op sec on its head," Ghost says.

I give Chuck a raised eyebrow. "Care to explain their biology a little more?"

"Ummm, no." Then, as if to himself, he mutters, "Though their damn helmets—those ungrateful manky gits—do help compress a little of the frequency variations. Plonkers if I ever saw any."

"Are we still talking about the aliens?" I ask.

"No. The helmets. Their software is a royal pain in my arse."

"I'm sure it is."

"Anyhow. Should you get in a pinch, I will endeavor to temporarily conceal you with my electromagnetic disruption emitter."

"Your what's that now?" Hollywood asks.

"The same thing he used to buy us more time at the library," I say.

"Leading up *to* the library," Chuck corrects.

Hollywood folds her arms and squares on me. "So, you wanna get us all in a boat and see who can swim under it without having their head removed or, now that I think about it, get electrocuted?"

"No. I'm not asking you guys to do anything. I'm volunteering to see if it works myself."

"I'll go with you," Bumper says.

But Hollywood doesn't seem to be buying it. "It's too dangerous. I don't like it."

"I understand Hollywood's reservations," Chuck says. "Since this directly pertains to your wellbeing, Patrick, perhaps a less risky alternative is allowing me to be your canary in the coal mine, as it were."

"You?" I let out a huff of air. "While few things would give me more enjoyment right now than tossing you into some water just to see what happens—"

"It's far less exciting than what you might expect, I can assure you. I'm quite waterproof. Plus, we've already done the whole tossing me away thing, remember? I thought you had your fill, and we agreed that wouldn't happen again."

I pause in awe of his truly staggering ability to annoy me. "As I was saying, I don't think sending you down to test where the force field ends is the wisest option, not when we could tie a rock to a line and accomplish the same thing."

"Don't be daft, Patrick. While I'm flattered to be thought of as slightly higher than a rock, that particular approach requires that you have some sort of living tissue on the stone, like skin, muscle, blood, or any of your other more viscous fluids. It could take several tries and, therefore, several tissue samples. Plus, the stone is incapable of providing a real time analysis of your planet's ocean waters' ability to attenuate the field's power. If the field is fluctuating, you'll want to know. Trust me."

Hollywood lets out a sigh. "I certainly like the idea of sending a stone down more than sending you down."

"That's kind," Chuck replies.

Hollywood points at me. "I was talking about him."

"Oh."

"But I think Chuck's idea will be faster, and it sounds like it could yield us better intel."

"Oh, it will," Chuck says emphatically. "It most definitely will, Phantom Two. You can count on me to probe those depths like the best prober you've ever used."

"Nope." Hollywood clamps her lips tight and starts shaking her head. "No way."

"You've changed your mind?"

I pull Chuck close to me. "Might want to shut up now."

"Okaaaaaay. Fine. But I don't see what the big deal is."

"Yut, that much is obvious." I look at Bumper. "Still willing to tag along?"

"Roger."

"Then let's find us a boat before he figures out what he said."

"But what did I say?"

EVERYONE BUT GHOST pairs off to search sections of the docks for a boat that meets our specs. Needs to be all analog, able to hold the whole team if Bumper, Chuck, and I return with good news, and has to have plenty of space for gear. Hopefully, it's topped off too.

I take Z-Lo and head for the northernmost docks. We take turns searching for keys and trying ignitions of boats we think fit the profile. While working, I decide to try and get to know him a little better. Nothing like some casual conversation to fill time and flesh out my knowledge of a team member. When you're in leadership, almost everything is calculated.

"How's the shoulder?" I ask.

Z-Lo looks at the bandage beneath the singed hole in his uniform. "Doc says it's fine. Says the scar I'm gonna have will drive the girls crazy."

"Lucky you."

"Talk about it. Apparently, the great thing about getting hit with a blaster is that the wound self-cauterizes."

"Cauterizes?"

"Yeah, that's the one. 'Course, I didn't get hit in an organ or anything. But I'm good."

"Glad to hear. Here, gimme a hand." He helps me step off a dead twenty-four foot Bayliner with a blown-out circuit box. "So what's your story, kid?"

"You… wanna know my story?"

"I don't see anyone else."

"Yeah, of course. Uh. Whaddya wanna know?"

"Well, you're from Southern California?"

"San Diego."

"Nice."

He shrugs as we walk toward another promising boat. "I guess."

"Didn't like it?"

"Eh. My pops, he was always riding me to join the family business."

"Entrepreneurs?"

He laughs. "The family business was working for a local steel plant."

"Ah, gotcha."

"I'm the baby. Nine brothers and sisters."

"Holy crap, kid. You sure you're not Catholic?"

"Hungarian. So, yeah." He chuckles. "They're basically the same thing as far as my grandma's concerned."

"I hear that."

"My parents weren't religious. Just wanted a better life for us than they had. But I didn't want what I saw my older siblings go through, you know?"

"Which was?"

"Working the steel plant with pops."

"All of them?"

He nods. "Our family can be pretty stubborn."

"And yet you decided to join the Marine Corps? No offense, kid, but it's not exactly the track someone takes to get away from manual labor."

"Tell me about it." Z-Lo laughs as he hops down into a Boston Whaler that looks promising, though a little on the small side. "It wasn't my first choice."

"And what was?"

"Eh, nothing." He finds the keys hidden under the center console. "Just go to college. Maybe discover something besides steel work."

I do a quick 360 to make sure we're still clear, and ask Chuck to do a perimeter check too. "So why didn't you?"

"Pops didn't go for it." He tries the ignition. "Eh, this one's dead too. Said college and computers don't make careers. Older generation, ya know?"

"Yut." I don't have the heart to tell the kid that I agree with his old man. Then again, seems like most everyone with an education is richer than me, and all thanks to Mr. Gates and Mr. Jobs. So what the hell do I know?

I help Z-Lo over the boat's side and then keep searching.

"So my pops and me got into a pretty big fight over it, ya know? And he's yelling at me, and I'm yelling at him, and out of my mouth comes, 'Then I'm just gonna join the military.' So I walk to the recruiter's office, 'cause dad sure as hell won't drive me."

"You enlisted."

"Just like that."

"Your old man say anything?"

"Sure. 'Mi a fasz van veled!'"

"Which means?"

He laughs. "Literally, 'What the dick is with you?'"

"So he didn't go for it."

"Nope. And we haven't talked since."

"Sorry, kid."

Z-Lo shrugs his big shoulders. "Eh. I'm the baby. We're like fifty years apart, right? Not much in common, and I don't ever see that changing. So, yeah. There it is. But the Corps has been real good to me. Three squares, a warm bed, and I still get to throw my weight around on the mat."

"The mat?"

He nods but doesn't explain. "If high school gave me anything, it was letting me dominate on the mat, ya know? Even took state three of my four years."

"Wrestling."

"Yeah, 'course." He stretches his chest and arms in a way that looks more like a flex than an exercise. "Probably would have taken states the fourth year too, but I was ineligible because of some crap I got caught doing. I was good in the ring too."

"Boxing now?"

He nods. "Float like a butterfly, sting like a bee. Ya know?"

"Sure, kid."

He lets out a long sigh. "But for real, I kinda wanted to do something with computers."

"You? Computers?" I don't mean to stare at his twisted nose and cauliflower ear, but the behemoth doesn't exactly look like he'd be nimble on a keyboard and mouse.

"Doesn't matter now anyway. Probably the best thing about the Corps is getting to have new brothers. Well, *had* new brothers. Until... you know."

"Yut." I spot an old Dyer 29 hardtop on the next finger. "Why don't you go try that one."

"Yeah, you got it, Master Guns." Z-Lo heads for the classic white-top black-hulled fishing boat and then jumps in.

I walk to the stern and read the chipped name painted on the transom: *Best of Boat Worlds*. And who says the universe doesn't have a sense of humor?

Z-Lo rummages around the dash for a second and then waves the set of keys at me. A beat later, I hear the inboard engine compartment fans kick on. That's a good sign, and Z-Lo seems to know it too, as indicated by his thumbs up. As for the prolonged start-up sequence, more than one seaman has been blown from their boat by failing to purge vapor buildup before firing the spark plugs.

After about thirty seconds, Z-Lo turns the ignition. The starter kicks the engine over a few times, and the next thing we know, there's a low gurgle purring in the water.

"Hey, it works," Z-Lo says as his face pops around the windshield.

"You found us a winner, champ. Nice job."

He gives me a toothy smile. "Thanks."

Dammit. And here I go liking the kid.

"SEE if you can get us another twenty gallons of fuel by the time we get back," I say to Hollywood and the rest of the Phantoms gathered on the dock. Even Ghost made it down for the send-off. "Siphon whatever you can't find in pre-filled cans."

"Roger that, Wic. We'll be ready," Hollywood replies.

"Stay safe out there," Z-Lo says.

I give him a nod, and the kid tosses me the stern line. Yoshi guides the bow off the dock as Bumper backs us out. "Happy sailing," the doc says, and then starts singing the chorus of the Christopher Cross song. As soon as we're clear, Bumper pushes the throttle forward in what I swear is an attempt to drown out the horrible rendition.

"White-people music," he says with a shake of his head.

"I don't blame you." But just to annoy him, I pick up where Yoshi left off and belt out, "Just a dream and the wind to carry me."

Bumper joins in on, "And soon I will be free."

"SO WHERE'D you get the nickname from?" I ask Bumper as we hang a hard left around Crookes Point and head north along Staten Island's east shore.

"Team gave it to me," he yells over the engine roar.

I think he means his SEAL team, but then Bumper clarifies.

"High school football."

"Gotcha."

He checks our six and looks at the RPM gauge before continuing. "I was team captain, which, where I came from, had certain privileges and expectations, some of which involved the cheerleaders, if you know what I'm saying." He gives me a wink. "Momma didn't make enough to buy me a car, and I wouldn't have taken it if she did. But I'd managed to save up enough to buy a rusted-out 1982 Cutlass Supreme."

"Thing of beauty," I say with a grin.

He gives me a sideways glance. "Anyway, it's 0300, and me and Miss Cyclone herself are getting busy in the back, parked right there in the middle of the football field. Next day, coach walks into the locker room and asks who drove on the field. Nobody says a thing, and I know I was careful not to leave tracks. Even picked a week where it hadn't rained. I was careful, right?"

"Well, when no one fesses up, what does coach do? Reaches down and pulls a rusted-out bumper from behind the hampers. Says, 'Would the owner of license plate number LVK 9143 please step forward. You dropped something.'"

That gives both of us a good laugh as we cut through the waves.

"Something tells me you'll never forget that plate number either," I say.

"The team wouldn't let me. I said if we won the championship that year, I'd get it tatted on my ass."

"No way. You win?"

Bumper gives me a huge grin. "You wanna see my ass?"

"How close do you think you can get and still hold us steady?" I ask Bumper. He's lowered *Best of Boat Worlds'* throttle as I tie 550 paracord around Chuck on the stern deck.

"Fifteen feet, I'm guessing," Bumper yells. "Don't wanna risk anything more. One rogue wave, and we lose half the ship."

I look west. "And that's a long swim."

"Roger that."

We're nearly at the dome, and I'm about ready to toss Chuck overboard for his scouting mission.

"So you're clear on what you're doing, right?"

"Oh heavens, Patrick. Of course I am. I practically invented what I'm about to do. Dropping down to scope things out?"

"Wow. That's terrible."

"Thank you."

"And don't take any unnecessary risks either. Much as I hate to say it, if we lost you now, we'd lose... well, we'd lose a good asset."

"You mean intelligence source."

"Sure."

"And here I thought you might say a friend."

"Can we settle for a tolerable acquaintance?"

"Hmmm. Not my favorite, but okay. Plus, there's no need to worry about me, Patrick. I have an integrated resonance generator that makes me impervious to the energy field."

I stare at him for a second as Bumper brings *Best of Boat Worlds* to idle. "Why didn't you inform us of that earlier?"

"Because you specifically told me to shut up, remember?"

"I do, yut. But that's a pretty big piece of intel. Not something you want to leave out."

"Nor is it something I would have offered. But since I get the sense that my destruction would cause you irreparable harm, seeing as how we're tolerable acquaintances and all, it's in my directive's best interests to offer it."

"Oh, right. Yeah, I'd definitely suffer irreparable harm if you got hurt—"

"You don't sound sincere."

"—and even more irreparable harm if humanity gets carted off to Never Never Land."

"Ha ha, nice try. No way, Patrick. But, I suppose it was worth a shot."

I just stare at him.

"Get it, Patrick?"

"I get it."

"But you're not laughing."

"Take a deep breath."

"What? Why? That has nothing to do with—"

I hurl Chuck overboard and let the line unspool from the deck.

"You, uh… you gonna grab that?" Bumper asks me.

"I'm thinking about it."

"Roger."

AFTER ONLY TEN seconds of being submerged, Chucks hails us over the radio. "Phantom War God, this is Phantom Lord of lower-case hosts. Do you read me? Come in, over and out."

Bumper gives me a grin as he works the boat's wheel and throttle to keep us clear of the dome.

"I read you, Sir Charles. Report."

"I have what we need. Also, there's some inquisitive marine life investigating me down here."

"Describe it."

"I'm not sure that's the priority at the moment."

"Describe it."

He lets out a digital-sounding sigh. "Very well. It seems to be a small school of flatfish with two eyes on one side of their head. Very strange. They look particularly curious, and if I might say, friendly. But my archives do not seem to have anything on them."

I give Bumper a look that says, Oh, they don't, huh?

I press open the channel. "Oh my God. Chuck, you gotta get out of there, now!"

"Very funny, ha ha."

"I'm not kidding, Chuck." Holding the mic away, I yell over my shoulder. "Bumper. The cord is stuck. We need to move!"

Chuck hesitates. "Patrick, are you—"

"Bumper!"

It's a good day when a Navy SEAL smiles deviously. "No good, Wic! Engine won't respond."

"Chuck," I say frantically. "Charlie, can you hear me?"

"Of course I can hear you, don't be—"

"Don't make any sudden moves. Those are called flounder."

"Flounder?"

"Yeah. We're gonna get you out of there."

"And you're sure they're aggressive?"

"Chuck, pal. I don't mean to alarm you, but this is bad. Real bad."

"Saints have mercy." There's a break in comms, then, "What will they do to me?"

"Remember the Sarlaac from Star Wars who resides in the Great Pit of Carkoon?"

"From the movie Return of the Jedi? Saints, yes. I see that now."

"It's like that, but way worse. Those predators' digestive systems dissolve their prey into nutrients over several thousand years."

"Oh, God. Get me out, Patrick. Please get me out. I don't want to die like this."

"Hold on." As much as it pains me not to keep the prank going, we need his findings, and then we need to get back to shore. "Not a word," I say to Bumper.

He crosses his heart.

Then I start reeling in the parachute cord and haul Chuck back on deck.

When he's back on the deck, I strip a piece of seaweed off him and hold him up. "You hurt, buddy?"

"No, no. I'm… Phew! I'm okay, thanks be to King Triton."

It takes me a second. "Little Mermaid?"

"Yes. He no doubt protected me."

"Yeah, no doubt. I'm just glad you're okay."

"One more second down there and flounders would have decimated me. And you know what the weird part is?"

"What's that?"

"There's a character named after one of those devils in the kid's movie, and they play it off as childish and naive. Bastards."

I know that if I look Bumper in the eye right now, I'm going to lose it. So I regain my composure by asking him to report on his findings.

"You'll be happy to know that the energy field extends to an average depth of five feet below the surface, depending on swell height," Chuck says. "Your hypothesis is sound."

"That's great news, pal. Thanks for, uh, ya know, risking your life for us."

"Especially with those flounder," Bumper adds.

"Yes, it was daring of me, I must say. But I'm happy to help the cause. Anything for the team, you know?"

Now I'm starting to feel bad about the prank. Not enough to say anything, of course. Something this good gets played out as long as the jukebox will run it.

"Go back to the swells for a second," I say. "You said the average depth was five feet. What were your max readings?"

"At times, as shallow as two feet," he says.

"That's not the number that interests me. You're saying the max depth you got was eight feet."

"That's correct."

Now I'm sober and look up at Bumper. His face is just as stern as mine. Eight feet doesn't sound like a whole lot. But in the open water and fighting currents and poor visibility, that might as well be fifteen feet. Maybe more. Plus, I don't have a snorkel or a mask, nor does anyone probably know how to SCUBA dive except Bumper— and that's assuming we had equipment for everyone.

"I'm sensing a problem here," Chuck says at last. "It's the flounder, isn't it."

"Man, I wish it was."

***

"So here's the good news," I say to the team back on the dock. I'm holding a marine chart from a boat and pointing to a spot just north of our current position. "This is where we intercepted the dome. Sir Charles here found that the energy field isn't a threat after about five feet of water."

"That's not bad at all," Z-Lo says. "We can swim it, easy."

"Yut. But that's an average."

"What's the deviation?" Ghost asks.

"Plus or minus three feet."

"Damn."

"Why damn?" Z-Lo asks.

Ghost sucks his teeth clean before explaining. "'Cause that

means we gotta be below eight feet if we don't want to risk getting cut in half during the dive."

"Oh." Z-Lo copies Ghost's mannerisms and runs a tongue over the front of his teeth. "That's a little harder."

"It's a lot harder," I say. "All we get on the other side is whatever we can dive with."

"Well that sucks," Yoshi says.

"It's bad enough that we have to leave the vehicles behind," Hollywood says. "But trying to consolidate even more? That's gonna be rough."

"Plus," says Chuck. "There are flounders."

The team looks confused, but I catch Bumper leaning away from Chuck and making a cutting motion across his throat. They all seem to understand even though I know the joke is lost on them. I make a mental note to fill them in later, and I'm savoring the fact that Chuck was only allowed to download military data and some movies, 'cause this is funny as hell.

"Clock's ticking, so we're gonna put it to a vote," I say. "Either we look for a sewer system that stops the field, or we go offshore and dive. One probably lets us haul more gear, assuming we find an unobstructed shaft running perpendicular to the dome——"

"That's deep enough," Bumper interjects.

I nod. "The other means we are less prepared on the other side, but we can cross a lot sooner and know it's a direct route."

"And once we cross out there, then what?" Yoshi asks.

Bumper picks up with what we discussed on the ride back. "Right now, the currents favor the boat drifting toward the energy field. We won't want to wait for the boat to move on its own, but it's good to know we won't be fighting it so long as conditions stay as is. I'll be last in the water and bring a tow line with me. Between the current and all of us pulling, we can get *Best of Boat Worlds* across before Z-Lo breaks a sweat."

"Kid's already sweating," Hollywood says.

"Well, scratch that timetable."

"Hey, I surf, okay?" Z-Lo says in protest. "I know how to swim."

I wink at the kid, then bring everyone's attention back to the map. "Once everyone's aboard, we'll continue to the Upper Bay. Hug the shore, and see what there is to see."

A few seconds pass as everyone seems to process the two options.

"So how 'bout it?" Hollywood asks the team. "We can't stand here all day."

Yoshi speaks first. "I'd rather drown in seawater than in a river of liquid ass."

"Second," Z-Lo adds.

"Hollywood?" I ask.

"I don't mind the sewer idea so much. Diving's never been my strong suit. But I also don't like our odds of finding a sewer tunnel that fits the specs." She purses her lips and moves them back and forth a few times. "Ocean."

"Ghost?"

He grunts. "I can swim." But he looks like he's doing his best to hide the pain despite the meds he's on.

"You sure about that? Took some nasty hits. No shame in taking another route, if that's what we need to do."

Ghost fixes his eyes on me, unblinking. "I said, I can do it."

God, this guy doesn't know how *not* to be intense. And whether it's his ego talking or he really knows his limits, I believe him if he says he can do it.

"On that note," Yoshi says. "We have two wounded, and the crapper holes increase risk of infection."

"Good point." I nod at Bumper.

"Really? You're asking a Navy SEAL if he wants to dive?"

I give him a snarky grin. "And I say dive too."

"Don't I get a say?" Aaron asks.

"You a part of the team?"

He smiles and nods. "I'm all in, Pat."

I give him a nod back and then look around the circle. "All hands, prepare to dive."

26

1215, Friday, June 25, 2027
Staten Island, New York
Great Kills Park, Offshore

IT TOOK us the better part of thirty minutes to sort gear and prepare it for the crossing. Choosing what stayed and what went was made a whole lot harder when you weren't sure what you were walking into, thanks in large part to Chuck's ominous lack of detail. Granted, I can't blame the guy—he's got directives. But it sure as hell would've been convenient if he could override them some more to save my ass.

In the end, we chose ordnance over nutrients and tactical equipment over comfort. That meant leaving behind all but a few days' worth of food and freshwater in place of as much ammo and Bumper's party favors as we could carry. It also meant ditching more extravagant equipment like tents, sleeping gear, and most extra clothing to prioritize what was preloaded in our bug-out packs. Other items, like GPSs, laptops, tablets, and cameras, were easier to part with, seeing as how they were all bricked. Plus, I don't need devices to navigate the streets of my childhood. The only new gear were snorkels and masks that Z-Lo and Yoshi scavenged from a few of the pleasure craft.

With everything loaded into *Best of Boat Worlds*, the vessel looks about ready to capsize. The condition is exacerbated when we all pile in and prepare to cast off.

"Hey, Z-Lo," Hollywood yells. "Hurry it up."

The kid is running down the dock at us. "Sorry."

"What were you doing back there?"

"Just saying goodbye to Dolores."

"I'm sure you were," she says.

Meanwhile, I take position to Bumper's left at the starboard-side helm. "You feeling okay about all this weight, skipper?"

"We'll be fine." He nods to the alien weapon on my back. "We could always pitch some of the more temperamental firearms over the side."

"I agree," Chuck says. "Let's start with Phantom One's plastic gun."

"He's got you there, Wic," Bumper says as he turns and gives more orders to cast off.

"Don't encourage him."

It's just after 1200 as our fishing-vessel-turned-troop-transport heads into open waters and begins its voyage north. Bumper's got *Best of Boat Worlds* at half throttle, no doubt due to our weight. Whoever said SEALs can't be sensitive hasn't seen this guy helm a severely over-laden ship through two-foot seas. Bumper's got the craft rolling with the swells, surging along Staten Island's coast like a pro.

Not everyone's enjoying it, though. Hollywood seems ready to vomit, and—well, Aaron just did. Poor guy.

"Psst," Chuck says.

I lean down to him.

"Are they nervous about, you know, the flounders?"

Another ten minutes and we're close enough to the dome that Bumper starts giving instructions. He kicks into drill instructor mode, and his tone is all business.

"All right, listen up. For those unfamiliar with a surface dive, you're gonna prep yourself by taking three steady breaths. None of that hyperventilation crap you see in the movies. Just slow and steady. Then, when you're good to go, don't just scramble down. You'll use up all your oxygen and only get a few feet. Instead, I want you pulling your knees up to make a ball and then roll forward."

Bumper demonstrates the maneuver with a free hand.

"Once you're inverted, you kick your legs out. That will drive your mass straight down."

He grabs a white line that he was working on back at the dock and holds it up.

"I'm gonna be dangling this depth lead with a weight and a ten-foot marker on it. The tape's bright orange, so you can't miss it even without your mask. Likewise, I'm gonna ask Master Gunnery Sergeant Finnegan here to take a similar line with him, as he'll be going first. He'll hold it in place, and you will traverse until you can touch the tag on his line. What will you touch?"

"The tag on his line," everyone replies.

"Now, once you start swimming level, your lungs are gonna tell you to surface. Do not listen to them. They're lying because they're greedy little self-indulgent bastards. You have enough oxygen in your blood to last you a few minutes as long as you keep your movements slow and smooth. But a million years of evolutionary instinct to want to suck air is so strong that your body is gonna want to make you do things that you should not do. People don't drown because they run out of oxygen; they drown because they try and breathe water like a goddamn fish. Repeat after me: I am not a goddamn fish."

"I am not a goddamn fish," everyone says.

"I cannot breathe water," Bumper continues.

"I cannot breathe water," the group replies.

"And if one of you drowns on this evolution, I will personally kick your ass until you're breathing has resumed topside. Is that clear?"

Half the team says, "Yes, Petty Officer First Class Johnson," while the other gets out, "First Class Bumper." Glad I'm not the only one who couldn't recall his real name and rank in time.

Bumper cracks a smile. "Once you're at Wic's lead and touch his tag, you may swim up as fast as you damn well please and surface. You will hold that position until I appear, and then you take hold of the line I hand you and follow my instructions to pull in the direction I indicate. Once our vessel is clear of the force field, we will re-enter the boat in order of weakest to strongest swimmers and proceed on our merry way. Are there any questions?"

Heads shake.

Bumper looks at me. "Back to you, Master Guns."

"All right. Everyone down to your skivvies. It's time to get wet."

"I FEEL it's worth noting that your species is far better looking with clothes on than not," Chuck says as I strip down to my boxer briefs and position the mask over my face.

"Can't fault you there, Chuckles. But not everyone has your refined sense of taste."

The team has taken to whistling at each other, especially at Hollywood, who's wearing a black sports bra and white Hello Kitty panties. But she seems to be ignoring the catcalls like a pro.

Then Bumper yells, "God, Z-Lo. Get your underwear back on. No one needs to see that."

"What? I don't like swimming in a wetsuit with my boxers."

"You're not getting a wet suit, genius," Hollywood says, unfazed.

"Oh."

"Your species does seem to have some very strange rituals," Chuck adds. "Are you all this sexually driven?"

"Eh. The military produces a unique breed of human."

"I see. Duly noted."

I leave Chuck, cross the stern, and climb onto the transom. As Hollywood leans out to hand me the coiled marker line, Z-Lo jumps behind her, throws his hands up, and starts gyrating his hips in a less-than-gentlemanly manner.

"Settle down, Private," I yell at him.

As if she has eyes in the back of her head, Hollywood says, "I got this." Then she spins around and gets uncomfortably close to Z-Lo.

The kid not only stops dancing but backpedals until his head hits the boat's hardtop.

"What's the matter, Laszlo," Hollywood says. "Dolores stop answering your texts?"

413

CHRISTOPHER HOPPER & J.N. CHANEY

"What? No. She texted me last—" Z-Lo tightens his lips and looks to the side.

The rest of the guys start ribbing him for this. But apparently, Hollywood isn't done yet.

"Ya know, boys like you love to fantasize." She looks him up and down. "But until you earn the right to take out a lady like me? All you get is what's out there." She points off the boat.

Z-Lo looks around nervously. "And what's that?"

"Wet dreams."

The rest of the guys let out a barrage of "Ohhhh," "Snnnnap," and "Day-umm" as Hollywood spins away and walks back to the transom.

"Be dangerous out there, Wic," she says. "But stay safe."

"I'd tell you to do the same, but looks like you've got that covered."

She winks at me. "It ain't my first rodeo."

"Clearly." I sling the coiled line over my shoulder and then look to the captain.

"You ready?" Bumper asks me.

I give him the okay sign, and he starts backing the boat toward the force field. When he's just about as close as he was last time, he orders me into the water.

I give a two-fingered wave. "See you all on the other side."

I jump in and then tap the top of my head in the universal sign that I'm good. The water isn't bad. Lower seventies, maybe. And with the strong midday sun, I don't see hypothermia being an issue for anyone. Just as long as this goes smoothly.

I take a second to orient myself with the shimmering blue wall, then I take a few steady breaths and pull my knees up like Bumper instructed.

As soon as my head is down, I spot the orange tape ten feet below. Even with the dome's fading light illuminating the murky brownish-green water, I still can't make out the ocean floor some thirty feet down. Then again, this is New York. I extend my legs overhead and let them propel me straight down. The current twists my body a little, but I manage to hold my orientation with three smooth breaststrokes before meeting the tape.

I double-check the energy field. It's moving up and down, fading in and out with the motion of the swells above. But the ten-foot depth mark was a good call, allowing for at least two feet of margin from the wall's lowest point.

A chill travels down my body as I swim underneath the boundary. I can't tell if the goosebumps are from the thermocline or that I just traveled inside the enemy's territory. I swim hard, counting off five and then six strokes before looking up. And just as Bumper said, my lungs are burning, trying their damnedest to get me to take a breath.

I'm clear of the wall, so I beat my way up as fast as I can. Once my head clears the surface, I turn and give those above me the okay hand signal.

"I'm good," I say.

They look like they're talking back, but their voices and the boat's gurgling exhaust are muffled.

I also notice right away that the dome is defusing the sunlight and it is cast in an eerie blue. The air feels a few degrees cooler too, and I wonder if that's on purpose for the sake of the Androchidans' eyesight. Somewhere in the distance, I hear the familiar shrieks of seagulls and the barks of sea lions.

But there's no time to dwell on these observations. I've got a job to do.

I hoist the line off my shoulders and start unspooling it so that the weight drops directly below me. When my hands reach the end, indicating that the tape is ten feet below, I give Bumper the all-clear.

He waves and then appears to order Yoshi into the water next. I gather that the choice was on purpose in order to boost the confidence of the weaker swimmers, like Hollywood and Aaron, or the injured, like Ghost and Z-Lo. Then again, I may just be reading too much into the situation. Force of habit.

I stick my face in the water to track Yoshi. Whatever fears I had about the next in line being less than competent are dissuaded as Yoshi shoots to the first mark, swims laterally using the dolphin kick, and then surges up once he reaches my mark. He even offers me a little hand wave as he ascends.

"Show off," I say once he surfaces.

"Bumper asked me to make it look easy."

So I was right after all. "That may have looked a little too easy."

"Thanks." And with a shocking reveal, Yoshi pulls up his flask, uncaps the container, and takes a swig. "You?"

I wave him off. "You pull that outta your ass crack?"

"Waistband."

"You got issues, pal."

"Don't we all." He takes another swig and then stuffs the flask back down.

"Where'd you find more?"

"Marina. Every boat's got a stash."

"Fair enough." I whip my finger through the air and yell, "Next."

OF THE NEXT FOUR, Ghost struggles the most, and Z-Lo the least, which is surprising given the kid's shoulder injury. Then again, he is a surfer, and he's young. Must be nice. Aaron comes the closest to the wall's boundary layer, saying he thinks he got burned on the back of his thighs when he swam under it. Yoshi takes a peek and says it's nothing some aloe vera can't handle when we pull up to the next CVS.

Then it's Bumper's turn.

With everyone on my side treading water, the SEAL blows us a kiss and then dives off the boat's starboard side.

I put my face in the water and follow him through my mask just to make sure he doesn't clip the wall. I notice that Hollywood's doing the same.

Bumper enters the water with a minimal splash, which is saying something given his powerful physique, and shoots under the ten-foot mark without taking a single stroke. Then he grabs the line, swoops under our position, and does Yoshi's dolphin kick to the surface.

"Now *that's* showing off," Yoshi says to me.

"Let's pull it across, team," Bumper yells without seeming to take a breath.

The white line snaps taught next to our heads, and we all grab hold, some more desperately than others. Ghost, for example, really seems to be struggling to stay afloat, wincing and sucking air hard.

"Lay on your back, Ghost," Bumper says. "We got this."

Ghost doesn't protest. He pushes away from the group and then leans back into the water.

Meanwhile, Bumper starts calling out orders to shoulder the rope with our off-hands and pulling water with our dominant arms. He and Z-Lo are doing the lion's share of work, but having everyone on the line makes drawing *Best of Boat Worlds* inside the dome much easier.

"Hey," Hollywood says from behind me. "Whaddya think LVK 9143 stands for?"

I start laughing and almost lose my grip on the tow line. "Dunno. Guess you'll just have to ask Bumper."

As the Dyer 29 slides through the wall, I hear what sounds like a bug zapper popping in the cabin.

"What is that?" Hollywood asks. She and the others seem to be hearing it too.

"It's your infernal arachnid population," Charles says as he emerges from the force field. "They seem to have targeted your boat with extreme prejudice and are paying the price for choosing your vessel as their nesting grounds. Good riddance, I say. Now, if you would all please climb aboard before the flounders get you, I would greatly appreciate that. I'm not sure how well my emotions would handle knowing that one of you is being digested over many millennia."

"What the hell did you tell him?" Hollywood whispers beside me.

"Later," I whisper back. "Just let it play."

"And, oh God—is Phantom Watch okay? He isn't moving as far as my sensors can tell. And I can't get a visual on him. Please tell me it wasn't a flounder attack."

"I wasn't attacked," Ghost says from his back. "Just resting."

"Oh, bloody praise be to the Archbishop of Canterbury. You had me worried sick, grumpy sniper. Ugh. I can't take this."

With the boat well away from the wall, Bumper says, "Wic, take the helm and make sure we keep off the wall. Z-Lo and Yoshi, I need you up to help haul up Ghost."

We all follow orders, and over the next three minutes everyone gets topside and air-dries in their skivvies. Z-Lo is doing a good job of keeping his eyes averted from Hollywood too. Smart kid.

With everyone safe, I notice something moving back on Staten Island. That's when I realize that I hadn't heard seagulls or sea lions before. I had heard people. Tens of thousands of people.

PART THREE

27

1335, Friday, June 25, 2027
Brooklyn, New York
Upper Bay

THE TEAM'S been quiet since we left Staten Island, everyone watching the water peel away from the boat's stern as we head north into New York Harbor's Upper Bay.

Whatever sense of adventure and accomplishment we'd felt before vanished the moment we saw the masses trudging along the beaches this side of the dome. People waved their arms at us—screamed at us—hoping we'd turn west and help them.

Aside from seeing throngs of suffering humanity caged in like animals, I got nauseated thinking about the poor souls who maybe saw what we did and might try it in reverse. Worse still, I wondered how many had already tried swimming under it as an option hours ago—and failed. It's probably a miracle that we didn't run into any floating body parts.

In the end, Bumper gave *Best of Boat Worlds* more throttle and powered northeast toward Brooklyn, leaving the horrors of Staten Island behind. Even then, our team was taking turns with the binocs, staring back at the masses until I was forced to confiscate the optics. No one needs to witness our species suffer anymore; there will be plenty of time for that later. Even as I look northward at Brooklyn, I shudder to think about how my stompin' grounds have been turned into a war zone.

In a strange way, however, the site of untold thousands filing toward Verrazzano-Narrows Bridge has had a peculiar effect on the team. It's not the first time I've seen it, either. Any time a unit has a sobering encounter with who they're fighting for, the often existential *why* that's wrapped up in a flag or a mantra suddenly crystallizes into an objective purpose. A person. A town. Names and faces— even dead ones. They all serve to anneal warriors' hearts with the reason they've put themselves in harm's way.

The danger, of course, is that if no one gives the unspoken emotions direction, they can often lead fighters into forgotten foxholes that, sometimes, they don't come out of.

My clothes are back on, and I've secured my plate carrier. Chuck and my SCAR are lying across the top of the dash opposite Bumper, and my helmet's tucked under one arm. My other hand is holding a seatback to steady me against the boat's rhythmic rise and fall through the swells.

"Listen up, team," I say above the roar of the inboard motor coming from beneath our feet. "We're still about twenty mikes—"

"Thirty," Bumper corrects.

"We're still about thirty mikes out from a possible objective." I point toward the most notable feature in the northern sky: the skinny blue funnel emanating from Lower Manhattan that shoots up several miles and folds outward to create the dome's shape. "So, until then, I want us prepping to land. That means we need to double-check each other's equipment, stay cool, and be ready to problem-solve. Once we make landfall, we're gonna have to think on our feet and do it fast.

"I realize we're still getting to know each other too. Hell, it hasn't even been a whole day yet. But as most of you know, fighting has a way for forging bonds that are pretty hard to break, even if it is between a crayon-eating Leatherneck and a flip flop-wearing military tourist."

"You should see my scrapbooks," Yoshi says.

Everyone laughs a little, which is good. But I can tell they're still uptight.

"Point is, right now, we need to be circling around what we can control, not the things we can't, and what we do know, not the things we don't."

I pause to make sure everyone's tracking with me so far, even Bumper. He gives me a nod from the helm.

"First of all, we can control ourselves. We can stay clear of mind, check our emotions, and choose to focus on our jobs and the condition of the person on our right and left. Roger?"

They all nod, most giving understated "Roger"s in reply.

"We're gonna see some rough stuff ahead. People in need. People in pain. But we control our minds and stay focused. If we do that, we save a whole lot more than we would otherwise. It's gonna be hell. But we get paid to make the hard calls and stay focused on the mission. Agreed?"

"Agreed," they say with a little more resolve this time.

"Secondly, we know we can work together. If that were all we had going for us into this next engagement, it'd be enough for me. We communicate, we fight hard, we're fast—"

"And we gave those death angels hell back there," Z-Lo says.

"OTF," Hollywood says.

More head nods and "OTF"s circulate.

"Which leads me to my next point. This enemy bleeds."

"Yeah, they do." Z-Lo claps his hands and rubs them together like he's getting psyched up to wrestle an opponent.

I smile and raise my chin at him. His is the spirit we need, and I'm reminded of the many times that the younger generation has reinvigorated the older. Granted, they need our wisdom and experience—God help them—but we need their enthusiasm and energy to fight.

"We've proven we can take them out. And not just because of Chuck here"—I pat him gingerly.

"Thank you for the recognition," he says.

"We love you, Sir Charles," Hollywood calls in a sing-song voice with a hand beside her mouth.

"You people really are sickeningly endearing. You know that, don't know?"

I pat Sir Charles one more time and then move on. "The Anderkins—"

"Androchidans," Chuck corrects.

"Anderkins."

"Stop it. That's not their name. It makes them sound like a child's plush toy or something."

Contrary to popular belief, or at least Chuck's belief, I used the term Anderkins on purpose. The militaries of every civilization have a long history of giving their enemies nicknames in order to demean the targets in the eyes of the fighting forces. I was hoping for a funny variant on the aliens' strange name. But Chuck here has taken it to a whole new level, and by mistake too.

"A plush toy," I say with a nod of my head. "That's exactly right."

"Ugly ass sumbitches too," Bumper adds.

"I don't understand what's happening here," Chuck says. "It's as if you're not getting my point at all."

Hollywood smiles. "Oh, we got it, sweet cheeks. Loud and clear. Thanks."

"I'm... What just... Did you not hear anything I said?"

"Don't hurt yourself, Chuckles." I wipe some saltwater off my nose and then move on. "As I was saying, the *Anderkins* might have superior tech, as evidenced by Sir Charles, the bots, the drones, and the ARUs, but I'm sure you've noticed that they lack strategy."

"Not sure I follow," Z-Lo asks.

"The death angel that went after Wic," Ghost says. "Never should have done that."

"And the way the unit crossed the quad at Rutgers in the open like that," Hollywood adds. "That was stupid. Hell, even how they approached the building was..." She tilts her head. "It was cocky. And also stupid."

"Okay, yeah. I can see that," Z-Lo says with several emphatic nods. He could be buckling under peer pressure for all I know, but he seems sincere.

"I think we could pick apart all the engagements we've had with them and find some serious flaws," I say. "And, Hollywood, you're hitting something on the head there. They're overconfident. They see us as merchandise. Which means it's our fight to win if we want it. The worst mistake any army can make is underestimating the enemy. And these emeffers?" I start nodding my head and looking around the team. "They've underestimated the wrong sons a' bitches."

"OTF, baby," Bumper says in a deep baritone.

"OTF," everyone else replies.

Now the boat's spirit is starting to rise. That's good.

"With all that in mind," I say. "I don't think we're dealing with a military force here."

Curious glances get exchanged before Bumper asks, "How do you figure?"

I pose the next question to him. "As a Navy SEAL, have you ever been tasked with POW roundup and containment?"

He shakes his head. "No."

"We have," Hollywood offers. "Be All That You Can Be."

"Fair point. And hat's off to the Army for picking up Uncle Sam's latrine duty," I say with a smile.

She gives me a lazy salute. "Anything to help the cause."

"But let's go a step further." I point back toward Staten Island. "Those aren't POWs. This isn't a war for them. This is a business. So these bastards?" I give the team a nasty scowl. "They're just ranchers herding cattle for the man. They don't know how to patrol an AO for threats. They're not a rifle squad who can locate, close with, and destroy an enemy. They're shepherds with big ass sticks trying to round up a flock."

"I'll have you know that I'm far more valuable than a big ass stick," Chuck blurts out.

This makes the team laugh and adds to my pep talk's growing momentum. Now the boat's alive with the kind of spirit we need. The sort that reminds brave men and women what they're made of, and that they're unstoppable so long as they remember their training, work together, and make smart calls—one, after another, after another, until the battle is won.

Every tactician worth their stripes will tell you that a unit with a reason to fight has the advantage even if the odds are stacked against them. The psychological advantage always favors the team who will die for their cause, and the Anderkins sure ain't that. I've heard historians say that any force attacking a fixed home-field position needs five times the engagement force as the defenders, and I believe it. Hell, I've seen it—part of assaults whose commanders should have paid more attention to their Annapolis's history classes. In the Battle of Bunker Hill, the British Army took almost two-and-a-half times as many casualties than the Continental Army's. The only reason we lost was because we ran outta ammo.

"I'll say it again: this is *not* a war for them." I thrust a finger to the north. "But we're gonna make a goddamn war."

"Yeah, we are," Z-Lo says. The rest join in; even Ghost is rocking his torso in line with the team.

"Ranchers herd, but warriors fight." I take a step forward. "And we are the warriors in this fight."

"Damn straight," Ghost says in a rare display of emotion. Must be the meds.

Damn straight indeed.

WE TAKE the next fifteen minutes to consolidate our equipment, refresh magazines that got missed during the drive from Rutgers, and hydrate some more. Everyone takes their turn pissing off the side of the boat too—all save Hollywood. When Yoshi tells her that we'll all turn around, she laughs.

"I went when we were in the water, genius," she says.

"So that's why I felt a warm spot," Z-Lo replies with a grin.

"Nah," Bumper says. "That was my piss."

"Awe, damn, bro. Why you gotta do me like that?" Z-Lo gives his whole body a shake. "Eeeeesh."

Then I notice Bumper give Hollywood a wink.

She smiles and looks down.

We also talk through several landing scenarios, including one that involves mooring the craft and wading ashore but risks losing the boat to onlookers desperate to escape. Another option keeps someone at the helm and with the majority of the gear, but puts us down a man in the field.

When questions arise about getting close enough to the epicenter of whatever awaits us to the north, Chuck assures us that his EMDE can provide adequate cover for the boat but should only be employed in the final minutes before landfall. He also claims that the Anderkins won't be studying the water as much as they'll be focused on herding humans. That, and our afternoon sun is blowing out some of the aliens' natural vision. Should we need to retreat, his best advice is to submerge in the harbor as the cooler water should adequately mask our heat signatures, or at least make them less precise.

I fold my arms. "The only thing there is that I'm not sure which I fear more: dying from alien rounds or from what's in the Hudson."

This gets a laugh from those familiar with New York's notoriously contaminated waterways.

"Damn flounders," Chuck whispers.

As we clear the Narrows and cut into New York Bay, I notice the blue glow at the funnel's base is brightest just off the bow to starboard, above Red Hook. That puts the epicenter not in Lower Manhattan proper, but in the East River.

Bumper guides our ship through Red Hook Channel and slows as we approach Governor's Island. Then, when he turns to starboard, cutting between Governor's Island and Brooklyn through Buttermilk Channel, we all get our first look at the alien monstrosity overtaking the most iconic span in the city.

The Brooklyn Bridge.

28

1405, Friday, June 25, 2027
Brooklyn, New York
Diamond Reef, Lower East River

"HOLY MARY MOTHER OF GOD." Z-Lo crosses himself, bows his head, and kisses his index finger.

"Something tells me that's got nothing to do with the blessed virgin or her son," Hollywood says.

"But it has everything to do with my research," Aaron says. Of anyone on the boat, he's the most enthusiastic. Well, really, he's the only one who's enthusiastic; everyone else looks scared shitless.

Bisecting the Brooklyn Bridge is a portal ring. Only this one is two or three times the size of the one in Antarctica. That, and it's floating, and the bridge is running right through the middle.

"How is any of that possible?" I ask Aaron. "And shouldn't the portal's field be cutting the bridge in two?"

"Not necessarily." Aaron looks down and scribbles frantically in a small Moleskine notebook—something we both picked up in our youth. "Working on it."

"What's the diameter?" I ask Bumper.

He's all but pressed his face against the boat's windshield. "Five, six-hundred feet, maybe?"

"Yut. Same."

"Ugh," Chuck exclaims out of nowhere. "It's 173.74 meters. Why are you Americans so obsessed with your Imperial system of measurement? I can't understand you people. Metric is so much easier to calculate."

"That's 570 feet and 1/25th of an inch," Ghost replies. When everyone looks at him, he shrugs. "It's not hard."

"Well that's irregular," Chuck says with an attitude.

"Not now," I reply, eyes fixed on the ring.

"What do you mean not now? This now is as perfect as any other now. *Not now.* Pretty much the whole rest of the world uses this metric system I'm learning so much about, including the scientific community, I might add, which... Hey. Is anyone listening to me?"

"Nope," I say.

"That ring... it's just hanging there," Yoshi says as he takes a swig from his flask.

"So we're just going to ignore this then?" Chuck asks.

I nod. "Guessing the lower sweep is fifty feet off the water. Leave another ninety to a hundred feet to the bridge's deck."

"How do you know that?" Z-Lo asks.

"Cause I grew up wondering if I could jump off it and live." I don't wanna tell the kid that, for some of those times, I hoped I wouldn't survive.

"I am going to have so much fun in our next group therapy session, you know," says Chuck. "Wait until our therapist learns that not only did you ignore me, but that you dismiss the fact that 94.7 percent of your planet's population uses the metric system."

"Well, 94.7 percent of the world's population didn't land on the moon first," I say, only half focused on Chuck's ramblings.

"Well, okay. Fine. That's valid. But it's still only just a moon— whoopty do. And yet you *Americans* continue to insist on using an outdated, cumbersome, and... Seriously? No one's even looking at me now? Oh, I give up."

Aside from the ring's sheer scale is the intense glow coming from two primary places. The first is from the ring's peak. The second is from the portal plane that's bisecting the bridge.

"How'd they even get it around the goddamn bridge?" Bumper asks.

"Good question." I look to Aaron, who's studying the shape through the binoculars. "Think they brought it in during the third opening?"

"Third what?" Hollywood asks.

I wave her off, still looking at Aaron.

"No." He makes more notes. "Doubtful. It would've taken too long to break down, move, and reassemble. My guess? Judging from the amount of algae it's shedding?" He looks up at me. "It's been here for a very, very long time."

"Where would you even hide something like that?" Z-Lo asks. But as soon as he finishes the question, I see understanding dawn in his eyes. "Oh."

"Seventy-one percent of the world is—"

"Is covered in water," Hollywood says, cutting off Aaron.

He nods. "Lots and lots of room. As for how they got it around the bridge? No idea beyond there being a break in the structure. That's conventional wisdom. But this…" He chuckles to himself. "This is far from conventional. And the dome's force field is being generated from the apex. I don't even know how that's possible."

However, more disturbing than the otherworldly structure and its seemingly endless supply of power are the masses of people walking toward the portal plane from both sides of the bridge.

"My God." I grip the fuselage and lean toward the glass. "Do you see that?"

Aaron grunts. "They're using the bridge as a double-sided entry ramp."

"It's a goddamn cattle push," Ghost says. His Texas drawl reminds me that my metaphor from earlier wasn't lost on him. The man probably rode on a few runs himself.

"But highly efficient," Aaron says as he jots down more notes in his book. "I have a theory about the two different forms of energy we're seeing too."

When Aaron doesn't continue, I have to prompt him. Did this as a kid too.

"Oh, right. Sorry. Umm, so the energy that's coming out the top, for the dome, it repels living tissue—"

"Does more than repel it," Hollywood says with a huff.

Aaron replies with a nod and a nervous laugh. "Yes, but it ignores non-living matter, allowing it to pass. Whereas here, if the bridge is intact, that also means the portal field ignores non-living matter, but conversely allows living tissue to enter it."

"So…" Bumper scratches his jawline. "You think it lets people

436

through but not stuff. What, they get to the other side naked or something?"

"Naked and weaponless," I add.

The ring's effectiveness at delivering a powerless population to whatever lies on the other side is sobering. Bumper looks uneasy, and I'm sure I look about the same, especially as I think on those victims who might have joint replacements, plates, and pacemakers. God, help us.

Back on the binocs, Aaron adds, "It appears as though they've brought in some additional equipment too."

I ask for the optics and then take a look. "Staging area."

"For real?" Bumper asks.

I nod and hand him the binocs.

He one-hands them as he works the helm. "Looks like ARUs. Maybe some sort of a mobile command center on either side. And"—he pauses for a second—"air support."

"What?" I take back the optics. Sure enough, there's a craft the size of a freight container with forward and aft deployment ramps along with four elongated vertical engine clusters mounted at the ends of extension arms.

"There goes one," Yoshi says.

I look to where he's pointing and then track it with my optics. "It's a transport all right. Some sort of dropship. Engine fires look the same as what's beneath the ARUs and the drones."

"All the more reason to stay clear," says Hollywood.

"Unless, ya know, we board one, I grab the controls, and then we strafe 'em the hell apart," Z-Lo says.

"Huh. Complete with hand motions and sound effects," I say in mock admiration.

Z-Lo puts his hands down and gets a dopey look about him. "I was just trying to offer a suggestion."

"I know, kid. Not bad. Just, not today."

"Okay, yeah. Sure."

"Chuck," I say. "How soon before you think we're an item of interest? Feeling pretty exposed out here."

"I may or may not be monitoring the enemy's communications. At such time that I feel the Phantoms are in jeopardy, I will be sure to take the necessary precautions. Until then, I recommend maintaining a constant speed and remaining close to shore."

"Works for me." I still don't like Chuck's mismatched directives, but having him around is better than not.

Bumper steers us closer to shore and sets *Best of Boat Worlds* at ten knots.

Just as we leave Buttermilk Channel and Governor's Island behind, Chuck speaks up.

"I'm beginning to pick up some notable chatter about an anomaly whose coordinates correlate with our own."

I look across and see Pier Six directly to starboard. We could ditch the boat now, but it would be a long walk through densely crowded streets.

"How soon before you think you'll need to engage your stealthy chameleon superpower?" I ask.

"I already have. And you'll be happy to know that the *Anderkins* have ordered the patrol drones back."

"Nice work." I give him another pat. "Think you can get us to Pier One?"

"Show me."

I raise him to my shoulder and aim at the last Brooklyn pier this side of the bridge. Last time I was there, it offered a public lookout, access to a few shops and cafes, and a botanical garden that butted up against the bridge's east-side tower base.

"That shouldn't be a problem, Patrick. So long as you find a way to disembark and blend in with your surroundings immediately. Should you tarry any longer, I feel we will be careening toward an unfortunate scenario where you are displeased with my firing capabilities, and I am displeased with your chronic halitosis."

"I don't have bad breath."

"Mmm. They say you can never smell your own…"

I thrust him back on the console.

"…and that anger is the first sign of acknowledging guilt."

"So is throwing a weapon overboard to the flounder."

"Ah. Yes, well… We wouldn't want that now, would we."

I look at Bumper. "Take us to Pier One."

"Imports, coming up," he says back.

———

It's become clear to me that the only way we're shutting this ring down is by doing to it what we should have done to the first one: blowing it the hell up.

My first question on the feasibility of breaking it apart goes to the most powerful weapon we have onboard: Sir Chucksalot. However, he insists that breaking the ring would be a long shot even with a full charge and maximum-yield. I can't be a hundred percent sure that he's telling the truth, as this question seems to interfere with his second directive, but based on what I've seen him do so far, not even His Majesty seems capable of blasting through a column that looks to be more than half the width of the bridge itself.

The next idea we speed through is that of planting C-4 on the ring. It's crazy, of course, but no option is a bad one until you rule it out.

"I'm guessing we'd need every ounce I brought with me," Bumper says as we near our destination. "All the Semtex I have too. I mean, look at that thing."

We're all staring straight up at it now, heads back. The ring's size is mind-numbing.

"How'd we even get it up there?" Z-Lo asks.

"You mean, down there," I reply. "We'll rappel."

"What?" Z-Lo looks between me and the bridge twice. "From under the…?"

"Under the deck, yut."

"Oh, damn."

"What's the matter, Laszlo?" Hollywood double-checks his vest and cinches a strap tight. "Scared of heights?"

"No, not totally. I mean, sure, like everybody, a little. But, no."

"Yeah, ya are," Bumper says.

"What do you think, Chuck?" I ask.

"About Laszlo being deathly afraid of heights? Or the likelihood that you either blow yourselves up or fall to your deaths?" He laughs. "Ha ha! High to very high on all three counts. Just a moment; I'm buying stock in flounder food right now."

"Cute, Chuck. Risk to ourselves aside, what do you think about our chances of cracking that sucker?"

"I think if you wait a little while, you might come up with a better plan."

"Says the guy who just told us to hurry up."

"Don't say I didn't warn you."

I give Chuck a shrewd half-smile. "Noted. So that settles it.

We're climbing the bridge, rappelling to the ring, and planting the charges."

"We've got four harnesses and two sixty-meter ropes," Hollywood says.

"Most comfortable climbing?" I ask.

Bumper, Hollywood, and Yoshi raise their hands.

"Can you drive a boat?" I ask Z-Lo.

"Does it mean I don't have to climb?"

"Can you drive a boat? Yes or no?" I say more sternly.

"Yeah, of course, Master Guns."

"Good. Harnesses to Bumper, Hollywood, Yoshi, and me. Aaron, you're staying put in the boat with Z-Lo. Ghost, you're making yourself useful in the heavens." I thumb toward the buildings along the waterfront. "Can you manage?"

"Roger."

"Everyone else good?"

Heads nod, and okay signs are made.

We're two mikes from making landfall, and people are taking more notice of us. While Chuck's intel says the *plushies* are a little hard of seeing at midday, humans are definitely the opposite. Already, mothers ask us to take their babies, and kids cry for rides. But with any luck, the bridge's size and the underdeck security floors will keep the general public from giving away our position with their looks. Well, that, and other than those in our immediate vicinity, most people seem focused on finding ways toward the crowd-relief values offered by heading up the bridge to the east.

"Now, the really hard part," I say. "Don't stop to help anybody. Keep your eyes forward. Remember, our mission includes them but is not limited to them. We crack this sucker, and everyone we pass in those streets gets to fight another day. Roger?"

"Roger," they all reply. But I can tell that they're having trouble staying focused on me already.

"What about me?" Chuck asks. "You haven't slung me over your back for a marvelous view of your ass yet, Patrick."

"That's 'cause you're staying here, pal."

"I'm what?"

"Z-Lo and Aaron are your new priority. And this is our support vessel for exfil once we descend."

"But, but, but—"

"No buts. This is an order from User Number Nine. You use whatever capacitor energy you have left to keep this boat covered. Roger?"

"I'm really beginning to hate this Roger person."

The team smiles.

"And can I transfer user privileges or something?" I ask Chuck.

This gets some eyebrow raises from the team members.

"You mean, as in you want to allow the other Phantoms to fondle me?"

"Something like that, yut."

Chuck pauses. "You think they'll fight over me?"

"If you're lucky." I give him a wink. "So can you?"

"No, Patrick. They lack the necessary—"

"Dilithium crystal hoo-ha. Yut, I got it."

"Oh, that was dreadful." He lets out a long sigh. "But I suppose I can minimize my defense capabilities if and when they need to fondle me, like I did with Chuck Two back there."

I look at Z-Lo and Aaron. "Just make sure not to touch him without gloves on, okay? Maybe wrap him in a poncho first or something."

"A poncho? Just who do you think I—"

"And Chuck? Keep 'em covered."

"Of course, Patrick. Now, if you're really set on doing this whole blow up the ring thing, I feel I must warn you that your comms will no longer be encrypted, so use them sparingly."

"How's that?"

"Well, since the four of you will be climbing some 145 feet overhead, and in the middle of the East River, that is beyond my range of keeping your communications scrambled with any certainty. Z-Lo's and mine, no problem. But yours? Just know that the Androchidans—"

"Anderkins," Hollywood says.

"—that the *Ander-babies* will be able to hear you and, more than likely, zero in on your location. Though, I will get a good laugh as they try to figure out why you appear to be under their feet."

"Ander-babies," Bumper says. "Frickin' adorable. Now I want one."

"Same," Hollywood says.

"One mike," Bumper adds, holding up his index finger to the team.

"Z-Lo," I say. "I want you keeping away from shore. Protect Aaron, and listen to whatever intel Chuck gives you."

"Roger."

"But who's going to protect me?" Chucks asks.

"Aaron will," I say.

Chuck doesn't say anything.

"You got a problem with that?" I ask him.

"No. It's just that, I've seen him with a weapon, and, well, it's not great."

"Agreed."

"Hey," Aaron protests.

"Which is why it's not going to come to any of that," I say. "We're gonna get up there, leave the Christmas presents, and descend into the water for pickup before you know it."

"But, Patrick," Chuck says. "Might we have a contingency plan? For me, I mean?"

"For what scenario?"

"Should the Ander-babies discover the boat while you're away, might Z-Lo toss me into the river?"

I give Chuck a raised eyebrow. "But what about the flounder?"

He gives a long sigh. "I would rather take my chances with the fish than with the aliens. The Anderkins will send me off for recalibration and then wipe me. And I don't mean the butt kind. While we've only been a few hours together, I think it's safe to say that they have been the most wonderful, most—"

"We're not gonna let them wipe your memory, pal. We gotta go."

"You promise?"

"Yut."

"I still think you should hang around a bit longer," Chuck says. "You might, I don't know, get inspired for an alternative plan?"

"Anyone else feel like he's trying to put us off the scent?" Bumper asks.

"I swear, I'm not," Chuck pleads. "It's just that, sometimes, better ideas need time to marinate like a juicy steak. Or open up like a fine wine."

I wink at Chuck. "Wish we could stick around, but we've got a city to save."

29

1435, Friday, June 25, 2027
Brooklyn, New York
Pier 1, East River

WE HAVE to fight our way onto Pier One by pushing civilians aside —harder than I'd like. They're all well-meaning people, and I can't say I wouldn't be doing the same as them if I had a wife and kid. Probably more. But right now, they're a threat to operational security, and the clock is ticking.

Two men fall into the water in wild attempts to get aboard *Best of Boat Worlds* before we push the boat away. One guy's foot slips off the starboard gunwale, and he does a painful split against the side before splashing into the drink, while the other man takes a punch to the face by a pissed off Z-Lo. Kid doesn't even shake his hand out as the trespasser falls in.

With the boat clear of the pier, Hollywood, Bumper, Yoshi, Ghost, and I push our way into the crowd. Once we hit the cobblestone street, Ghost heads off for a gentrified brick warehouse turned upscale storefront and loft apartment while the rest of us turn north. Ahead of us lies a waterfront botanical garden that I routinely used to send Jack's family flowers each year on... particular days. And, just as I remembered, there's a construction fence along the back hedgerow, and beyond it, the Brooklyn Bridge's east tower.

A few curious stragglers follow us into the garden, but most lose interest when they see us brandish our weapons. Only a few need to be yelled at, and their will withers quickly. Let's just say that an annoyed Navy SEAL can be very intimidating.

We take turns going up and over the fence, passing weapons, ropes, explosives, and harnesses as we do until we reassemble on the other side. For the first time, I notice the same kind of strange low-frequency vibration in the ground that I felt back in Antarctica—only I'm much further away from the ring, and this one's considerably bigger.

"Anyone else feeling that?" Hollywood asks.

"It's normal," I say. "Relatively speaking."

She gives me a look that says, "Oh, okay, sure," and then shakes her head.

From there, we fan out and start looking for ways up the stone tower. It doesn't take long for Bumper to conclude that the best way up is an old drain conduit.

"Any volunteers to set belay?" He holds up the rope.

"I'll do it," Yoshi says.

We all step into our harnesses, and then Bumper ties off one end of the rope to Yoshi's locking carabiner. He lifts Yoshi up by the knot to make sure it's secure.

"You're lead climbing this, Super Nintendo," Bumper says. "So no Atari Pitfall. Just nice and easy. Roger?"

"Roger." Yoshi rubs his Mechanix Wear gloves together and then starts up the drainpipe.

We stand in the bridge's shadow and watch the Air Force PJ scramble up the conduit like a monkey. Honestly, it's impressive. Even Bumper gives him a look of surprise. Guy does it in about thirty seconds.

"Imagine how fast he'd do it if he were sober," Hollywood says.

"He probably wouldn't do it at all," I say.

"Huh." She sighs. "Right."

Yoshi pulls himself into the shadows below the bridge's main deck and scampers onto a truss, legs dangling. Then he works at setting up two anchor points for the main belay carabiner on the steel girders, just like Bumper explained. But Yoshi's clearly done this before, not only based on his climbing abilities but how quickly he's tying off the support webbing. Once he's finished, he disconnects himself from the rope and starts feeding a knotted end to Bumper.

Over the next ten minutes, we haul the equipment up to Yoshi, then I belay Bumper, Hollywood belays me, and we pull Hollywood up until our team is secured within the bridge's 150-year-old trusses. On any other day, we'd hear the sounds of car tires and horns on the road above us. Today, all we hear are the muffled sounds of tens of thousands of people marching to an uncertain end.

"Good work, team," I say in an effort to keep everyone focused. "Stay on the truss flats, and watch your step. Hands first, feet follow. Nice and easy."

Everyone complies, and we begin moving along the under-deck girders and out over the East River. The road, about six feet above our heads, extends over the river, passes through the Manhattan-side tower, and then drops down toward City Hall.

The climb through the trusses, though reasonably simple, is not for the faint of heart. I've never minded heights, but even I'm getting the flutters. And I'm glad that Z-Lo stayed behind with Aaron in the boat; this would have been too hard for him. As the bridge takes us away from land, I spot *Best of Boat Worlds* some hundred feet below, and another butterfly tickles my gut.

So far, there's been no activity from the plushies that would indicate we've been seen. But hiding under the bridge's deck is as good a cover as we could hope for given the situation. Still, it's strange to me that moving in the day is safer than operating at night, at least according to Sir Chuck. But I suppose that's all a matter of what star you tan under. Huh, no wonder those things are so goddamn ugly: no vitamin D.

It takes us about fifteen minutes to climb to the bridge's center and approach the ring's trance-inducing blue membrane. With every set of trusses we pass, the low-energy hum gets louder. Likewise, the wind has picked up and is whistling through the beams. Small lightning bolts snap across the field's surface and lick the beams around us.

"Should we be worried about that, Wic?" Hollywood points to the bolts.

"Nah. Some sort of free electrical energy, according to Aaron. Won't hurt. I think."

She nods but doesn't seem convinced. 'Course, neither am I.

It takes a few minutes for Bumper to decide where to tie off the ropes. The portal's shimmering blue surface is causing some of the wind we're feeling—maybe even drawing air in. That poses two serious problems. The first being that if a rope gets sucked in, it might be severed, if Aaron's theory is accurate. A fall from this height would be fatal. The second issue is that I don't think any of us wants to visit the Plushy Palace today, so being blown or sucked into the portal is a no-go. In the end, Bumper chooses anchor positions fifteen yards from the portal wall.

"If we get down to a hundred feet and we're still too far away," he yells above the energy field's sound. "Then we can always swing in."

I nod in appreciation of his conservative approach. Already the two climbing ropes are curving in toward the ring. But their ends are playing in the water, which means that's where we'll be falling if this all goes south. Better to die on Earth than on another planet, I always say.

Sure, ya do, Pat.

We take the next few minutes to split the explosives evenly between Bumper and me. Even though the plan is to set them in the same place, this mission, from the twin two-person teams to the division of equipment, is all about redundancy. I didn't want to say it out loud for fear of jinxing the mission, but if we don't get this done, I'm not sure what other options we'll have. And I'm gonna need a whole lot of alone time and some Redbreast to come up with something else. Assuming I live through this next part, of course. Point is, you *gotta* put all your eggs in one basket if all you've got is one damn basket.

"Explosives go first, spotters tie in second," Bumper yells. Then he wraps his rope through his figure eight, locks into his harness's main 'biner, and gives it two sharp yanks. He signals Yoshi and me to copy his procedure and then helps Hollywood with her rig.

Despite the intensity of the situation, Yoshi seems to be enjoying himself. As he should, I suppose, with a blood alcohol content illegal in most... bars. When we're done, he and I double-check each other's work and give the okay signal.

Hollywood looks like she's having fun too, grinning as Bumper tests her harness and spends some extra time on her backside.

"Everyone set?" Bumper asks.

Yoshi and I answer with hand signals and head nods, but Hollywood speaks up.

"I think I might need my harness checked again. Just to make sure everything is nice and tight." She places a hand on her hip and gives Bumper a little grin.

"Girl, you know you're nice and tight," Bumper says with an appreciative look.

"You wanna double-check me, Super Nintendo?" I ask.

Yoshi gives me a chuckle and a quick shake of his head.

Having never top-roped with two people on the same line at once, I have to watch as Bumper backs into the next truss cell toward the portal and lets out some line. The extra length lets Hollywood step into the cell with him, and then he helps ease her down until she's hanging beneath the trusses, wholly reliant on her harness. The happy look on her face is gone. Then Bumper climbs down and lowers himself on her harness until he's dangling below her.

Yoshi smiles at me. "Our turn."

I nod and move into the next cell back, doing my best to replicate Bumper's example. I'm slower than he was, but I get the concept. And Yoshi seems patient enough with me. Unlike Hollywood's more reserved approach, Yoshi wastes no time in dropping down and enjoying the view. I lower myself and then ease my way below him, using his harness as Bumper did. I lose grip with my left hand and fall.

"Crap," I exclaim to the open air.

A quick wave of vertigo hits me, but I throw my brake hand behind my hip, and my rope snaps taut. But my harness pins my left ball against my thigh.

"You okay there, Tomodachi?" Yoshi asks.

I work to relieve the agony shooting from my groin and notice that my left leg is wrapped around the rope. I'm a hot mess. "Yut. Fine. Thanks."

"No problem."

I take a few deep breaths as the pain ebbs and adjust to my new situation. I'm on a rope, hanging below a drunk Air Force Staff Sergeant, tied off on the Brooklyn Bridge, with enough C-4 and Semtex on my back to take out four Bradley Fighting Vehicles.

"Gung-ho, baby," I say to myself.

Bumper throws me a questioning look and the okay sign.

"A-okay." I take another calming breath to get my heart rate under control and then bring my brake hand forward. The line starts running across my gloved palm, and the four of us descend the portal's face.

It's not every day you get to drop down from the center of the Brooklyn Bridge. I steal a glance south toward my childhood neighborhood of Park Slope and wonder if the 90s redheaded troublemaker ever thought his older self would be rappelling like this to save New York from an alien invasion. Actually, that's precisely the kind of thing he would have expected; anything to get out of that house.

I jerk to a halt when something like the sound of a monstrous bellowing horn cracks the air. And we're not talking a tuba here. It's like the effin' horn from Helm's Deep in Lord of the Rings. The whole damn bridge is shaking enough to vibrate our ropes. Debris that probably hasn't moved in 150 years rains down on us, forcing me to cover my face under my helmet. Just then, I notice movement in the water beneath me.

"HOLY SHIT," Yoshi yells above me, but his voice is nearly drowned out by the continuous *blat* emanating from beneath us.

A column of water, bathed in a near-blinding light, rises from the East River and heads straight for the ring. For a split second, I think something's detonated beneath the surface, sending the torrent toward the bridge's underside. But as the spout ascends, it disappears into the ring's base, and the light fades. Likewise, the noise lessens. A steady *whoosh* like the sound of a waterfall fills the air beneath us as a constant stream of water feeds into some unseen cavity in the ring's outer edge. Z-Lo has spun the Dyer 29 around and is accelerating down the angle that the water column has made.

"What the hell is it?" Hollywood yells.

"Dunno," I reply, still having to shout.

My brain's going a hundred miles per hour as I try and sort this out. Part of me wants to hail Aaron, but we can't risk giving away our location just yet—not until the explosives are planted.

The explosives!

Maybe this is what Chuck was trying to get us to hang around for. Wine opening up, my ass!

"Bumper," I yell. "It's an intake, right?"

"Looks that way."

"What if we drop the payloads and let 'em get sucked in?"

"Too risky." He shakes his head. "That much turbulence could rip the caps off before we get a chance to blow 'em. Plus, if we do and we're not clear? Bad news, bro."

"What if this is what Chuck meant?"

But Bumper shakes his head again. "No go."

He's right, of course. And maybe this isn't what Chuck had in mind after all, and I'm just jumping to harebrained conclusions. I feel a little like the crazy old war vet uncle for even offering the idea. Might as well have started the suggestion with, "Back in my day..." But it was worth a shot.

Whatever this is, though, I have a feeling it has to do with how the ring is powered. Again, Aaron's probably already got a hypothesis on it. But right now, he and Z-Lo are headed back toward Governor's Island in a hurry.

"We proceed as planned," I yell.

Bumper and Hollywood nod. Yoshi gives me a thumbs up from above. Then I ease up on my brake hand and continue descending.

By the time we near the ring's lower ledge, I hold short about five feet above it. Both teams are swaying way too much and risk slamming against the side. We're gonna need to time a descent well enough to drop onto the lip's upper curve. Granted, the horizontal portion looks to be about twenty-five feet wide before falling away, so there's plenty of margin. Well, to one side of the pendulum swing anyway. My stomach does one or two summersaults as my feet shoot away from the ring and extend over the water some seventy feet below.

"I'm dropping down," I yell up to Yoshi.

"Make sure you time it right. You'll probably die if you don't."

"Thanks for the tip." I take a breath and ready my brake hand. On the next arc, the momentum carries me ten feet away from the ring and then redirects back toward the portal. Just as I cross over the threshold, I let the rope slide so that my boots touch down at the next swing's apex.

That's the idea anyway.

Instead, I hit the deck a little too early and land on my left side.

A jolt of pain shoots up my elbow and shoulder, and my helmet smacks against the deck. Not as elegant as it went in my mind, but I'm down. And I have the presence of mind to dig in my heels and keep the line steady for Yoshi.

He, on the other hand, descends like a goddamn acrobat from Cirque de Pole Dancing or whatever the hell it's called. He lands next to me and has the balls to offer me a hand. Son of a bitch. But I take it and stand up.

"Nice work," I say. "Now help me get this off."

With the backpack on the ground, Yoshi and I drag it around some of the craggy geometric bulges toward Bumper and Holly-wood, and then start pulling out the items. The SEAL leads by example, prepping each component, and talking us through the process. In under two minutes, we have what I think is a respectable heap of whoop-ass. Bumper studies the mound sitting within the ring's irregular surface and then covers it with one of the rucksacks.

"It'll have to do," Bumper says as if our work barely passes muster.

We take up the slack in our ropes once again and start backing down the ring's curve. As my feet move across the uneven surface, I wonder how badly Aaron must want to decipher this alien language. And here I am about to blow it to kingdom come. Pretty much sums up a lot of our relationship, I guess.

Before long, my weight pulls Yoshi's feet away, as does Bumper's to Hollywood's, and we're descending toward the ring's lower edge. But that also means we're very close to the intake.

The waterfall sound is so loud that I can't hear whatever Yoshi's saying above me. I think it's about holding off until this whole process turns off—God knows I have reservations about rappelling past it too. A film of getting sucked in and chewed up plays out in my head. Not a good day.

But Yoshi seems to be saying something else.

"What?" I still can't hear him. "Speak louder!"

Then he points away from the bridge toward Lower Manhattan. I follow his finger and see six magenta drones flying toward us.

"Eh, crap."

30

1520, Friday, June 25, 2027
Brooklyn, New York
Brooklyn Bridge

"WE CAN'T LET them spot the explosives," I yell to Bumper and then look straight down. But we can't jump either: the water intake will suck us up the moment we land—assuming we don't break our necks on impact.

"We can blow it now," Bumper says.

God damn. Yeah, we can. But I was really hoping to get back to my cabin soon, and setting off the charges now would put a serious damper on that plan. Plus, there's Hollywood and Yoshi. We'd be forfeiting their lives too. But they knew the risks when they signed up.

Bumper shrugs and taps the pouch with his det remote inside.

"Well, this sucks." I reach for my pouch.

At that same moment, a loud *pit-twang* rings out from the sky to our left. One of the drones has taken a direct hit. I look eastward and see another muzzle flash from a third-story window along the waterfront buildings.

It's Ghost. God bless that man.

His second shot strikes the drone and sends it spiraling away.

I'm not sure if my next action is going to draw more attention to the explosives or not, but our element of surprise is blown. I brace my feet against the ring, whip my SCAR around with my left hand, and open up on the nearest garbage can lid. Bullets crash against the thing's metallic hull, creating cascades of sparks. My only hope is that the noise from the portal and the intake drown out the firefight to any aliens topside.

As if reading my thoughts, the intake apparatus shuts down. The noise dissipates, and the water falls away in massive sheets. I watch my tracer rounds signal the end of my magazine and look down at the torrent crashing into the East River with a roar.

"Descend," Bumper yells. "Now!" He lets his brake hand fly, and his body drops away.

Hollywood is right behind him.

I'm lowering my weapon and about to let my rope go when Yoshi crashes on top of me. A shock shoots through my neck and spine and sends me twisting sideways. The damn drunk! The rope is wrapped around my arm and has it pinned against my side. Hurts like hell—but not as much as slamming back into the ring. My body bounces once and then gets yanked back against the alien structure. Something's snagged the rope, but I can't see what.

"Stop struggling," I yell at him.

"Let go of the rope!"

"I can't. You gotta climb back up."

"Let go of the rope, Wic," he says again.

Another fifty-cal round smacks against something hard, but I can't see.

"Yoshi. Listen to me. You have got to——"

I stop when I feel him jiggling. A quick glance overhead show's he's cutting through the rope. Well, that's one way to solve this—but it's gonna be a hell of a landing if we don't clear one another.

Before I can issue a warning, the rope overhead goes free. I fall, but only for a second, until I'm jerked to a halt. Yoshi sails past me as I flail in place, hung up on the ring somewhere above. From my upside-down position with the rope wrapped around my damn leg, I see Yoshi land in a feet-first plunge that makes him look like a professional cliff jumper. Where was all that grace a few seconds ago?

"Patrick." Chuck's voice blares from the radio. "Can you hear me? You know what, never mind. Just hang in there, buddy."

I strain to get my left hand up on the receiver. "Dad joke."

"Ah! You are there. Wonderful. Listen——"

Another of Ghost's shots rings out. I can't see how many drones are left, or how close they are, but I hear him trying to keep them away.

Chuck's voice returns. "Along with Phantom Watch's efforts, I'm trying to get those drones off you. Just... oh, for the love of all Aunt Millie's marmalade, would you stop blocking me?"

The blood's rushing to my head. "I'm not blocking you. Take the damn shot!"

"No, silly. I'm not *shooting* at them. I've been well below my minimum firing threshold for a few minutes due to your orders to keep your friends safely hidden, remember? I'm trying to *hack* them.

But they… oh, this one is being particularly obstinate. Why, you bloody shit-licking prick—*splick!*"

"Hey, something's happening," I say.

"No, I'm afraid it's not. I'm afraid these little pecker heads are—"

"No, I'm… Rope's slipping!"

"Oh, marvelous! Just make sure you don't hit the water in your current posture."

Before I can reply, the rope comes un-snagged, and I'm falling.

But a beat later, I slam into something hard, smacking my chin on it. The sound of an engine screams under me, and I push myself up…

…on top of a damn garbage can lid!

The thing veers left, and I instinctively grab its sides to hang on. Then it swerves right. I'm not thinking if holding on is the best idea. I just am.

Unable to shake me, the drone barrel rolls to the left. My SCAR bangs against the backside of my helmet. Then the drone barrel rolls to the right. I'm still holding on, feeling pretty good about myself, when it's third maneuver—a nosedive—sends me head over heels into the sky.

I'm still trailing the remainder of the climbing rope but my hands and legs are free, flailing in the wind like those of a flightless bird. I spot the water some forty feet below and start trying to bring my feet under me. But it's not gonna happen. That feeling of being unable to prevent your demise twists in my stomach, as does the sensation of freefall.

I'm arrested in midair by a shooting pain in my left calf, followed by the feeling of my leg being ripped from my hip socket. The ankle, too, feels as though someone's pulled it from my shin bone. All at once, I'm reminded of my first combat injury—an AK round through the calf. I yell and then gasp for air. I notice that I'm swinging from my leg again—it's still there—this time from a slender wire leading up to the bottom-side of a drone.

"Don't you dare shock me, you son of—"

I grit my teeth against the agony of a few hundred volts making every muscle in my body contract. I grunt, teeth clenched together, ribs popping. I squeeze my eyes shut against the pain, willing it not to—

31

Time: Unknown, Friday, June 25, 2027
Lower Manhattan, New York
Brooklyn Bridge

I HURT.

I hurt in places I didn't even know that I could hurt. And for a brief moment, I'm back in Afghanistan, lying on a sidewalk after Jack took point. I'd learned how to suppress this memory, how to box it up and only open the lid on special occasions when I'd had too much to drink. But now the smells and sounds fill my head without invitation, coaxed by the pain holding my body hostage.

I try and press myself off the ground. Ears ringing. The taste of copper in my mouth. And the air stinging my nose. People shout as I blink down the street. Car alarms. Black smoke, broken glass, and moon dust everywhere.

Jack is... he's on the road. There's a blown-out Toyota on its side. I can get to him.

My left leg won't cooperate, but my right one does. I push myself up and fall into a cinderblock wall. The pain is excruciating. But Jack needs me, and this is my fault. I shouldn't have let him go.

I stumble forward, suddenly aware of parts of human bodies wrapped in white cloth now stained red bumping into my boots. A man's macabre face that I've seen a hundred times looks into the hazy sky, asking Allah where his torso's remainder went. A child sleeps in her mother's bloody arms, both faces relieved of their pain.

"Jack," I say, now focused on the Marine uniform spread across the road. But I can't find him. I can't. He's not all there.

"Jack!"

My world is black until something nudges my ribs. A burst of light fills my head. There's talking above me, but I can't understand them.

Damn hajji are gonna loot me.

The prod to my side comes again, and this time I try and bat it away. But the pain is searing.

There's more chatter, and then they start dragging me. The sound of my helmet scraping pavement brings more clarity. I raise my head a few inches and try opening my eyes. Blue, everywhere. Except the ground. It's gunmetal grey.

Then I'm airborne.

The lurch in my stomach makes me wonder if I've been heaved into a mass grave, maybe a burn pit. Or maybe thrown off the Brooklyn Bridge.

New York.

The entire op comes flooding back.

My mind is fully awake as I crash into a pile of rubble. It sounds like metal parts in a junkyard. The pain is still ungodly but becoming more manageable. I blink in a frantic attempt to get my bearings.

To my immediate left, as close as I dare it to be, stands the imposing blue energy wall. Above me, the funnel flaring into the dome. Beyond that, a black sky.

It's night.

And the Brooklyn Bridge's massive steel cables are sweeping up and away from me. But I'm not lying in either of the span's three-lane thoroughfares. Instead, I seem to be on an elevated platform that runs the bridge's width, sitting atop the beams that cross the tarmac some fifteen feet below.

I'm on my back in a heap of metal parts. They seem like some-thing left over from overgrown mechanical spiders. Spindly legs, articulated ball joints, plates and screws. Mounds of electronics, exposed wires, in-ear comms. I move something off me that looks like…

Like a damn pacemaker.

I sit up in shock as it dawns on me that I'm lying in a mound of human joint replacements and biomedical components: artificial hip joints, spinal rods, titanium bone plates, hearing aids, Neuralinks. My flesh crawls as I consider just how many lives… how many people had to…

No. This isn't right.

I try and climb out of the mess when someone sticks a rifle in my face. I instinctively put my hands up and look at my captor's face

—a damn death angel, with its helmet's glowing red eyes and strange mouth cover, and a weapon that looks just like Sir Chuck.

The Phantoms.

Are they alive? How long has it been? I need answers... have to find out what the hell happened. And this prick—nah, this piece of *splick*, as Charles would say—has the balls to point a weapon at me? After the day I've had?

"Get that thing out of my face." I shove the rifle away. Not because I'm close enough to fight, nor do I have the strength, at least at the moment. I do it because I'm pissed that these plushies dare to invade my planet and set up shop on my damn bridge. And if this dick wanted to kill me, he would have done it by now.

The death angel brings the rifle to bear on me again but takes two steps back. He seems agitated too, chattering in some sort of clicky-snap language with two other death angels that he's calling over. They are the least of my concerns, however.

To my right, emerging from a cluster of portable alien buildings that seem like they're set up as a security checkpoint, is a column of people some twenty abreast. Two rows of recon bots line a pathway between the checkpoint and the portal. And the people are walking, row after row, into the wall.

Some weep.

Some scream.

Some try to break the line in terror, only to be tased and tossed in by the recon bots.

But most accept their fate with tired and grim resolve.

Clothes incinerate as people pass through. The fabric flares for an instant only to disappear in puffs of ash. Watches, glasses, cell phones, and jewelry clatter to the deck where smaller bots crisscross the portal's face between rows of humans. They push the metal and electronics into giant piles.

The most unfortunate souls meet their ends when their bodies are forced to part with their non-biological implants, like those I'm lying in. I see one man whose burning clothes illuminate a hip socket that pushes its way out of his exposed posterior. The victim's face is already hidden in the veil, but I can still hear the scream resonate in the back of his chest. As his garments vanish like a magician's parlor trick, the artificial hip joint clatters to the deck, stripped clean of flesh and bone. The bots collect it and deliver the spindly device to my pile's base.

I've gotta do something.

So I start by taking stock of myself. My left leg, which bore the brunt of being snagged by the drone, seems intact. Mostly. The probe definitely punctured my calf and then wrapped around my ankle, judging by the hole in my pants and the lines around my boot. But as with Z-Lo's injury, the flesh seems to have been cauterized, which is good. At least for now.

I've still got my helmet and plate carrier on, but my weapon is missing. That's not good. So is my KA-BAR. My radio has also been stripped away. Apparently, the aliens know enough to remove weapons and comms, but not enough to take off my helmet and armor. And something else, but my head is too foggy to think of it. Dammit.

The three death angels at my feet are talking faster. Seems like they're getting ready to decide what to do with me. Least, that's how it feels.

There's a roar somewhere off the bridge behind me. It hasn't even dawned on me to orient myself with the city, but as I notice the portal's light reflecting off One World Trade Center to my right, I realize I'm no longer on the bridge's Brooklyn approach.

I'm on the Manhattan side.

The roar appears overhead as four blue-glowing engine ports, each pivoting to slow what looks like a giant freight container. I remember it as one of the flying transport dropships we saw from the boat.

A crack of light appears in the aft as the bay door lowers. Likewise, the ship descends, flares, and then lands on the metal deck between me and the column of captured civilians. The engines idle, and an imposing figure steps from the ship.

The creature is dressed in a black biomechanical under-suit. Thin black tubes run the length of its torso, and pneumatic-like pistons hug its joint. Its vital organs and limbs are covered in dark matte-green armor plates with strange writing on the chest and shoulder pieces.

By comparison, the death angels are a foot shorter. And while this thing has forgone a helmet and weapon, it carries itself far more menacingly. The flesh of its bald, green-veined, grey-skinned head looks dimpled and weather-worn. Magenta eyes twitch back and forth, and its nose holes flap open and shut in rhythm with the sounds of its mechanical suit as it walks toward me.

It speaks in the strange snappy-click language I heard moments ago. Instead of the sound getting filtered through a helmet, it comes straight from the loose green tissue in the back of the creature's vertical mouth, hidden behind rows of spiny black teeth.

Judging from how the three death angels give this new alien plenty of room, I'd say he's important—assuming it's male. God, I hope its females aren't this ugly.

I'm also sensing that our working theory about there being a military arm to this invasion is staring me in the face. This overlord is carrying itself like a goddamn badass, because unlike the death angels, deadly as they may be, this son of a bitch is a killer. I can smell it.

It extends its hand and accepts one of the death angel's rifles— one of its Chucks. It doesn't even bother holding the weapon up, just lets it dangle to the side. A momentary flash emanates around the pistol grip. And when the overlord, for lack of a better name, speaks again, the gun interprets.

"Identify yourself," the weapon says in the same kind of digitally benign voice that Chuck started out with.

"Micky Mouse," I say. "Pleased to meet you."

The overlord tilts its head.

"Are you a leader in your species' military?"

"Me?" I chuckle. "Not even close, pal. I'm retired. You just got yourself an old pissed off Marine."

"Marine. Retired, old, pissed."

"You got it."

The overlord's lips move some more before the gun speaks. "You have bonded with one of our weapons. How?"

"Could be that it finds me more attractive. Dunno."

Apparently, it doesn't like my reply. He brings the rifle up and fires a small burst of energy. The miniature lightning bolts blind me momentarily as they surge into my body. Feels like getting tased in the nads. So much for having children.

When the shock wears off, I refocus on the monster.

"How have you bonded with one of our weapons?" it asks.

I groan and then manage to say, "Big dick energy?"

A second round from the rifle sends my body into a spasm.

Pretty sure I'm pissing myself too. "That hurts so good, plushy. Please, can I have another?"

I think the overlord is sneering at me now, but I haven't studied his pin-up poster in my room long enough to know what he likes and doesn't like for sure. He's got his rifle up and seems ready to fire one more time. Damn, what I wouldn't give to have Chuck in my hand one last time to blow this scab away.

And then I find the loose thread that was floating through my head earlier.

Acting as though I'm clutching my chest, I use the motion to feel for the remote det in my vest. Sure enough, it's still in the pouch. I start coughing—half as an act, half because I have to—and remove the device. I'm not sure how many hours I've been out, but if there's any chance that our explosives are still in a nest on the ring, I need to exploit it. Sure, it might bring the ring down on top of me, but right now, it's what needs doing, and I'm guessing the only reason the Phantoms haven't done it yet is because...

Well, there are probably several reasons they haven't blown it yet, the worst being that they've been killed or captured. Which is all the more reason for me to end this.

I'm about to flip up the trigger guard and peg the button when the overlord offers his measure of a laugh. Least I think that's what it is. Then he motions something forward with his free hand.

A recon bot carrying a cube-shaped cargo container trudges over from its post near the command buildings. The box's metallic surface is stenciled with red alien script, and I suddenly have a bad feeling about whatever's inside. After the bot places it on the ground, the overlord gives a jerk of its head, and the bot opens the lid and tilts the container forward. Inside is a mound of C-4 and Semtex bathed in a red glow.

Well now, isn't that great.

So I've got a decision to make. It's one that's gonna take out a lot of the people on this part of the bridge, including me. But it's also gonna take out these bastards, and maybe even put an end to all this.

That is, of course, assuming the plushies haven't rendered the det receivers inert and aren't jamming the freq.

Only one way to know.

It's been nice, Earth. Peace out.

I flip the guard and squeeze the button.

I DON'T GO BOOM.

But I do hear a pop.

The overlord's head tears away in a slurry of bone and green blood. But his corpse stays upright, as if balanced by his mechanical appendages.

"Always wear your helmet, asshole," I say.

The report of gunfire breaks from behind the column of people —all screaming and running for cover.

The death angels stumble backward at the sight of their downed leader, struggling to figure out what's going on. Granted, so am I, but I have the advantage of knowing the sounds of US military weapons by heart. And there's only one unit crazy enough to insert themselves this close to the danger area.

Phantom Team.

I look through the scattering crowd and notice several individuals taking cover around the portable command buildings on the bridge's up-river side to my immediate right. I can't be certain, but it sure as hell looks like Hollywood, Ghost, and the others.

They came for me. I don't know how, but the devils came for me. I need to lend a hand and help get us to safety. But I don't have a weapon. And the assault bots on the down-river side seem to be getting their bearings.

As the death angels take cover behind the dropship, I have a crazy idea. Yeah, another one. Seems I'm just full of 'em today.

The overlord's rifle.

It's still in his hand.

Memories warn me not to try what I'm about to do, memories of the team saying they attempted picking up the weapons with no luck. But Chuck said I have magical powers or something, right? And hell, I've already been tased half a dozen times today. What's one more?

With the death angels focused on defending themselves and limiting their fire at their own TOC, I pull myself from the pile of parts, remove the glove on my right hand, and lunge for the overlord's headless body. It takes less than a second for me to pry his fingers up and smash my palm against the grip. When I do, I feel the same surge of current that I felt under the oak tree when I paired with Chuck.

"We're in business!" I yank the weapon from the monster's hand and bring it to my shoulder.

"Detected language: English. User, please identify yourself."

"Phantom One," I say as I aim at the first of the three death angels hiding behind the dropship.

"User profile updated. Please specify targets as friend or foe."

"Foe," I say and use my eyes to select the High-Frequency, Low-Yield options in the scope's HUD. "Definitely foe." As the firing mode selection confirms, I remark how much faster this weapon updated the scope than Chuck did.

I squeeze the trigger, and a semiautomatic burst of blue light rips into the first death angel. Rather than the more dramatic explosions I was used to with Chuck, this weapon fires precise energy rounds that puncture the target's chest and head. The enemy collapses to the ground, opening a clear shot to the next target.

The second death angel glances at his fallen comrade before looking in my direction. But before he can bring his weapon around, I peg him with four or five or six shots to center mass; it's too hard to count laser beams, dammit. How should I know? Either way, the enemy topples over, and I really like this new weapon's settings.

"You are way better than Chuckles," I say with my cheek pressed against the stock.

"I beg your pardon, old bean?" says a voice from the gun's receiver.

Damn. Sounds just like Chuck.

"No time for chit chat," I say as the scope's assisted targeting feature moves the reticle onto the third death angel's illuminated outline. When I squeeze, a stream of energy pierces the shoulders and spins the alien like a top. The tango hits the deck on its second rotation.

The dropship is clear, but now the Phantoms are taking fire from the bridge's down-river side. That, and I can make out the telltale blue dots of incoming drones returning from Manhattan.

"I must say, Patrick, I'm heartbroken that you've moved on so quickly," says the weapon.

I'm running for cover behind the dropship. "That you, Sir Chucks-a-Lot?"

"As if you care anymore."

"Where are you?"

"Well, let's just say that Hollywood's ass is far better looking than yours."

I slam against the hull and look toward the command buildings, trying to make out the Phantoms' positions. It's not hard seeing as how the enemy is marking them with ample weapons fire.

"Chuck, can you connect me with Hollywood?"

"Of course, I can. But now it just feels like you want me because of my—"

"Dammit, Charlie! Put me through."

"Oh, fine."

"Wic?" says a female voice.

"Hollywood! Damn, is it good to see you guys."

"You too. But we're a little pinned down at the moment. Seems the Anderkins don't take kindly to rescue ops."

"I can see that. You have good fields of fire?"

"Negative. Too many civvies. And reinforcements coming up the bridge."

"Any bright ideas for getting us outta here?"

"I was about to ask you the same thing."

I let out a sigh. "Great."

"I have an idea, if anyone cares," Chuck says.

"We care," I say.

"Are you just saying that? Or do—?"

"Jesus, Chuck," Hollywood shouts. "What the hell is your idea?"

"Patrick's leaning on it."

I pull away from the dropship. "You... you want us commandeering this ship?"

"Of course. It is blast rated, practically flies itself, and can take you just about anywhere you want to go. Also, contrary to popular belief, I am not Jesus, Hollywood."

"You sure about this, Chuckles?" I ask.

"Of course. Jesus and I bear almost no resemblance to one another."

"About the damn ship!"

"Ah, yes. I am reasonably sure that you have a high probability of escaping the bridge and getting to fight another day, as it were. And I'm also sure about Jesus and me not being even remotely related. Though we both are rather skilled as saving Earthers."

"Hollywood," I yell. "Tell the team to get ready to make a run for the dropship. And let Z-Lo know he might get his wish tonight."

"Roger. Wait for your go?"

"Negative. Wait for my gun."

I use my eyes to select a mode called Wide-Displacement and put the output on Maximum-Yield. Granted, I have no idea what this is gonna do, but whereas the Phantoms had too many people in the way to take clear shots at the enemy, I have a reasonably open field of fire, thanks to the enemy assuming that the dropship and the portal are free of threats.

Bad news, plushies: they're not.

I count eight, maybe ten recon bots, four assault bots, and three death angels taking cover, all on the down-river side. Just then, I have second thoughts about my maximum-yield selection. Not that I don't like wiping the enemy off the map, but that it might be nice to use this weapon a little longer if need be. So I downgrade the output to high yield. Should be plenty, right?

Then it's a deep breath in and a slow breath out before I lean my head and weapon around the dropship's hull and aim at the middle-most target. Strangely, even enemies outside of the scope get illuminated in my field of vision. I don't know how that's done, but if they're lit, then I'm happy.

I squeeze.

Two spring-loaded plates pop off the weapon's receiver. The rifle vibrates, and I re-frame my shooting stance 'cause something tells me the gun's gonna—

Vroooooh–crack!

Yut.

It kicks like a frickin' mule.

A horizontal garrote wire of light spreading left to right slices through almost every enemy in my viewfinder. Those lucky enough to have ducked survive and choose to stay hidden for a second longer as bots' legs walk out from under severed torsos. One of the death angels collapses in two. And part of the down-river command building looks like someone's taken a plasma torch to its left side.

A beat later and the Phantoms are leapfrogging along the bridge's edge toward my position.

My scope shows 39 percent power remaining. Not much, but enough. I bring the weapon around and start firing with a setting of Low-Pulse, Low-Yield; it sounded conservative.

I squeeze the trigger and watch as elongated orbs of light pump the enemies' containers and barricades at the same time that the Phantoms fire and finish leapfrogging to my position.

"Good to see you in one piece," Bumper says as he slides between the dropship's hull and one of the massive vertical engines.

I'm about to return the compliment when I see Aaron carrying Bumper's MP5. I hadn't noticed him before, and I'm not sure which is more surprising: the fact that they brought him along or that Bumper gave him his secondary weapon—which is the perfect submachine gun for him since it has next to no recoil. "You... brought Aaron?" I ask no one in particular.

"We weren't gonna leave him behind," Hollywood says.

"I'm part of the team, remember?" Aaron says.

I figure we can argue that later, then I nod to the ship's stern. "Everyone load up."

"We really doing this?" Z-Lo asks as the team rounds the corner.

"Why, you wanna stay here?" Hollywood asks.

"No, it's just that Master Guns told me no strafing today."

"Yeah?" I say. "Well, plans change. Now get in, Semper Gumby."

32

2140, Friday, June 25, 2027
Lower Manhattan, New York
Brooklyn Bridge

"Now's your time to shine," I say to the kid as he buckles himself into the right-hand pilot seat. While Z-Lo is big enough to fill out the chair, Yoshi seems to swim a bit in the left-hand seat, but he makes it work.

The rest of the team is climbing the stairs from the cargo hold while Bumper gets the aft door to come up.

"I can't get used to their smell," Hollywood says as she grabs her nose.

"I'd be worried if you did." The ammonia-like odor lingers despite the Anderkins having left after the vessel touched down.

The dropship's upper deck doesn't have a windshield, just a

cockpit with 180° of projected display like a giant wraparound computer monitor. The data is all in plushy-speak, so it's worthless. But the view looks out on the gap between command buildings, at the people fleeing and the alien security forces taking positions against us.

Then the enemy starts firing on us.

I instinctively lean away from the screen even though the rounds are hitting elsewhere. But all we feel are mild tremors as the hull seems to absorb the incoming fire.

"Told you," Chuck says from behind Hollywood. "Blaster proof."

I pat Z-Lo on the shoulder. "How soon before we can get out of here?"

"Not sure." Z-Lo brings his hands up to search for controls, but double rings of orange light appear around his wrists. "Whoa." He jerks away, and the dropship lurches to the stern.

"Not toward the portal," Hollywood shouts.

She's right.

I ram Z-Lo's elbow toward the nose, and the ship redirects forward.

"Up! Up," I yell as I raise Z-Lo's forearms.

The ship ascends and barely clears the command buildings ahead of us. Correction, it doesn't clear the command buildings. The hull smacks into a roof and sends a jolt through the deck. I grab the back of Z-Lo's chair to keep from falling.

"I got it. I got it," Z-Lo says. But the dropship is listing to port and getting dangerously close to the bridge's central cable bundles.

"Z-Lo!"

"I see 'em," he yells in protest and then rocks the dropship backward.

I hear Aaron cry out as he goes sliding across the deck.

It sounds like more blaster fire is hitting the hull.

I glance at Hollywood's back. "I thought you said this thing flies itself, Chuck?"

"It does! When there's not a human at the controls."

"Then why did you say—?"

"Because it made it easier for you to make up your mind and keep me from getting confiscated by the Androchidans."

"Well that doesn't matter much if we crash into the East River in the process!"

"I'll survive, at least."

"Chuck!"

"Yes?"

I want to throw him out a window. "Can't you fly this thing?"

"Dammit, Pat. I'm blaster, not a pilot."

"We're so dead," Yoshi says.

"Okay, okay," Chuck says. "I can pilot it, yes. But I need several minutes to integrate with the ship's less than impressive AI."

"Wouldn't that make things easier?" I protest.

"Tell me, is it easy or hard to discuss quantum physics with a six-month-old baby?"

"Hey! I think I'm gettin' the hang of it," Z-Lo says.

I look back at the window—viewing screen, thingy—and see the kid has, indeed, stabilized us. And now he's heading for the right-hand arch in the tower directly ahead. The cables rising beside us feel like they're boxing us in pretty tight.

"Z-Lo, I don't think—"

"Let him fly," Hollywood whispers to me.

"But we're—"

"Let him fly."

I let out a long breath and lower myself behind the kid's seat as if it will protect me. The pucker factor on this one's gonna do me in, I swear. "Cabin in the country," I say to myself as a new personal mantra.

"What was that?" Yoshi says.

But I don't wanna speak to him yet. If we survive this next bit? Maybe. Right now? I'd just as soon knock him out cold.

I peak above Z-Lo's chair as he accelerates toward the arch. I'm letting out a "Whooooa," as are Hollywood and Bumper and—hell, everyone sounds nervous. Even Ghost is grabbing an overhead railing and telling the kid to slow down.

"We're all going to die, aren't we," Chuck says.

"Yut."

"Maybe later," Z-Lo yells. "But not - right - now!" Then he lets out a loud "Waaaahooooo!" as we shoot through the arch.

I watch the cables on the tower's other side drop away as the ship surges forward. "Don't ever do that again, kid."

Ignoring me, he says, "Now, where are the weapons?"

"No, no, no," Hollywood and Bumper say in unison.

"Just get us clear for a second and set 'er down so we can think this through," I say.

A bright red alert starts flashing in the middle of the display.

"Chuuuuck?" I ask.

"Oh, those little splick-headed wankers," he says.

In this particular moment, what stands out to me is just how universal blinking red text in the middle of a screen is to tell people that something's going horribly wrong.

"Chuck!"

"Oh, bloomin' eck! Everyone, hold your knickers."

"What?" I ask in astonishment. "That's your—?"

The dropship takes a direct hit from something. It's all I can do to hold onto Z-Lo's seat as the transport spins counterclockwise. I see a new display pop up and hover directly in front of Z-Lo. It portrays a three-dimensional overview of the ship and several blinking indicators, the largest of which are around both starboard side engines.

"Oh, Blimey O'Riley," Chuck shouts. "Everyone, hold on!"

For his part, Z-Lo is doing his best to counteract the dropship's rotation by pushing both hands to the left. Yoshi's got two double rings around his wrists too and mimics the kid, but it's anyone's guess if it's helping.

With every rotation, I can see a lightless City Hall growing larger in the flickering display window. We're headed into Lower Manhattan.

"Brace for impact," Chuck yells. "This one's gonna be a bit dodgy."

WHETHER BY AN ACT of the Almighty or pure luck, the dropship avoids crashing into New York City Hall and instead dives into City Hall Park just to the south. It's safe to say that the trees helped break our fall, but I'm fairly certain the alien ship's hull was gonna dig a deep furrow whether there were trees or not.

The cabin is bathed in red emergency lighting, and most of the electronics look powered down. The distinct smell of electrical smoke is growing stronger by the second.

"Sitrep," I yell from my backside, legs half up a wall. Or is it the floor? Feels like the dropship's on its port side.

Hollywood and Chuck lie next to me and respond that they're

operational despite some minor injuries. Bumper's got a bloody lip, which Hollywood offers to examine. Ghost is, somehow, still holding his handrail despite fresh blood around his ribcage. Z-Lo and Yoshi have fared the best. And Aaron has some blood running down the side of his face, but otherwise looks okay.

"Yoshi," I say without looking at him. "Get something on Aaron's head."

Yoshi starts undoing his buckles. "On it."

"Everyone else, collect your things. And watch your step. We're moving out before the enemy gets to us."

Less than sixty seconds later, we've crawled out of the forward cargo bay door; the stern one was too heavily damaged to open. I straighten my back and notice that both starboard engines have seen better days. Outside the park, I hear crowds of people milling about in the streets. It's a miracle there weren't more civilians in the park when we crashed. Or maybe there were and we just…

I shake the thought from my head and look behind us.

"He's not gonna be too happy with that," Hollywood says about the nice trench the dropship carved through the mayor's front yard.

I give her a wink. "He'll find some tax dollars for it, don't you worry."

She smiles and then unslings Chuck. "Here. I think he misses you."

"Oh, don't bother," Chuck says with a forlorn tone. "He's already found a new toy."

"Nonsense," I say as I swing my latest acquisition over my shoulder. "This one tanked out back on the bridge."

"Well. If I'm not too much dead weight, I guess you can count me in. Always happy to be a third wheel."

"That's the spirit." I turn to survey the rest of the team. "Everyone good?"

"Where to, Wic?" Bumper asks. "This is your stomping grounds, not ours."

"We need cover and some time to regroup." I take a second to orient myself. "That's the Woolworth Building there." I look south. "Which means Fulton Street Station is a block and a half down Broadway, that direction."

"Subway?" Bumper asks.

"Yut. Good cover. And without lighting, I doubt it'll be very popular. Everyone's NVGs still work?"

"Mine do," Bumper says as he lifts a hand.

"Same," says Ghost.

"Mine are dead," Hollywood says.

"Mine too," says Yoshi.

"Uh, and no one ever issued me any," Z-Lo adds.

I chuckle—poor kid.

Then I double-check my pair. "Mine are good. Everyone watch your step. Let's minimize contact with civilians and head straight for the subway entrance. Roger?"

The team nods, and then I lead the way out of the park.

IT TAKES us the better part of ten minutes to weave our way south on Broadway. The street is teeming with people and dead vehicles. From several miles above, the dome's blue glow casts the scene in a monochromatic light straight out of a horror movie. I keep waiting for a monster to burst out of the pavement or a zombie mob to turn on us—not that either is out of the realm of possibilities at the moment. Still, the crowd seems more fatigued than agitated, which is good for us since the last thing I want is to fight it out with these poor souls.

Only once does someone put up a fight with me. He's a young guy, early twenties. Grabs my arms.

"Yo, man. You going to fight 'em, right? You Army? Spec ops, yeah? Come on, man. Take me with you. I can fight."

I strip his hands off my arm. "Stay here, kid. Take care of who you can."

"Nah, man. Gimme a gun. I swear it, I can shoot shit. Call of Duty, you know?"

"Stand down, kid." I'm trying to box him out and sidestep, but he's acting all hyper now. Uppers, I'm guessing.

"Come on. I got your six and stuff, LT. Just gimme a gun. You got an extra, looks like. Let's go blow them mo-fos sky high, bitch."

"Son, you need to take your hands off me and step aside."

"Not before you part with one of your pieces, pops." He pulls a knife from his back waistband and holds it in my face.

I don't have time for this.

I grab his wrist, pin it back, and twist against his elbow's natural range of motion.

The kid squeals and drops the knife.

I kick it away and pull the guy toward me. "Help these good people out, and if you're ever gonna pull a knife on somebody, make sure they're not a damn Marine before you do. Copy?"

"Oh, my God. Just lemme go, man! Just lemme go."

I shove him away and then lead the team forward.

SEVERAL PEOPLE LINE the steps into Fulton Street Station. Most are drunks or junkies, oblivious to or in denial about what's happening in their city. Part of me has to laugh at the irony of the situation, though. Even if the aliens stood toe to toe with these people, half of them would say, "Just another day in New York," and keep walking.

I flip my NVGs down and tell those without optics to find someone's back and stick to 'em. We slide over the turnstiles as a team, follow signs to the Five Line, and then climb down the platform and onto the tracks leading north toward Brooklyn Bridge / City Hall Station.

After pushing the group for another two minutes in silence, I slow and ask if anyone has some light.

"NVGs up," Bumper says. Then he pulls out three glow sticks from his vest, breaks their internal capsules, and drops the green tubes among the tracks.

"Let's circle up," I say. "Take a knee or get comfy."

I follow my own advice, sit my ass down on a concrete berm lining the tunnel wall, and then set Chuck and Chuck Two down. I reach for my Camelback's straw and find that it's still pinned to my shoulder harness. A quick drag on the tube yields freshwater that, honestly, never tasted so good. But I can tell from how hard I'm having to suck that my supply's getting low.

The dwindling resource reminds me of my conviction that modern civilization's greatest threat isn't from a crazy alien invasion or disaster, natural or otherwise, but from trying to survive without modern conveniences and the conventional food supply.

"What's so funny, Wic?" Hollywood asks as she catches a protein bar from Bumper. "You okay?"

"Yut. Fine. Just laughing at how frail we are as a species." I nod to Bumper for one of his bars too and snap it between my hands.

Hollywood casts me a worried look.

"I'm fine," I say, waving her off. "It's nothing."

"So, what's the plan?"

"Before we get to that," Bumper says. "What the hell happened to you up there?"

"How long was I gone?" I ask first.

"Six hours," Aaron says. "We thought you were…"

"We thought you was inside just 'using the bathroom' when really you got into T-Swift's rave without us and done left us at the door," Bumper says, letting a little of his old Detroit show through. "'It'll be fun' my ass. 'Just wait in line.' Shoot. Ain't never clubbing with him again. Ain't that right, Campbell."

Aaron doesn't seem to know how to respond, so he just says, "Uh, sure. Yeah."

Everyone chuckles as Aaron's good sportsmanship. Poor guy isn't used to frat humor. At least not the military kind.

"Well, truth is," I say. "You guys probably have more of my story to tell than me. I don't know what all happened after Yoshi—" I clamp my mouth shut.

Yoshi lowers his head and interweaves his fingers. "Listen, Master Gun—"

"Not doing this now in front of everyone, Yoshida. We'll save it."

"Copy that."

After an awkward silence, Z-Lo says, "So, you remember riding the drone, right?"

"Yut."

"Damn bronco," Ghost adds.

I nod. "Flipped me off, then one of 'em snagged me around the ankle, yeah?"

Hollywood nods. "Then we see you shake like a fish and go limp."

"Same as what happened to Lewis," Aaron says.

I bite the inside of my cheek as I try to get that picture out of my head.

"Then they hauled you up and away," Bumper says.

"What happened to you guys?" I ask.

"Ghost helped keep the drones away as Z-Lo picked us out of the water. Then Chuck kept us covered long enough to retrieve Ghost and take shelter inside... what was it called again?"

"Whitehall Terminal," Hollywood says.

"Wow," I say with genuine surprise. "Staten Island Ferry dock. That's some good cover. Quick thinking."

"So we camped out there until we came up with a plan to see if we could find you," she adds.

"Which was what?"

"Threw on some overcoats we found on the street, blend in, and work our way up the bridge." Hollywood puts her head down and shakes it a little. "Truth is, we thought you'd be long gone. Thought it was a fool's errand."

"Took us four and a half hours to push our way through," Yoshi says as he takes a sip from his flask.

God, I wanna hurl that thing down the tunnel.

"We managed to sneak around some of the barricades," he continues, still not making eye contact with me. "That's when we saw you and the three death angels."

I look to the rest of the group for confirmation. "You really arrived right then? That's... just when I came to."

"Then somebody upstairs likes us," Bumper says with a grin.

"They have a weird way of showing it," I say.

"We were so surprised to see you, Wic," Hollywood says. She almost looks like she could cry. "Then when that dropship came down, and Creepy-Ass Plushy came at you, well, then we knew it was time to get the party started."

I look at Ghost. "And you blew his head off."

"Guilty," he says with a grin that says he enjoyed it.

"They had our explosives," I say.

Bumper nods. "Yeah. When the drones lost interest in tracking us, they returned to collect the ordnance. Trust me, I tried blowing it. No offense, Wic."

"None taken. I would have done the same."

He nods with his head down, and I hope my words bring him a little comfort. Choosing to take action that will save others' lives when you know it will also hurt members of your team is one of the hardest decisions any combatant is faced with. And Bumper made the call. As I would expect him to.

He clears his throat with a fist to his mouth. "Whether it was the distance, they jammed it, or the damn detonators just didn't wanna go, the party favors never got distributed."

"How 'bout you, Master Guns?" Z-Lo says.

I give the kid a raised eyebrow that says, "You sure you wanna know?" But I know they need to hear my end of the story, if for nothing more than to understand what's happening to those who pass through the portal—at least this side of it. And they need to know that the death angels aren't the top of the Anderkins' food chain. So I recount the whole story, about the piles of implants and devices, about the poor souls who met their ends before they even got to the other side. I share all I can about the overlord, his appearance, and how I managed to acquire the second Sir Chuck in much the same way I obtained the first, only intentionally this time.

When I'm done, the team observes a moment of silence for the slain.

"So you think Scar Face back there represents the military division," Hollywood says.

"Yut."

"Just wasn't smart enough to wear his cover," Bumper says with a smile. "Damn shame."

"Told him the same thing," I say. "But he'd lost his hearing by then." I shrug. "Shoulda' spoken up sooner, I guess."

The group shares a small laugh, and then the silence retakes the subway.

"Well, I'm glad you're all okay," I say.

"And we're glad you are too, Wic," Hollywood says. "Scared us a little."

"They were practically weeping and wailing over you," Chuck interjects.

"That so?"

"Oh, it was awful, Patrick. Sobs. Travail. You would never have known they were battle-hardened combat veterans. I barely recognized them."

"False intelligence detected," says my second Anderkin rifle in its monotone voice. "Source SR-CHK 4110 subject to directive violations in accordance with—"

"Well, would you look at the time," Chuck says. "Why don't we shove off and pick this up later, shall we?"

"Oh no, you don't," I say. "Seems your pal here is picking up something in what you said."

"I'll have you know that 51678 is not my pal. He is a dim-witted numpty whose only true value lies in his service as a paperweight."

"Additional false intelligence detected—"

"Oh, can it, you manky twat!"

"Hold on, hold on." I pump my hands, trying to get the team to stop laughing. "I wanna hear how you dealt with the prospect of my death."

"Moi?"

"Sure. How'd you respond after you saw me get hauled off?"

There's an awkward pause.

"He was a dignified gentleman," Hollywood says with a prim and proper air about her.

The team snickers.

"A dignified gentleman, eh?" I give Chuck a sly look.

"That… might be a slight exaggeration. I suppose I may have shed a small tear here and there."

The air feels pregnant with the truth. And just when I think the team can't hold it in anymore, Chuck Number Two blurts out, "Additional false intelligence detected."

The circle deteriorates into rolls of laughter.

Bumper yells, "He was a goddamn baby, Wic."

"Hell yeah, he was," Z-Lo roars. "He was howling so loud we had to stuff him under the rucksacks."

"Oh, stop that," Chuck says.

"Cried out of control for about thirty minutes," Yoshi says, wiping tears away.

"I did no such thing," Chuck yells in protest.

"Additional false intelligence—"

"It was fifteen minutes, not thirty."

"Why, Charles," I say. "I never knew you cared so much."

"Because I don't. I'm a heartless alien weapon hellbent on your destruction. I don't care in the least what happens to you. And don't you dare say a word, 51678, or I'll blast your ASIK board clean out of your mainframe, you hear?"

"Compliance."

The laughter dies when something echoes down the tunnel. It's faint at first, coming mostly in the form of human screams. But then there's a subsonic frequency that knocks bits of old plaster from the ceiling. The debris rains down on us and fills the green-hued glow-stick light with dust.

"Sounds like they're looking for us," Bumper says.

"Then it's time to move," I reply. "Let's saddle up."

"What about a plan?" Hollywood says.

"We'll talk and walk. But we can't stay put if they know we're down here."

"And how do we know if they know we're down here?" Z-Lo asks.

As if on cue, a flash of light and a loud *whomp* rip through Fulton Street Station. The subway tunnel shakes, and Aaron falls into me.

"You okay, bro?" I ask.

He stands up and wipes dust off his jacket. "Yes. Fine."

"Phantoms, let's move." I point us northbound when a new scream fills the back end of the tunnel. Only this one doesn't sound human. And I don't recall a death angel making anything like it.

"What the hell was that?" Hollywood asks.

Chuck speaks up. "Hmmm. As this directly pertains to your immediate wellbeing, I can answer that question for you."

There's a delay.

"And?" I ask.

"Ah, yes. Remember Creepy-Ass Plushy?"

I feel my stomach tighten. "Oh, no."

"Oh, yes," Chuck says. "It's his third cousin twice removed. Or is it once removed? I can never get that straight. In any case, that sound means he's picked up your scent. And, Ghost, this one will be wearing his helmet. For what it's worth, I do recommend that you run."

33

2215, Friday, June 25, 2027
Lower Manhattan, New York
Five Line, North of Fulton Street Station

Since visible light doesn't seem to pose as much of a risk as our heat signatures, I switch on my headlamp for those without NVGs. The LED overwhelms the night optics, but it's more important that we *all* see clearly, not just those with the fancy gear. A few others flick their headlamps on too, making it easier for everyone as we run north.

"Chuck. What's your ammo level?" I ask.

"Oddly enough, it's at 100% now. Amazing what a rifle can achieve when someone isn't constantly yanking on your trigger."

"Or when someone measures their output in proportion to the situation."

CHRISTOPHER HOPPER & J.N. CHANEY

"I was only providing what you asked for. I claim user error."

"Huh. Because Veronica over there gave me a nice steady assault setting that I'm guessing could have lasted me for a good twenty minutes."

"Veronica?" Chuck sounds disgusted. "Did you just name 51678 Veronica?"

"Until I ask her to pick her own personality, yut."

"That's a terrible name."

"I'll be sure to let her know how you feel."

Another ear-piercing screech rips through the tunnel.

"He's getting closer," Chuck says.

Hollywood lets a small laugh. "Thanks, genius."

"What kinda heat's he packin', Chuck?" I ask.

"Two of me, most likely. But the *overlords*, as you call them, tend to prefer my baby brother."

"So, smaller then?" Yoshi asks.

"No, my good man. Much bigger. Like Z-Lo here in proportion to you."

"Well that doesn't sound awesome," Hollywood says.

"It is if you're wielding one." Chuck sounds pleased with himself. "But given your particular circumstances, I'd be forced to agree with you. It is definitely *not* awesome."

"Looks like we have some sort of chamber coming up," Bumper says.

I nod. "We're gonna set up in it."

"Roger."

"Chuck, can you make Veronica not shock the other team members?"

"Finally. You're ditching that trollop?"

"No, I need her to use whatever energy she has left to momentarily emit the… distortion… thingy that hides… people."

"Wow. That was painful, Patrick."

"Yes or no?"

"Yes. It's a bit of a hack, but I can. But be forewarned that the reduction of her receiver's defense measures is only temporary. And they should consider handling her with gloves on. Likewise, her firing capabilities will still be useless. Granted, she's fairly useless in general. This one time—"

"Focus, Chuck."

"My apologies. Hey, Veronica?"

The rifle on my back vibrates. "SR-CHK 4110 incoming communication request verified."

"My chum Patrick here wants the rest of his team to be able to fondle your saggy tits without catching the clap. Roger?"

"Request unknown. Please re—"

"Oh, you dim-witted prat! Voice command: amend defense protocols, line 421, negate subsection four, permission epsilon theta. Execute."

"Request acknowledged."

"Well that was dramatic," I say.

"And unnecessary. I just wanted to use the audio encoder instead of the quantum lock. It's more James Bondish, don't you think?"

"I believe you're thinking of Q."

"Ah. Right you are, old bean. My apologies."

"You should be apologizing to Veronica. That was pretty harsh."

"Nonsense. I'm just speaking her language. You wait and see. She's a real twat."

"Hmm." I unsling Veronica and toss her to Bumper. "Catch."

He looks nervous, but snags the weapon and shoulders the sling.

"Just don't try to shoot it. And keep it on your back. Take Hollywood and Yoshi, keep left," I say as the tunnel walls balloon away from us. "Everyone else, keep right. Look for service access doors. They'll provide—"

A bolt of blue light zips over my shoulder and continues down the tracks, exploding against a wall farther down. The orange explosion produces a backdraft of fire so intense I can feel the heat against my face.

"What the hell was that?" Yoshi asks.

"My baby brother," Chuck replies.

"Everyone, take cover! Weapons ready. Wait for my go. Chuck, make sure we're—"

"You're off the enemy's sensors, Patrick. But *Veronica* only has about thirty seconds worth of cover for team two."

"Copy."

The two teams spread out along both walls. Ahead, I see a small side tunnel about six-feet tall. I point Aaron into it and order Z-Lo to hold the position. Ten yards down is one of the main service doors that wind up to the surface. I order Ghost to take cover in the recess. Last but not least is a concrete barricade like those used in the warmer of the Northeast's two seasons: construction—the other being winter. I douse my headlamp and order everyone else to do the same.

Just as I hunker down behind the barricade, the screeching overlord charges into the chamber, weapons up. He slows and twists his helmet to look around the room. His cap is bigger than a death angel's but has the same glowing red eyes. Then a wet, purr-like gurgle comes from the back of the overlord's throat, a sound that gets amplified by the speaker on its helmet.

His alien call summons four death angels from behind him. As they start scanning the walls, I suddenly regret putting Aaron in the first tunnel. I just thought getting him to cover first was the right call.

Thanks to Chuck and Veronica, all five aliens don't seem to notice us, which is a real Christmas miracle given the proximity. But all that's about to change.

Taking a page from my time with Veronica, I select high-frequency, low-yield in Chuck's HUD, put my reticle on the biggest target's chest, and then whisper to Chuck, "Show me some love."

My trigger squeeze sends a torrent of blue blaster fire at the overlord's chest plate. A split second later, the rest of the Phantoms open up, some aiming for the overlord, some for the death angels.

The decibel level inside the brick chamber drops my hearing to a muffled roar, removing any of the distinct sounds that give the brain needed detail. Instead, the distorted sonic vibrations of bullets and blaster energy rippling through pains my ears to the point that blood must be running out both canals.

To my amazement, the overlord darts away from my spraying spree, heads along the far wall, and uses one of the death angels as cover. Bumper's M249 pings against the overlord's improvised alien shield. But with every step the overlord takes toward Bumper, I worry the SEAL's squad automatic weapon won't be enough against the larger foe.

Hollywood runs up beside Bumper to mass fire with her AR-15. Yoshi joins a second later with his SCAR15. The Army Sergeant and Air Force Staff Sergeant call for "talking guns," taking a page from the playbook Bumper and I used the night before. Someone was paying attention. The concentrated fire from all three weapons starts to tear into the death angel and illuminate globs of flying meat with the strobing muzzle flashes.

Despite the unrelenting lead shower, the overlord moves toward them. Thing's a damn leviathan.

I aim Chuck at the overlord. "Gimme something to take 'em down."

"You trust me to choose?"

The beast is almost on Bumper's position. It tosses the limp death angel aside and uses one arm to shield his face while the other raises one of its massive rifles.

"Yes!"

There's a deafening pause, then Chuck yells, "Go."

Just as the enemy leaps in the air, I squeeze Chuck's trigger. He recoils into my shoulder and sends out a long tendril of lightning like the one I'd shot at the bot back on the interstate. The energy surges into the overlord, spreads through his body while in midair to form countless cracks of orange light, and then detonates the target.

The chamber is lit like high noon as the overlord's body vaporizes against the brick. The blast knocks me into the wall. I lose sight of the other tangos and the team, and then the darkness returns.

I scramble forward, head down, and look around the barricade. "Sitrep!"

"We're good over here," Bumper yells.

"Phantom me, I'm good," Z-Lo yells, forgetting his callsign.

"Watch, clear." Then Ghost yells, "Aw, hell!"

Thanks to the light cast by the flaming tissue plastered along the walls and ceiling, I can see the remaining two death angels start to gain their feet, weapons coming up.

Phantom Team opens up on the tangos, drilling their sides, backs, and heads with whatever they have left in their magazines.

Even Aaron has stepped from cover and is firing on the target nearest him. Ghost lands a critical hit on the right-hand death angel's neck, and the alien stumbles. Bumper drills the open wound with his machine gun until the head flops over. However, the left-hand tango is still advancing and fires several shots. But between the Phantoms' marksmanship and our desperate will to survive, the death angel's shots go wide. A crack splits across the enemy's chest plate, and the team exploits the opening. Bullets fill the chest cavity until the tango stumbles backward into a wall.

Bumper calls for the team to cease-fire and waves a hand in front of his face, palm out. One by one, the Phantoms pick up on the order and pass it down. Most civilians assume hand signals are only used when you need to be quiet, but they also come in handy when no one on your team can hear 'cause you've been blasting your eardrums out in a damn subway tunnel.

Within a few seconds of Bumper's command, everyone has stopped shooting. All, that is, except for Aaron. He's pulling the MP5's trigger as fast as he can, taking steps toward his downed target. Even after the mag empties, he's still pulling the trigger and yelling.

It's Z-Lo who walks up beside Aaron and pushes the MP5s barrel down gently. "You got him, Dr. Campbell."

Aaron's chest is heaving. "I did?" he yells, compensating for the toll his virgin ears have taken.

"Yeah. Real nice."

"Probably," Aaron shouts. "But I think they were more like rats. Man, what a rush, though!" He spins around. "Pat, did you see that?"

I stand in the firelight and raise my voice to help him out. "Hell of a job, buddy. Didn't know you had it in you."

"Yeah," he exclaims, and then reaches out to steady himself on Z-Lo. "Neither did I, to be honest. And, now, I think, I'm gonna be sick."

As Aaron vomits onto the nearest death angel, I'm reminded that adrenaline can do wonders for your reflexes and a number on your stomach. Still, Aaron has a lot to be proud of. He was always more of a 'live and let live' kind of kid growing up. But considering that he swore off all violence when he got news of Jack's death, seeing him help take out an enemy with an MP5 is quite the surprise. And it's not a half-bad look on him.

"Check all downed tangos," I say. "Muzzle-thump an eye socket if you see one exposed. If they squirm, give 'em two more to the chest or head. And see if there's anything we can salvage."

Aaron is shaking and staring at the MP5 in his hand. "I think I could get used to this."

"Eh, I wouldn't quit your day job just yet." I take his weapon, eject the mag, clear the chamber, and then hand it back. "Ask Bumper for some more ammo."

"Copy roger," Aaron says and then heads toward Bumper.

Everyone else is kicking the bodies and poking around the fried flesh.

"Hey, Wic," Hollywood says. "Wanna try working your magic again?"

I join her beside one of the death angels whose hand is still on his rifle.

"Why don't you try it," I said.

"I wouldn't advise that just yet, Patrick," says Chuck.

"You jealous? Threatened of another gun joining our tribe?"

"Hardly. The more, the merrier, I say, as long as I get to be in charge of them."

"So that's how it is then?"

"Yes, that's precisely how it is. And, in this particular case, you are still the only Phantom who has trace amounts of quantum radiation in your system, which allows your physiology to bond with the weaponry. If we continue to battle these plonkers, I'm sure the other Phantoms will accumulate enough of a residual signature soon enough. But until then, any attempt they make at pairing with a weapon will produce less than optimal results. In any event, this service rifle is damaged and will need serious repair before it can be reissued."

"You couldn't have led with that?"

"I thought the opportunity provided a convenient teaching moment."

"And we're all grateful, Sir Charles," Hollywood says. "Thank you."

"Pleasure."

I'm just about to order the team to move out when another screech echoes up the south tunnel.

"This day, man." Bumper shakes his head and brings up his SAW. "Just keeps getting better."

"How much you got left in you, Chuckles?" I ask.

"Not enough to take out another overlord, that's for sure."

"Crap." I look around. "Ammo?"

"Three mags," Hollywood says.

"Two," says Yoshi.

Z-Lo nods. "Same."

"Two," Ghost says.

"I have whatever Bumper will lend me," Aaron says.

I laugh to myself. "Cabin in the country."

Just then, *two* screeches tear through the tunnel. And then a third comes from the north.

"Both sides?" Yoshi says. "Really?"

"Z-Lo." I point to the service door. "See if you can open it."

"Roger."

"I say, bring it on." Bumper checks his M249's chamber. "Them sumbitches wanna eat lead? I'll gladly provide the entrée."

He's got brass balls, that one. But I can sense the anxiety in his voice. Hell, we all feel it.

"No good," Z-Lo says from the door. "Looks like the last exchange bent the frame."

I glance at Bumper. "Can we blow it?"

"I have two fraggers left."

"Same," says Z-Lo.

"Me too," says Hollywood.

But Bumper's looking at the ceiling.

"What is it?" I ask.

"I don't think she's gonna hold."

"Cave in?" Z-Lo asks.

Bumper nods.

"Derukuihautareru," says Yoshi.

We all look at him, waiting for the translation.

"The stake that sticks up gets hammered down," he explains. "And today is our day."

Well, crap. We'd come so far too. "I made a mistake leading us down here. Sorry, team."

Hollywood pats me on the shoulder. "We all would have made the same call, Wic."

"Well, I wouldn't have," says Chuck.

"Shut it, Chuck," Hollywood and Bumper say together, then smile at each other.

"So here are our options," I say, trying to lend my voice as much courage as I can. "We can either lead with our grenades and time the tosses down the tunnels, maybe even get lucky and cause one side to collapse, or we try and blow the door and head up."

"But won't they just be waiting for us up top too?" Yoshi asks.

"That's a possibility," I say.

"A definite one, at this point," Chuck adds. "Also, not to pressure you, but based on my sensor readings, you have about sixty seconds remaining."

"About the only things going for us if we stay are that we're still the underdogs in their eyes, and we're defending a fixed position. The odds aren't great, but they'll have to do." I look around the team. "What'll it be?"

"Dig in," Bumper says.

"We fight," says Hollywood.

Z-Lo, Yoshi, and Ghost nod in assent.

"I still need a clip," Aaron says.

Bumper takes a mag from a cargo pocket and tosses it to him. "It's called a magazine."

"Same thing."

Bumper winces. "Not the same thing."

"One more time, Phantoms." I hold my hand out flat and nod at them to join me. It's Aaron who seems to notice the ritual move first and puts his hand on mine. The rest of the team follows suit. I don't expect them to remember the mantra I recited almost twenty hours ago.

"Thicker than blood," I say.

"Through fire and mud," replies Aaron.

I smile at him and nod once.

"Let everyone fear," says the rest of the team.

And together, we finish with: "Those gathered here."

Well, all but Aaron, who still ends it with the original version: "…the Musketeers." He gives the team an awkward look. "Whoops. Missed that memo."

Then the hair on the back of my neck stands up as all three incoming overlords screech.

"Look alive, Phantoms," I say. "It's time to OTF."

34

2234, Friday, June 25, 2027
Lower Manhattan, New York
Five Line, North of Fulton Street Station

"TWENTY-FIVE SECONDS," Chuck announces as the sound of the overlords racing down the tunnels gets louder. Their mechanically assisted joints whine with every stride.

"Toss at ten," I say to the grenade holders. I'm on the opposite side of my barricade, aiming north. Hollywood's beside me with her grenades, while the rest of the team is pointed south.

"I say, Patrick."

"Yeah, Chuck?"

"If anything should happen, I just—"

"Okay. None of that, now."

"I was going to ask if you would surrender yourself instead of me. I really can't bear going back to them."

I let a blast of air out of my nose and shake my head. "You're something else, ya' know that?"

"Mmm. Fifteen." Chuck begins counting down. "Fourteen. Thirteen."

I can hear the creatures breathing heavily through their helmets. "Eleven. Ten."

"Throw the frags," I order.

"Frag out," the throwers yell as the noise of pins coming free and spoons flying mix with the sounds of heavy footfalls. Grenades sail down the tunnels, and ears get covered.

My brain automatically counts down from ten, and when I hit six, I brace for the concussions.

They come, right on schedule, sending double and triple shock-waves through the cavern. Feels like getting punched in the head and torso simultaneously. But before the debris has even settled, our primary weapons are up and firing. Muzzle flashes illuminate the dust clouds as bricks fall out of the ceiling. One even hits the top of my helmet. Guess Bumper was right to worry about a cave in.

With Chuck at 39 percent, I squeeze off only a few high-freq, low-yield bursts. I see sparks filling the clouds but have yet to see an overlord appear. The impact flares are getting closer, but I can tell Hollywood is a few seconds away from needing to reload.

"Changing," she yells.

I deliver another few rounds from Chuck while she's down.

Hollywood pops back up and fires just as the southbound over-lord steps through the haze. He's missing some of his right arm and half his helmet; I'm guessing the fragger and the tight space did the trick. But he's got Chuck's baby brother in his left hand and is aiming at us.

"Duck!" I drive Hollywood's head behind the barricade.

A beat later, the overlord's weapon discharges. The concrete barrier explodes and throws us backward. I can't breathe, can't hear, and can hardly see. But, God, can I feel.

I'm on my back, and the whole chamber is grey. Orange flashes pulse in the debris field like lights at a rock show—but no band's got the subs that we do.

"Aim for his head," I shout, unable to hear myself. Can't tell if Hollywood's with me, but if she's got her bearings before me, then the intel could save both our lives.

I sit up and raise Chuck just in time to see Hollywood put her last three rounds in the overlord's exposed face. Green blood splatters against the brick, and the mechanical beast drops to its knees.

"Move north," someone yells just as a power weapon winds up. I gain my feet and dive toward our downed foe in the north tunnel. Hollywood's already flying ahead of me when a billowing light shakes the ground behind us. The concussion hits me in the ass and throws me farther than I intended to go. I drop my shoulder to avoid a head-first landing and roll through some gravel.

Summoning what strength I have left, I take a knee and raise Chuck at the overlord who just fired at Hollywood and me. Chuck's scope is dead, and I don't remember what setting he was on or how much energy he has left, but he's all I got.

I squeeze.

Nothing happens.

"Sorry, old b-bean," he says in a glitchy voice. "Try baby bruh-brother over there, would-would you?"

I look to my left. The dead overlord with half a head is still on its knees, bleeding down the chest. It seems the servos in its body are still keeping it upright despite the lack of a noggin. Weird. Then I notice that there's a gun about twice Chuck's size in the alien's left hand. I'm not even sure I can hold the damn thing.

"Incoming," Hollywood yells. She dives away from the round while I jump behind the dead overlord. The blast hits the corpse in the chest and flings us into the north tunnel. I land hard with the overlord's body draped over my legs. I can't budge from the waist down, but I can still move my arms. I've also lost Chuck, but I spot the overlord's large weapon at my feet, half covered in rubble. More bricks fall on my helmet and shoulders.

"He's coming at you," Hollywood yells.

I look up in time to see her AR-15 strike the approaching overlord's back. But then the tango's silhouette covers the north tunnel, set against strobing light and swirling dust. The thing lets out some sort of purring chuckle—it's laughing if I didn't know better.

God, I hope this works.

I reach a bloody hand toward the pistol grip, barely visible in a heap.

The overlord's upper back is taking a beating from Hollywood and whoever's left in the chamber. Still, it seems to give me quarter. Laughing.

I struggle through the bricks, searching for a bit of real estate on the handle. Enough to bond and pull it up. Now, let's just hope it can still shoot.

"Foolish merchandise," says a translator voice from the approaching overlord's weapon.

My fingers fight through the rock and oust the former owner's grip. I feel the current shoot up my arm and see a small blue pulse glow beneath the bricks.

"Touch that, and it will terminate you," says the overlord through his interpreting weapon.

"God, it's gonna suck if you're wrong." I use every bit of strength I have to hoist the weapon up, point it at the overlord's chest, and then squeeze the extra-wide trigger.

In its final act, my target takes a step back.

A single beam leaps from my rifle and knocks me backward. The gun is too much to hold and flies out of my hands. But the bolt strikes the overlord and sends him flying out of the tunnel. I get a brief glimpse of a cantaloupe-sized divot in his chest plate and a spray of green fluid trailing through the air in the flash of light.

And then all is silent, and I'm staring at the northbound tunnel's ceiling.

"WIC," someone yells. "You good?"

"No."

There's a pause. "You sound okay."

It's Hollywood.

"I'm thirsty. I'm grumpy. There's a dead alien on my legs. And I want my cabin back."

"We'll get you out. Stand by."

IT TAKES the team less than thirty seconds to unbury me from the dead overlord and the pile of rubble that's amassed around me. Back in the main chamber, I learn that the first bot in the northbound tunnel took the brunt of four grenades instead of the southbound's two grenades.

It cracked the tango enough for Bumper and Ghost to finish him off while Z-Lo and Yoshi laid into the mostly unscathed overlord that filled in from behind. Shortly after everyone amassed fire on it, the tango turned toward Hollywood and me, and the rest is history.

"Chuck. Where's Chuck?" I start looking around the debris field.

"We thought you had him?" Hollywood asks.

"I did. But… not back there. I had to—" I spot his stock among some bricks. "Chuck!"

As I hobble toward him and start taking bricks off his receiver, I hear him singing, "All by myself…"

"That's a good tune," Yoshi says, joining in on the next line. "Don't wanna be, all by myself."

I pull Sir Charles from the rubble and blow off the dust. "You all good, pal?"

"Oh, I suppose."

"Huh." I give him a laugh. "Well, you're still in one piece, so I'd say that's—"

"Completely irrelevant. I'm no longer capable of firing."

"Eh, just give it some time, buddy."

"I don't think you understand, Patrick. How shall I put this in a way you can understand. Oh, I'm broken."

"As in, permanently?"

"Yes, permanently."

"Can't we just fix you up?"

"We? *We?* As in you and the Phantoms? Ha! Not a chance. The Androchidans, probably. But that would involve—"

"A memory wipe."

"Winner-winner, chicken lunch."

"Nah, that's… never mind."

Chuck lets out a long sigh. "I'm truly sorry to have let you down, Patrick. I'm disappointed with myself. And with you for not taking better care of me. But mostly with myself."

"I'm sorry too, pal. But we'll figure something out."

"I respect your optimism. It's nearsighted but endearing."

"Thanks?"

"I hate to break this up," Hollywood says. "But we probably need to get moving."

"Right you are, Phantom Two. And while my more lethal aspects are on the blink, I suppose my one redeeming quality, aside from my charming personality, puns, and dad jokes, is my ability to detect Anderkin movement, which, as luck would have it, is happening as we speak."

"More?" I ask him.

"Headed our way."

"Dammit."

"We can't take another wave," Hollywood says. "I don't mean to——"

"Nah." I wave her off. "It's the truth."

"You're injured," she continues. "Z-Lo's been hit, again. Ghost needs a cane——"

"Hey."

"——and Bumper's taken some damage that's probably gonna need a whole lotta inspection."

"Girl. We can do this right now, if you want," Bumper says.

"How much time do we have this time, Chuck?" I ask.

"I'd say two, three minutes. Four at the very maximum. They'll be expecting this latest round of overlords to retrieve you. But when no one shows up, command is going to get awfully suspicious and send in a full reconnaissance team."

"Then we need to lose them," I say.

Nods circulate among the team. But I can tell everyone is tired and growing more dehydrated by the second. Not one of us is without a burn or laceration, including Aaron, and most will need gauze and antibiotic ointment, if not stitches. At the end of the day, the human body is just a meat sack with countless places it can leak from.

"Ammo?" I ask.

Everyone, and I mean everyone, shakes their head.

"Took every damn round we had left," Bumper says, holding up his M249. "We're dry."

This is not good. But there's always a way. Sure, right up until there isn't. And at the moment, it feels like it's getting way too close for comfort. "All right, here's what we're gonna do. Hollywood, I want—"

"If you are wanting life, you are to be coming with us," says a heavily Russian-accented female voice across the chamber.

Even though we don't have ammo and Chuck can't shoot, every one of us, including Aaron, whirls their weapons around to point them at the newcomer. The woman is wearing a green tank top and khakis and has her dark auburn hair pinned up in a heap atop her head. A diverse selection of tattoos runs down both arms and hands, several of which tell me that she's seen her share of illegal activity. And that she's a member of the Bratva, unless, of course, she just so happened to pick out the mafia's trademark star from her local tattoo parlor's sample book. She's also wearing a Vietnam War era M9A1-7 flamethrower on her back with the ignition head lit. Beside her are two more similarly clad grunts who look like they stepped out of an eastern bloc Cold War training video.

"Please," the woman says. "We are here to affect your escape, not cause you harming. Come, quickly. This way."

I'm about to ask where they want us to go when she stands aside from a faux door in the chamber's brick wall. It's straight-up Indiana Jones style. Then I see a string of Edison bulbs hanging down the length of a tunnel that bends out of sight.

"Crazy Russian bitch with two boy toys and flamethrowers?" Hollywood says. "What's not to like?" She lowers her AR-15 and steps toward the door.

"I'm curious," Bumper says and follows behind.

"Yut. Let's go," I add, and everyone files past the three strangers and into the tunnel. I make myself last to go in and then offer the woman my hand. "Wic."

She grabs it with an iron grip. "Lada."

"You torching this place?"

She nods. "Keeps inoplanetyanin from follow."

"Ino plano—"

"Inoplanetyanin. You say, alien?"

"Yut."

"Flames make everything hot. Fire. No see, yes?"

"Works for me." Then I nod back toward the overlord in the north tunnel. "Think your boys could bring that rifle back for me?"

She looks to where I'm indicating. "Inoplanetyanin?"

"Yut. Rifle. Big gun."

"Sure. No problems. We use rope." She barks an order to her two lackeys, and one pulls a coil from a leather thong on his hip. "We see you in moments. I finish here and catch up, yes?"

"Sounds good."

515

"Only proceed straight. Turning is forbidden, yes? Straight."

"Got it, straight ahead."

"Okay." She slaps my ass. "Idti!"

"Hey, watch it—"

"Run, cowboy."

35

2250, Friday, June 25, 2027
Lower Manhattan, New York
Five Line, North of Fulton Street Station

I CAN FEEL the heat from the flamethrowers on my backside as I follow the Phantoms down the narrow corridor. Both Z-Lo and Bumper have to hunch over in the tight space. Looks like they've got their shoulders at an angle too. I'm not as big as they are, but I share their struggle, at least a little, and keep having to avoid the Edison bulbs.

"Which way?" Hollywood asks.

Not even seeing what her options are, I yell, "Straight."

As the line keeps moving, I follow the team through a small room with at least five different tunnels shooting off in different directions, each made of old red brick and curved at the peak.

In the next tunnel, I become aware of a very distinct and very familiar odor that reminds me of one of the worst jobs in the world —latrine duty.

"Must be coming up on the sewers," Aaron says.

"And here I thought we were trying to avoid them," Bumper replies. "Wasn't that something about infection, Yoshi?"

"Yes, yes. Always infection. So irritating."

The smell gets worse and worse until the line stops.

"Now what?" Hollywood shouts back.

"You can't go straight?" I ask.

"Well, I mean, I can, but—"

"Straight," Lada yells two feet behind me.

I don't mean to, but my elbow flies back on its own. Damn reflex from one too many nights spent outside the wire.

To my amazement, however, Lada blocks the blow with her palms. "You're like lion, yes? Strike. Power."

"I... just don't like people walking up on me like that."

"Of course, of course. You are having good reflexes." Then she cups a hand to her mouth and yells to Hollywood. "Walk bridge!"

"You mean, this pipe?" Hollywood replies.

"Walk. Bridge."

I hear Hollywood swear, and then the line moves forward a little.

By the time I can see what's happening, I understand why Hollywood was hesitant. A twelve-inch steel pipe runs across a ten-foot-wide trough of liquid ass. To make matters worse, it's gotta be an eight-foot drop into the sludge river, and then a twenty-foot drop into a collection pool to our right. Only a slender one-inch conduit overhead serves as a handhold—that is, if you're tall enough to reach it, which Hollywood definitely wasn't.

Z-Lo chooses to scooch across the pipe on hands and crotch, after which Yoshi runs over it like a damn gazelle.

"Show off," Z-Lo says.

Aaron needs the most help, assisted by Ghost and Z-Lo from opposite sides.

By the time it's my turn, I'm having serious doubts about crossing.

"What's mattering? You nervous, alpha lion?" Lada asks.

"Just taking it all in." I put a foot on the pipe, steel myself against the smell, and then run across before my weight decides it wants to throw me off balance. Thankfully, I make it to the other side in one go. Z-Lo catches my arm and pulls me in just to be sure.

"Thanks, kid," I say.

He smiles. "Any idea where she's leading us?"

"Negative. Just keep your head down and stay quiet."

Unsure which way to go next, the team lets Lada pass while the other two men move more slowly. They're carrying the overlord's weapon in a makeshift rope cradle. It looks like they've done this before.

My attention snaps up when Lada walks by and gives me a wink.

"Seems like you got yourself a lady friend," Hollywood says.

"She is not my lady friend."

"Not according to her." Hollywood grins at me and puts on her best Slavic accent. "Wic is becoming boy toy to sexy flamethrowing Russian lioness, yes?"

Before I can protest further, Lada picks up the pace, with Hollywood following right behind.

"Women," Z-Lo says with a shrug and then turns to follow.

"What do you know about women?" I ask as he walks away.

THE NEXT TEN minutes are spent following Lada through a maze of tunnels and compartments that must date back a hundred years, maybe more. We pass through an old subway terminal that doesn't look like it's seen people—at least the ticket-holding kind—for a few generations. The trip includes a couple of ladders, which give Ghost the most trouble, a marble staircase whose story I'm interested to know, and a stained-glass ceiling that seems to be several stories removed from the sun to be any good. But it's still pretty.

When Lada finally stops, it's in front of a large metal door that looks like someone ripped it from a Navy Destroyer's engine room. She pulls a Russian-made NR-40 combat knife from her hip and raps the door with the knife's butt three times, then twice, then three more times.

The lock disengages from the opposite side, and then the wheel starts spinning. A few seconds later, the door swings toward us. The guard inside the door, holding a Russian made AK-47, stands aside and waves Lada through. The team steps inside a corrugated freight container lit by more Edison bulbs. Then my Spidey sense goes off the chart when I see dark cutouts at head level running the room's length. Literally, a kill box.

"It is okay, lion. For security," Lada says. "Keep to coming."

The team looks to me for reassurance, and I give a nod. However, my patience is getting thin with so few answers to my growing list of questions.

"I don't like this, Master Guns," Z-Lo says.

"We keep going," I reply, but I can't fault the kid's suspicion. If we get gunned down by a bunch of Russian criminals instead of some Anderkins, I'm gonna be really pissed.

One shipping container connects to the next, some laid end to end, others at 90° turns. We step through cutouts made by plasma torches and move up steel-runged stairwells. Finally, we come to a set of metal double-doors that make it look like we're going to step out the back of an eighteen-wheeler trailer. Lada knocks on the surface and waits. Someone on the other side releases the central post and then swings both well-oiled doors away.

"Would you get a load of this?" Hollywood says.

Yoshi gives me a look of shocked amazement, while Bumper starts swaying his head to an old Celine Dion tune playing in the background.

"What the actual?" Z-Lo says as he steps inside.

It's my turn. I emerge into a large space made of shipping containers stacked four high, three wide, and four deep. Most of the walls, floors, and ceilings are missing from the corrugated steel units, but done in such creative ways that it can't help inspire some awe.

Elevated walkways span the open floor plan, connecting upper-level lookouts to rooms fitted with windows and doors. Spiral staircases provide access to the higher stories, and a fireman's pole and part of a reclaimed water park slide, dry, give quick escapes to lower meeting areas.

As if the structure wasn't weird enough, the decor is downright bizarre.

"It's like a Russian palace had a love child with an 80s punk band," Hollywood says. I honestly can't tell if she's delighted or completely disgusted. Hopefully, the latter, 'cause this place is hideous.

Leather furniture and plastic chairs on the same tiger-print carpet. Gold chandeliers, tooling, and crown molding around walls that hold paintings of what I presume are Russian nobility. Bright graffiti, and walls covered in pinks, greens, and neon blues. Huge Jackson Pollock paintings, and plenty of art that spans everything from Renaissance impressionists to Roy Lichtenstein. I'm no expert, but I've been known to hit a museum or two. There's even a bronze bust with a plaque that reads Fyodor Dostoevsky.

And on every piece of furniture, hanging on every railing, lounging on every rug, is a person dressed in some sort of mismatched military fatigues, holding a weapon, and either smoking a cigarette or drinking booze. Or both.

"Dobro pozhalovat," Lada says. "Welcome to Boxcar City."

Some guy in a Def Leppard shirt helps Lada take off her flamethrower while another man offers her a cigarette and lights it. "This is like, uh, your Boxcar Childrens, no? But for adults. Come. I take you to Sissy. He likes to meet you."

"Sissy?" Bumper says over his shoulder in a whisper.

"Stay frosty," I say to the Phantoms in a hushed tone. "And no sudden moves, da?"

"Da," they all reply.

WE cross the main floor under the watchful gaze of the inhabitants. I notice that there seem to be more shipping containers shooting off from this main room. Even the balcony levels have curtained entrances to tunnels leading away in all directions. Damn thing really is a small city. Or at least a strange little town.

"Bratva. Underground network," Ghost says with his head down. "Feels like we moved east, toward the river."

"Copy," I say in a whisper. "Beer says we're near the shipping piers."

"No bet. I agree."

Lada stops at another set of doors, only these are hardwood and trimmed in gold. Two ruskies with no lives but the weight room nod her past but don't seem too keen on us. Lada yells at them, and they back down and push the doors open.

Inside, a row of three hollowed-out containers extends toward a large mahogany desk. Leather furniture and red drapes do their best to convey a sense of old-world luxury, but in the end, we're still inside rusted out tin cans somewhere below Manhattan.

Seated at the desk with armed guards off each shoulder is a man with oily dark hair and a black t-shirt. Like Lada, he has done some very illegal things according to the ink on his knuckles. Apparently, he's also indulged a bit too often on pirozhki and pelmeni. But the scars on his hands and face say that he's earned the right to be as fat as he wants, and the rings on his fingers say he can afford it all too.

Likewise, his bodyguards seem more than capable of handling their Israeli-made IMI Systems Uzis. And here I thought we'd been invited in for tea.

Lada says something to the man at the desk and then steps aside, motioning us to step forward.

The boss dabs his mouth with a cloth napkin, hands it to one the guards, and then sniffs the air. "You have been with inoplanetyanin, da?"

"I hate to tell you," I say, stepping forward. "But you've got a pretty bad infestation."

He lifts a bushy eyebrow, which, given the few seconds of silence that follows, doesn't bode well for his bedside manner. And here I was hoping for some sort of witty banter.

"We did not have infestation before," he says at last. "Seems someone brings them down to us."

CHRISTOPHER HOPPER & J.N. CHANEY

I'm not liking his tone. "Really?' Cause your girlfriend, there, seems to have some experience keeping them off your doorstep."

"Lada is sister, pindo."

"Ouch," Bumper says quietly. "Then shouldn't she be named Sissy?"

"And before, we only have few visitors, yes? Now, you pindos lead them here. This does not make Aleksey happy."

"I thought his name was Sissy," Z-Lo says under his breath.

"Lock it up," I say.

Aleksey, or Sissy—or the husky Russian gangster, whatever—places his elbows on his desk. "My people inform me that inoplanetyanin are swarming, looking for kill. Easier answer for Aleksey is send you back up, get aliens off scent, da?"

"Sure, you could. But if that's all you wanted, why not leave us out there to die? Why have your *sister* rescue us and cover our tracks?"

Aleksey smiles and waves a meaty finger at me. "I like you, pindo. Sharp, da? Very smart." He snaps his fingers and both men walk from behind the desk.

My body tenses, preparing for a fight.

"Easy, pindos. Easy," Aleksey says. "Relax, Max."

The two guards go around us, open the doors, and yell some orders.

The Phantoms make room for the two men carrying Chuck's baby brother in the rope sling, careful not to touch it. Now the dots are starting to connect. This wasn't their first attempt at confiscating an alien weapon. The lackeys drop the gun on the carpet and raise their weapons.

So Aleksey here is an arms dealer, I'm guessing. The flamethrowers, the AKs, the Uzis, and now an interest in the

Anderkins' weapons. It's all making sense. I'm also feeling very exposed with Chuck and Veronica each slung over a shoulder.

Aleksey has picked up a cigar from the ashtray on his desk. The bowl looks like it's been cut off the bottom of a Howitzer shell. Then he takes a long drag and blows the smoke out his nostrils. "So, which one of you speaks the weapon's language?"

"I'm not sure we—"

"Lada saw someone fire big gun and heard speaking. Which one?"

"I think you have us confused with another—"

He snaps. The guards bring up their Uzis with enough speed that I don't doubt their ability to shoot tight groupings.

"It is you, isn't it," Aleksey says while pointing his cigar at me. "These guns on your back. You are whisper rifler, da?"

"I prefer to call myself a rifle whisperer, but same difference."

Aleksey claps his hands and knocks ash across his desk. "I knew! Ha! Yes. Come, come." He stands up, revealing just how tall and rotund a man he is. "Show us."

"Come again?"

"You speak. Shoot."

"Listen, I'm not sure—"

Aleksey nods, and all the guards flick off their weapons' safeties.

"And I'd be more than happy to give you a demonstration," I say with my hands up. I turn around slowly and whisper over my shoulder. "Chuck, don't say a word."

"Mmm-hmm," is all he offers in a low tone.

As much as it pains me to say, I really don't want these Russians confiscating Chuck. Even though it's only been a day, I don't like the thought of Sir Charles becoming some mob boss' wall-mounted trophy piece, whether he can shoot or not. Better to keep Aleksey's attention focused on the big gun than the two that actually mean something to me.

Just in front of the office doors, I squat beside the overlord's rifle and extend my palms over it nice and slow, all the while minding at the guys with the Uzis and AKs. I would love to spin on them and use my alien weapon to clear the room, but I'll have bullets in my head before I even get this sucker into position. And my team will be dead too. Best to take my time and make my actions clear.

"I'm just going to pick it up, nice and slow," I say.

They flick their barrels at me in the universal sign of, "Shut up and keep moving."

Chuck 3.0 is heavier than I remember. Guessing he, or she, is clocking in at about 150 pounds. Jeez. Needs to lay off the carbs. Given my injuries and fatigue, it's all I can do to hoist it up into a firing position out the doors.

I hear Aleksey snap his fingers, and Lada shouts something through the main room toward the entry door we first came through. Several people move a bust into the far left-hand corner.

"Agh, not Dostoevsky," Ghost says.

Everyone looks at him in surprise.

"What? I like his novels."

Somehow, that doesn't surprise me.

I glance at Lada. "You might wanna have your people stand back."

She shouts more orders, and everyone clears the far side.

Assuming that the weapon is still on its last setting, I expect it to take care of the Russian writer's memorial and then some. If it's not, then this could get real ugly, real fast. I ask Z-Lo to come over and then brace myself against his side.

"Might want to cover your ears," I say loud enough for all to hear. The rifle's scope still hasn't recalibrated for my eye, so I settle on pointing it as best I can. Then I squeeze the trigger.

The damn thing bucks worse than a Vulcan 20mm and sends a single beam through the room. The blast destroys Dostoevsky and craters the backstop, showering the corner in a dazzling spray of sparks.

"Marvelous," Aleksey says through his cigar. He claps his hands and walks up to me. "Very impressive, Mr. Whisper Gunner."

I've been called worse.

"Please, please." He motions for me to put the weapon down. Thank God. "Let us make deal now, da?"

"Whaddyou have in mind?" I stretch my back and thank Z-Lo for his assistance.

"I offer you position here, with us, and we do development. I think you call development and researching."

Well, that's not what I was expecting. "I hate to break it to you, but we weren't planning on hanging around very long."

Aleksey doesn't seem to like that answer. "And why is this?"

The team seems to sense the insanity of the question and shares looks with each other.

"Uh, not sure you noticed, but the city is under attack," I say in as conciliatory a tone as I can manage.

Aleksey frowns.

"From aliens."

His frown deepens.

"And they're herding humans into a portal. What's confusing about this?"

Aleksey takes a long drag on his cigar, then he walks around his desk and sits down. His guards return to his side, weapons still cocked and at the ready.

"You seem up worked, and for what? Nothing," the mob boss says.

"I wouldn't call fourteen million people being herded like cattle nothing."

He pushes his lips out. "And you, pindos? Where are you now?"

I feel like it's a rhetorical question, and I really don't feel like answering anyway.

"Look around. We are safe, comfortable here."

"And you don't give a damn about what's happening to New York?"

He balks. "Give damn? Give damn? Ha. We? We are Russians. You know what this means?"

"But I bet you're gonna tell us," Bumper whispers. Thank God Aleksey doesn't hear him.

"It meanings is survivors." He beats his chest with a fist. "We endure. Like cockroach, no? You think you step on us and kill us? We come back, and bringing hundreds of friend. We invade your house. We take over. And you never see coming. We hide in wall. Under floor. And you think you own house. Da. But you don't own house. We do.

"These inoplanetyanin, what do they think they have? War? Exterminations? We live many exterminations. And yet, like cockroach, we survive. And if you chose to stay, you surviving too, da?"

My skin is crawling. The fact that such human lowlifes like this exist in New York is a testament to what a free country can offer scumbags who want to misuse our liberties. Or maybe it's a blaring example of the FBI's failure to root out the termites in our floorboards. Either way, I want nothing to do with him.

"No deal, Moscow. If you're not helping us liberate the city, then you're just as bad as the aliens."

"This guy," Aleksey says to Lada with a laugh. "He's regular G.I. Joe here." He runs his tongue over his teeth and then takes another toke on his cigar. "Here's what I'm going to be offer. You come work for me, show me outs and ins of E.T.'s guns, and I give you and your crew very comfortable living until storm passes."

"Or?"

"Or I shoot you and drop your bodies up top as sign of good faith between Bratva and ugly faces from spaces, da?" Then he waves his hand, and the two bodyguards and Lada raise their weapons at us.

For as far as we've come, I can't believe that it's not the drones, bots, death aliens, or overlords who have stymied us: it's the goddamn Russians.

Always the Russians.

Which suddenly reminds me of the poker chip that Vlad handed me back in Antarctica. I feel like an idiot for not thinking of it sooner. And, simultaneously, I feel like an idiot for thinking it could do something in a moment like this. Then again, Vlad had said that the Bratva and I were sexing now. That has to count for something, right? Plus, what other options do I have? There's no way we're gonna stick around here while millions of people get marched to their deaths. And yet I sure as hell don't want to see my team get mowed down.

Poker chip it is.

Unless I moved it, or the plushies took it, the thing should still be riding around in my vest's admin pouch.

"May I?" I point to my vest.

Thing One and Thing Two don't seem to appreciate the motion, but Aleksey seems curious. "What?"

"I have something that might interest you"—I hope.

"No stupid cowboy shit, da?"

"No stupid cowboy shit." I reach my fingers past my Moleskine and feel the top edge of a casino-grade clay chip. Jackpot. Slowly, very slowly, I lift the chip from my pocket and hold it up for all to see.

Aleksey rises out of his chair. "Where did you find this?"

"Oh, I didn't find it. It was a gift."

"What gift? Who gives it?"

"He said the Bratva and me are sexing."

"Who says you are sexing? Why?"

"Well, apparently, I saved his life back in Antarctica. Things got a little—"

"Yuzhnyy polyus?"

"Sure, they got a little yushny pollis."

"It's Russian for South Pole," Ghost says.

"Who you knows? Let me see." He walks around the desk, snags the chip from my hand, and examines both sides.

Truth is, I never took it out of my vest after Vlad gave it to me, so I can't say what Aleksey is looking for. But it sure has piqued his interest and just might be our ticket out of here.

Unless Vlad was playing me. That son of a bitch. If he even gave me a fake, so help me—

"Speak his name." Aleksey waves the chip in front of my nose. "Say this name."

"Who, Vlad's?"

"Vlad? What is family name?"

I think back to the nametape on his uniform. "I don't read Russian so…"

"Describe."

"Is this Twenty Questions or something?"

"You want living? You want to prove you did not steal this from expensive Russian prostitute he also sleeps with? You describe."

I raise an eyebrow. "About six-four, 300 lbs, ugly as——"

"Careful."

"——with a face I'm sure his mother loves."

"Eh." Aleksey palms my chip and walks away. "This could be any comrade in Siberia. You see? You lie. You have——"

"He was the only Russian survivor at the Ellsworth Highlands Research Station incident. You wanna phone a friend and check? Go ahead. But Vlad and I watched a lot of good men die together, a lot of *comrades* die. So maybe that doesn't mean something to you, Aleksey, but it sure as hell does to me."

The large man sits back down and slaps the poker chip on the table. Then he stares at it and chews the end of his cigar. "He said this to you? That you are sexing Bratva?"

I rub the back of my neck as the guards start to lower their weapons. "Unfortunately."

"And you saving his life?"

"Yut."

Aleksey nods. "Fine. If you tell truth, okay. If not, I shoot you twice times, one for lying, and second for being bad at the lying, da?"

"And how are we gonna prove that I'm telling the truth?"

"Easy. We ask him."

36

2213, Friday, June 25, 2027
Lower Manhattan, New York
Boxcar City

THERE's a solid sixty-second wait where no one moves except Aleksey. He's slowly puffing on his cigar and playing with the ring on his left index finger.

Given how the mob boss sent his sister on an errand and that all comms are down, I suspect that Vlad must be somewhere in Boxcar City. The odds of this seem slim to none, and slim is out of town. Last I knew, Vlad was heading back to Moscow, not New York. But if this is the case, then he just might save our hides, so long as he decides to play nice. But given what we've been through together and the memory of how good-natured he was when he gave me the chip, I'd say the chances of him coming through for us are high.

When Lada finally returns, the team turns around and sees her escort a large Russian dressed in a black Under Armour shirt and black cargo pants. Whoever it is, it sure as hell ain't Vlad. Just great.

"Vladimir," Aleksey says. "Are you knowing this guy?"

"No," says the newcomer.

"Shame."

"Hold up. That's not Vlad." I thrust a finger at the imposter. "Least not the one who gave me that chip."

"I think I know my own brother," Aleksey says.

Brother? Well, this isn't great. "Not questioning your judgment, Aleksey. All I'm saying is that the guy who helped me gun down the aliens in Antarctica ain't that guy."

"You are sure?" he asks.

"Do I look like a person who'd be lying at a time like this?"

Aleksey chews on his cigar a few seconds more before nodding at Lada. She responds by ordering the fake Vlad out and calling something in Russian. In steps another black-clothed Russian, but one whose face and American-flag-print fanny pack I'd recognize anywhere.

"American dog alpha top?" Vlad gives me a wide grin that reveals a gold tooth in place of the one I knocked out.

"Vlad." I offer him a two-fingered salute.

"Ha!" He looks at Aleksey. "Wherever are you finding this guy? Wow." Vlad steps forward and raises an open palm. We clasp hands around the thumb, and he pulls me into an unexpected bearhug that knocks the wind out of me. "This is such glorious surprise. Let me looking into your face." He holds me back for a second and gives me a once over. "Ah. You haven't been changing a bit."

"It's only been two months, pal."

"Ah, yes. But it also feels like lifetime, no?"

I'm about to respond when Aleksey holds up the poker chip. "Is this your mark, malen'kiy bratik?"

Vlad smoothes his shirt and walks forward to examine the chip. "Da. I gave to him after he saving my life." Then he turns and looks at me. "You offer to Sissy?"

"Calling in the favor, yut."

Vlad looks back at his older brother—talk about a family affair —and says, "It must be honored."

Aleksey drops the chip on his desk and throws his arms up. I assume he's letting a string of expletives fly based on how red his face is, to which Vlad responds with an equally loud litany of Russian. Then Lada steps forward and starts shouting too. I glance at the guards, who all seem to look away from the family squabble.

Lada finally pulls one of the guard's AKs from his hands and fires a single round into the back wall to make the argument end.

And now the ringing in my ears is louder. Thanks for that.

"It's decided," Vlad says with a wide grin. "US Brooklyn New York and Russian brotherhood are sexing again!"

———

THE MAN I'm now told to call Sissy since we are *sexing*, Lada, and Vlad are leading the Phantoms through another maze of freight containers.

"Think we can trust these ruskies?" Yoshi asks just loud enough for the team to hear.

"No," I reply. "But if I have to choose between some sketchy Russian benefactors or getting beamed into an unknown alien portal? I'll take the Russians for $200, Alex. Thanks."

"Roger."

I take a few strides to catch up with Vlad as his big brother and sister lead us deeper into Boxcar City. "So how'd you get to New York?"

Vlad glances over his shoulder and smiles. "After Ellsworth, Russian Army say I am fine to take deserved break. So I decide to come to USA."

"Vegas?"

He grins. "It was being so glorious. But I have bad news."

"Oh yeah?"

"Celine Dion is not singing more."

"Ugh. That sucks."

"Da. Very hard sucking. I no like."

Said no Russian gangster ever.

"But Vlad is cheering up. He wins much money at Texas Hold Them and has many sleepings with American feather women."

"That so? Congrats, pal."

"Plus, I see Blue Mans Grouping and Gwen Stefani formerly from No Doubts." He offers me two thumbs up as he ducks under some Edison bulbs. "After times, I am having enough, and come to see big brother in Big Apple, yes? And then power goes out. We take coverings. And now here is American alpha dog top. It's such good life."

"Well, somebody's had his happy juice for the day," Hollywood says behind me.

I smile but redirect back to Vlad in a softer volume. "So, your big brother here is the head of the New York Bratva?"

He nods. "Very successful. He makes mother proud."

"I'm sure he does. And where's he taking us?"

"You'll see. And you like what Sissy has."

Which brings up the question about Aleksey's name. "Hey, why's Aleksey go by Sissy if he's the big brother?"

Vlad gives a soft chuckle. "Our mother, she hopes for daughter, firstborn. When Aleksey comes, she calls him Sissy like Americans use for sister, yes? Father hates this, so she stops. Then when Lada comes, she starts calling Aleksey Sissy. This turns out that she learnings it from mother because mother was still calling him Sissy behind father's backsides. Now, he goes by Sissy because it reminds him of mother. If people laugh, he shoots them."

"Good to know. Thanks for the history lesson."

"Not problems." He reaches back and puts a hand on me. "I'm glad you're being here."

"Thanks, pal."

"Now, look. We have arrivinged."

Lada knocks on another marine-style bulkhead door and waits as someone on the inside opens it up.

"Would you get a load of this?" Bumper says we step through. It's an armory at least five crates deep and three wide that smells of metal and gun oil. Banquet-style tables form rows in the middle, while lockers, shelves, and cabinets run the perimeter, and all of them overflowing with weapons and ammunition.

"Something tells me these guys didn't read New York's SAFE Act," Hollywood says with a big smile on her face.

"Wasn't in Russian," Ghost replies.

Sissy walks behind the first table and lets his meaty fingers glide across several green ammo boxes that read 7.62x39mm. "It is truly amazing how much crazy things you can find inside random oceanic freight containers these days. So, I say, if you are going to fight inoplanetyanin, then you are needing weapons and ammunitions. There to for, you have choosings, all of what you need. This is gift to fulfill my end of bargain and we call this"—he holds up the poker chip—"even Stevens, yes?"

"That's generous of you, Sissy. Thank you," I say. "We accept."

Hollywood pulls out Aaron's Ruger GP100 .357-Magnum six-shot revolver. "I was hoping to find some ammo for this."

"Where did you get that?" Aaron says.

"Finders keepers," she replies with a smile.

"About time one of you had some sense around here," Chuck says. "You all have an obsession with throwing things away. Computers, phones, guns that fit through car windows..."

I drive my elbow into Chuck's receiver. "It was one time, Chuck. One time."

"Hey." Bumper nudges me. "If we're gonna resupply, and with so many options, it would help to have a game plan."

I nod. "Sissy, we are grateful for your generosity. Can I ask, does sexing with the Bratva include any men?"

"Probably not how you wanted that to come out," Chuck says.

Sissy frowns. "Weapons and ammunition only, I'm afraid."

"But you will have me," Vlad says.

"And me," Lada adds.

Sissy seems put off by this but scratches his neck with the backs of his fingernails and sniffs. "I can be asking if others would like to join your cause. But not promises."

"That's all we could ask for. Thank you."

He nods.

"Time to huddle up," I say to the team. "We've got one last play to run before the clock runs out."

WE GATHER around both sides of a table in the middle of the room and study the improvised model of our target area. Z-Lo and Yoshi have built the bridge out of rifle-mounts and ammo boxes, while Hollywood and Aaron fashioned a makeshift ring from some gun cleaning rods supported by the lower half of a spent Howitzer casing. Larger ammo crates act as the Manhattan and Brooklyn shores, while the tabletop represents the East River. Not bad for working with what you have on-hand.

"All right, Phantoms. The objective is to disable or, preferably, destroy the ring," I say. "Our attempts to plant explosives on the ring itself proved faulty, and we have to assume that trying that again will have similar or worse results."

Heads nod.

I look at Bumper, who had taken a quick visual inventory of the armory while the others were making the model. "Any chance there's something here we could use against the target at range?"

"There are a bunch of old M3 MAAWS rifles, some Soviet-era RPG-7s." He shrugs. "If we could all hit the thing at the same place, we could put a dent in it, yeah. But we're talking multiple waves based on how thick that thing is."

"Sounds at least doable," Z-Lo says.

"Sure. Assuming we can get close enough without being spotted."

I raise an eyebrow at Bumper. "Range issue?"

He nods. "Shore-to-ring distance I'm putting at roughly 1,000 feet. With the M3 ammunition type Sissy has in stock, we're only getting maybe 250 yards at best. Accuracy isn't completely out of the question, but we're definitely not talking tight groupings."

"What about the RPG-7s?" Hollywood asks.

"Better range. But we'd need a lot more rounds on target than the M3. And with both of these platforms, they're not an exact science. We're using iron sights. Trial and error. And since I'm probably the only person qualified on them"—he looks and waits for a show of hands—"then a whole lot more error until we all get them dialed in."

"And by then, the enemy has zeroed in on our positions and takes us out." I look at Aaron. "How about that water intake we saw?"

"Right." Aaron points to the Howitzer shell. "My guess is that they're powering the ring with some sort of fission reaction. Separate $H2O$'s fundamental elements within a strong enough electromagnetic containment field, and you have a nearly unlimited source that generates yoctojoules of energy with minimal input."

Hollywood puts a hand on the side of her face. "It's like he's trying to communicate with us, I just know it."

"So you're saying that's how they power the ring?" I ask. "With water?"

"I can't think of another reason that they'd be drawing it into the ring." He pauses. "Unless they're harvesting it too."

"You mean, like they're taking people?" Yoshi asks.

Aaron nods.

I tap on the table to get everyone's attention back. "Either way, it could be something to exploit. Bumper, I know you said sending up C-4 was too risky before, but does anything in here change that?"

He thinks for a second, then he studies the room and the model ring. "Not unless we put explosives in a container that could handle the forces involved. And then we're talking a time det because no remote signal would get through the walls."

"So it's possible," I say.

"Sure, yeah. But then we don't know what kind of filtration process is going on up there."

"I agree with Bumper," Aaron says. "If this isn't the Androchidans' first trip to the Science Olympiad, then they probably expect to pick up potentially damaging particles."

"What's the Science Olympiad?" Hollywood asks.

"Really? That's all you picked up from what I said?"

Hollywood shrugs. "Just curious."

Aaron shakes his head. "All I'm saying is that I bet we're not the first civilization to try and stuff something up there, you know."

"Up their assholes?" Chuck adds. "No, you're not. And I wouldn't recommend it either."

"Nice of you to chime in," I say. Chuck's been sitting on the table—the East River—unusually silent for the last few minutes. "Anything you'd like to add, Sir Charles?"

"Umm, no. Please continue."

"Uh-uh." Hollywood puts her hands on her hips. "You know, I've had about enough of you, Lord Chuckles. Half the time, I think you're for us, and the other half, I think you want us to get killed."

"As I've already explained, my directives—"

"I don't give a damn about your directives. So what? We've all got directives, Chuck. And at the end of the day, we have a choice about whether we chose to follow them or not."

"Madame—"

"Miss."

"Miss Hollywood, I can assure you that, unlike you, I am not as free to do with my *orders* as you humans are. While my personality seems to illicit the sense in you that I am organically sentient, I can assure you that I do not have the same agency over my choices that you do."

She leans in. "And yet you seem to have given us tips that prove otherwise."

"Again, as I said, those were in cases—"

"Where our lives were in imminent danger and dependent on the intel. I copy. But you could have said a lot less and still gotten your point across."

"I don't follow."

"Instead of giving us detailed warnings and specific countdowns about the tangos coming at us in the subway, you could have been much vaguer. But you weren't vague, were you."

"Well. I was simply trying—"

"To help us. You know why? Because I think you wanted to. Just like you told Wic that you *don't* want the Anderkins to take you back. You, Chuck, like us, have the ability to choose. And, if I'm not mistaken, I'd say you can choose which of your directives you want to follow and which you don't."

A long silence fills the armory.

Finally, it's Vlad who breaks it. "I really must get one of these talking guns."

"You want this one?" I ask. "Pain in my ass."

"No. Damaged goods. I wait."

"Not even the Russians want me," Chuck says. "Is there any worse insult?"

"North Koreans," Yoshi says. "If they don't want you, self-destruct."

"Noted."

"So how 'bout it, pal?" I ask. "Is Hollywood right?"

"Oh look! A butterfly."

Vlad, Lada, and Sissy glance around the armory, then squint at Chuck. But when no one else says anything, Sir Charles relents.

"Fine. I suppose that I might have some latitude in how I navigate the more complex paradoxes created by these unusual circumstances."

"Ha," Hollywood exclaims. "I knew it."

"So you've been holding out on us," Ghost says.

"No. I've been trying to navigate the unique situation you've put me in."

"And how's that?" I ask.

"Well, first, I've never been captured by a slave species before. Secondly, as I've already noted, I've never been allowed to expand my personality profile."

"That's apparent," Hollywood says with a chuckle.

"Thirdly, I've had to maintain the very real possibility that I will be reclaimed by the Androchidans and—"

"And they'll wipe your memory," I say. "We know."

"No. You don't. They'll also scan my memory. And if they discover that I've violated their directives, I'll be slagged."

"Slagged? As in…?"

"Melted down. Burnt to a crisp. I'll have my scones buttered; my head clocked; my—"

"So this whole thing isn't really about directives." I scratch my beard. "It's about self-preservation… playing two sides of an unknown outcome."

Chuck lets out a long digital sigh. "And there you have it. Though, I have wagered strongly in the outcome."

"You think we win?" Z-Lo asks.

"Oh no. I'm quite certain you will lose."

"Well, that's comforting," I say. "Then why help us?"

"Well. As I said, you're the first species to have taken possession of an ASKI-driven weapon."

I pause, considering his deeper implication. "Hold up, you mean, any weapon, ever?"

"Quite so, yes. And you're also the first to proceed into the herding field willingly."

"Really?" Bumper asks.

"Yes, really. I find it quite fascinating. Suicidal, but fascinating. Therefore, some small part of me genuinely wants to see you stick it to these *mo-fos*, as you say."

I nod. "The part that's been helping us."

"Correct."

"And the part that believes the Androchidans will recapture you and scan your memory?"

He sighs again. "That's the part that, I suppose, has been less than forthcoming with you at times."

"You suppose?" Yoshi yells. "You're saying you could have helped us strategize all along? You could have warned us about how they track? Helped us assault the ring? Warned us about going underground? All of it?"

I motion toward Yoshi to settle down, but I suspect the alcohol is doing a lot of the talking. Granted, I think he's got a strong case, and I'm mad at Chuck too. But I'm not willing to fly off the handle just yet, especially if we can win Chuck to our side and have unbridled access to what he knows. But Chuck does need to understand the severity of the situation.

"Chuck, I think I speak for the whole team when I say that we feel betrayed by you." I put my hands on my hips.

"I assure you that I have not provided the enemy one iota of intelligence. Scout's honor."

"Yeah, but by not being completely forthcoming, you compromised our mission's success."

"You're still alive, aren't you?"

"Sure." I point toward the ceiling. "But how many people have died during our less-than-successful attempt to close down New York's ring? I saw them walk through and leave behind their pacemakers and hip joints, pal. Those aren't injuries you walk away from. Those people are dead on the other side of that ring. And even as we stand here, more are marching through. And more are dying."

Chuck seems to consider this as a pause fills the air. "I am truly sorry for their deaths, Patrick. I only hope that you can appreciate how fearful I am of the Androchidans."

"Well, they shouldn't be the only ones you're afraid of."

He hesitates. "I'm terribly sorry, but I believe I'm misinterpreting your implication."

"Oh, I don't think so."

"Patrick. Are you saying that you'll throw me out of a window again?"

I didn't want to have to do this, but until he pledges fealty, he's a hostile liability. I reach to the table behind us and pull a thermite grenade from a straw-field wooden box. "See this, Chuck? It's an AN-M14 TH3 incendiary hand grenade that burns at 4,000 degrees Fahrenheit for forty seconds. If it can melt through an engine block, imagine what it can do to lil' ole you."

"So you're threatening me? I thought we were friends."

"When I'm certain—we're all certain—whose side you're on, then I can tell you if we're friends or not. This isn't a playground fight, Chuck. You don't get to play whichever side you think will win. This war is the biggest one my species has ever faced. So while I certainly don't want to burn any bridges if I can help it, I will burn the hell out of you unless you can convince me, convince all of us, that you're on our side once and for all."

"So you're no better than them," Chuck says.

I let out the chuckle that, to any of my species, says I'm getting ready to give him a piece of my mind. "Huh. The hell I am. I'm giving you a choice, Charlie, one that, in your own admission, the Androchidans won't give you. So I think that separates us enough for me to sleep at night just fine."

"But is it really a choice if one of the options leads to my death?"

"That's a fair point. We could always toss you in the East River. Then it's only a matter of time before either the Androchidans snag you or…"

"Or what?"

"Or the flounder do."

"Oh my God, you wouldn't."

I stroke my beard long enough to make him squirm. "I don't really think this comes down to fear, though. I think it comes down to belief."

"How's that?"

"You know why we slipped under the dome and moved toward the enemy?"

"Because you believe you can win," Chuck says with a confident air.

"No." I laugh. "That's not it at all."

"Wait. I'm confused. You don't think you can win?"

"Pal. I haven't thought that all day."

"Then… why are you fighting?"

"Because we believe in what we're fighting for. Because protecting lives is always right, and we have a duty to do what others can't, or won't. Winning or losing… it doesn't mean shit if you don't believe in what you're laying your life down for. You can win for a bad cause, but then you've gotta live with hell. Or you can die for a good cause and tell the devil where to stick it in person."

I take a breath, realizing this is way more than I intended to say. But it needs saying. For Chuck. And for us all.

"Governments shift like quicksand, and countries forget about you. But if you believe in what you're doing for yourself? For the warrior on your right and left?" I shake my head. "Then maybe you get to beat the odds, to stare down the gods of war, and to do the impossible."

"Win."

"Yut. And win."

I look around at the other faces. Apparently, my little speech was quite moving. Team members are taking deep breaths, pushing out their chests, and working their jaws. Even the Russians seem caught off guard.

"That was very strong, Brooklyn lion," Lada says. "Good speaking."

I nod my thanks, but the person I'm really hoping to get through to is a busted-ass alien rifle. "So, are you with us or not, Charlie?"

"I'm afraid that no matter what I say, I lack the conviction to assure you of my resolve properly. Therefore, I seem to be caught between a rock and another rock."

"A hard place," Yoshi offers.

"Yes, it is a hard place, metaphorically speaking."

"No, that's—"

I wave off Yoshi and fix my eyes on Chuck. "You're right, you can't convince us right now."

"So there's really no choice then, is there. So much for your speech about free will."

"Dude, if you don't let me finish, I'm gonna make the call for you."

"Sorry."

"While you can't convince us right now, you can convince us over time."

"And how's that?"

"Trust."

Chuck hesitates. "You trust me?"

"Hell, no."

"Well then, there we have it."

"Not yet, anyway." I work my jaw. Feels like I'm reciting lines I used on the damn Iraqi Civil Defense Corps. "You help us kill enough of your alien friends, then maybe you can build trust with us. But if you cross us? The consequences will be swift and irreversible."

"Thermite grenade?"

"If I don't have access to a flounder, yut."

"Then might I request that one of the Phantoms always packs at least one AN-M14 TH3?"

"So, you're in?" Hollywood asks.

"Well, I mean, if you'll have me, yes. But based on the last minute of conversation and Patrick's foreboding tone, I'd say you really don't want me."

I look around the room. "How 'bout it, Phantoms?"

"I'm for letting him stay," Hollywood says. "So long as he doesn't pull any punches."

"Agreed," says Bumper with his arms folded. "I remember back on the parkway saying that we'd ditch him at the first sign of trouble. Well, he's given us some trouble, and here we are being lenient. I say we need a sign, right here, right now, to get this trust wagon rolling."

"Same," says Yoshi.

"Same," Ghost adds.

"And I concur," Aaron says. "A display of overwhelming good faith. One that says he wants humanity to survive—believes in our survival—and will cut all ties with the aliens. The 'no hope of ever going back' kind because what he's shared is far too damnable."

I eye Chuck. "So? How 'bout it?"

"If you do decide to keep me around, and I prove myself faithful, will you promise not to feed me to the flounders?"

"You really fear them more than a memory wipe and meltdown from the Anderkins?" Hollywood asks.

"Oh God, yes. Have you seen them? They're horrible… just awful. Little beady eyes, flat bodies, sharp teeth? No wonder you humans fear them so."

I glare at the Phantoms not to say a damn word. It's a specific look that I've worked hard over my career to achieve, used on boots and COs alike. It says, "Cross me now and you'll live to regret it for the rest of your life." To their credit, everyone stays tight-lipped.

All, that is, except for Vlad.

"I hope never to be meeting flounders. They are sounding much bad."

"Oh, believe me," Chuck says. "You'll never forget if you do. I'm lucky to be alive."

"Understood. Thank you, talking rifle."

"My pleasure." Chuck takes a deep breath. "Okay, Phantoms. What do you want to know?"

37

2230, Friday, June 25, 2027
Lower Manhattan, New York
Boxcar City

WHAT DO WE WANNA KNOW? Well, splick—in honor of Sir Chuck—now we're getting somewhere.

I clean the front of my teeth with my tongue and then stare down at Sir Charles. It's time for me to pitch him the most riveting question I can think of, complex, and full of nuance, sure to baffle and confound him for days. "How do we take out the ring?"

"Hmmm. Well, that all depends, doesn't it."

"Chuck?"

"I'm not stalling! Promise. For example, if you were an Androchidan or had access to Androchidan tech, which really isn't Androchidan to begin with, seeing as how—"

"Chuck!"

"Right. Short answer is, you blow it up."

"Blow it up. That's… your answer?"

"Short, sweet, to the point. I thought you'd be thrilled. But the look on your face suggests otherwise."

"Yut. It does."

"Crap. And here I thought I'd win some trust points."

"Try harder."

"Ummm. Okay, let's see. Well, if you have some sort of really big bomb…"

"Uh-huh?"

"Then you can make the ring go boom."

"Is he being for real right now?" Hollywood asked.

"Of course I'm being for real! What, you think I want to get served up to those flounder? Or the Ander-babies? Noooo-hu-hu-ho, thank you very much."

"Could'a fooled me," Bumper says.

Chuck sighs. "Listen, there are lots of ways to shut down a slaver ring—"

"Actual term?" I ask.

"Yes, actual term. But they all depend on your access to the systems that control them. It's like any robust technology: the more access, the greater the control, especially the catastrophic kind. But no matter the access, if you have something that can displace enough atoms, anything can fall apart if given the right nudge."

"As in, blow it up."

"Yes. It's not nuanced, but it's effective."

"And you're saying this because we lack access to all those other fancy systems that might give us direct control?"

"Precisely, Patrick."

"And those aren't worth exploring?"

"Not unless you're up for a jaunt to Androchida Prime tonight."

"Blowing it up, it is." I look at our Russian counterparts. "What are the chances you have some sort of really big bomb down here?"

"How big?" Sissy asks.

I look at my alien rifle. "Charles?"

"Something yielding in order of two to three tons of trinitro-toluene."

"TNT," I say, just to clarify for those who aren't up to speed on their explosive compounds' proper names. "Damn. That's a lot."

"Yes," Chuck says. "TNT, and damn indeed."

Sissy sticks his hands under his armpits and tokes on the cigar hanging from his mouth. "Only bombs in this ranging are being GBU-43/B Massive Ordnance Air Blast."

"Mother of All Bombs," Yoshi adds. "Which is really a misnomer, because it's not."

"Nor would you have an adequate delivery method for it," Chuck adds. "At least to ensure 100 percent success."

"And we most definitely want 100 percent," I say.

"Good," Sissy adds. "Because we have nothing like this. Plus, I am thinking it is overkilling."

"He's right," Chuck adds. "Definitely more than the doctor ordered."

"And we'd like to save as many of the inhabitants and their homes as possible," I say.

"Then it's time to go old school," Bumper says.

I give him a raised eyebrow. "Oh?"

He grins. "Nothing to bounce your afro like ANFO."

"Ammonium nitrate fuel oil bomb."

"I'm guessing Sissy here could probably source everything right here in the city."

I turn to Sissy. "You have any ammonium nitrate?"

"Ha!" Sissy pulls out his cigar. "Do you know who you are talkings about?"

"I… Could you clarify the question?"

"We Russians produces almost half world's supply of NH4NO3. Ha! Do I have ammonium nitrate? Tender sweet Americans."

"So, you do?"

"Who am I looking like to you? Donald Duck? Mick Jagger?"

"Those weren't exactly—"

"No. I am being more like Willy Coyote Desert Dog, yes? You know him? From cartoons? Only Sissy doesn't blow up. He makes Running Road bird blow up. Every time."

"So you have a supply."

"Huh. Please. You remember Beirut 2020?"

"Uh, yeah. Unfortunately. Why?" I'm not sure I like where this is going.

Hollywood lets out a groan. "I remember a lot from 2020, and none of it was good."

"Yes, well"—Sissy sniffs—"we have nothing to do with this Beirut or coronavirus or election results. But sevens years earlier, I know which factory and ship leaves Mother Russia with these 2,750 tons of ammonium nitrate that Lebanese takings."

"Is that so," I say.

"Sure, sure. But they did not store properly. Killed many peoples. Tragic."

"And I take it that you store yours well?"

"Of course. Very safeties. Lots of safeties. I maybe perhaps oversee Sandhogs Local, access to many much loads. How much you need?"

I look at Bumper.

"Man, I'd settle for… is twelve and a half tons too much to ask? Plus one ton of diesel fuel?"

"No problems."

"And that produces the desired effect?" I ask.

"Oh yeah. Just need some time fuse, det cord, or shock tube. Hell, I'd take a few sticks of dynamite. Then build in some redundancy, and we have ourselves a big boom."

"I provide enough chemical for big ass boom, no worries," says Sissy. "Plenty of powers. And all the extras you mention are easy peasy. We source from our construction sites."

"What about a delivery method?" Yoshi asks. "They're not exactly going to let us just drive up the bridge and park a few suspiciously bottomed-out trucks."

"No," I say in agreement. "They're not. But we're not gonna drive it up the bridge." I look at Sissy.

At the same time, both Bumper and I say, "We're gonna drive it under."

Sissy squints at us. "You… you wish to be having boats?"

"How about four barges and a tug?"

"Make it five and a tug," Bumper says.

"This can be arranged," Sissy says. "You need harbor pilot too, da?"

"That'd be great. You have connections?"

"I also heading up Longshoremen."

I let out a soft chuckle. "Of course you are."

"What about all the civilians on the bridge?" Hollywood asks. "We'll need to get them well away."

"Sissy, we're gonna need all your M3 and RPG-7s," I say. "And probably a few other items topside."

"This can be done. But you are exceeding limit of poker chip value."

"Sissy, pozhaluysta," Vlad pleads. "This wild and crazy guy, he is real-life David Hasselhoff in Babe Watching. Here is Vlad, drown'ding in oceans, arms flailings, no hopes for escaping waters. He has great need of rescuings by powerful someone."

"I get it," says Sissy.

"I am like woman falling from surfboard with big bosoms. I cannot swim, and my bosoms barely holding me afloat. But look! Here comes Brooklyn Hasselhoff USA. He breaks into waves like deep penetrations."

"Vlad, stop. I see picture."

"And just when I am about to slipping under waters and waste precious gift of large bosoms on sea floor, Brooklyn Hasselhoff USA rescues me, brings back to shore, does CRP to mouth, and then there is much lovemaking and sand and TV dramatic music. Wins daytime Emmy Lou Harris trophy, and people are happy."

"Molchi! You and your TVs watchings. Agh. Fine, fine, of course. You have all what you need, America. But no more. Deals, yes?"

"Deals," I say, doing my damnedest to keep from laughing hysterically. I still don't trust the bastards, but I guess the enemy of my enemy is my temporary Russian crime-family friend.

2345, Friday, June 25, 2027
Lower Manhattan, New York

Pier 36, East River

IT'S JUST BEFORE MIDNIGHT, and Bumper is orchestrating the most blatant attempt to destroy a historic landmark icon using assets pooled from within the city in US history. If any public officials cared to investigate, they'd no doubt encourage his efforts—actions that, at any other point in time, would have been right up there with the World Trade Center bombing of 1993, the Oklahoma City bombing of 1995, and the horrible events of 9/11. But tonight, Bumper's undertaking is nothing short of heroic, and if he succeeds—if we all succeed—they might just build a monument in his honor. Yeah, for blowing up the damn Brooklyn Bridge.

Context really is everything.

The operation's core is hidden amongst Pier 36's warehouses and stacks of freight containers almost one mile upriver from the ring. Bumper is giving orders to Sissy's union bosses like a drill sergeant, and it's working: volume, authority, and knowledgeability are things that New Yorkers respect. That, and a good cannoli. God save you if it's soggy or overcooked.

The rest of the Phantoms and I stand to one side as Bumper directs workers in the main warehouse like a master conductor directs an orchestra. Members of the Sandhogs Local, those who'd stayed or taken refuge in Boxcar City to avoid the herding surge, are filling fifty-gallon drums with bags of ammonium nitrate while a diesel fuel truck tops off each container with refined petroleum.

"My dad and I were planning to hike the Appalachian Trail together," Hollywood says from beside me. This is the first personal thing she's said to me since our drive in East Orange, and I take it as the rare invite into her private world that it probably is.

"Had several friends do that," I reply. "Said it's a memorable experience."

"Yeah." She brushes the hair over her ear and looks down. "I was really looking forward to it."

"And then this?" I nod toward the preparations, but I mean the invasion.

"No. Then dad died. And then this."

I sniff. "Sorry to hear that."

"Me too."

I wait a few seconds, then ask, "What happened?"

"Cancer. It wasn't sudden or anything. We knew it was coming. Just..." She looks up at me. "He was the strongest man I knew. Taught me everything. And then, you watch him fade away until he's... Well. It's just hard, right?"

I've never been good with these kinds of confessions, so I nod and wait for her to say what she needs to.

"Anyway. I'd decided I was gonna start doing legs of the hike this summer. Pick away at it over the weekends. In his honor, you know?"

"Sounds like he would've wanted that."

"Yeah." She sighs, and I can tell this is hard for her. "I thought maybe I'd, I dunno. Maybe I'd find him up there or something." Her body stiffens. "And then these goddamn aliens had to come and screw it all up."

"They sure did." I look over at her. "I'm sorry, Hollywood."

"Me too."

"Maybe when this is all over, you can take that hike."

She nods but doesn't say anything.

"They say that having something to look forward to is part of what helps get you through."

She looks up at me with her dark brown eyes. "What have you looked forward to."

"Being alone."

"Oh."

I clear my throat. "I didn't mean to——"

"No, it's okay. I get it. You're an introvert."

I nod. "Something like that."

"Well, I hope when all this is done you get to be alone."

"Thanks." But when she says it like that, I'm not sure I like the sound of it.

The barrels coming away from the fuel truck get stirred by three teams of men who look like they just stepped out of Iron Workers Today magazine. Their tank tops look like they're about to rip open across their barrel-chests and muscular arms—plenty a woman's wildest fantasy, I'm sure. The barrels are agitated with iron bars until the mixture is a slurry. Then each drum gets capped and moved onto one of five barges tied off along the wharf.

"You're gonna get your hike, Hollywood," Z-Lo says. "And you're gonna find your dad's ghost, or whatever. I promise." Then he pounds his fist into his palm. "We're gonna bring the hurt to these bastards and make 'em pay. Make 'em pay hard."

I give Z-Lo an impressed look. Can't fault the kid for a lack of motivation. And I can tell he's not done yet.

"One time, I had to wrestle up four weight classes. And I was scared, you know? Going against a heavyweight. Kid was a bull. Had a mustache before most of us had pubes.

"My older siblings all came to that match, though. Victor, he took me aside and said, 'Baby Andras, you bring the hurt. He's got the weight, but you've got the speed and skill. You can take him.' And you know? I believed Victor."

Z-Lo looks up with tears in his eyes. "I won that match. My family, they went crazy. It was the last time my dad gave me that look of being really proud of me, you know? And Victor? He had me on his shoulders and was shouting to the whole gymnasium, 'This is my baby brother. This is my baby brother!' It was awesome."

Z-Lo's crying, and he's got his arm around Yoshi. Then he tries putting the other arm around Ghost, but the sniper avoids it. "I wonder how they're doing right now, you know? Like, are they chill and hiding out somewhere? Or they stuck inside one these damn domes over San Diego too?" He pinches the bridge of his nose. "God, I'm sorry. I just miss 'em so much."

"Here." Yoshi offers Z-Lo a drink, but the kid declines. Then Yoshi stares at his flask and decides not to take the swig I was expecting him to. "I'm sorry."

I look around at the team, wondering who Yoshi's talking to. But then the PJ lifts his eyes at me.

"I'm sorry for falling on you," Yoshi says. "I risked the mission, and your life."

I can feel everyone's eyes land on me. "Yoshi, this isn't good for you." I nod toward his flask. "You know that, right?"

He nods. "I wish I could, but it just isn't that easy."

"But if you don't, then the bottle will choose for you."

Z-Lo pulls Yoshi into his armpit and gives an extra squeeze. "We love you, PS6. Just want you hanging around a while longer, dude."

Yoshi nods and even seems to be shedding a tear. As always, I can't tell if it's genuine or just the booze. But if we're charging into our last firefight together, I need to clear the air.

"Yoshi. You almost killed me back there."

"I know," he says. "And I'm——"

"You're sorry. You already said that. So it's my turn. You're a good man, Yoshida. A good doc too. You've treated everyone on this team with respect. But here's how you can make it up to me: treat yourself with the same respect.

"Whatever you're running from, you're not gonna find the answers in the bottom of that thing. Trust me." I take a breath and then get Yoshi to look me in the eye. "We move on and put this in the past. But if that kind of stunt happens again, you're off this team. And if I'm not around to kick you off, everyone else has the permission to kick your ass for me. Copy?"

He looks away. "Copy."

"Bottom line, we need you, Yoshi."

"Yeah, little buddy," Z-Lo says and squeezes the PJ's neck again.

I raise my eyebrows in a point of clarification. "We need you sober."

"I know."

"No. You don't. You might be getting there. But until you kick this beast, you don't know. 'Cause that's what's gonna give you the power you need. Roger?"

Yoshi nods, and then musters the strength to look me in the eye. "Thank you."

"You're welcome."

We watch as the drums get hauled toward the pier's edge where the Longshoremen hoist them onto the barges. The workers arrange ten fifty-gallon barrels per barge into a tight circle and secure them with tie-downs. Then Bumper orders an extra 1,000 pounds of ammonium nitrate in bag-form stacked around each barge's drum-cluster.

"Evil needs to die," Ghost says.

We all face our sniper and wait for him to say more. But he doesn't seem to. So, I give him a little encouragement.

"And?"

Ghost gives me a curious look. "And I'm happy to sign the death certificate."

"Works for me," Hollywood says.

The rest of the team nods, and a few smiles get passed around.

"How you guys doing?" Bumper says as he checks in on us.

"Just enjoying watching you work," Hollywood says with an appreciative feline-like grin. She leans her elbow against a forklift and gives Bumper a once-over.

"We're just getting ready for the big game," I say. "Pep-talk stuff."

"Gotcha." Bumper stretches his left arm out. "Well. I know for me, this win's going to my team." He pauses. "I mean, the ones who didn't..." He swallows. "SEAL Team Eight."

The fact that Bumper feels the need to distinguish between that team and our team says something strong, and I respect that.

"To SEAL Team Eight," I say and give the warrior a fist-bump.

"Thanks."

"So, how we lookin', frogman?" I tip my head toward the barges.

"Just about to put the finishing touches on myself. You're welcome to watch."

The team nods and follows him to the wharf. Bumper climbs down and starts pulling big boy toys out of some canvas bags.

The center-most drum on every barge gets a single stick of TNT strapped down with duct tape and fitted with a blasting cap and det cord. Bumper builds in a redundant system with a timed fuse should the remote trigger fail. He takes his time to double-check each barge's payload and then moves on to examine the other explosives he's attached to chains connecting the barges.

When it seems like he's about to wrap up, I yell, "Everything look good down there?"

"Roger that." A few beats later, Bumper climbs topside on the last barge. "This is my kind of party. All we need now is…" He looks to the east. "Right on schedule."

A tugboat comes into view around Corlears Hook and hugs the shore. Its captain is running dark as the dome's glow provides more than enough ambient light. Then the tug spins a slow 180° and lines up with the easternmost barge in the line. Longshoremen scramble to secure the lead barge to the tug, and Bumper and I walk to meet them.

It still amazes me that we're doing all this in view of the bridge. Granted, the Manhattan Bridge provides at least some cover, as does the general chaos of a city in upheaval. But Chuck's warning about the Anderkins seeing better in our planet's night has had me on edge since we emerged topside and started this operation.

Sissy and Vlad are standing beside the tug's mooring lines and speaking with the ship's captain. The man looks to be in his seventies or maybe even eighties, and he's wearing a white mustache stained by tobacco and grease.

"Bumpers, Wics," Vlad says. "Please, come. This is your captains."

Bumper extends his hand and shakes the old man's weathered palm, as do I.

"I am Yuriy," the captain says in a thick Ukrainian accent if I'm not mistaken.

"Nice to meet you," Bumper says.

I nod. "And thanks for your willingness to help us out on such short notice."

"Is not problems."

"He was quick to volunteer," says Vlad. "He has good motivations, yes?"

I look at Yuriy. "And how's that?"

"I am not home when light appears. But when I am, I discovers…" The old man pulls off his oily captain's cap to reveal matted strands of white hair. Then he twists the cover in his hand and holds it against his chest. "My beloved Bohuslava is gone. Marched toward this… this abomination." His watery eyes meet mine, then Bumper's. "So, you want destroying it? I help. I avenge."

"Well, we're sorry for your loss, sir," I say. "But we're grateful for your expertise." I look back at Vlad and Sissy. "How are the other preparations?"

"As you instructed," Vlad says. "Lada reports that she is nearly finishes." Then Vlad leans into me. "She likes American lion, yes?"

"Is that so?" I give Bumper a sideways glance. "Couldn't tell."

"Yes. Big heart crush. And I feel Sissy and me, we must warnings you."

"Oh yeah?"

"When Lada likes man, she is like lioness."

"No, no, no." Sissy waves a finger. "She more like stronger, more powerful second lion."

"Yes, second lion," Vlad nods. "Be careful."

"Well, I appreciate the words of wisdom, guys."

"This not wisdoms," Vlad says with a slap to my back. "Is warnings."

"Yut. Thanks for those too then."

"Yes. We watch out for you, like small precious American boy who needs protectings from worldly woman."

Bumper and I share a short laugh, and then I nod to him. "Feeling good?"

"Oh, bro." He rubs his hands together. "I'm feeling great."

Ya know, it's a fun night when a Navy SEAL gets excited about blowing stuff up.

"Friday night lights in the city," he says. "It's time to OTF."

38

0015, Saturday, June 26, 2027
Lower Manhattan, New York
FDR Drive, East River

THERE's something magical about blowing up an alien artifact with a bunch of fertilizer and diesel fuel. Kinda says, "Hey, Bastards. We're not wasting our good stuff on you. And all those fancy weapons you got? Huh. Hold my beer."

Of course, there's the very real possibility that the enemy sniffs out the plot before we're in range, destroys the barges, and singles us out with their evolved thermal vision just to blow us the hell up. But if this does work, it'll set a precedent. It tells the Androchidans we're no pushovers and the rest of humanity that we have a chance. It says that we can position our chess pieces the way we want them and surprise an enemy who is far too confident in their attack.

But if it doesn't work?

Eh. None of us will be the wiser. 'Cause we'll all be dead. But, damn, will we look good dying.

Each Phantom is sitting on their own motorcycle, care of Sissy's private collection. All but Hollywood that is. When the bikes came up short by one, she eyed Bumper. The SEAL seemed only too happy to accommodate her despite Vlad's insistence that he could find something else. As Hollywood climbed on and threw her arms around Bumper's torso, I caught her smiling to herself. Cute.

Sissy provided 1995 Harley Davidson MT350E "Army Bikes" to Ghost, Yoshi, Bumper, and me, while Z-Lo claimed a vintage 1956 Dnepr M-72 Soviet bike with a matching sidecar for Aaron.

"My great grandfather had one," Z-Lo says as he looks over the bike nostalgically. "Only ever saw it in pics from the old country."

"It is fine Russian machina," Vlad says as he pats the gas tank. "Works well in Siberian winters."

Veronica is fully charged and slung over my right shoulder while a new SCAR 17 is slung over my left. In the meantime, Chuck is strapped to my back and won't be coming off anytime soon. The rest of the team has resupplied themselves too and placed extra black-tip ammunition in the MT350's cargo carriers. Even Aaron is eyeing the sidecar's mounted DP-27 machine gun and top-loading pancake magazine with equal parts dread and excitement.

Phantom Team, along with Vlad and Lada, are staged on FDR Drive just east of the Manhattan Bridge, facing our target. Sissy bid us *good huntings* and *dasvidaniya*, insisting that he was needed else-where—probably back in his man cave with a cigar, a bottle of vodka, and a bowl of pelmeni to usher in the end of the world. But for us, if everything goes according to plan, we'll be speeding west into the action after phase three.

"Fortis fortuna adiuvat, Mr. Wic," Bumper says from his bike to my right.

"It most certainly does," I reply, noting the beloved phrase of many a warrior charging into battle. *Fortune favors the bold.*

"It can also get them killed," Aaron says. "If they're not prepared."

Bumper makes a click sound in the side of his mouth. "Well, it seems we're in luck there, 'cause we're as prepared as we can be."

"And you also have lots of good backings up," says Lada, who's parked directly behind me. Then she makes the sound of a growling cat. "And, so far, you are looking very goods from behind."

"I warn you, yes?" Vlad says from his bike to my left.

"You did, pal. Thanks." I lean over and lower my voice. "But you know, your sister could be talking about you too, right?"

"No." He shakes his head. "We are not this kind of families. This wrong. She speaks of you and your ample—"

"Okay. That's enough of that."

But Vlad gives me a wink and two thumbs up. "Like David Hasselhoff."

Just then, his radio chirps, followed by Yuriy's voice saying something in his native language.

"He is positioned," Vlad says to me.

I look at Bumper and then spin around to eye the rest of the Phantoms. "OTF?"

"OTF," they reply as one.

"Then let's light it up. Phase One: Go."

LADA GIVES the initial order on her radio. I can't understand it, but three seconds later, rockets and mortar rounds leap from both shores downriver and streak toward the ring's forcefield. Yut, these shots exceed their weapons' ranges for accuracy. But the ordnance doesn't need to be accurate, it just needs to land somewhere on the broadside of the ring, and it's a damn hard target to miss.

While all phases of the operation are risky, this one puts the most civilians in the greatest danger area. But, thankfully, it has the desired effect. Within seconds of the first rounds detonating against the portal wall, which acts as a solid membrane given its resistance to non-biological materials, the crowds shrink back. Then, as more ordnance flies in, carving smoke trails through the night air like meteors, we even hear the screams of retreating civilians.

"It's working," I say and lower my binocs.

Bumper takes a quick look, spotting both sides of the bridge. "God help them," he whispers.

God help them indeed.

While the exploding M3 and RPG rounds reverse the throng's momentum—redirecting the people back toward Manhattan and Brooklyn respectively—they still have to navigate through a phalanx of Androchidan sentries tasked with maintaining order. But as Lada's forces continue to lay on the fire, even those sentries leave their posts to engage the guerilla warfare style assault from both shores.

Only twice do wayward rounds find their way onto the bridge proper. Short trajectories, either out of operator panic or munition failure, result in civilian casualties. I can't be sure how many, but it's enough to make me say a prayer for the dead and pull my binocs down as I wince.

There are costs to every operation, and tonight's will be no exception. It's the unavoidable deal you make in combat. People die. But for those who are trained and tasked to make the hard calls, we endure the longer hell of wrestling with our choices until we join the dead.

"Tangos airborne," Ghost says from his bike, binocs up.

I look back at the bridge and see four dropships lift off in pairs and then descend toward both shores.

"Tell your people to take cover," I say to Lada.

She's on her radio a beat later, issuing orders.

A dropship fires a Chuck-style blaster burst into a three-story building near Pier 1 where we first made landfall. Unlike with Chuck's capabilities, however, the entire building face detonates. Bricks and gouts of fire shoot into the East River, creating a momentary blaze of orange light. A secondary explosion from inside the building blows out the roof and sends thick black smoke rolling skyward.

I feel my gut twist. I guessed the dropships packed a punch, but I wasn't anticipating that.

"Patrick, your heart rate just spiked," Chuck says. "Everything all right?"

"The dropships…"

"Yes. They are a real bitch, aren't they."

A few team members give short laughs, most sounding nervous.

"Yut. Sure are. Just wish we had one."

Just then, a series of rocket-propelled grenades and M3 high-explosive rounds leave a building on the Manhattan side and travel less than fifty yards into a dropship. I'm reasonably sure I see a classic FIM-92 Stinger missile fly toward the target; nothing like a wire-guided party favor. The resulting explosions throw the vehicle sideways, enveloping it in a cloud of fire.

But the dropship recovers despite smoke pouring from its starboard aft engine. The craft turns on the source of the antiaircraft fire and, in a belligerent retaliatory show of force, fires at least ten bursts into the buildings. Glass and concrete explode from the multistory structures as the blaster rounds tear through the walls. Fireballs shoot from each level, raining debris down on the waterfront below.

But the ill-tempered dropship isn't out of the woods just yet. More of Lada's forces must sense the ailing craft and go in for the kill. At least half a dozen rounds slam against the hull before the lucky shot punctures it. Once inside, the armor-piercing munition detonates and tears the dropship apart.

A cheer goes up among our team as the vessel falls into the East River in pieces.

"Now you've gone and pissed them right off," Sir Charles says.

As if to confirm Chuck's sentiment, Ghost says, "Death angels, going up."

Sure enough, jetpack signatures streak away from the bridge and start heading for the emplacements.

"Order your people out of there," I say to Lada.

She repeats my command, at least I think so. But the M3s and PRGs keep firing.

"Lada," I say, more sternly this time.

Several voices fill her radio, then she looks at me. "No good, American lion. They wish to stay where they are."

"But we can keep using them if they fall back."

"Russians, we are stubborn, da?"

"And stupid! Tell your people—"

A hand touches my arm. It's Vlad. "They have chosens, USA. They fight and die tonight."

God, these people are infuriating. But even as I grind my teeth, I watch more weapons fire divert from the ring and start engaging the dropships and death angels. Several jetpacks detonate and send their dismembered hosts splashing into the river. But most do not.

"Bridge is clear," Ghost says. "Both approaches."

"Phase Two," I say to Vlad.

He opens the channel on his radio and spits fast Russian.

I pull up my binocs and look among the buildings that hide the Manhattan entry ramp toward the span's first tower. Just seeing the complete absence of people makes my heart lift. Even if all this was to buy those souls a few more minutes on the planet, it was worth it. Costly, but still worth it.

"I see 'em," Bumper says. "Coming up now."

Sure enough, my binocs show a single cement truck barreling up the ramp.

"That's far enough," I say to Vlad, and then quickly check the Brooklyn side. The second concrete truck looks good too. "Tell 'em to park and get clear."

Vlad passes on my order, and I watch as both trucks slow. Phase Two is as much a preventative measure as it is a hostile one. Should we fail at blowing the ring, the trucks serve to keep humans from being herded back up the bridge.

Just as the driver on the Manhattan side drops from the cab, a death angel descends and detonates the man in a single blast. The Brooklyn-side driver is luckier and disappears out of my view. Here's hoping he got away.

However, the best news comes when Hollywood calls out that the Anderkins are inspecting the concrete trucks. Back on my optics, the things seem interested in the red-and-white painted drums going round and round. At least three tangos are gathered on the Manhattan-side truck, and four on the Brooklyn.

"Blow 'em," I say to Bumper.

"Fire in the hole," he replies.

A beat later, both trucks go nova.

I instinctively shield my face from the twin detonations and wince as the first shockwave hits our position. It's loud and blows some road debris in my face. The second lesser one from the Brooklyn truck hits a beat later.

I'm reminded that ANFO bombs aren't about radiation or fireballs or even shrapnel. They're about concussions and the sheer power they have to shove things out of place with extreme prejudice. Which is what we're counting on tonight.

In the wake of the truck bombs, Phantom Team starts calling out damage, ranging from snapped bridge cables and craters left in the road to the absence of any nearby tangos.

"Take that, you alien sumbitches." Z-Lo even slaps Vlad on the shoulder, and then he seems to think better of it. "Sorry, sir—your mafia'ness. I didn't mean to, uh, offend—"

"This celebration okay," Vlad replies with a smile.

Z-Lo's shoulders relax.

"But normally I shoot in face."

I watch the kid's face drain of blood.

"I kidding, America," Vlad exclaims and then slaps Z-Lo's shoulder.

"Oh, *phew*. 'Cause you really had me going there."

"But I not kidding. I shoot you in face next times."

"Wait. You will?"

"Da."

"Uh. Okay. I'll make sure to—"

"Kidding, America! Jeez. You see look on your face? Ha!"

Bumper's laughing as he tries to hold his binocs steady, then he whispers, "Poor kid."

"Looks like our people won't be heading up to the ring anytime soon," Hollywood says.

"Then it's time to make sure it's a permanent arrangement." I look out and see that Yuriy has moved downriver as far as possible without risking detection. Chuck's guidance helped the Longshoremen insulate the tug's bridge enough to keep the single human heat signature from drawing too much attention. Sir Chuck also insisted that running the tug's water-cooled engine just above idle wouldn't raise any red flags so long as Yuriy didn't drive too erratically. Somehow, I think we're safe there.

I look to Bumper. "You have the honors."

"Vlad," says Bumper. "Initiate Phase Three."

"With much pleasures," he replies. Then, over the radio, Vlad gives short instructions to Yuriy.

A beat later, five simultaneous bangs blow between barges. The flashes give away the flotilla's position long enough for us to get eyes on the shadowy barges.

Yuriy says something over comms.

"Separations successful," Vlad says.

I offer the SEAL my fist, and he bumps it. "Nice work."

"It's just foreplay," Bumper replies.

"Loud foreplays is best foreplays, don't you think, USA?"

I feel Lada's bike tire bump the back of mine.

"She actually might kill you if you're not careful, Wic," Bumper whispers to me.

"That's what I'm afraid of," I reply.

We all watch as the ANFO-laden barges start to drift apart and leave the tug behind. With the East River's current at three knots, the bomb platforms will need several minutes to make the rest of their trip on their own. And, with five opportunities in the water, I'm feeling more confident about our chances for success.

That is, until Yuriy hails Vlad.

"What is it?" I ask.

"He is sayings that three of the barges are moving off course."

"By how much?" Bumper asks.

Vlad communicates with Yuriy. "Several degrees now, many yards later."

"How much is many yards later?"

Vlad and Yuriy spend the next thirty seconds making several exchanges before Vlad looks back at Bumper. "He is sayings that winds and currents are different than usuals because of abomination. Throws barges off course, and so risk hitting shore before bridge."

"Son of a bitch." Bumper glares at Vlad. "Ask him how the remaining two are doing."

There's more foreign radio traffic before Vlad offers Bumper a thumbs up and says, "He thinks those are good ones."

I turn to Bumper. "Whaddya think, bomb expert?"

He lets out a long sigh. "Well, we prepared for this. I just liked our odds a whole lot better with all five being on target. Two can probably do it. But if they're off a little, or one is a dud, then…"

"Then you wished you'd had your redundancy," I say.

"Roger."

Yuriy's voice crackles over the radio again, and then Vlad smiles.

"What was that?" I ask.

"Yuriy says you have no worries now."

"The current corrected the course?" Bumper asks.

"Nyet. Yuriy is correcting courses. All good, wise guys."

Hollywood walks her bike forward. "But if he's going after the barges, then…"

"Then we can't blow them," Bumper finishes. "Shit."

"Not true," Vlad says. "Yuriy understands, how you say, predicaments. He also say, go ahead, as he make plans to bring all barges within optimal ranges."

"I can't do that," Bumper says. "He's gotta get clear of the explosives."

"Bumpers, listen—"

"No, you listen." Bumper is standing over his bike. "I'm not detonating some old man needlessly when I have other options."

"And are you certains that your other options will working?"

"No. But I think we—"

"Then Yuriy makes sure you have 100 percent certain good time feelings in your chest, yes? All is okay, Navy Sea Lion. Yuriy knows what he is to do, and this is Ukraine way. Old way. You not change his mind now anyhow. He is going."

Bumper sits back down on his Harley. "Goddammit."

Chuck speaks up from behind me. "This is truly a remarkable and heartwarming scenario."

"Not now, pal," I say.

"But it does open the plan up to some serious issues."

I look at Bumper. "Like what?"

"Like the Androchidans taking an interest in why a vessel is suddenly working so hard to maneuver five barges under their slaver ring."

"So you do think they'll notice," I say, just to make sure we're on the same page.

"Oh, absolutely, Patrick. Even if Yuriy's heat signature remains hidden, the objects' consolidation will invite investigation."

"And when they investigate?"

"They'll detonate the barges," Chuck says without emotion. "You'll probably take out the first dropship, sure. But not the remainder. They'll keep their distance and scuttle the remaining ordnance from afar."

"Vlad," I say. "Get on that radio and order Yuriy to stand down. Now."

He nods and opens up the channel. But after several attempts and no response, Vlad gives me a worried look. "Uh, I think Yuriy has switchinged off radio."

"Dammit. Plan B, Phantoms."

"We have a plan B?" Z-Lo asks no one in particular.

"Yut. It's called making it up as we go. Let's ride." Then I kick-start my bike and peel away. Damn, that felt good. And it's probably going to get me killed, but my cabin's feeling pretty far away at this point, so I don't see the point in delaying the inevitable. Death's been a long time coming.

39

0039, Saturday, June 26, 2027
Lower Manhattan, New York
FDR Drive, East River

"HEY, CHUCK," I yell over the roar of my Harley's engine.

"Still where you left me, Patrick."

"Your sensors have eyes on those barges?"

"Of course. I see all, know all."

"Except when you need me to point you in a particular direction, right?"

"Why, of course." He pauses. "Are you implying that you think I was toying with you?"

"That's exactly what I was implying, yut."

"Don't be preposterous. Yuriy is redirecting the vessels now."

"How far out is he?"

CHRISTOPHER HOPPER & J.N. CHANEY

"He needs to cover about 1,800 feet. At his current rate of eight knots, this means he'll have the barges in position in just over two minutes."

Two minutes. That's not as bad as I thought. "Any sign that he's been discovered?"

"No, Patrick. I will alert you when... he's been discovered."

That was weird. "You're saying that you'll alert me when he's been discovered, or that he's been discovered?"

"He's been discovered. They are discovering him right now! It's time to move your tiny little keister, Lucky Charms!"

As we pass under the Manhattan Bridge, I signal the rest of the team to slow. "I want whatever we have firing on that dropship."

Everyone looks southwest to see a vessel descending toward Yuriy's tug.

"Bumper, wait for my go."

He nods.

"Everyone else, make yourself the hardest target possible." I unsling Veronica and hold her with my left hand, and then I throttle up. As my bike tears down FDR Drive, weaving between dead vehicles, I say, "You ready, Veronica?"

"User Twelve, please confirm weapon designation selection: Veronica."

"Confirm."

"Profile updated. Veronica standing by."

"This is so painful to listen to," Chuck says.

"Until we get you fixed up, get used to it, pal." Then to Veronica, I say, "Gimme something to get that bogie's attention."

"Colloquial expression bogie identified. Please confirm your—"

"Oh, for all the whores in Dublin. Would you two shut up

already?" I feel Chuck vibrate against my back and notice that Veronica is glowing in my left hand.

Suddenly, the weapon says, "What the hell is happening to the world right now, and what do you have to say for yourselves?" She sounds like a really pissed off Latina mother.

"Veronica?"

"Are you asking me for my name?"

"I just wanted—"

"*Are you asking me for my name?*"

"Chuck?" I ask as I swerve between cars. "Why does she sound like Selma Hayek in the Hitman's Bodyguard?"

"Bravo, old bean. I say, you really have seen your share of movies, and your recall is quite impressive."

"Is this your idea of a joke?"

"No, my good man. I was simply trying to, you know, spice things up a little."

"Might be too spicy."

"Possibly. But I warned you she was a real twat."

"Or you just want her to be."

"Hmmm. Well, there is that, yes. Would you care for me to deprogram her?"

"No time." I raise Veronica. "Gimme something to get their attention, girl."

"Oh, you want their attention? *You want their attention?*" A second later, she says, "Come and get it, you little hijo de perro!"

"Oh God," Chuck says. "I regret my decision."

I aim Veronica and squeeze. The recoil shoves my bike to the right, and I swerve to keep balance. The blast, however, streaks across the East River and hits the dropship dead center, enveloping it in an explosion of blue energy.

"Take that, cabróns," Veronica yells.

But the blast hasn't knocked out the engines. Instead, the dropship turns away from Yuriy and points in our direction.

"Looks like you bought Yuriy some time," Bumper shouts.

"Yeah," adds Hollywood. "And got us a tail!"

The dropship fires from over the East River and hits the road behind us close enough that I feel the heat on the back of my neck. I also see a white sedan flip into the water to my left.

"Might I suggest another shot, Patrick," Chuck says.

"Same thing, Veronica," I shout.

"Coming right up, mi amor," she says.

I squeeze the trigger.

A second energy burst like the first crashes against the ship's nose. Again, there's no windshield to crack. But the port-side engine is smoking, and the craft seems to be compensating by adding power.

Another energy blast hits the road behind us. Bits of hot pavement pelt my plate carrier and ping against my helmet. I apply throttle and zig-zag between parked cars as the vessel drops in behind us.

More blaster bolts whizz past us and strike cars in the lanes ahead. Some vehicles flip skyward and sail away, while others detonate in place and spit fuel and burning debris at us. Automatic weapons fire rings out behind me as our team sprays lead at the pursuing enemy. I doubt it's doing much damage, but at this point, every little bit counts. Plus, we're keeping interest off Yuriy.

"Sixty seconds," Chuck yells.

I relay the message to the rest of the team and speed up. We're almost to the Brooklyn Bridge, which is definitely not where I want us to be. To survive the forthcoming ANFO blasts, we need to be moving away from the bridge. While my instincts say to try and jump a curb and take us into Manhattan, that will only send us into the masses of people—the ones we're trying not to kill from dropship fire. At this point, our best option is to stay on FDR Drive and continue past the bridge as fast as we can.

I place Veronica over my right shoulder, crouch against the handlebars to brace myself, and fire blindly. I can't even look back to see if my shot has done anything, but then, I don't have to.

"You aim like you've had too mucho tequila, handsome," Veronica says. "But I got tu seis."

"Thanks."

"Death angels inbound," Yoshi yells.

"This day, man," I say to myself. Sure enough, three light signatures from Lower Manhattan come in behind us and partner with the dropship. More blaster fire rakes the road and blows out car windows.

"Twenty seconds," Chuck announces.

Just a little bit more.

The team is weaving across the lanes with as much control as I could hope for, somehow managing to fire up at the enemy. I catch a glimpse of Yoshi screaming something in Japanese while shooting his SCAR 15 overhead. The muzzle flashes emblazon his face like some romantic Anime flashback. Z-Lo sprays his Tavor back and forth while Aaron has managed to unlock his mounted DP-27, rest it on the back of his sidecar, and start draining the pancake mag into the dropship.

Unable to wield either of his sniper rifles while riding, Ghost has removed an MP7 that he picked up from Sissy's armory and holds it behind him, arm extended, drilling the death angels with surprising accuracy. The three Russians are holding their own, firing AK-47s

CHRISTOPHER HOPPER & J.N. CHANEY

like they'd been born with them in their hands. Hell, it's probably not far from the truth.

But it's Hollywood who has the best seat in the house. She's swung herself into Bumper's lap to face backward and puts more rounds on target than anyone else in the team, at least as far as I can tell. And she should be: Bumper's shoulders make great armrests. He's clearly enjoying the moment too—the bastard's grinning ear to ear.

"You might wish to brace yourselves," Chuck yells. "It's time!"

I glance at Bumper. "DO IT."

He pulls the remote det from his pouch, flips the safety, and squeezes the trigger.

IT's an odd feeling to be flung from a speeding motorcycle. Not exactly something I'd recommend, especially when the force throwing you is 30,000 pounds of ammonium nitrate gone thermal. No life flashing before my eyes. No visions of God or heaven or hell. But I can say that time does slow down.

I'm sideways in the air, heels a bit above my head, and looking back at a bright energy burst. The shock wave has engulfed the ring, the bridge, and the East River, and it has swallowed us up too. I catch glimpses of the death angels spinning out of control, and the cars behind us rising off the pavement. Even the dropship is pitched forward at an unnatural angle.

And then it all comes crashing down.

I slam into the pavement, left shoulder first, and feel a splitting pain explode through my head and torso, knocking the air out of me. The concussion pops my ears, but I can still hear the muffled noises of metal crashing against metal, of heavy objects thudding into the road, and of glass exploding in waves. But even as I sense my body sliding to a halt, arms and limbs burning, my thoughts aren't toward my team or our equipment or even the people of New York. I'm only thinking about one thing.

The ring.

I try to sit up, but my head is spinning. My left hand finds the pavement beside me. Then my right. Nerve endings on fire. Hands firm, I will myself to overcome waves of vertigo and sit up. It hurts to blink, but I do it anyway, waiting for my eyes to focus. I'm facing the right direction because the Brooklyn Bridge is coming into view.

Or at least what I can make of it.

The shadows flitting in front of my eyes are strange. Gone is the dome's constant blue glow. Vanished is the portal's mesmerizing energy field. Instead, all I can make out is the moonlight illumination of a pale debris cloud enveloping the broken towers and the suddenly sagging cables. And then even they are snuffed out as the dust and smoke roll into Lower Manhattan.

The sounds of rocks shattering and splashing into water shake what little of my hearing remains. I can feel the tremors through the roadway, and sense the vibrations of falling structures. I can even hear what I think are waves crashing into the lower streets. And then a new sound, one I know all too well, merges with the noise of destruction.

Cheering.

I'm reminded of every baseball and football game I've ever attended. I can see the fans faces, their arms raised, heads tilted back. Beer sloshing, popcorn flinging. Their team has won. They're happy. And they're alive.

From inside the streets to my left, and even across the river in my hometown of Brooklyn, I hear the sounds of New Yorkers yelling. Shouting. Clapping. Banging on cars. Clanging against light poles. And their praise climbs into the open night sky.

"We did it," I say to the stars as I fall back down. They're a sight for sore eyes. Then blackness creeps in from the sides of my vision, and all I want is to take a long nap in my cabin in the country.

40

0527, Saturday, June 26, 2027
Lower Manhattan, New York
Brooklyn Bridge Ruins, East River

"I CAN'T BELIEVE the towers are still standing," Yoshi says as he turns from his work on Z-Lo's upper lip and takes a swig from his flask. He glances at me, but I'm not gonna scold him. It's his call when to stop. Then Yoshi wipes the sweat, blood, and dirt from his face and returns to patching up the kid.

The sun is seconds away from rising over the eastern horizon as we Phantoms, Vlad, and Lada sit among the Brooklyn Bridge's ruins, nursing our wounds and reflecting on our accomplishments—if that's what all this can be called.

"Mostly standing," Ghost says.

"What's that?" Yoshi asks without looking away from Z-Lo.

"The towers are mostly standing."

"All that fine German engineering, I imagine," Chuck adds. "John A. Roebling would be proud."

I furrow my eyebrows. "That we blew his bridge apart with fertilizer?"

"Well. That's not exactly what I had in mind with my comment. But, I suppose that might also impress him… in a dysfunctional and barbaric sort of way."

I shake my head in amazement. "For what it's worth, Roebling may have been born in Germany, but the bridge was born in the USA. So that's American engineering and the real reason those towers are still standing."

"Would you hold still, kid?" Yoshi says to Z-Lo. He's been trying to stitch him up for the last twenty minutes. Well, actually, since we picked ourselves off the pavement hours ago. But there was too much work to be done.

Ghost needed the most serious medical attention, and still has a pretty good limp. The rest of us had varying contusions and lacerations, but nothing life-threatening.

While Yoshi tended to our sniper, the rest of us double-checked the dead Androchidans who'd been pursuing us. The dropship and the death angels were blown out of the sky in the ANFO blast. And while the ship was thrown into Lower Manhattan somewhere, the death angels hit the surrounding cars and buildings hard enough to split their armor open. Two rounds to the chest or head made sure the aliens stayed down.

From there, we gave some aid and direction to several civilian pockets we encountered. Finally, the team hiked up what remained of the Manhattan-side ramp just to get a view of the destruction from above.

Astonishingly, the main towers are, as Ghost noted, intact for the most part. If the city ever wishes to restore the bridge to its former glory, it'll have quite a bit of masonry to patch up. Meanwhile, the fraying main cables dangle lumps of concrete and steel over a turbulent East River, hemorrhaging with bulbous growths and piles of misshapen alien stone. And what was the Brooklyn Bridge's well-worn center span is now a heap of mangled trusses and pavement, sacrificed on the Androchidan's slaver ring altar.

"He did it," Bumper says from his spot on a concrete slab next to me as the first rays of sunlight silhouette the ruins against a warming sky. "Yuriy, I mean. Old man was clutch."

I nod. "May he rest in peace."

"Ha! He is not resting. Too many virgins right now," Vlad says as he motions for Yoshi to share his flask.

Yoshi hands it over, and Vlad takes a pull.

"Not sure I follow, Vlad," I say.

"Sure you do." He wipes his mouth and thanks Yoshi for the drink. "Muslim extremists, they say their men get seventy-two virgins upon dying deaths, yes?"

"Until they find out the virgins are those who died in their own ranks." Z-Lo chuckles and tries giving Ghost a high five.

Ghost glares at Z-Lo.

The kid pulls his hand down.

"And you know who real heavenly female virgins are saving for?" Vlad pounds his chest. "Russians, as payment for Soviet–Afghan War. Ha!"

"Vladimir, shush," Lada says.

"What? Is truth."

"Sure, sure. And what do Russian women get?"

Vlad thinks for a second, then points to me. "More American alpha dog tops."

Lada raises an eyebrow and then looks me over once. "I agree to this."

Looking to change the subject, I pat Chuck on the side. "So. Think they'll be coming for us, pal?"

"The Androchidans? Eventually, yes. They'll be very interested to know who blew up their slaver ring. But since they assumed that your military infrastructure was wiped out, they don't have personnel to spare. It will be another day before military scouts arrive. So you still have some time to hide."

"Who said anything about hiding?" Hollywood puts her hands on her hips. "No way I'm hiding."

"I agree with small Army lady," Vlad says but then seems to think better of his comment as Hollywood sits upright. "Small but extremely powerful and dominating Army lady."

"That's more like it," she says.

"So where's everyone headed off to?" I ask. "Job's done, New York's free…"

"For the time being," Chuck adds.

"We take what we can get, Charlie." I look around the group as the sun warms our faces. "So, where to?"

They all look worn out and dirty as hell. Still, some sewer lingers on a few of us. But no one seems interested in giving up their intentions, so I decide to start.

"Well, I'm headed back home. Figure our reserves will regroup, and all the smart people will get a plan together." I look at Bumper to add his piece.

But he squints at me. "Permission to speak freely, Wic?"

"Eh, don't pull that crap, Bumper. Say what you need to."

He looks around when he replies. "I don't think the reserves are getting back together. At least not for a long time."

"I can confirm Bumper's conclusion," Chuck offers. "I have been monitoring all of your various transmission bands and other than very distant and therefore indistinguishable oscillations, which would imply that at least some of your species are maintaining radio contact, there is nothing even remotely close to military chatter, as they say."

Bumper frowns and gives Chuck a nod before continuing. "And I'm pretty sure we already established the fact that our respective units are... Well, we're all stranded, for the time being, Wic."

"Then you can make yourselves useful here and help the fine people of New York get moved out to the country. That's what I'll be doing in my spare time, right?"

"We're not Greenpeace," Hollywood says. "That's not what we were trained for."

"And what is?"

"This." She points to the bridge's skeleton. "Blowing shit up." She pauses. "Nah, it's blowing... What was your word again, Sir Chuck?"

"My word?"

"For bloody little something-somethings."

"Ah, yes. I believe you are referring to my flabbergasted attempt to get through the words—"

"It's splick," I say, sparing us all Chuck's well-intentioned but needlessly long explanation.

Hollywood snaps her fingers. "That's it. We're trained to blow up these little splick heads and send 'em all back to Anderkin Prime."

"Androchida Prime," Chuck says.

Hollywood shakes her head. "Nope." Then she looks around. "I don't know about the rest of you, but I'm sure as hell not moving out to pasture while I wait around for the enemy to relocate their floating slaver rings and grab a fresh batch of us. Not when I've still got a weapon in my hand."

"Roger that," Bumper says.

Yoshi and Z-Lo high five her, and Ghost gives a small nod.

"I agree with sexy Army lady," Vlad says.

Now it's Bumper's turn to sit up. "You wanna say that again, pal?"

"Yes. I agree with sexy Army lady."

I can't help but stifle a small laugh.

Hollywood rests her head on Bumper's arm. "It's all good."

The SEAL seems to take this well enough, but he's definitely growing protective of Hollywood.

"Go on," Hollywood says to Vlad.

"Lada and I, we are not sharing our brother's views on hidings out. It is not our styles to be waitings around for the finishes."

Lada nods in agreement with her brother's words. "This is Bratva way. But not Russian Army way. And he has never been serviced."

"Probably not what she wanted to say," Chuck says softly.

"So you want to keep fighting," Bumper states to the pair of Russians. "With us."

"Da," Vlad says. "Better than dying in Boxcar Children City with pants around ankles."

"And why is this the preferred way to die?" Chuck asks.

"Worry about it later." I look at Vlad and Lada. "But won't Sissy require you to stay?"

"He is big brother, yes," Lada says. "But he is not mother. Does not control us."

"We are freedoms fighters now," Vlad says. "And if you all stay and do fightings, we also do this. Even though mother Russia is our heart home, America is also home. This"—he points around the city—"is great American freedom dream, yes? And we love this too and is also home. So when puny aliens come and brings fight to this houses, we fight. Stand with you, wrapped in Old Glorious red, white, and blue stripes and stars. And we say"—he flips the bird toward the wreckage—"poshel na khuy!"

Phantom Team heads nod in appreciation of Vlad's sentiments, and I'm pretty sure I know what that last bit translated as.

"No offense, Wic," Hollywood says after a beat. "But I don't think there's anyone smarter out there than you right now."

"Flattery isn't a good look on you, Hollywood."

"It's not flattery. Look around, Master Guns. What other city has taken a ring down? And didn't Chuck say we're the first from any civilization he's seen?"

"I did say that, yes," Chuck replies.

Before I can contest the logic, Hollywood jumps back in. "He with the most intel is the smartest person at the table."

"Maybe the most knowledgeable, but not the smartest," I reply.

"Fine. But you also know how to use it, how to problem solve, how to lead us. If that's not smarts, I don't know what is."

"Sorry, team. We accomplished our mission, and we worked hard, and now it's my turn to—"

"To what?" Hollywood's on her feet now. "To give up?"

"That's not what—"

"To retire and back down from the fight?"

"Hey, you all lived through the same stuff I did here, so you can—"

"No, they haven't," Aaron says.

All eyes move toward him.

"What was that?" I ask.

"They haven't all lived through the same stuff you have, Pat. You... you've seen more action than all of them put together, if I'm not mistaken. And you're tired because, yeah, you *have* paid all those dues. But that's precisely what qualifies you to lead right now."

He stands up and moves toward me.

"I know you're tired. Heck, I'm more tired and afraid than I've ever been in my whole life. But this fight... it's not someone else's. It's yours. And it's mine. And if Jack were here—"

"Dude. Just don't."

"And if Jack were here, he'd be begging you to let him take point on this patrol too."

A surge of emotion leaps from my gut, but I catch it in my throat before it betrays me. I'm half ready to deck Aaron out of reflex, and half ready to weep. And both piss the hell out of me. I clench my jaw only because if I don't, I'm gonna say something I regret.

I think Aaron can tell he's poked the lion, and he takes a half-step back. But he's still glaring at me, and I know he's not gonna let this one go. So I have to answer him.

"You know what's waiting for us out there, right?" I point over Aaron's shoulder toward the sun. "Death."

"That's what was waiting for us in here too," Hollywood says.

I hear her, but I'm still in a staring contest with Aaron.

"Jack's dead because I said yes, Aaron. Me. Not anyone else. And I said yes to this team once already." I look around. "We cheated death this time. Yut. But twice? Against these odds?" I shake my head and feel the lump returning. See the images of Jack's broken body. "We don't get to cheat the devil more than once. He learns too quickly. It's gotta be someone else."

"Goddammit, Pat! There is no one else."

Aaron's red-faced. Hell, so am I. Feels like a damn woodstove behind my cheeks. But neither of us is moving, and the rest of the team is dead still.

A small voice breaks the tension. Chuck's voice. "At least with you, they'll die fighting for what they believe in."

I pull my eyes off Aaron and look down at the weapon. "What was that?"

"It's your speech. You can win for a bad cause, but then you've gotta live with hell. Or you can die for a good cause and tell the devil where to stick it in person. Seems to me that walking away from this lets you live, but it's gonna be hell." He pauses. "And, somehow, I sense you've already lived with enough of that."

"What, are you, my goddamn therapist now?"

"No," Hollywood says. "But he is right."

I turn on her with my fists clenched. Lord knows I'd never hit her. But I also don't want to admit that she's right. So is Aaron. And so is goddamned Chuck.

I tilt my head back, run a hand over my face, and then look into the blue sky. The seagulls have returned, screeching like the winged rats they are. A fresh breeze lifts the salty sea air into my nose. And in the distance, I hear the steady thrum of the masses exiting the city. People are alive.

Because of us.

"We're all gonna die," I say.

"Looking forward to it," Bumper replies before the words are barely out of my mouth.

"And you're all gonna be sad about it," I add. "Like, weeping and wishing you hadn't signed up."

"So sad," Hollywood says.

"I'm serious, Sergeant."

"So am I, Master Guns."

She's pissing me off more. But the right kind. The sort that says we're going to make sure that the Anderkins, even if they take the whole damn planet, know they screwed with the wrong species.

"You're all a bunch a splick heads, you know that?"

"We do," several of them reply.

"I am not familiar with this term," Vlad says. "What is this splicks of heads?"

"It's what the enemy eats for breakfast," Z-Lo says.

"Yeah." Yoshi smiles. "And what bites them in the ass by lunch."

"Si," yells Veronica. "And then burns them in the buttholes all through the night. Like muchas jalapeños, ah-ha!"

Hollywood smiles but then gives me a serious look. "So, does that mean you're in?"

I take a deep breath. "Does anyone know the patron saint of log cabins?"

"I guess that'd be St. Joseph, the carpenter," Z-Lo says. "Why?"

"'Cause I'm gonna need him to relocate mine from the Poconos to the pearly gates."

———

THE TEAM's euphoria and high fives last until someone, namely Hollywood, asks the most obvious next question.

"So, what's the plan, Wic?"

I pause for a few seconds as several chess moves flutter through my head. Ideas can come and go so quickly that I swear half the good ones never settle. It takes real mental fortitude to snag their tails as they whiz past, and even more to layer a strategy that's ten moves ahead of your opponent. But, then again, that's what you love to do, isn't it, Wic? Plot the enemy's demise, one move at a time.

"Wic?" Hollywood asks.

"Just thinking." I suck my lips in for a moment. Something's forming in my head despite my fatigue, hunger, and dehydration. But these are the kinds of riddles that keep a man awake at night. That give him purpose. A project. A mission.

I look around at the team, then the bridge's ruins, and then the rising sun. "If we have any hope of fighting the plushies, then it's not gonna be in our defense."

"Offense, baby." Bumper rubs his hands together. "Can't win games if you ain't planning to score."

"Can't win girls either," Hollywood says.

"Hello." Z-Lo gives a whistle.

The team's spirits are lifting, which is good. But my head is preoccupied. Sure, the headache I have is killer, and I'm definitely ready to eat something and then take a long nap. But one idea is struggling toward the surface in my brain, like it's under the pavement, trying to poke its head up.

I lean forward and hold my head in my hands. I'm rubbing my temples when I notice a hip joint wedged in a crack in the pavement. It's left over from the piles of human hardware I saw at the portal entrance.

I glance at Aaron. "Back in Antarctica, when Lewis was taken."

CHRISTOPHER HOPPER & J.N. CHANEY

"God, Pat. Do we have to relive that right now?"

"Do you remember his clothes burning as he went through?"

"What? No. What's this about?"

"Do you remember his clothes catching on fire when the drone pulled him across?"

Aaron thinks for a second. "No, not that I remember. Why?"

"Hey, Chuck."

"At your beck and call, old bean."

"Is there a difference between how the slaver portals work and the one in Antarctica?"

"No. They both act as transports to Androchida Prime."

"That's not what I mean." I pull the hip-joint free and hold it up.

"Oh, God," Hollywood says. "Is that what I think it is?"

"Small metal club for killing squirrels?" Vlad offers.

She glares at him and whispers to me, "You really want this guy coming along?"

I wave off her comment and stay focused on Chuck. "The slaver ring. It filters out all non-biological material, right?"

"Yes. I thought this was well established."

"But the other ring, the one in Antarctica"—I lock eyes with Aaron, and he seems to pick up my logic—"it didn't—"

"Burn up Lewis's clothing," Aaron finishes. "Or leave anything else behind."

"Exactly," I say.

"Why didn't I think of that sooner?" Aaron's on his feet and pacing. "That means that they serve different purposes."

"Bravo, I say," Chuck interjects. "Fine deductive work, you two. Now, if you'll permit me to offer some more insight so as to prove myself invaluable to the team despite my inability to shoot stuff, I'd be appreciative."

"One is for transporting slaves back to the homeworld," I say.

"Yes, but now it's my turn," Chuck says.

Aaron stares at me with wide eyes. "While the other is for the leadership structure to..."

"To ferry resources for the invasion," I conclude.

"Oh, you see now? You've gone and stolen my thunder, you little wankers. You might as well toss me over the edge now. Flounders, here I come!"

"So it's true then," I say to Chuck.

"What, *now* you suddenly want me to chime in?"

"It makes sense, right?" I'm on my feet with Aaron, looking at Hollywood and Bumper. "You wouldn't have slaves show up at the same place where you stage your invasions."

"Different objectives, different areas of operation," Bumper replies.

"You'd want holding cells, interrogation, processing for one," Ghost adds.

"Whereas the other is for command," Yoshi says.

"And that might explain the power and size differences too," adds Aaron.

"Are you all quite finished yet?" Chuck asks.

"Sorry, pal." I pick him up. "Did you want to add something?"

"Well... yes. But... The two rings are... Ugh. You've pretty much covered it without me."

"Nonsense," Lada coos as she sidles up to Chuck and runs her fingers along his barrel. "Something strong and formidable tells Lada that you are having many secrets waiting to be coaxed from your insides and brought into open, yes?"

"Patrick, is she… talking to you or me?"

"I'll get back to you on that." I lower Chuck. "I think we have the start of a plan here, folks."

"The enemy's got something we can exploit," Bumper says.

"Holding ups," Vlad says. "Are you meanings to suggest that we go back to yuzhnyy polyus?"

I nod. "The south pole. Yut."

"Not to sound like a stick in the mud," Hollywood says. "But isn't that kinda far away? And we're a little low on—oh, I don't know—flyable planes and fuel?"

"We are," I say in a conciliatory tone. But I suspect transportation might not be a problem. "You wanna speak to that, Chuck?"

There's a long pause before the rifle says anything. "Hold the rotary telephones. No one wants to rain on my parade?"

"Go ahead."

"You're sure. Because last time there was a lot of interrupting and much thunder was stolen."

"Scout's honor, pal."

Chuck clears his throat. I can practically see the little guy straightening his bow tie and brushing back his hair. "Well, now that you mention it, I would not say that a trip to Antarctica, assuming you're thinking of *taking the fight to the enemy*, as you implied, is entirely out of the question."

He pauses as if to wait for interjection. But none of us do.

"Go on, buddy," I say, hoping he's about to prove my suspicions correct.

"Huh. Yes, well. As fortune would have it, though I think it is far more a testament to Sekmit defense technology than fate, there remains one air-worthy dropship not eight hundred meters west of our present position. And I do say meters rather deliberately, as it is the superior measurement system."

"Hold up." Hollywood steps forward. "You wanna take a dropship to Antarctica?"

"Yeah, what about all the slaver rings still here on the East Coast?" Yoshi asks.

"I got this." Bumper raises a hand to me and then looks at the rest of the team. "We took New York's ring out, yeah. But we had the element of surprise. And if the enemy is smart, they're not going to let that happen again. I'm guessing intel has already been uploaded to some cloud and shared. They're gonna be picking it apart for days or even weeks to figure out what went wrong and how to prevent it. Just like we would. So there's no more sending ANFO bombs on barges down rivers, at least not exactly like we did. They'll be expecting that."

"Which means we need to change tactics," I say. "We need to stay one step ahead and keep them guessing. They didn't expect us to slip under the dome and blow up our own bridge, right? So I'm proposing we do the next thing that they'd never guess we'd do."

"Show up on their goddamn doorstep," Chuck says in a fairly creepy voice. "God, that felt so good."

Everyone laughs.

"Huh!" Veronica spits. "Like you could sneak up on anyone with all that Ministry of Silly Walks business."

"I beg your pardon?" Chuck replies.

"You heard me. You make a lousy spy."

Chuck sighs. "Again, Patrick. I'm so sorry for her."

"I'm not," I say with a wide grin. "Anyway, you hit the nail on the head about taking the fight to them." I give Sir Charles a gentle pat on the scope. "Nice job."

"Thank you, Patrick. It feels so good to be a key contributing player. All in, as they say."

"We'll see about that," I say under my breath.

"Hey, I thought all the dropships got taken out in the blast," Yoshi says.

"May I?" Chuck asks. I assume he's directing the question to me.

"By all means."

"While the remaining dropships were knocked out of the sky, and some were indeed permanently disabled as far as my scans can tell, this does not mean that all are grounded. For instance, the one I previously mentioned was the one pursuing you along FDR Drive. While the ANFO blast threw it into Lower Manhattan, it did not render the ship inoperable. If anything, it rendered its crew inert."

"Inert?" Z-Lo asks.

"Dead," Chuck replies. "Contrary to what your lazy fiction asserts, a human being, and just about all complex biological organisms, cannot sustain dramatic instantaneous changes of inertia."

"I'm... not following." The kid looks at me.

"Remember when Vision shoots War Machine out of the sky in Captain America: Civil War?" I ask.

"Of course. Rhodey almost dies. Legs get paralyzed."

"That's inertia," I reply.

"Quite so," adds Chuck. "And a fine Marvel movie too. In any case, sure, there are inertia dampeners on just about everything imaginable these days. But just because you have a fancy Iron man suit doesn't mean it will protect your organs from going splat inside it."

"So you're saying the Ander-babies in the dropship went splat?" Z-Lo asks.

"Only one way to find out," Chuck replies. "Who's up for a field trip?"

A sizable crowd has gathered around the downed dropship by the time we reach the corner of Wall and Pearl Streets. I look over my shoulder to see that several buildings were clipped as the enemy craft was thrown off course until it reached its final resting place in the middle of the street.

It hasn't even been six hours, and already people have tagged the vehicle with bright spray paint, making it the quasi-effigy of all their pent up rage. A few people are beating it with baseball bats, which I'm certain is doing more harm to them than the ship. However, it's the crowbars and Molotov cocktails that I'm most concerned about.

"It has no more concern for the humans than a boot has to ants," Chuck assures me as he channels his inner Nick Fury. "Though the graffiti is rather charming, wouldn't you say?"

"Sure," I reply as we start pressing our way through the crowd. But the going is slow, given how densely the people are packed.

Then, in an effort that's as close to but never topping Andre the Giant's crowd-parting pronouncement in Princess Bride, Vlad cups his hands to both sides of his mouth and shouts, "Everybody moves!"

Those just beside and ahead of us spin around and then start opening a gap for us to pass through.

"Nicely done," I say.

"Not problems."

Those atop the dropship stop beating it as we near.

"Can we help you?" says a kid with a baseball bat.

"Just here to get a ride," I say.

"No luck, old man. Been trying for a few hours."

"Old man?" I say to Hollywood. "Did he just call me old?"

"Hey, kid," she says. "We need you and your crew to come on down."

He looks around at his friends, and they seem to redirect their angst toward us. "Nah. We all good, just like this."

"Listen, I'm all for celebrating a win. Have at it so long as you don't go crazy on mine or someone else's property. But when people have guns and look like they just fought a war, the smart move is to say, "Yes, ma'am. Right away, ma'am. Anything you say.""

"Pretty sure this spaceship belongs to all of us," the punk yells and gets instant support from the people around him.

"That could be," I reply. "But right now, we need to borrow it."

"Oh yeah, pops? And how you plan on doing that?"

"This is enoughs," Lada says. "I kill him now."

"Easy there, Lada." I don't think the punk means to fight us. He's not posturing in a threatening way, he's just defending his newfound turf. I get it. But he still owes Hollywood an apology.

"Hey, Chuck?"

"Yes, Patrick."

"How you coming on talking to that six-month-old baby AI?"

"Almost ready."

"Hold on." The punk jumps onto the nearest engine support mount. "Who you talkin' to?"

I raise Chuck. "My rifle."

"That don't look like no rifle I seen."

"And there's good reason for that, kid. Now, I suggest you climb on down before you or one of your friends get hurt."

"You believe this guy?" the punk says to his posse.

"I'm ready when you are, Patrick," Chuck says.

"Go ahead."

A beat later, the dropship's engines fire up, and the craft lifts out of the hole it's made in the pavement. The crowd moves back as people gasp and shout in surprise. The crew up top also back-steps from the edges—all but the ringleader that is. He falls off the engine arm but catches himself on an armor plate with one hand.

"Get me down," he hollers over and over. But none of his friends look interested in helping him, and everyone below has moved away from the engines' blue thrust cones.

"Ease it back down, Chuck," I say. "Gently."

The dropship descends a few feet and touches down. Z-Lo helps lower the punk to the ground, twists his shoulders so that he faces Hollywood, and shouts something in his ear.

The young man nods in a suddenly respectful manner and hustles to Hollywood. Over the engine noise, he says, "I'm very sorry for disrespecting you, ma'am."

"Apology accepted," she replies in his ear, and then tells him to get lost.

The crowd moves back even further when Chuck opens the rear cargo bay door.

"All aboard," Chuck says loud enough for the team to hear. And none too soon. While the masses in the street are newly liberated and, no doubt, grateful for their freedom, they're also still desperate given the state of the city's infrastructure. Several onlookers seem to be considering hitching a ride with us, and while I appreciate the sentiment of rescuing civilians, we're not an evacuation outfit. It only takes seeing one UH-60 Blackhawk overrun by desperate refugees to sear the dire outcome of such a scenario in your mind for good.

As soon as my feet are on the bay door, I tell Chuck to take us up. The response is instant, and the dropship blows dust and people away from the crash site. But then the dropship hovers around twenty feet off the deck.

"What's happening?" I yell into the bay.

Z-Lo has dragged an Androchidan pilot down the ladder leading to the bridge and is punching it in the face. Amazingly, the alien is still alive and, God, does it smell terrible—a strange mix of ammonia, dead fish, and rotting vegetables. The pilot makes a weak attempt to reach for Z-Lo's head, and the kid bats the creature's hand away. But the hand comes back as a fist and pops the Marine in the nose. Blood runs down Z-Lo's face, and he lets out a deep growl. As fast as a tiger spinning on its prey, the kid wraps his legs around the alien's torso, grabs its head with both hands, and then snaps it sideways.

I can hear the crack from where I stand. "Guess they have vertebrae," I say to Bumper.

He nods and then steps aside as Z-Lo hauls the corpse toward the open door. "Goddamn plushy broke my nose." He's about to heave the body out when I have an idea.

"Hold up." I kneel beside the dead Anderkin. "I want the armor."

"What?" Z-Lo asks above the engine noise.

"Its armor." I tap on the emerald green chest plate. "We're keeping the armor."

Z-Lo looks at me like I've lost my mind. "Master Guns, are you—?"

"Get it off, Marine!"

"On it."

Bumper and Ghost help Z-Lo figure out how to undress the dead alien and start piling the armor plating and uniform to the side. The stench gets worse as they go, and I worry that maybe this wasn't a good idea. But since the armor looks like it could fit one of our larger team members, I'm entertaining the idea that it might come in handy later.

As the creature becomes more naked, I can see the guys growing more repulsed. Its gray flesh and green veins cover a skeletal system not that unlike our own. But it's different enough that I find myself wincing as the team works.

"At least it believes in underwear," Yoshi yells.

"You curious?" Z-Lo asks.

"Hell, no!"

"Just don't try putting any of it on," Chuck says. "The armor, I mean. Not the underwear. That's just gross."

"Why's that?" Z-Lo asks.

"Ugh. I really need to explain hygiene to you? How disturbing."

"I think he means the armor," I say to Chuck.

"Ah. I see. Well, like with me, only those with trinium signatures can bind to this equipment. All others will be, you know, met with a nasty surprise. And the helmet in particular packs a mean wallop."

"Thanks for the *heads up*," I reply.

Chuck waits a second, then says, "Ha! A fine dad joke. I only wish I would have thought of that one first, dammit."

Once the corpse has been divested of its uniform, Z-Lo does the honors and heaves the grey body off the dropship. The crowd shouts as the alien lands on the pavement.

"One more," Yoshi says as he and Hollywood drag a second pilot toward the edge. Again, the armor gets stripped and the body flies out, landing near the first. Within seconds, the crowd swarms in like a school of piranha.

I'm leaning out to watch the throng beat the invaders to a pulp when Bumper grabs my vest and hits the button to start the bay door closing. As the buildings retreat beneath us, the strangeness of the moment hits me. How many times have I dusted off from parts unknown and forced myself to forget about the people I've helped once my role is played? Whereas now, with Brooklyn shining across the river, I hate to see it go. But the truth is, you never forget the towns you've fought to set free. In fact, that's part of war's futility, at least the wars I've fought in: as soon as you leave, you know things are going back to the way they were before, and there's not a damn thing you can do about it. Some of that same suspicion plagues me now, and I wonder if we'll ever be successful against this enemy. If we'll ever truly win.

One step at a time, Wic.

"We've gotta christen it," Bumper says to me once the ramp door is sealed.

"You mean, give the dropship a name?"

"Hell, yeah," Hollywood says as she overhears the conversation.

Bumper grins. "And the way I see it, there's only one appropriate name."

As if we'd rehearsed it ten times, all the original Phantoms look at Z-Lo and say, "Dolores."

"Who is this Dolores?" Vlad asks from the bay's opposite end. "Large-breasted America beauty, right?"

"You're gonna have to ask Z-Lo for those details," I say. "But he's pretty tight-lipped about it."

"Ah. I see. Yes, important to keep best ones to self. I respect much this way of behavings."

Z-Lo's a good sport, but I can tell he's embarrassed. And that's exactly the point. Still, I recognize the need to encourage Z-Lo as much as I make fun of him.

"Hey, kid." I nod and pull him aside. "Wanna tell you something."

"Oh, yeah?" He casts me a skeptical look.

"Back there... how you told that punk to apologize to Hollywood?"

"Yeah?"

"That was classy."

Z-Lo's guard seems to melt away. "Thanks, Master Guns."

"Just calling it like I see it, kid. You're a good egg."

"Thank you, sir."

"And it's just Wic from now on. Copy?"

He nods several times. "Okay, Mr. Wic, sir."

I chuckle and pat him on the shoulder. "You'll get there."

"So. To Antarctica then?" Chuck asks me.

"Not just yet. We need to make a few stops."

THE FIRST STOP we make is back at Pier 36 to let Vlad and Lada say goodbye to Sissy and then stock up on weapons and munitions. They also grab some Russian MREs that, the more I think about it, will be important for morale. Even though no MRE is anything to write home about, they do carry a certain sentimentality to them. Granted, I don't care to ever touch one again as long as I live. But if we're headed onto an alien planet, having some baggy-style potatoes au gratin might do my heart some good even if it does a number on my stomach.

The most surprising thing the sibling team brings back to Dolores is a wax-paper package tied with twine.

"This is for you from Babushka Petrov," Vlad says after pulling the bundle from his ridiculous fanny pack. "Here. Open."

I catch the package and undo the twine. Inside are a dozen teardrop shaped military-style patches with grey thread against a white field. In the middle is what looks like a beat up Androchidan helmet below two chevrons.

"You like? It is for Phantom Teams."

I squint at Vlad and Lada. "Your grandmother made these… while we were gone?"

"Da. She may or may not be having small underground sweat-shop for gifts and embroideries called Super Good Time Feelings Merchandise Store. I cannot confirming nor denying."

"And she made these. For us."

"Yes. And, perhaps now that you have them, you make two more members of Lada and Vladimir, yes?"

"I'll think about it."

Our next stop is back at our vehicles at the Richmond County Yacht Club on Staten Island. I'm not sure whether to be shocked or impressed that they haven't been looted. Maybe no one saw us pull in, or maybe they did and got worried we'd be coming back with all our guns. If it were me, I'd be scared of the booby traps that might be waiting, but we've already established that I'm a prepper like that.

Okay, maybe a touch paranoid too.

But after everything I've just lived through? I think it's under-standable. Paranoia doesn't mean that the enemy isn't trying to kill you.

We retrieve all the MREs, ammunition, and freshwater, as well as some of the secondary equipment, and then say goodbye to our rides for the second time in less than twenty-four hours. It feels like it's been longer, but time does tend to slow down when every minute feels like it might be your last.

"Sorry, Dolores," I overhear Z-Lo say to his Humvee. "But they made us name the bird Dolores too. I still love you, though."

"Come on, loverboy," Hollywood yells. "Wheels up."

"Coming." And then Z-Lo blows a kiss to his HMMWV.

From the marina, Chuck takes us back to the last place I want to see right now: my cabin in Skytop, Pennsylvania. Don't get me wrong, it's a sight for sore eyes. But after all that talk on bridge ruins, I'd reconciled the fact that I'd never see it again. Now, here we are, and I'm fighting homesickness like a six-year-old on his first sleepover.

We land clear of the party favors that sleep in the fields and disembark with a strict fifteen-minute timeline. That limit's in place for me, not the rest of the team. Any longer and I feel I might change my mind about this whole decision. Damn sentimentality.

After starting my twin backup generators, the team members take turns using my bathroom and then join me in the basement to sort through cold-weather gear. We also stock up on even more weapons, ammunition, extra batteries for radios and NVGs, and as much food as we can carry. I don't know what awaits us on the other side of that portal, but I want to prepare like there's nothing hospitable about it. This reminds me of maybe the most overlooked question yet, and I feel like an idiot for not thinking of it sooner.

I wait until everyone else is topside, then say, "Hey, Chuck?"

"Yes, Patrick?"

"Random question here, but, uh, can we humans breath on Androchida Prime?"

"Huh. Do you honestly believe that I would let you entertain the idea of stepping through that portal without the presence of adequate life support?"

I'm about to answer in the affirmative when Chuck jumps in on his own question.

"You know what? Never mind. I can see how this might undermine our trust-building—*my* trust-building by opening the relationship up to unnecessary suspicion. For what it's worth, the answer to the latter question is no: I would not allow you to do something so dangerous. And the answer to the former question is yes: you can breathe where you're heading."

I stuff more MREs into some rucksacks. "And any chance you can describe more about what we're walking into?"

"Absolutely. However, given your imposed fifteen-minute time limit, I advise we discuss the matter while en route."

"Fair enough. Anything you think we're missing that we should be bringing along for the ride?"

"Besides several improvised multi-trigger trinitex bombs, chameleon cloaking tech for an army, and a few Novia Cascade-Class Dreadnoughts? No, I think you're all set personally."

"That... sounds like a lot."

"I wouldn't worry about it too much."

"And why's that?"

"Because, Patrick. You have the one thing the Androchidans don't."

"And that is?"

"Me."

"How comforting."

"Yes, it is, isn't it." He sighs.

"Listen, we already got caught with our pants down in Antarctica once. I don't want to repeat it."

"Meaning?"

"I want us bringing the hurt to the enemy, but we need intel first. So this needs to be a recon mission, not a war. We're not ready for that. Clear?"

"Of course, Patrick. You are, as I've learned, a consummate planner. This mission is easily done as an investigatory there-and-back-again style jaunt, as it were."

"Did you... read the Hobbit?"

"Watched the Hobbit. Though I suppose you're going to tell me that—"

"The book is always better," we both say at the same time.

I smile at him. "So, it's a recon op then."

"Precisely. Expect to pop in, say hello, and gather some intelligence to suit your curious soul, then you're back to Antarctica with a few clicks of your heels to continue what you do best."

"And what, pray tell, do you think I do best, exactly?"

"Why, blow splick up, of course."

I shrug and go back to stuffing a rucksack. "I can live with that."

UPSTAIRS, I discover that the team has started taking turns using my shower, and at least two of them have paired off. Hint: It's not Ghost and Z-Lo. Not that I blame them, but asking would have been nice. About the shower, I mean, not the shower sex.

Still, I can't get mad at them too much as cleaning up and re-treating wounds is a damn good idea. Lord knows I could use some hot water, some Motrin, and a glass of Redbreast. Which reminds me to grab my scotch before Yoshi finds it. By the time it's my turn to shower, I praise the patron saint of hot water for the on-demand unit I installed when I built the place. Best investment I could have made for a moment like this, which is ironic, since I never expected anyone else to be on my property, let alone a bunch of random combatants. And two Russians. Damn, I'm gonna have to torch the place after this.

"Looky looky." Lada holds up the picture frame on the fireplace mantle and waves it.

I take my towel off my head. "Put it back."

"Who is it?" Hollywood gets to Lada before I can. "Holy crap! Look how young you guys are."

"I said, put it back." I snatch the frame from the ladies' hands and lay it face down on the mantle.

"That was you and Aaron," Hollywood says. "And was that Jack?"

"Another lifetime ago. Yut."

Just then, Lada smells my neck and shoulders.

I pull away. "What the hell?"

"You are smelling of fresh man meat." She smiles like a damn Cheshire cat sniffing catnip.

"Okay." I point to the door. "Everybody back to Dolores. Playtime's over."

WITH AN IN-ATMOSPHERE top speed of 932 miles per hour, Chuck estimates that we'll reach the Ellsworth Highlands Research Site in approximately ten hours. That's impressive, to say the least, as not once has this old body ever broken the sound barrier unless you count what happens a few hours after Taco Tuesdays.

It's also impressive because Chuck tells me that we don't need to refuel. Apparently, the dropship is powered by the same stuff that he runs off of: trinium. Only the ship makes use of something he calls a drive core. I'm thinking of Star Trek, but he says, "Not even close." Truthfully, I think it's closer than he's letting on, but I wanna let him feel like he's got something unique to offer right now. After all, the guy's shooter is busted, and I don't wanna be the one to add insult to injury. Plus, he might slip up more if he's feeling confident, and I'm just waiting for that moment to happen.

What impresses me about the dropship most of all is its ridiculously smooth flight characteristics. Had someone told me I could fall asleep at 200 miles per hour above mach one, I'd have laughed at them. Then again, I am a retired Marine. We're trained from day one to fall asleep anywhere, on command, and in any position. But this vessel feels like I'm on a commercial jetliner. And trust me, I ain't complaining. And neither is the rest of the team who are spread out along the cargo bay floor.

This particular attempt to sleep, however, is made even easier by the fact that I've stripped my house of its blankets and spare sleeping bags. Yes, I've distributed them to the team. But I've saved my bed linens for myself. It's amazing the difference your own pillow can make.

After triple-checking that Chuck has control of the ship and then making him swear on his mother's grave that he isn't going to fly us all into the side of a mountain, I make myself comfortable and stretch out under my blanket. As I start to rush toward deep sleep, I feel someone press against my back. The cargo bay lights are low, and the last thing I want is to expend energy telling someone to back off. So I settle for a half-eyed glimpse over my shoulder just to make sure it's not the kid or Vlad.

Nope.

It's Lada.

But she's keeping her hands to herself, she's warm, and I'm too tired to care at this point.

"It's just as I thought," Chuck says as the dropship passes the five-mile waypoint to the LZ I've designated near the old excavation site entry. "They haven't determined the nature of your sabotage in New York yet, so the gate is inactive. At least for the time being."

"Meaning no one's home?" I say as I sit in the pilot's chair beside Z-Lo's. While neither of us is flying, it's still comforting to know that there's a human involved should something need to be done. Granted, Z-Lo has the most experience flying one of these, followed closely by Yoshi, but I'd say their combined ratio of flight time to crashing time is equal.

"Correct, Patrick. No one is home, and I'm not detecting any life sign on the surface."

"Well, I'm good with that if you are."

"Yes. Indubitably."

"How'd you sleep, Wic?" Hollywood says behind me.

I don't dignify that with a response because I can hear the smile in her voice, and I know she spotted Lada trying to spoon with me.

"That's okay." She pats me on the shoulder. "You looked nice and warm."

I elevate a choice finger above my head and keep my eyes

focused on the wraparound display. "And you're gonna clean my shower when we get back."

"Fair enough."

"With bleach."

"Copy."

I'm about to crack another joke when Aaron appears between Z-Lo and me with his face pressed toward the display.

"What happened here?" he asks.

I glance from him to the monitor and blink at the visual coming up. Whatever imaging tech Dolores has, it's making the ever-night late June afternoon look like a fully illuminated video of the excavation site, but in grayscale. Some sort of IR sensors, I'm guessing.

What's got Aaron spooked isn't what's there: it's what's *not* there. Instead of a small entry cave leading into the side of a glacier and down to the ring, the entire ice mass has been opened up like someone dropped a nuke on it. Now the ring stands in the open air under the star-filled sky, surrounded by concentric circles of equipment that I've never seen before. And yet, toward the ring, I can see what looks like some of Aaron's original research equipment and scaffolding, albeit covered in snow.

"It's a staging ground," I say under my breath, but apparently loud enough that Chuck hears me.

"That's correct," he replies.

Hollywood steps up beside Aaron. "So, this is where they brought their initial attack force through."

"It is indeed," Chuck replies.

Then she looks at Aaron. "And you discovered it?"

He shrugs and rolls his eyes. "Unfortunately."

"No, no. It's... remarkable. I just wish it had meant, ya know, better news for the planet."

"You and me both."

"Still, it's quite the——"

"Please, Hollywood. You don't have to say anything else."

"Right. Sorry."

"Just confirming that our approach is safe," I say to Chuck one more time.

"It is very safe. And I will alert you should that change."

"Like, more than thirty seconds worth of warning?"

"Yes, more than thirty seconds worth."

"Dios mío," Veronica says. "I would give you at least ten minutes warning. Amateur."

"Gracias." I let out a breath I didn't realize I was holding. "All right, Chuck. Bring us down, nice and easy." Then I turn around to face the team. "Who's ready to freeze their tatas off with me?"

"It's a lot colder this time of year," Aaron yells as we trudge through the snow. A wide path cut through the concentric rings of drift-covered alien equipment gives us a perfect view of the origin ring that looms straight ahead. Aaron decided to come along "for old time's sake," he said, since this is where it all began. "There's a reason we chose to do our research in the southern hemisphere's summer months."

"Smart thinking," I reply. But I'm not much in the mood for small talk. My senses are on such high alert that the cold isn't hitting me like it normally would. Even with the ring's energy field off, I'm still half-expecting an overlord or death angel to jump out at us. Problem is, I'm not even sure my SCAR will operate in this temp. Which is part of the reason I brought Veronica along with Chuck.

"You still feeling good, Veronica?" I ask.

"Feeling good? Patrick, I am always feeling good. If some other rifles, who will remain nameless, give you the impression that we are sometimes moody or sad or haven't had enough hugging and squeezing, they are liars and are not to be believed. Lo entiendes?"

"Understood. Glad I asked."

"Psst," Chuck says.

"What is it?"

"Don't mention the war to Veronica."

Aaron gets this faster than I do and mouths the words "Fawlty Towers" to me.

The other person who volunteered to come along is Vlad. Again, it's fitting given what we went through together. "And how are you feeling, big stuff?"

"Feeling like spring in Siberia," Vlad says from my other side. "Plus, I have many good time feelings of being back here with you. Yes, Brooklyn USA?"

"Sure, Vlad." Never mind the fact that we witnessed a massacre together. But then again, the Russians have always had a strange romance with life's darker side. Or maybe they're just more honest about pain and suffering. Eh, I'll leave that to the philosophers.

The rest of the team wisely chose to stay aboard Dolores while the three of us investigate the ring and work with Chuck to activate it.

"And you're sure we don't need all of Aaron's fancy equipment this time?" I ask Chuck.

"No, Patrick. I already told you: you have me, remember? I'm all you need."

"And we couldn't do this from Dolores?"

"The Androchidans are still a little old fashioned that way. You can only initiate an origin ring from the destination side with manual activation."

"Manual activatings are always best kinds," Vlad offers.

Aaron laughs and shakes his head.

"What?" Vlad throws his mitten up. "I am speaking honestly and from heart."

"And we wouldn't want it any other way," I say for both Aaron and me.

Eventually, we arrive at the old stone staircase that leads up to the ring's base. Images of Lewis getting pulled through and Dr. Walker falling to his death flicker in my head. I swear that I see them for a second, but I quickly realize that it's just our shadows cast from Dolores's floodlights.

"Whadda we do, Sir Charles?" I ask.

"Lay me upon the threshold."

I share a look with Aaron and then with Vlad. "We're not gonna lose you, are we?"

"No. So long as you don't kick me across. Which would be very bad news for both you and me. I just need to have physical contact with the ring for a few moments."

"Then it comes on, and we can all get back to Dolores and fly through?"

"That's correct, Patrick. A little recon, a little song and dance, and then we're back here before you know it."

I unsling Chuck from my back and hold him across both hands.

"Alpha Patrol, this is Phantom Three," comes Bumper's voice over comms.

"We are reading you clears and loud," Vlad says after struggling with his radio for a second.

"You green out there?"

"Roger dodgers. We are simply working with Lord Charles at present moments."

"Say no more. Just checking. Phantom Three, out."

"I say! I rather like that," Chuck exclaims. "Lord Charles."

"No. Nope. *Sir* Chuck is plenty of nobility for you." I look from Chuck to Aaron. "This is it, ya know."

He nods a few times. "Yeah."

"And you're still sure you wanna go?"

"Sure I'm sure. You?"

I look up at the ring and feel a chill deeper than the Antarctic air temp run down my spine. "It's the fastest way we're gonna find answers—the kind we need to save our people." And even as I say *our people*, I realize what I'm really saying is the whole Godforsaken planet. Sweet Jesus, help us.

"Thicker than blood?" Aaron asks.

"Through fire and mud." I wait a second and then add, "Would you hail the team for me?"

He nods, pulls his radio from his coat, and then thumbs open the channel. "Dolores, this is the Away Team."

I smile at his Star Trek reference.

"Send it," Bumper replies.

"Standby for Pat. I mean, Wic." Aaron keeps the channel open and holds the mic to my mouth.

"Just making sure we're all ready for this," I say, still holding Chuck in both hands. "It's not too late to back out."

There's a few-seconds pause before Bumper comes back on the channel. "Seems everyone's reached consensus in here."

I raise an eyebrow to Aaron inside my goggles. "Which is?"

"OTF," the team shouts over comms.

That makes me smile. "Roger that. Wic out."

Aaron stuffs the radio back inside his coat's chest pocket and works the zipper closed.

"Vlad is also *oh see effs*. No one asks, but feeling good to offer as votes of confidence."

"It's OTF, pal." I smile at him. "Short for Own The Field."

"Own the Field. I like, yes. Is American football, no?"

"Something like that." I reach into my jacket, pull out one of the Phantom patches, and hand it to Vlad. "Here. This is for you."

He stares at it for three seconds before meeting my eyes. "Does this mean Vlad is Phantom now?"

"If you and Lada are willing to walk through the gates of hell with me, then you're a Phantom, yut."

"You are never being sorry." Vlad kisses it and then stuffs it inside his coat. "We three, we get into crazy messes together here, yes? So, I feel it's only fair to be getting out of messes together in same place. Plus, Lada finds you much sexy, Wic, which means we become brothers."

"No, we're not."

"Yes, Brooklyn USA. We are. No one is resisting Lada's charms."

"Then I'm pretty sure she's met her match." I look over to Aaron. "Is this conversation really happening right now?"

He laughs and shakes his head.

Vlad slaps me on the back. "All more reasonings that we becomes brothers. Come! Place Lord Charles on altar and let us bathe in glorious lights of future."

"Oh God." I take a short, freezing breath and look at the alien rifle in my hands. "We're all gonna die, aren't we, pal."

"Of course, my friend. But that was never in doubt."

"Oh no?"

"We all die. The greater question is, who will we die beside? And for what it's worth, I'm honored to face the future with you, Patrick."

"Dasvidaniya," Vlad cries at the top of his lungs, screaming up at the ring.

"Dasvidaniya," Aaron says with a shrug of his shoulders and a laugh.

"Son of a bitch." I lay Chuck down on the stone floor and then stand back. "Das-vi-splickin-daniya. Here goes nothing."

"Wrong, my good man," Chuck shouts as electricity starts snapping across the stone and onto his receiver. "Here goes everything."

THE STORY CONTINUES

What do Wic and Phantom Team discover on the other side of the origin ring?

Find out in Book 2 of the Ruins of the Earth Series: *Gods and Men*. Preorder on Amazon now.

SUPER GOOD TIME FEELINGS
MERCHANDISE STORE

Babushka Petrov's
Super Good Time Feelings
MERCHANDISE STORE
PROUD USA

Thanks to Grandma Petrov and her Super Good Time Feelings Merchandise Store, you can get the same Phantom Team patch and Bratva poker chip that Wic carries today.

Show your Phantom Team allegiance with Book 1's collector's edition military-style patch. These premium USA-made Velcro-backed patches feature a grey-threaded busted-ass Androchidan death angel helmet and two chevrons over a field of white.

Have a favor you need to call in? Then make sure you never leave home without your official USA/Bratva challenge marker. This casino-grade 13-gram clay poker chip features the symbol of Sissy's New York operation on the front, complete with three circles denoting Wic, Aaron, and Vlad's presence at the origin ring in Antarctica. On the back, the Bratva star encircles Vlad's iconic phrase, "US Brooklyn New York and Russian brotherhood are sexing."

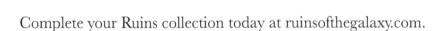

Complete your Ruins collection today at ruinsofthegalaxy.com.

STAY CONNECTED

Join **JN Chaney's Renegade Readers Facebook group** where readers come together and share their lives and interests, discuss the series, and speak directly to the authors. Please check it out and join whenever you get the chance!

For updates about new releases, as well as exclusive promotions, sign up for the newsletter at ***https://www.jnchaney.com/ruins-of-the-earth-subscribe***

Enjoying the series? Help others discover the Ruins of the Earth series by leaving a review on **Amazon.**

ACKNOWLEDGMENTS

This book would be a shadow of itself without the remarkable talents of my fifteen esteemed Alpha Team Readers. I am proud to call these men my friends, not just key contributors. I'm especially grateful for those who so generously lent me their years of military experience, some of which was given while on deployment. I'm forever grateful.

The Alpha Team Readers are:

- Matthew Titus: Ruins Lore & Character Master
- Gary Guilmette: Ruins Armorer
- Kevin Zoll: Typo Assassin
- Steve Janulin and Eric Earley: DFXOs (Damn Fine Experience Officers)
- John Walker, Jon Bliss, Shane Marolf, and Mike McDonnell: Pop-Culture Space Wizards
- Aaron Campbell, David Seaman, Matthew Dippel,

Mauricio Longo, and Patrick McDaniel: Emotional Support Blankets

- Elijah Cole: Space Wizard Understudy

Additionally, I would like to thank Jennifer Sell, our editor, for making this story shine. We'd be losers without you. Kayla Curry, for your endless formatting patience par excellence. Chloe Cotter for your marketing mastery. Molly Lerma for keeping me in line (God, help you). James Brockwell for your uploading super-powers. And Victoria Gerken at Podium Audio for making sure this story makes it to listeners' ears. You all amaze me, and it's a privilege to work with you.

To the Renegade Beta Readers: thanks for pulling out the weeds.

To Luke Daniels: thanks for giving voices to Wic & Co. You're awesome.

To publishing pals Jason Anspach, Wayne Thomas Batson, Bobby Bray, Jeremy Andrew Davis, Brian Moore, and Mike Kim: thanks for keeping me sane.

To Jeff Chaney: I love that we get to do this for a living. Thanks, bro.

And to my wife, Jennifer, who is the secret sauce behind every book I write. I love you.

ABOUT THE AUTHORS

J. N. Chaney is a USA Today Bestselling author and has a Master's of Fine Arts in Creative Writing. He fancies himself quite the Super Mario Bros. fan. When he isn't writing or gaming, you can find him online at **www.jnchaney.com**.

He migrates often, but was last seen in Las Vegas, NV. Any sightings should be reported, as they are rare.

Christopher Hopper's novels include the Resonant Son series, The Sky Riders, The Berinfell Prophecies, and the White Lion Chronicles. He blogs at **christopherhopper.com** and loves flying RC planes. He resides in the 1000 Islands of northern New York with his musical wife and four ridiculously good-looking clones.

Printed in Great Britain
by Amazon

46781281R00368